PE
WI

Manik Bandyopadhyay, widel
post-Rabindrik writer of fiction,
at the age of twenty and in his sho
and sixteen collections of stories   over 200 stories
in various Bengali periodicals. Manik Bandyopadhyay died in 1956.

*

Kalpana Bardhan was born in 1940 and grew up in Calcutta. She studied in
Presidency College and Calcutta University. After obtaining a Ph.D. in
economics from Cambridge University and working for many years in
research and teaching positions in Calcutta, Delhi, and Berkeley, she now
works primarily at home on translating selections from Bengali literature. Her
translation of a set of Bengali short stories on the theme of oppression,
Of Women, Outcastes, Peasants and Rebels, was published in 1990. She has
also translated a novel by Advaita Mallabarman, *A River Called Titash,*
published by Penguin Books India in 1992.

Manik Bandyopadhyay

WIVES & OTHERS

Short Stories and a Novella

Translated with an Introduction by Kalpana Bardhan

PENGUIN BOOKS

Penguin Books India (P) Ltd., 210, Chiranjiv Tower, 43, Nehru Place, New Delhi 110 019, India
Penguin Books Ltd., 27 Wrights Lane, London W8 5TZ, UK
Penguin Books USA Inc., 375 Hudson Street, New York, NY 10014, USA
Penguin Books Australia Ltd., Ringwood, Victoria, Australia
Penguin Books Canada Ltd., 10 Alcorn Avenue, Suite 300, Toronto, Ontario M4V 3B2, Canada
Penguin Books (NZ) Ltd., 182-190 Wairau Road, Auckland 10, New Zealand

First published by Penguin Books India (P) Ltd. 1994

All the stories and the novella in this edition are taken from various volumes of *Manik Granthabali*, vols. 1-13, published between 1963 and 1976.

Typeset in Times Roman by Digital Technologies and Printing Solutions, New Delhi

Contents

Translator's Introduction

Manik Bandyopadhyay was born on 19 May 1908 in a remote town called Dumka in Bihar where his father was posted as a settlement officer. His parents were from Bikrampur, Dhaka in Bangladesh (then East Bengal). His uncles stayed on in East Bengal and Manik spent long periods of his teenage and early youth there, in explorations among fisherfolk and other communities, venturing out in their company for days at a time, equipped with his curiosity and his flute. This experience of Bengal's variegated rural life went into his most famous early novels.[*] By the time he died (3 December 1956) in Calcutta at the age of forty-eight, he had known life in the city inside out. Starting with his college days, he had lived in its dingy north, the city of the impoverished urban and the recently migrated rural people, and in its affluent south, where his father had built a family house after his retirement; he had walked its alleyways and avenues, travelled in its buses and commuter trains, and closely known the lifestyles of both lower and upper middle-classes, often among branches of the same family, even his own family.

Manik's creativity was fired by his intense experiences in the Twenties and Thirties, in a social environment that was in a state of major flux. On the one hand, society was reeling from the economic, political, moral shocks of the time, with people trying to cope with the destabilization of familial and social relations, and on the other, it was a period that saw a great deal of mobility, both upwards and downwards. Calcutta of the inter-war period—with its teeming slums of labourers, the elite lifestyles of the patricians and the nouveau-riche, the buffeted lives of the middle-class—was at the heart of his life and his art, the immediate context of his knowledge of conflict and contradiction in life.

---

[*] See, *Padma Nadir Majhi* and *Putul Nacher Itikatha*, available in translation as *Boatman of the Padma* (tr. Hirendra Mukherjee, 1948, Bombay: Kutumb); *Padma River Boatman* (tr. Barbara Painter and Yann Lovelock, 1973, St. Lucia: University of Queensland Press) and as *The Puppets' Tale* (tr. Sachindralal Ghosh, 1968, Delhi: Sahitya Akademi) respectively.

This knowledge, and the agonizing awareness of the gulf between the life he knew and the literature he grew up on, powered Manik's creativity. It drove his search for the clues hidden behind the facades of social and familial life, or exposed in the wrecks left from crises. His fiction depicted his perceptive search for structures in life's turbulence and turmoil, the indeterminate logic unfolding in the chaos, the instabilities and warps produced by the gaps between expectations and reality. The whys and the hows of this search of his, at once subjective and objective, inform this selection, mostly from his pre-1944 work. It captures social and familial conflicts, the crumbling edifices in changed contexts, the questioned premises of personal relationships.

Despite the clear-eyed originality and boldness of his social-psychological portraits in both theme and narration, it would be wrong to see Manik as an outsider to the Bengali literary tradition till then. His art was partly an insider's inspired reaction to and conscious departure from the literary mainstream of his time, the work of one who felt driven to look in unexplored areas, tease out the puzzles, ask the unasked questions. Manik himself considered his relation to the existing literature thus, 'No literary work comes to be born without the strong influence of the existing literature. Even before actually picking up the pen and writing, the work goes on in bits and pieces of thought . . . . The time before I actually started writing can be divided in two parts. From school to the first year or two in college, I worked my way through the literature influenced by Rabindranath and Saratchandra, then I tried to familiarize myself both with the noisy event of creating a 'modern' literature going on in Bengal as well as with foreign literature from Humsun's *Hunger* to Shaw's plays and Freud and so on . . . . I read stories and novels eagerly to understand real life. Deeply moved from reading them, I searched life to understand the life in the stories and novels. My question (often) concerned the problem of romantic love and the physical side of it, love in literature and love in real life. I could not find the literature's rarefied love in either the middle-classes or the underclass . . . . Being given to genteel sentiments myself, I started to see their familiar expressions as foppish, revolting lies . . . . The very literature that moved me at one level, held me in spell, also aroused a furious complaint, made me ask·bitterly, angrily, if there was no remedy to this (chasm) . . . . This conflict grew unbearable in my youth—after I started writing, its ferocity subsided with increase in my ability to acknowledge and accommodate the complex reality.'*

In the twenty-eight year literary career of his short life, troubled by

---

* See, essay titled "Sahitya Karar Age" (Before I started literary work) in Manik Bandyopadhyay, *Lekhaker Katha*, pp. 18-19, 20, 23-25.

financial and health problems, Manik wrote thirty-nine novels, 226 short stories, aside from a play, a number of essays, and poems (brought out posthumously). More striking than the prodigious pace and feverish intensity of his work is its departure from the immense influence of Rabindranath Thakur on Bengali prose fiction of the time. Interestingly, Manik always regarded Rabindranath as primarily a great poet, and although he often remarked on Saratchandra's novels, he made almost no written remark on Rabindranath's novels and stories. Interestingly, too, he never tried to publish the poetry he left in his notebooks, and later in life, made this categorical remark: 'My love of science and propensity to pursue the questions of life in terms of a born scientist's why-is-it-so . . . clearly told me that though I could perhaps become a poet if I wanted to, it would be both natural and right for me to write novels (fiction).'[*]

Young Manik's novels and stories came out all very different from the luminary Rabindranath's in prose style, in theme, tone and perspective. Even among the noted post-Rabindrik[**] fiction writers of Bengal, Manik was seen from the beginning as breaking new ground—a restlessly energetic and uninhibited investigator of the familiar sentiments, the much-cherished genteel emotions, one who felt them deeply, yet could look at them unsentimentally. His work in the Thirties and Forties gives a startlingly different kind of neo-realist portrayal of a cross-section of middle-class lives, then rocked by economic crises and moral doubts and by the loss of security and faith in life's familiar order.

He was the product and the artist of a turbulent juncture in time and place. Relationships were turbulent from the interpersonal reactivity of hopes and frustrations, of attitudes and expectations, acted upon by the changing socio-economic parameters. The clashes of sentiments with reality, which he knew in himself and in others, he examined with sympathy and empathy, but resisted moralizing about or answering normatively. He said later: 'I haven't quite offered a well-defined ideal for living, but I certainly have remedied to some extent the absence of realism, the realities of life, in Bengali literature . . . . There was a need for that too. At least as a step . . . .'[+]

In the 1920s, when a teenaged Manik was voraciously reading, a new generation of writers was struggling to come out of the influence of half a century moulded and dominated by Rabindranath's work. Saratchandra and Nazrul Islam were then among the few loners young Manik admired

---

[*]   See, essay titled "Upanyaser Dhara" (The tradition of the novel) in Manik
      Bandyopadhyay, *Lekhaker Katha*, p 58.
[**] That is, in the tradition influenced by Rabindranath Thakur.
[+]   See, essay titled "Sahitya Karar Age" in Bandyopadhyay, op.cit., p.31.

much. By the 1930s, a wave of neo-realism had arisen in the Bengali literary scene, commonly referred to as the Kollol Yug,* which, in Manik's words, tried to 'create literature at the ground level, close to the people, leaving the world of imagination.' Though Manik was variously claimed to be part of this new wave, the significance of his work defied any such classification. As the publisher of his collected works remarked, 'Even among the most notable of the so-called Kollol-Yug writers, Manik occupied a special place because of his viewpoint, characters, his focus on conflict, and his use of the language . . . (the) most striking aspect of his work was . . . the exposing of pretenses, the contradictions behind the orderly facades.'

When Rabindranath was in his seventies, and still in undiminished efflorescence of his exquisitely crafted, sublime prose and poetry, Manik in his twenties and early thirties was pouring out his startlingly different early work, in which he looked for neither the sublime nor sublimation, but the wheels and gears of living multiple lives—the scarcely revealed psychic processes of coping with conflicting emotions that bent and refracted the flow of energy in close relationships. In his short stories, especially of this period, which overlapped with his being newly married, he charted the unsettled pathways in the subterrain of conjugal relations, searching for the forces at work underneath the surface, particularly in the various middle-class contexts of clash between sentiments and circumstances.

His early work gives unsparing yet empathic accounts of the rankling conflicts of expectations and their effects on life. Particularly in the arena of conjugality, in the relations between the sexes and interdependent psyches—relations that are a function not only of individualities, but also of family background and location in social strata. The stories and the novella in this collection explore the dynamics of interaction in relations of love, hate and love-hate. They chart the resulting shifts in the relationships revealing the structures of contradiction, the shifts in the clouds of doubt, the flashpoints of volatile tension breaking through surfaces that were calm till then. They show how individuals affect the relationship *and* vice versa.

If harmony and poignancy—of transcendence or sacrifice, of transformation or redemption—are the highlights of Rabindranath's fiction, for Manik's they are conflict and tussle, disintegration and instability of close relations, the tension of opposites reaching points of

---

* The term is derived from the name of a journal, *Kollol,* which had been started to encourage and publish young new-wave writers. Manik himself, however, never wrote for this journal.

explosion or implosion in those relations. Unlike in Rabindranath, there is no presiding deity of life (*jiban-debata*), only a mind-trapping hunter (*jiban-byadh*); no cosmic order or reason, no prospect of redemption, no recourse to transcendence in the face of conflict and loss. The complex interactions of different psyches, divergent reactions to given situations and to unexpected events, produce outcomes that are neither quite determinate, nor totally indeterminate. Most of the stories end by revealing a puzzle, leaving us with insight, but no resolution or answer, no light at the end of the tunnel. The narrative voice is that of a rationalist unbeliever, the tone brisk from a sense of the compelling tension of the puzzle, and wry from the irony of the situation. It is a more distilled form of what came across in the novels he wrote in his early twenties, a good ten years before most of the pieces in this collection. In one of his early novels,[*] the passively fatalistic view of life—our wanting one thing and getting something else, puppets in the hands of an invisible puppeteer—moves the rationalist hero to rage: 'If once I could get hold of that scoundrel.' Death merely terminates the complex structures of conscious reaction, as the meaning of life is all in the process of living.

By the 1930s, Manik's work was established as one of the robust departures from Rabindranath's integrative, normative perspective and poetic, evocative prose. Manik captured, uniquely and perceptively, the angst of his generation, the generation gap in an age of doubt and uncertainty, the inner turmoils set off by surface tensions, the volatility of pressures unknown to earlier generations. Manik's early work proved galvanic for a whole new generation of writers, not just readers. With powerful analytics and quick eyes, and an empathic yet sardonic voice as of an insider standing slightly outside, his perspective is knowing but skeptical of the genteel romanticism. Critics have duly noted what in Manik's style and theme the younger readers of his time hungrily took to—'the striking absence of Rabindranath's influence on his language, the plain, unadorned use of verbs, the brisk, cutting dialogue ... his themes and treatment of those themes thoroughly original, analytical, and expressed in a language sharp as a blade.'[**]

At the heart of Manik's neo-realism is his investigation of middle-class romanticism—a searching, questioning look at the Bengali bhadralok (genteel) culture then in the throes of economic decline, and the breakup of the extended family with both its shackles and its safety

---

[*]   See, *Putul Nacher Itikatha* translated as *The Puppets' Tale* by Sachindralal Ghosh.
[**]   See, Suneet Sengupta, in a review of *Putul Nacher Itikatha* titled, "Grantha Samiksha: Putul Nacher Itikatha" on the occasion of its tenth reprint (1968) published in *Ekshan*, 1969, vol. VI, no. 6, p.92 (excerpt in my translation).

nets. The *Bou* (wives) and other stories he wrote during the Thirties and early Forties form an engaging arrangement of sketches of men and women in various relationships of marriage and non-marriage. In vividly drawn contexts, they look at forms of deception and pretension, conflict of sentiments with reality, the new tensions in family and social life as the previously quiescent (women in particular, the young in general) question and reject customary norms and face unfamiliar choices and their sometimes harsh consequences. But there is as yet no clear, unambiguously preferred resolution.

While the focus in Manik's pre-1944 stories is on family life, especially conjugal relations, his later stories focus on the emergent class struggles, and even in those relating to family life and conjugal relations there is now a positive outlook—a new faith in a fresh set of values with which the underclass regroups and forges ahead to assert their place in society as the labouring class. In his later work there is also a faith in struggles within the middle-class toward possibilities beyond the mind-numbing clutter and torment of dead-end conflict. But, in his early work, 'during the nine or ten years from 1936 to 1944–45, such an experience of existential crisis found expression in Manik Bandyopadhyay's writing . . . such an unmitigated experience of god(order)lessness . . . of collapse of the distinction between anarchy and rule of order . . . that remains unparalleled in Bengali fictional literature from its beginning till today.'*

Yet, as Manik himself noted later on, the perspective in his early work was not all negative, most definitely not nihilistic. 'The meaning of a certain social group starting to crumble is taken by many as the people themselves getting completely crushed—actually, those people's lives find motion in new directions, start taking new forms.'** Still, in his early work about the middle-classes at the time, the focus is relentlessly on the working of the tensions and pressures, not on presuming, prescribing, or predicting the forms and directions of the outcomes. The pieces are meant to provoke the readers' thoughts as much as they did the writer's.

Despite the thematic and stylistic differences between Manik's early work and his later work, to characterize the one as apolitical and skeptical, the other as political and positive, would be rather simplistic. Aside from Manik's own remark cautioning against the false dichotomy between 'crumbling structures' and 'changing people'—false for the simple reason

---

* See, Jugantar Chakravarty "Samagra Manik Bandyopadhyay ebang tnar kabita" in *Ekshan*, 1973, vol. IV, no. 5, p.26. (excerpt in my translation).

** See, Sudhiranjan Mukhopadhyay's article (April, 1957) in Appendix B, p.442 of *Manik Granthabali*, vol. 13 (excerpt in my translation).

that in the process of coping with the crumbling structure, people themselves change and move towards a new structure—the work of putting together this selection further convinced me of the narrowness of this common characterization.

The point is that gender is a major aspect of a society's power relations, and the personal relations between the sexes is the arena in which the conflicting forces actually interact and work out one way or the other. The stories of couples in this collection focus primarily on the women involved, the tragedies and the triumphs at their conclusion are those of the respective female protagonists. In the titles of some of the stories, Manik uses the descriptive/ascriptive common words 'bou' or 'stree' (wife) to powerful ironic effect. While the word symbolizes supportiveness in a multiplicity of physical and psychological senses, the prime mover of each story's course and outcome is the wife; in each, the heart of the crisis and the mode of its resolution belong to her. In the ultimate analysis, none of the central female characters, not even in the most dire of situations, comes out as either a victim or a goddess, a candidate for either our pity or our adoration. Neither childlike and helpless nor idealized and mystified, she is seen as accountable, at least partly, for the course of her life, no matter how oppressive the circumstances are. Isn't it so for any striving, self-willed individual? Isn't there always an option, for a price? She is seen exactly as *any* thinking-acting human agent deserves to be seen. Manik's portrayal of women as genuine characters rather than stereotypes, as agents, even if imperfectly free agents—thinking, scheming, acting, reacting, no matter how restrictive the assigned role, how relentless the socialization, how harsh the control—offers one of the savviest social commentaries in the literature. Neither condescending nor vilifying, Manik lets their personal complexities stand up to the challenge of dramatic spotlight, unmodified one way or the other. Each one faces moments of personal decision, in matters however seemingly minor, which prove pivotal for herself and for the relationship. By playing the game differently, she affects the other player and the rules indirectly, even if she can't alter them directly. The emotional aspects generate complexity and leeway in the conjugal power struggle.

Besides, if these stories describe from close quarters, as they do, the complex dynamics of interpersonal exchanges, then what we are looking at is 'process rather than state, of becoming rather than being,'* which in a basic sense cannot be considered apolitical and devoid of potential. Today, with the principles of chaos theory much bandied about in

---

* See, James Gleick, *Chaos: Making a New Science*, p.5.

psychology and the social sciences, it is worth remembering that good literature does indeed search for those, and becomes of timeless value by doing it perceptively in well-defined specific contexts. The structure of interpersonal relations within family and society move over time not linearly along a path of cumulative change, but through periodic instability and realignment. The process of shift from an existing order—troubled as it is by doubts, conflicts, unravelling moral consensus—has in fact resurfaced since then in other forms, in both conjugal and social life. The confusion and ambivalence, the turmoil and transformation experienced by the particular women in these stories from half a century ago (in relation to the particular men they are wedded to, in love with, trying to or failing to love) remain of interest and immediacy.

Aside from their literary value and sociological acuity, the veracity of Manik's early stories reaches beyond their immediate context. Even with a less than complete coverage of his early work, these stories offer plenty of insights into, and food for thought on gender relations generally, and conjugal relations particularly, in another era of doubt and disillusion, for still other couples' grappling with the moral anguish and ironies of questioning in a different context. Had Manik lived on to a ripe old age like Rabindranath, and continued writing about the ongoing processes of turmoil in familial and social relations, we might have gained his insights into the angst of today's Bengali middle-class couples.

Manik's short stories are large in number and variety. Even focusing on the husband-wife (couples) theme within socio-psychological themes generally, the choice is huge. The task of selection proved to be quite a challenge. Aside from the thirteen titled as someone's wife, I have included ten not titled as such but directly relating to conjugal relations, and a novella that is about three young men and a woman, idealists in different ways, in their mutually frustrating interactions owing to both miscommunication and conflicting self-perceptions.

As already noted, Manik's work is generally seen as divided in two groups—the novels and stories he wrote in his twenties and thirties, and his later work in the period following the 1943 Bengal Famine and the social ravages that were but local by-products of the Second World War. The thirteen *Bou* stories came out between 1939 and 1946, most of them written in the author's early thirties, then a newly married man himself. Six of the remaining eleven stories and the novella were published by 1938 before he was thirty. One story ("More Precious Than Life") in this collection can definitely be said to have been written while he was in his early forties, in the post-independence context. It is clearly part of the class-struggle inspired work in the last quarter of his life, the context for personal relations in the story being the emergent class consciousness.

However, if we define the political more broadly, as power struggle not just in the public arena of changing class structure and class relations, but also in the domestic arena, and in relations between the sexes, particularly in the conjugal context, then this collection drawn mostly from Manik's early works is unquestionably political. His investigation reveals the dynamic tensions that characterize the relations between men and women, caught as they are in the web of opposites—love and hate, sympathy and resentment, trust and distrust, strung in emotions in all areas of daily life. The political significance, in this broader sense, of this body of Manik's work, would seem all the more striking if we remember that the perceptive portraits of this most complex of human relations, too intimate and too much in conflict for generalization, were drawn half a century before gender relations and sexual politics became a brave new frontier in the study of power relations in various contexts of conflicting emotions.

In 1928, as an undergraduate student of science and mathematics in Calcutta's Presidency College, Prabodh Bandyopadhyay had aspirations to become a writer, but decided against starting before the age of thirty, not even as a hobby. His reason was not only to gather enough experience as raw material before writing, but also to arrange the material aspects of his life so as to have adequate time free of the work and the worries of earning a livelihood. As it turned out, by the age of thirty he was near the peak of an intense literary career and one of the foremost names in the post-Rabindrik literary scene of Bengal, with six novels and three collections of stories to his credit.

His first story he wrote and published to prove a point to his friends. As he recounted later, 'One day some of my college friends were discussing current literature . . . . The discussion rolled on to the topic of the monthly literary magazine editors' stupidity, partisan mentality and indifference. They don't publish anyone except the well-known; they publish if the author is one of the club—that's it . . . . Three pieces by one of them had been returned from the monthlies' offices. He used an ugly epithet about editors—the way college youths do . . . . I said, "Why talk rubbish? Is good writing so easy to come by that even after getting one, editors will return it? Are they crazy that they'll reject good stories and print bad ones? If they get a reasonably good, let alone excellent, story, I'm sure they print it eagerly." The bet offered was this. I would write a story and get it published within three months. If I failed—why go into that? I knew I could . . . . One morning as I debated whether or not to go to college that day, a gentleman came to see me. He was the editor of

Bichitra . . .; putting in my hand cash for my story "Atasi-Mami", he demanded another . . . . I dropped everything and started writing . . . . To this day my folks say with regret, "Look at you brother . . . and what have you done with your life, Manik?" What do you say?'*

The twenty-year-old undergraduate, Prabodh, had used his nickname for the story: he didn't want people to bring it up and find fault with it later when he would be writing really well in his official name. He remained known to his readers by his nickname. The story, "Aunt Atasi," one of the two dozens in this collection, first came out in 1928 in a top literary magazine of the time. One of its editors later reminisced about meeting the unhesitant young writer fresh with his first story: 'There was this sharp agility in his eyes and face, flashing intelligence. The expression said: I just finished writing one and it'd better be sent to the press without any delay . . . . Not the slightest hesitancy or appeal in his manner. Not a doubt as to whether or not it'll be accepted, not a drop of curiosity expressed as to when he should come back to find out about the decision.'**

As he recounted later, Manik's thoughts behind the writing of his first story reveal the dynamics underlying much of his work: a creative tension between emotion and reason, between romantic yearning and aversion to sentimentality, between fantasy and fact—in life *and* in the life in art.

> Some practical considerations went into writing the story . . . . For a total beginner, it's just not possible to pull off a story on a new theme, from a new angle, using a new technique; too much of 'novelty' the editors may not like either . . . I decided to write a love story . . . a romantic story of idealized love. But it won't work if it's all imaginary, there has to be a real foundation too to the story. If I weave a story out of romantic fantasy, then I've to make the characters real, out of people of flesh and blood . . . . So I used two closely known people as the hero and the heroine of "Atasi-mami" . . . . The husband played the clarinet exquisitely, but he played it mostly at home, to his wife, and he played for hours until his throat

---

*   See, essay titled "Galpa Lekhar Galpa" (The story of my writing stories) in Manik Bandyopadhyay, *Lekhaker Katha*, pp.5-10.

**   These were the words of Achitya Kumar Sen, then an established writer, who was in the *Bichitra* office when Manik went in with his story. Sen has been quoted in "Manik Bandyopadhyay: Mawn O Shilpa" (Mind and art) by Rathindranath Roy in the introduction to Part 1 of *Manik Granthabali.*

started to bleed. As a young boy, I was befriended by the couple and a few times I joined her as his audience, I sensed the very unreal romantic love in the real form . . . ; even at that early age I knew from the way they talked with each other and the language of their glances that their bond was far stronger than of other couples I knew . . . . In writing "Aunt Atasi" I kept the two of them before my mind . . . . I myself entered the tale as an adolescent and had him narrate it . . . . The plot . . . is a ridiculous sort of romantic fantasy. To this day when I think of the idea of Aunt Atasi taking a trip every year on the night of the train accident to be alone in the fields by the tracks to feel her dead beloved's company through the night, I myself want to laugh. (Yet) even today, reading the story from the start, I do not find it possible to smirk even inwardly. Because, though the plot is a fairytale, the hero and heroine are real people . . . . *

The conflict between romantic sensibility and what Manik called romantic disease, the central tension in his creative inspiration is expressed with characteristic insight and analysis in the present collection about couples.

The novella, *Amritasya Putrah* (translated here as *The Children of Immortality*), stands at a brief transition point between his more famous novels of the early period and those of the later period, **between the shift of focus from interpersonal psychological process to social struggle as catalyst for consciousness, before an ebbing of the preoccupation with romantic sensibility as 'romantic disease'. In its three youthful central characters, idealism takes a plunge into an abyss and the dramatic tension around romantic sensibility turns almost schizoid, estranging the head from the heart in a lethal way, literally for one of them and spiritually for all three. If "Aunt Atasi" is about uncommon romantic love in maudlin characters, *The Children of Immortality* is about the dissipation of romantic sentiments (love and idealism) in characters at a higher level of intelligence and sensitivity than what we are likely to come across in strictly average people. Interestingly, the former story is projected through an adolescent's tender longings and eager voice, the latter through the mature author's sense of irony, humour and analytical voice.

It is Manik's sixth novel, a short one, the only one he published between 1936 and 1940, as against three collections of stories. It was written during a period that in more than one way was destabilizing for

---

*   See, essay titled "Upanyaser Dhara" by Manik Bandyopadhyay in *Lekhaker Katha*, pp. 64-6.

**   See, *Shahartali, Chintamoni* and *Sonar Cheye Damee*.

his own life. In late 1936, at twenty-eight, with three major novels just published and, along with a collection of stories, received with immense acclaim, his health suddenly sounded the alarm with epilepsy.* The recurrence of seizures at short intervals was preceded by two years spent in a series of anxious dislocations. He had to leave his room-and-board life in Calcutta to be with his younger brother and family caught in a devastating earthquake in Munger, stay with them at his elder brother's place in Ranchi, and back in Calcutta, had to have two changes of rented home with them before moving into the family house in Tollygunge his father got built. Persistent financial difficulty (his novels had brought him little money despite the literary acclaim, as was quite usual then) and family pressure made him push aside his resolve a remain a wholetime writer, and take up a job as assistant editor of the *Bangashree* magazine. Near the end of that year, 1937, he got married. *The Children of Immortality* was written during that year and serialized in this magazine, which had earlier done another of his novels.

The impression one gets from most commentators is that the process of writing this stark novel about the loss of idealism and hope, about demoralization and dissolution, was less smooth than the torrentially energetic writing of the earlier novels.** It also took me an unexpecteldy long time to translate, perhaps in part because its bleak perspective on human striving rings distressingly true, and because it is so compelling a study of despair and disintegration of the young and the bright of an era. This novel, I believe, is truly unique in its painfully clear-sighted and dry-eyed view of the social situation of interwar Bengal, an environment of doubt and moral crisis concurrent with the decline of many

---

*   In a letter to Atulchandra Gupta dated 9 February 1955, Manik wrote: 'At the beginning, being preoccupied with writing several novels like *Putul Nacher Itikatha*, when I myself had forgotten that I had a human body and the people in my family had also become cruelly indifferent, one day I fainted. It kept occurring after a gap of a month or two.' (*Parichay*, 1965, Autumn issue).

**   The reasons by various accounts were: fatigue partly from the seizures, the distractions and demands of starting on a new job and married life, the fact that Manik was much too spontaneously frenzied a writer for time-bound serialization. 'It was never possible to keep Manik tied up in set rules. His writing habit was absolutely unruly. He used to be given a week of leave from work for writing his instalment of *Amritasya Putrah*. But he would come back after the seven days (and say to the editor Kiran Roy), "I'm not done, Kiran-da." To extract the instalment, he had again to be put pressure upon. For that reason the novel turned out an oddity . . . .'(Sarojmohan Mitra, *Manik Bandyopadhyay: Jiban O Sahitya*—life and works of Manik Bandyopadhyay). This, however, is far from my view of the novel, which I admire deeply for its stark portrayal of alienation from hope and ideal, in the crosscurrent of economic crisis and political movements in the Thirties' Bengal.

middle-class families in poverty, their bourgeois mentality lagging far behind in adaptation. This novella is not just about the 'ugly realities that stay neatly hidden behind the appearances of middle-class gentility,' but also about how the pressures of this conflict fell the hardest on the young idealists and the old moralists amidst the spongers and climbers thriving in the economic stagnation and spiritual paralysis of the Thirties and early Forties in Bengal.

In the novel's last scene, two young men sit in dazed silence staring at each other, thinking of the losses they have in common—the suicide of the haughtily idealistic young widow they both loved, their unimagined slide into demoralization, and their being manipulated by the cynically self-centred. Step-cousins and former friends, estranged over the girl who saw romantic love as mere folly, they blankly take leave in the paralysed last meeting while a ruthless climber, the wife of one of them, cheerily goes about offering her 'ambrosia-like cordial'. In a counterpoint scene earlier, on the day they first met, they sat in embarrassed silence, sensing the mortification of their upright grandfather before the upright widow of his elder son who had spurned him for marrying a second time, when one of the youths is curiously assailed by a sense of moral guilt as he falls in love with the spirited widow he saw for the first time there.

Around its interconnected central story of the three young idealists' self-destructive fall and two moral elders' dissolution, and the sub-story of a son's guilt-ridden failure to live up to the superficial idealism of his parents' self-righteousness the novella's fabric explores, once again, 'why and how is it that the false notion of gentility persists in middle-class life in spite of its reality of conflict, hypocrisy, meanness, selfishness, artificiality and tradition-fixation.' Manik later remarked about this conflict in himself in his early years, as a driving force behind his creativity.

'I hated the expressions of sentimentality at the same time that I was sentimental myself. I liked the genteel, cultured life, my middle-class friends, I did not entirely drop my middle-class hopes and aspirations. Yet I found my mind constantly poisoned by the narrowness of that life, its artificiality. Sometimes, I ran away from my own life to the company of the low-class peasants and labourers just to be able to breathe. Other times, tormented by the relentless harshness of their deprived lives, the naked reality of their daily existence, I ran back to my own life just to be able to breathe. This conflict got worse and worse through my early youth—until I learnt to acknowledge it in my writing. My enraged rebellion against the middle-class sentimentality forced me as a writer to keep looking into the reality of middle-class life.'*

---

* See, Manik Bandyopadhyay, *Lekhaker Katha*, ch.3, pp. 19, 23-4.

The early Forties was a time of convulsive lurches in Bengal. The country's worst man-made famine and wartime corruption of the economy had shattered lives, families, kinship, social cohesion, and demoralized society to the core. At the same time, politicization was starting to take place at the mass level, reassessment of values and mores was in the wind, the freedom struggle was growing along its various branches, one of which was the sharecroppers' movement known as *Tebhaga* which spread through Bengal's countryside before it was suppressed, then drowned by the horrors of the Partition. There was intense concern at the time with the question of what constituted progressive realism in literature. Manik expressly differed from the position of some of the prominent progressive writers when he remarked:

> To think, or give the impression, that the peasants', and other common peoples' struggle against oppression is expressed only in the form of confrontation and battle is to deny the very core of their struggle. . . .The reality of their struggle lies in its centrality to their lives and their minds. The peasant's struggle today is not just for two-thirds of the crop he grows, but also in his thinking that it is wrong to treat his wife the way he used to. He may still lower his head to the priest or the mullah in the temple or mosque, but he does so with much less conviction.[*]

One story ("More Precious than Life") in this collection illustrates very well Manik's radical leftist political work in the post-1943 period, a period both traumatic and revolutionary in Bengal, a period also of clashes between the old and new attitudes and norms of behaviour in the personal, familial relations as well.

Manik's earlier work powerfully explores the anxieties, uncertainties, sense of disillusion and impatience, especially among the middle-class urban Bengalis, himself included, living in the Twenties through Forties as youths and young adults. Premendra Mitra, a contemporary writer, remarked: 'the slight shadow of sickness in his work is the reflection of only that in ourselves.'[**] Yet what seems to be the sickness of a generation would from hindsight turn out to be part of a reintegration process, the passage of the self through 'the dark nights of the soul' from which it would emerge reintegrated at another level. Besides, despite the unique characteristics of the so-called malaise of each

---

[*]   Manik Bandyopadhyay, *Lekhaker Katha*, pp.113-5.
[**]   See, obituary titled "Manik Bandyopadhyay" published by Premendra Mitra in *Desh*,
         12 August 1956.

generation, their different processes may share broad similarities of pattern.

Although radically different from his predecessors', Manik's work is not as unconnected with the mainstream literary tradition of the time as has often been implied by contemporaries, critics, followers and readers. Jugantar Chakravarty, Manik's son-in-law and a scholar on his work, has argued this point well.

> It is sometimes said that Manik Bandyopadhyay's work did not arise from any of the Bengali literary traditions established before him—he is the only great writer in the language without precedence in literary tradition . . . . It is inconceivable that any writer could be unconnected with his society and literary tradition in the language . . . . Sometimes, in some contexts, contradicting may become the only way in which a writer can reveal relationship with the established literary tradition. Conscious conflict is a kind of relationship too . . . . In the history of all literature, we find, once in a while a writer appears, out of historical necessity, who in the role of an outsider born in and shaped from inside, forces the contradictions to attention . . . contradictions between literary imagery and reality that became increasingly sharp in our society since the turn of this century, but did not quite find adequate expression in our literature till the mid-1920s . . . . In his writings, the unbearable contradiction between the changed realities of life and the unchanged literary sentiments came under ruthless scrutiny in all its forms.*

Eight of the central set of the thirteen *Bou* (wives) stories first came out in 1941 from a short-lived, small publishing house Manik had started with his younger brother in an attempt at financial supplementation. The second edition in 1946 by another publisher included all thirteen. As one of the editors of Manik's collected works remarks, this is a thoroughly unconventional collection of short stories about women married to people in different walks of life, a wonderful portrait gallery, almost Chaucerian in its conception and the variety it has to offer—the shopkeeper's wife who is one up on her husband; the clerk's wife who has the dire experience of growing up a girl with a sexy figure in a lower middle-class family,

---

* See, Jugantar Chakravarty, editor of "Manik Bandyopadhyayer Diary" (he kept several between 1945—1950), published in *Ekshan*, Autumn 1974 and a special issue of 1975.

doubly harassed by male leering and incessant female suspicion, so that the suppression of a passionate nature becomes her lifelong vocation, with occasional venting of steam in hysteria; the leper's wife, filled with hatred for the deformity of his mind that becomes worse than his body in the course of the disease, who finally hits upon a way to live and breathe by turning their home into a shelter for street lepers, tending them her only means of escape from a sick husband's oppressive selfishness.

About the seemingly simple yet eerily haunting "The Priest's Wife", Manik himself made this brief remark in his diary, 'The priest is a believer in God, he's unperturbed, nothing shakes him: not even the deaths of his babies; the other, turned unbeliever, is now unmoved by anything having to do with God,'* even about stealing the temple deities' water pot and desecrating the temple pond by drowning herself in it, using the weight of the filled pot.

"The Widower's Second Wife" and "An Elderly Man's Childbride"—both have a catalytic last scene in which the husband notices that the new wife has put a garland on the photograph of his much-grieved dead wife, the one whose shadow hangs over her, stifling her in one way or another. The meaning of her act and the denouement that follows his noticing it is very different in the two stories: in the former, it is a grown woman's resentment and romantic frustration; in the latter, a child's unthinking gesture to please an aloof authority figure and the unforeseen success of her childlike response in prompting fatherly affection where she failed to find romance.

Of the remaining eleven stories about couples in various modes of attraction or disattraction, in two ("The Widower" and "Death by Hanging") the wife is led to suicide, but the dynamics leading to it and the nature of the responsibility, are quite different. In one case it's the humiliating cruelty of a boorish, complacent husband reaching an unbearable extreme that drives her to it. In the other it's the frustration of her conjugal pride and urge to take charge and distance the marriage from oppressive surroundings, in the form of the suffocating pressures of relatives' and neighbours' pity for the wife of a decent, ordinary man who has fallen into stigma and social disgrace from a false murder charge. Yet there is a subtle commonality, as each reacts in an extreme of hopelessness that the husbands, different as they are, fail to sense, let alone understand. One, narrated in the husband's smirking first person, is an indictment of his smug viciousness, without contriteness or possibility of redemption. The other, narrated in a mellow, neutrally perceptive third person, highlights the tragic mutuality of misunderstanding in conjugal love,

---

* See, "Manik Bandyopadhyayer Diary", Part II, edited by Jugantar Chakravarty in *Ekshan*, 1975.

arising from a difference in the way the society affects the respective individuals.

In both "The Wife of a Man Gone Blind" and "The Wife of a Leprosy-stricken Man," unexpected physical affliction suddenly ends a young couple's marital bliss. However, the striking difference is in the dynamics of the interaction that follows, which is largely a consequence of the differences in the nature of affliction. But not entirely. Also at work is the difference in the strength of the emotional bond, the personalities, and in the mental disorder that follows a progressively disfiguring disease as opposed to a speedy one-stroke disability. These two stories offer fascinating, graphic sketches of the different ways in which the nature and the circumstances of illness feed back into the couple's interactive personality traits and shape the course of psychological morbidity and the almost unconscious coping strategies of each.

Although a reader would come upon light touches of Manik's sardonic humour in even the most tragic of this collection of stories, perhaps by far the most hilarious are "The Shopkeeper's Wife"—about the dead-earnest game of staying one step ahead in the mix of deception and intimacy which play in the power struggle of a relationship, a game in which the fine shades of gray make it rather hard to decide which side to sympathize with—and "The Know-it-all's Wife"—about the painful farce life can be for the spouse of a compulsive show-off, obsessed with instructing and enlightening one and all on everything under the sun.

In "The Ascetic", a husband turned charlatan and guru gets a kick out of seducing a long-deserted wife and abandoning her a second time as revenge for her rejecting, years ago as a new bride, his invitation to elope, to join him in 'renouncing home' when she was ready for nothing more daring than getting on with the difficult enough task of settling down into a conventional marriage in a large, joint family. The husband/guru has the instinct of a killer who returns to the spot of crime to improve upon it.

My inclusion and juxtaposition of "Chor" ("The Thief") and "Sadhu" ("The Ascetic") aim at the contrast between the vulgar, yet sweetly guileless character of the thief and the righteous, yet·smugly vicious character of the guru, brought to light the way it is by the contrasting personality traits underlying their wives' discontented strivings. In one case, the love-for-money mentality of a 'material girl' who happens to be the object of a mere thief's hopelessly deep love; in the other, the passionate longing of an abandoned woman, a starving heart, who happens to be married to a sadistic quitter who beats her with his psychological impotence in the name of righteousness. Both the thief and the ascetic would have been flat cutouts but for the emotional counterpoints played by their respective wives.

"The Widower", first brought out in 1938 in a collection titled *Mihi O Mota Kahini* (Stories fine and course), is about a smugly remorseless creep of a husband who has just found out that with false accusations he has driven his meek wife to hang herself. The only thing that bothers him a bit about it is that he can't get over the unfamiliar resourcefulness she demonstrated in devising her suicide, how in her unequipped pursuit of death in the dead of the night, she contrived to pull the rope through the ceiling hook. He feels vindicated about his vicious accusation, taking her suicide as her admission of guilt, but he is upset from this blow to his conceit about having perfect knowledge of her dumb-meek character. On discovering her suicide following his insults, it is not grief he feels or guilt, just an irritating bit of intrigue that mocks at his boastful condescension towards his inferior, a mere wife who is to be ever beholden to her provider.

"Aunt Atasi", "Serpent-like" and "The Saqi Made of Mere Clay" are among Manik's earliest stories, from his first collection published in 1935. In its introduction, he wrote: '"Aunt Atasi" is my first piece. My writing has changed much since then, as will be quite obvious.' A story of blissful marital love as seen through the sensitive, yearning, adolescent eye. The subject of the other two is the despair of dead marital love as seen through a critical adult eye over a yearning adult heart—one about an insanely jealous husband's murderous deviousness, the other about a self-pitying, emotionally starved husband's comparison of his own wretched marriage, diseased from childbearing amidst poverty, with his affluent neighbour's seemingly blissful marriage, in concealed neurosis resulting from childlessness amidst opulence. The dark heart of "Serpent-like" is in the intelligent wife's knowingly self-destructive stay in a nightmarish marriage with a hideously jealous man. The redemptive grace of "The Saqi Made of Mere Clay" is in the self-hating deprived husband's gaining the insight that a sense of deprivation is part of the human condition. In both, the grim, almost macabre, contents are set off with a bright, lightly sarcastic narrative tone. The even lightness of the voice narrating terrible events and disturbed emotions reminds me of a remark I read recently about Muriel Spark's work,[*] 'cruel things happen while this even, nonchalant tone is maintained.' And Spark's own statement: 'I've put a lot of tension into it, and I've left the emotion out.' Something like this remark would hold also for much of Manik's work. He wrote the pieces in this collection nearly two decades before Spark was published and became known, and in a literary tradition florid with emotion, ornate in

---

[*] See, Stephen Schiff, "Muriel Spark between the lines" in *The New Yorker*, pp. 36 and 41.

language. Another related remark by Schiff on Spark also holds more or less of this entire Manik collection. 'The tone . . . is always at least latently satirical, but it's not ungenerous. She sympathizes with her figments as easily as she lays them waste.'* To the young generations of the 1930s-1950s, this tone rang refreshingly true, it felt electric. The tone permeating his work is illustrated especially well in *The Children of Immortality*, in the portrayal of the three young protagonists in the course of their interactions.

While differing from many other post-Rabindrik, 'new-wave' contemporaries in the disinclination to shock and sensationalize, Manik's work, however, unhesitatingly means to disturb, not soothe, the reader's mind; clearly his purpose is to focus attention on the contradictions that disturbed him, not indulge the need to be uplifted consolingly. His characters are rarely in black and white, the mixing of honesty and deception common enough to be seen as part of human nature. The characters lacking such a mix, like Taranga and Sadhana, succumb as if from an auto-immune deficiency. If the consideration of motive and awareness somewhat blurs the distinction between good and bad, then the reader is best left with the questioning and the self-questioning, to reach a final judgement if possible, but not at the price of too definite a philosophy. A jealous husband's camouflaged murder of his wife in "Serpent-like" is horrible because of the pathological nature of the deceit and his incapacity for enlightenment. A clear-eyed woman's use of a camouflaged murder threat, in "The Accidental Death of Shipra," to bring her manipulative rival and ennui-stricken beau, an irresolute young man, to their senses, refusing to stand by against her own better senses, does not strike us as deplorable because of her unerring perception and effectiveness. She is only a teacher, not a killer—'. . . you shouldn't have gone that far so soon after learning to swim,' she remarks of what she has done, 'I saved her with a lot of difficulty.' We feel pleased with her because her counter-manoeuvre has not only worked for her, but exposed a complacent falsity, made it unviable; we abhor the homicidal husband because not only does his malice come from blind jealously, but he is steeped in deceit.

On one side a hateful husband ("Serpent-like") hypocritically forges a suffering wife's murder to look like an accident to the outside world if not to the bitterly resigned wife; on the other side, a professional thief fallen in love ("Poisoned Love") persuades himself to become a caring husband in order to save the woman he has finally been able to rob from an unintended, accidental death at his hands. Perhaps not unexpectedly,

---

*   See, Stephen Schiff, "Muriel Spark between the lines" in *The New Yorker*, p.41.

given Manik's interest in the schism between appearance and reality in middle-class life, the former is an educated, urbane gentleman and the latter an uncouth underclass swindler. The woman in the one case is sophisticated and highly intelligent, but one whose instinct for survival is paralyzed from marital bitterness; in the other case she is an illiterate, thoroughly plebeian woman, but one whose metier is the harmlessly canny pursuit of purely self-interested survival, a talent that grows robust, not anaemic, from her affection for a man.

The children of immortality are sensitive and brilliant, seductive in their idealism and high-spiritedness, who fall in self-defeat and mutual letdown partly as a result of their very earnestness, their lack of antibodies to the antigens of cynicism and dishonesty. Three young men and women in an age of transition in the moral realm, they could perhaps be saved, at least through mutual understanding and support, which they are foolishly too proud to seek, too self-focussed to offer, too naive to generate on their own—not so unlike most first-generation idealists in any country that has been conditioned to the customs and practices of social stagnation. In the destructive dynamics of their mutual attraction and disattraction, the vulnerability of their puristic idealism gets exposed to the exploitation by the cynical, manipulative world around; their engagingly unconventional traits end up in self-destructive mutual alienation. The maverick assertiveness of the young widow and the sensitive softness of the two young men could potentially make their lives fulfilling and creative, had they consciously befriended each other, instead of leaving each other in the isolation of false pride; had they been more concerned with survival in their apartness from conventionality, instead of acting and reacting on received models and norms. The bravely unconventional, the forbears of a fresh way of life, before it becomes quite the viable or even the dominant mode, often become casualities not only of the leaden weight of existing norms, but also of their own ambivalence and contradiction. Perhaps they are in a greater need of self-knowledge and mutual support in order to survive than are the hidebound, the conventionalist.

This account of three bright young people's interaction gone awry from insufficient engagement in mutual knowledge, compounding a problem of unripe self-knowledge and leading to the emotional ruin of each, gains some fine complexities from the added dimension of intergenerational communication gap in the pursuit of morality, as against conventionality. A hardworking upright woman, devoted wife and mother, Sadhana's fierce loyalty to her personal standards of love and duty ironically produces in her son the demoralization of double failure—proving less than the assigned standard and unable to form his own, caught in a vicious circle of self-loathing.

Altogether, the principal attempt of this collection is to put together

Manik's varied depiction of relations between the sexes (not all marital) in various states of mutual attraction or disattraction, at various levels of society, under different kinds of pressures. Many of these were written when he himself was newly married, almost all before he turned thirty-five. This bit of biographical information helps appreciating, and getting a perspective on, the restless pace of the stories and their keenly enquiring aspect. It is important also for speculating how his angle might have evolved had he lived and worked to a ripe old age, a relevant speculation when comparing the bodies of work of writers subject to the arbitrary factor of unequal longevity.

Comparison in terms of stylistic difference and aspects of literary form may be less limited by this biographic factor. Manik's forte, as this collection amply reveals, is his unflinching portrayal of deceit and disorder in relations, even intimate ones, and his relative freedom from both romantic illusion and cynicism in the interpretation. His viewpoint is skeptical, ironical, wry, but rarely cynical or bitter. These portraits of psycho-sexual relations are striking in their complexity, clear-sightedness, and lack of sentimentality, except in "Aunt Atasi" narrated in adolescent idealization.

In the literary scene of the second quarter of the century, and not just in Bengal for that matter, this kind of investigative empiricism towards the interaction patterns in conjugal life was indeed an exciting, pathbreaking approach to work with, much the same way as chaos theory of non-linear dynamical systems has become in the sciences in its last quarter. Viewing it today through a consciously post-modernist window may fail to appreciate the groundbreaking quality of this approach, fictional depiction of the dynamical systems of psycho-social relation.

Here we may perhaps usefully quote from a Jungian psychotherapist, on the relevance of the logic of chaos theory (as opposed to the Newtonian mechanics under near perfect conditions) to the conceptual framework for understanding the behaviour of the Self:

> . . . like describing the air currents passing over the surface of a falling leaf, as opposed to the surface of a falling pine cone, for instance. No one could ever know enough about the conditions of the leaf's release from the tree, and the condition through which it falls, to predict precisely where it will land or how it will be oriented . . . . Order is impinged upon by all the surprising and unexpected caprices of events in nature and the psyche, the unpredictable twists and turns . . . we broadly think of as fate. We repeatedly emerge from the operation of fate into new configurations of wholeness that could never have been

precisely predicted because of their sensitive dependence on initial conditions, to say nothing of impinging variables along the way . . . . The chaos represents the breakdown of the [previously] ordered side of the Self, which will then be unified into . . . wholeness, through the alchemical process . . . (of) the disintegrations, disorientations, falling apart . . . that many of us—if not all of us—have experienced in the dark nights of the soul . . . in passage from order, through chaos, to new wholeness, over and over throughout life.[*]

If Rabindranath Thakur was an artist of processes of reintegration in relationships and in individual psyches, Manik was that of chaos, those alchemical processes of disintegration which tend to generate whatever uncertain outcome is to follow.

References

Bandyopadhyay, Manik. *Lekhaker Katha* (The author's story), 1957. Calcutta: New Age Publishers.

Chakravarty, Jugantar (ed), "Manik Bandyopadhayayer Diary" published in Calcutta in *Ekshan,* Autumn 1974 and a special issue of 1975.

—. '*Samagra Manik Bandyopadhyay ebang tnar Kabita*' (Manik Bandyopadhyay's works as a collectivity and his poems), published in Calcutta in *Ekshan,* 1973, vol IV, no.5.

Gleik, James, *Chaos: Making a New Science,* 1987, New York : Viking Press

Hill, Gareth S., *Masculine and Feminine: the natural flow of opposites in the psyche,* Boston & London: Shambhala; 1992.

Mitra, Premendra, "Manik Bandyopadhyay" in *Desh*, 12 August 1956.

Mitra, Sarojmohan et al, *Manik Granthabali,* 1963–76, vols. 1-13, Calcutta : Granthalaya.

---

[*] See, S. Gareth Hill, *Masculine and Feminine: The Natural Flow of Opposites in the Psyche*, pp.193, 195, 207, 209.

——. *Manik Bandyopadhyayer Jiban O Sahitya* (Life and Works of Manik Bandyopadhyay); 1970; Calcutta: Granthalaya.

——. *Manik Bandyopadhyay*; 1974; New Delhi: Sahitya Akademi.

Roy Chaudhri, Gopikanath. *Manik Bandyopadhyay: Jibandrishti O Shilpariti* (Manik Bandyopadhyay: View of Life and Artistic Style); 1987; Calcutta: G.E.I. Publishers.

Schiff, Stephen. 'Muriel Spark Between the Lines,' in *The New Yorker*, 24 May 1993.

Wives

The Shopkeeper's Wife[*]

Sarala keeps her anklets on all the time now. Jingle jingle—she walks with the anklets ringing at each step! She doesn't take them off even when she needs to move soundlessly, secretly; she just pushes them up and jams them against her calf muscles—that stops the jingling. Initially, Sambhu was unaware of this. He had thought that the sound of her anklets would reach him before his wife came anywhere near him, like the blare of a horn when a car is approaching from behind. But after getting into trouble a few times, Sambhu stopped relying on his wife's anklets for warning.

Sambhu's shop sits on a bamboo platform in the front portion of a large tin-roofed room in a path running right through the middle of the Ghosh neighbourhood. The low stool he squats on doing his business, with the cashbox stashed under it, is surrounded on three sides by merchandise held in clay pots and basins, open-top cubes made of scrap wood, small and large-size deep wooden dishes, burlap sacks, and so on. Most of these he can reach from his seat by just extending his arm and with the aid of an iron ladle. At the back of his seat stands a row of five wooden shelves to nearly a man's height. The shelves are packed on one side with small, square tins with front panels of yellow glass, containing pearl tapioca, arrowroot powder, crystal sugar, and jars in many shapes for the expensive kinds of spices, like cardamom and clove. These are followed by stacks of glass domes for hurricane lanterns, matchboxes, laundry soap, bath soap, little tins of shoe polish, a variety of candy lozenges in jars, and other such fancy items of grocery and stationery for sale. Three cubits behind the row of shelves is the wall of mud-plastered panels of woven bamboo slats which separates Sambhu's bedroom area. The narrow, dim corridor formed by the space between the wall and the row of shelves is Sambhu's passageway between his home and his shop.

Being a young wife, Sarala is supposed to stay well inside the house. But every now and then she jams her anklets into her calves and stands

---

[*]   The Bengali title is *Dokaneer Bou.*

quietly behind those shelves, her eyes to a gap between the containers, watching her husband's shopkeeping and listening to his conversation with the customers. At home, Sambhu is a rather quiet sort, timid and reserved. But while sitting in the shop, much to Sarala's amazement, he chats and jokes and laughs with his customers. Depending on the customer, he comes up with such funny jokes that Sarala, standing behind the shelves, has a hard time stifling her giggles. But she is amused by Sambhu's conduct only when the customer is male. Regrettably, not all those who come to buy things from his shop are male.

Sarala waits in the corridor until he has finished the transactions on hand. Then, releasing her anklets, and stamping her feet as though she were kicking the floor, she goes inside jangling them. Soon after, Sambhu comes in and finds the fire in the coal stove gone out, the cooking pot for rice and lentils rolling empty on the porch, and Sarala herself on the floor. Sambhu does not take the other signs too seriously. It's the sight of her slumped on a torn mat on the floor, in rejection of their comfortable wide bed on the large bedstead that has come down through three generations, her contorted face and her deaf-mute-blind expression that makes him feel weak. Then for a long time he has to weigh his words, show loving concern, express regret that a person couldn't understand that there's nothing wrong with another person being good-humoured and keeping fellow human beings in good humour, and he has to use a lot of the lozenges he keeps in his shop to pacify her. She's an ogress when it comes to lozenges, and she is not to be pacified with the less expensive kind! She devours the kind he sells only two for a paisa and never spares one as a bonus even to the buyer of four-paisas worth of it.

It is only then that her speech, hearing and sight are restored and the fire of her fury put out. Still, for days she stays in an indifferent and negligent mood, ready to weep at the smallest imagined slight. For a full remedy, Sambhu then has to buy her a new sari, not a very expensive one, just an ordinary sari for regular use, preferably in thin horizontal stripes.

It has been only a year since Sambhu started his shop, and already in this and other similar ways, Sarala has exacted seven new saris. Ordinary, inexpensive saris in the thin stripes she likes.

Yet, close to the year's end, early in the month of Chaitra, Sambhu brings her another new striped sari, without any such compelling reason. He, of course, says it's a gift of love, but he says it a bit too eagerly, a bit too explicitly. Who makes such a gift to a wife who has already exacted seven penalties in a year for no great offence? However, the unexpected sari makes Sarala too happy to stay confined to her husband's house for even another moment. She wears it and goes for a visit to her in-laws' house on the other side of the fence.

Only a section of the house, about a third, is Sambhu's—the large room divided into the bedroom and the shop, a very small room off the building on the north, a little thatched kitchen next to it, and a triangular piece of the central porch separated by a sturdy fence of double-layered split bamboo from a corner of the bedroom to a corner of the kitchen. Sambhu is one of three brothers. The home they inherited from their father was divided thus only a year ago. Sambhu and Sarala live on this side; his elder brother Dinanath and younger brother Baidyanath live on the other side, with their wives and children, Sambhu's widowed mother, an aunt and two sisters. Fencing off his portion to live alone with his wife may seem to indicate extreme selfishness, but that would not be quite true. A year ago when Sambhu was unemployed, Sarala's shopkeeper father Bishnucharan gave his son-in-law the money to set up his shop on condition that he would fence off his share of the property exactly like this. One must therefore concede that Sarala got her present comfort and independence not by making a sheep of her husband, but by using her father's money.

How comfortable Sarala is, how independent! How proud, how precious she feels walking on this side of the fence with her anklets jingling all day for those crowded on the other side to hear, those to whom she had been merely the wife of an unemployed bloke. The shop is doing well. Compared to the tough time those others have, making ends meet, she's almost affluent. A new sari arrives every time she pouts, and now it seems to arrive even without that little effort.

Sarala's appearance in the new striped sari on the other side of the fence draws various comments. The harshest remark comes from her older sister-in-law, Kali, always in a shabby raglike sari. Her withered face charged with envy, she snaps: 'Aren't you ashamed to appear before your elders dressed like a dancing girl? Go back, go and charm your husband with your dance.'

Her younger sister-in-law Khenti is a bit soft in the head, but not envious. She giggles and says, 'From the amount of jingling we hear all day it would seem our middle sister-in-law dances all day, right Didi? Want a paan, middle sister?'

At the sudden appearance of her older brother-in-law, Sarala quickly covers her head with the pallu of her sari, and with a silent shake of the head, turns down Khenti's offer of a paan. Noticing her, he enquires sternly of his sister, 'Punti, why is the second daughter-in-law in our part of the house at this time?'

The reed-thin Punti, dropped by her husband within three months of marriage, says, 'Just visiting, no special reason.'

'Why should someone visit for no reason?' So saying, Sambhu's elder brother Dinanath goes back in.

Immediately Sarala flips the pallu off her head, and as the youngest brother Baidyanath comes out now, her younger sister-in-law covers hers. He is a jovial sort of fellow. While Shambhu reserves his jolly banter for his choice customers at the shop, Baidyanath is not picky about right or wrong time, right or wrong person. Perhaps it is from constantly having to suppress the urge to laugh at his jokes in bed at night that Khenti developed her habit of crazily giggling at anything and everything. He says, 'This must be a lucky day! Middle sister-in-law honouring us dressed in her finery! What luck! Whose face did I see upon rising this morning to get so lucky, eh? Punti, get going, seat her properly, go fetch a good rug from Chhinath-babu's house.'

Such are their responses to Sarala. Only Sambhu's old mother, impervious to all this, sits in a corner of the porch facing the large room, turning her beads silently. She doesn't even look up when Sarala comes to her to pay obeisance. And when Sarala proceeds to touch her feet, she says sternly, 'Don't touch me, dear, in a new sari that is still unwashed!'

Sarala's teeth are a bit on the large side; normally, they're never fully covered. After spending twenty minutes at her in-laws' place, when she returns home, her lips are pursed tightly together.

How terribly they mistreated her before she got her separate home. Before the fence went up in the porch, Sarala was thin and weak. How little she ate, how hard she worked, how much scolding she put up with through each day, and never a sweet word from Sambhu to soothe the ears ringing from the harsh words!

Being in her own household has in one year made her body plump and round, and filled her mind with peace and happiness. Sarala lives almost like a queen, with little work to do except cook for the two of them; the rest of the work is done by a poor neighbourhood widow hired to come daily. The money her father promised Sambhu for the shop was not given all at once, he gives it in instalments as incentive to improve his performance. Every month he comes to inspect the stocks and the transaction accounts. Each time he also enquires of his daughter if there has been any, even temporary, drop in Sambhu's love and attention. The man must be a particularly suspicious, distrustful sort—otherwise he would not be asking this of his daughter so directly, even after seeing her many new striped saris and her oozy pleasure.

If Sarala still has any unhappiness, that is only from the loneliness of living this greatly beneficial separate life. Day and night she can hear all the sounds from the trouble-ridden household on the other side of the fence. Sitting in her home on this side, she follows everything small and big that goes on there. She knows when the children cry from hunger and when they cry from a beating, when her older sister-in-law shouts with reason and when she shouts without any, when her younger sister-in-law giggles inappropriately and gets scolded, with whom her younger brother-in-law jokes, which relatives come to visit and when they leave. Sarala has made several pairs of tiny holes on the partition fence from one end to the other. Moving from one pair of holes to another, she spends hours watching the goings-on in that household. Every now and then she gets an irresistible urge to go for a twirl in that chaotic whirlpool of happenings.

Back from the visit to her in-laws', Sarala does not stop to change out of her new striped sari, or get ready to cook. She watches Sambhu's shopkeeping for a while, and still feels restless. Her father is coming this afternoon; she considers whether to go away with him for some time. All kinds of thoughts turn in her mind, disobedient from the indulgence of idleness. Earlier, they tormented her because Sambhu was unemployed. Now, they are rude to her because she has her separate household. Suppose the fence were pulled down and the split households rejoined, would they treat her well considering the amount of money Sambhu makes, and how much more he will make in the future? But then the problem is that if they start getting a share of the profit from the shop now, the time will never come when Sambhu will make enough to keep in the iron safe. No matter how many new striped saris she exacts and lozenges she consumes, Sarala roughly knows the balance of income and expenditure in the shop. She goes to the bed and lies down. She feels frustrated at not being able to figure out how long it would take her to be wealthy enough to buy up the love and respect of all those in the other household.

She gets up after a long time, walks to the fence out of habit, and puts her eyes to a pair of holes in the middle part of it. She sees Sambhu sitting in the porch facing the big room on that side, talking to everyone gathered there. She has from time to time seen Sambhu on the other side of the fence. That doesn't surprise her. If she, as another family's daughter, could visit them, he certainly could visit them sometimes! What strikes her as astonishing is their behaviour with Sambhu. No one seems the slightest bit upset, let alone angry with him for splitting up. As soon as he crosses the fence, he blends easily in that household as if he were one of them. Punti brings him a glass of water. Sarala can't make out what he's discussing with them; they're all listening to him attentively and talking happily to each other. Even after Sambhu gets up and leaves, the rest of the family keeps talking among themselves. Sarala wonders what serious matter her husband could be linked with that she doesn't know of, that required so much consultation.

'Nothing important,' he says when she asks. 'Just talking about dividing up the land, because I'm thinking of selling my share.'

'Why? Why'll you sell it?'

'As if you don't know why!' Sambhu says with a glum face. 'How long have I been saying that there's no money in selling salt and oil, I want to set up a variety store in the market? Doesn't that take money? Where can I get it, unless I sell my share of the land?'

'But the land also brings you some money,' Sarala reasons.

'The shop will bring a lot more.'

Still worried, Sarala asks, 'When will you start this other shop in the market?'

'I'm thinking of the first of Baisakh, now it's all upto my luck.'

Sambhu lets out an enormous yawn, snaps his fingers before his wide open mouth, shakes his head and turns to sit at an angle away from her saying: 'Your father said he'd give six hundred rupees in all for the shop, but after giving one hundred for starting it, he held back the rest. In the one year since then, he gave me only two hundred more—how can a shop be run like this? Running even a little shop requires a lump sum.'

Doing a complex bit of mental calculation, she says, 'Father's coming today. Shall I ask him for it?'

With a doleful face Sambhu says, 'What good is asking? He won't give more than twenty or thirty rupees at a time.'

'He certainly will if I press him,' Sarala replies smiling widely.

Sambhu then gives her some lozenges, brings an invisible blush on her dark cheeks, and whispers in her ears his own secret scheme. Sambhu is counting on the money his mother has got; he's her favourite son, as Sarala knows, so he's trying to get hold of that money. Otherwise, why does he have to go to that household so often! Sambhu will be starting a big store in the market—no mere shopkeeping, doing real business this time—Sarala mustn't forget to ask her father for the rest of the money. Goddess Durga be praised! And no need to cook lunch now! Some fruit and stuff will do just fine—he understands how hard it is for Sarala to cook in this heat.

Sarala knows some error has entered her calculation and there's a possibility the scales will not tip in her favour; still it's not good to do a lot of shopkeeping with one's husband. With her father's money she has bought her husband for a whole year; it may be well now to let him off the leash, whatever that might bring her. After all, one day she'll have to consign herself to her husband's hands without the help of any protective talisman. Besides, the way her husband has loved her during this one year should not be taken as all show merely because of her own nagging suspicions. It would, of course, be best if she could postpone letting go until after the baby is born, for she knows well from living with him this long that his hardened shrewd heart will turn soft and green at the sight of his own son's face. But the son will still be a while coming. If before that Sambhu opens a variety store in the market with money from selling his land, he'll think all the credit is his and he has no reason to be grateful to anyone. Going by things from the past, of course, Sarala isn't sure how much value gratitude enjoys in Sambhu's mind. Within a year or two of starting his variety store in the market, if he makes so much money that Sarala can tear down the fence and live without fear, in peace with the others, almost as the undisputed mistress of the entire house, then perhaps with rocklike hardness and ingratitude he himself will keep her down. Still, as a slight possibility has arisen that even in future he may remain under her influence, it's better to leave the helm this time and see what happens.

Sarala's suspicion-prone, distrustful father is at first taken aback by his daughter's demand. Three hundred rupees all at once! He was in fact thinking of not giving his son-in-law another paisa; the way the shop is running is enough for two people to live on well with food and clothing, at least as well as the poor can, though not like the rich. He has not taken it upon himself to make his son-in-law rich. True, he promised to give six hundred in all; but people say all sorts of things in all sorts of situations in life. Should they or could they follow all those to the letter? The arrangement must change with the situation. Besides, if Sambhu has the foolish idea of starting a variety store in the market . . . .

Sarala makes quite a fuss crying and protesting. She cries and fusses more than she needs to in order to impress Sambhu about how much trouble she's taking to extract the money for him from her father. 'You said you'd give, now you're saying no, Father?' Sarala sounds as if her heart is going to break with the agony of disappointment and sorrow. It's not easy for her father to hand out three hundred rupees in a bundle, yet after resisting her campaign for a good part of the day, he concedes defeat. He has three sons, but no other daughter; she's his one and only motherless little girl. After asking Sambhu a lot of questions like where the shop would be, goods worth how much would be stocked in the store and how much he would have at hand as capital, he takes leave with a worried unsmiling face.

Triumphantly Sarala says to Sambhu: 'See!'

Sambhu thanks her in response. Not quite the way a husband expresses gratitude to his wife, but modestly, politely, almost respectfully. At this point suddenly, the giggle of Sarala's younger sister-in-law Khenti is heard on the other side of the fence. Has she been spying through a hole in the fence, listening to them? Sarala at once goes around the kitchen to the other side, and finds the yard empty except for Khenti and Baidyanath and the dog. Standing between the fence and the paddy storebin, jovial Baidyanath has been joking with his wife.

'Where's everybody?' Sarala asks her younger sister-in-law in a huff.

Khenti steps up close and whispers that they're all inside.

That's plausible. The sun is harsh outside and the wind hot on this Chaitra afternoon. But don't these two have a room to stay in? What are they doing out here at this hour, laughing and joking? Back in her own place, she and Sambhu leave the porch and go inside. Sarala lies down on the three-generation-old huge bedstead (to this day she hasn't figured out by what trick Sambhu extracted it from his brothers' clutches when dividing the property) and closes her eyes. Sambhu sits smoking his hookah. Ever since his wife left him to dress his own hookah, he puts in so much tobacco that Sarala becomes impatient waiting for him to finish smoking after lunch and dinner. Today she falls asleep. Perhaps she's tired after wrestling with her father all day, or irritated from finding Baidyanath joking privately with his wife behind the paddy storebin out in the hot sun.

After about a week, Sambhu leaves one morning to see Sarala's father for the money. Before leaving, he stops by at the other household. He has already stopped replenishing stocks; his shop has run out of many things and many customers go back empty-handed. Still he doesn't want to close the shop for even a day as he wants to sell off the staples like rice and lentils and spices, stuff that would not be sold in the variety store. Baidyanath will sit in for him today—unemployed, jolly Baidyanath, Sambhu's younger brother, who hides behind the paddy storebin in midday sun, having a laugh with his wife. Sambhu too was once unemployed, and he too had a wife—with rickety bones like an overused hackney carriage—still a wife is a wife. Khenti is no fairy either, is she? She's soft in the head too, giggling for no reason even as she works hard and eats little—the way Sarala did until a year ago. Sarala never saw Sambhu laugh when he was unemployed; after he started the shop, she has seen him laugh a few times, but only with his customers. But then Sambhu buys his wife striped saris. Baidyanath laughs with many besides his wife, but he never buys his wife a sari. How can he when he has no money? The difference between the two brothers is amazing. Even their names have just the qualifier 'nath' in common. Drop that and one is Sambhu, the ascetic, the other is Baidya, the healer!

Silencing her anklets, Sarala stands behind the shelves, watching Baidyanath's unpractised shopkeeping, and studying the shop's forlorn, denuded look with the few stocks left.

Sarala hasn't been feeling happy the last few days; her buck teeth have remained hidden behind pursed lips most of the time. Daughter of a seasoned shopkeeper and wife of a beginner, her instinct keeps telling her she's making a mistake, one that'll bring her not just loss, but bankruptcy this time. For quite a while now, things around her are becoming curious, incomprehensible; yet, as though with eyes and ears closed, she has been allowing these ungrasped goings-on move towards culmination. Sambhu's frequent visits to that household these days may be explained by his desire to divide the land, as he told her. But how to explain the behaviour of those people towards him? Are they gods and goddesses that, even after Sambhu partitioned the house over a year ago and now wanted to divide the land, they treat him as their very own? Besides, why should the subject of Sambhu closing the shop and opening another in the market cause such a current of excitement in that household? What difference would it make to them? Her eyes at the fence holes, she clearly senses the grown-up members of the family going through something. They are acting exactly as they would at the immediate prospect of a big family event like a wedding or a youth's sacred-thread ceremony. Of course it is possible that some big event is going to take place in that household at the same time that Sambhu is to open his new shop. But then why is Sarala without any knowledge of what it is. Whatever is about to happen on that side of the fence is unlikely to have stayed unknown to her unless they had conspired to hide it from her. And would something they are all trying to hide from her ever be to her benefit?

Sarala regrets not having consulted her father about these strange goings-on, trying only to make him give the money. A mere woman, how could she singlehandedly deal with so many conniving against her? At least if she knew what the conspiracy was about, she could try to defend herself with her own wit. But she has been groping in the dark, floating with the current, she even thought it might be better to slacken control over her husband. As a mere woman, and a new wife, could she allow a condition to develop in which they could secretly conspire against her?

At one point, seeing there are no customers at the shop, she calls Baidyanath in. 'Tell me, brother-in-law, what was it my husband came to discuss at your place?'

Jolly Baidyanath replies, 'Don't you know, second sister-in-law? He came to speak ill of you—that you pull him up by one ear, and pull him down by the other, making his ears ache so . . . .'

Irritated, Sarala interrupts, 'You talk just like the low folk, you know. The way you talk, with not one paisa to call your own, burns people. How much you'll be pinching out of the money from the sales today, you alone know!'

Thus rewarded for tittering with his wife a few days ago behind the paddy stack, Baidyanath goes back to the shop. Sarala sits on the porch, cheek on her palm, worrying about the future. Her father had been impressed that Sambhu's older brother was a lawyer's clerk and Sambhu himself, only two years short of matriculation, was an account-keeper in a godown. Falling for these things, he gave his dark-complexioned daughter with buck-teeth in marriage to Sambhu. Perhaps he shouldn't have. There was another proposal from a farmer by the name of Jagat from the next village—maybe her father should've picked him. That man would've stayed subservient to her without any effort on her part, and if it was in her luck, she could slowly have got him to improve things so that one day she would have walked around in striped saris and ringing anklets, doing no housework and taking no one's hard words. A shopkeeper's daughter with dark skin and buck-teeth is better off married to an illiterate farmer. A man who after studying upto the eighth grade works in someone else's godown and does shopkeeping with yet another's money must be this wicked and deceitful . . . .

When Sambhu returns late next day, Sarala at once senses that he is no longer quite the same man he was when he left yesterday. He left almost holding his breath, he is back breathing freely. Sambhu was once involved in litigation. She remembers the difference between the state he was in when he left home on the day of the verdict and the state he came back in after hearing it go in his favour. There is a very similar change in him now after seeing his father-in-law.

'Got the money?' Sarala asks him.

'Yes,' he says, grinning from ear to ear.

'All of it?'

'All of it. Where's the fan? Come on now, fan me a little.'

She merely points at the palmyra fan resting against the fence, and goes on: 'Tell me, didn't my big brother make any fuss about father giving you this money? At the time of our wedding, my brother had such a tiff about my four hundred rupee dowry!'

His triumphant smile already gone, he glowers at her. 'I come back sweating in this hot sun, and you can't even fan me,' he says. 'Any other wife would've fanned her husband without even being asked.'

With a smile Sarala says, 'My little sister-in-law does that sort of stuff, and that's because your brother makes her laugh so much.'

Though she brings the palmyra and fans him, it doesn't cool him. Sarala says, as if to herself, 'Poor thing, my little sister-in-law! I wish her as many years of life as there is hair on my head!'

'Why?'

'Last night I had a nightmare about her choking to death giggling! Burn that sort of nasty dream!'

Sambhu's temper flares up. 'Trying to be funny with me, eh? You won't get away with this sort of thing, I tell you. I come home tired and hot from walking in the sun . . . .'

Offended by his reproach, Sarala throws down the palmyra fan, marches out to the porch, and lies down on the torn mat. After a while Sambhu comes out massaging himself with oil on his way to bathe, and asks her in a matter-of-fact tone, 'What's it now? What did I say to be so upset about?'

Getting no response from Sarala, he leaves for the pond for his noon bath with the towel on his shoulder. The sight of him walking slowly away seems to her like an optical illusion in the dazzling glare of the Chaitra sun! No new sari, no lozenges, no caresses, no sweet words. Merely asks casually if she is upset and walks off to the pond! Sambhu's behaviour has deteriorated so much in just one day? Maybe at lunch, he'll even shout at her for burning the lentils! What a mistake she has made not disclosing things to her father and seeking his advice!

At lunch Sambhu says nothing about the burnt lentils; instead, he deigns to ask her once not to sulk. In a tearful voice Sarala complains, 'Why did you scold me?'

'I didn't scold you. It's only because I came back so sweaty and tired . . . .'

After lunch today Sarala dresses the hookah for him. She dresses it, but doesn't blow at it to light the charcoal and tobacco; she had tried it out once before the mirror and knew that blowing made her face look quite ugly. Sambhu takes the hookah from her, blows at it himself, and smokes contentedly. Sarala says, 'Take an account from brother-in-law of all the sales he made.'

'I will,' says Sambhu.

Sarala persists. 'Forty-one pounds of rice bought by Rakhal-babu's house, five pounds of mung lentils from Chhinath lawyer's house, a pound and a half of crystal sugar and a bar of soap, and a lot of small sales besides. Yesterday brother-in-law took home a large amount of oil in a clay cup, and today some lozenges and a container of something. Ask him about it.'

'Okay, okay, I'll take care of it.'

Then at some point Sambhu goes to sleep. Sarala goes to the other house. Nobody asks her either to come in or to sit down, but she is used to this. The older sister-in-law is lying down, Khenti is stitching a rag quilt, Baidyanath is knocked out in sleep. The mother-in-law, squatting, turns the beads, and her daughter sits beside her silently. Knowing that her older brother-in-law is out to work at this time, Sarala goes about quite freely looking into one room after another with her head barely covered. Afterwards, she sits with Khenti for a while. Khenti whispers some inanities and giggles but Sarala is not able to extract even a word from her on the real matter she is after. Back home, she climbs onto the grand bedstead and just sits on it. The clothes arranged on the bamboo pole hung from the ceiling are swaying in the strong draught; her two striped saris among those catch her eye. Her attention is also caught by the large hairy birthmark near the back of her husband's neck. Sambhu is asleep on his side, with his broad back bearing the imprint of the woven mat. He turned on his side when Sarala came in, facing away from her. Maybe this was a sign of an impending change of fortune, who knows! Ill luck signals its approach in advance, in so many ways. Just before her marriage was fixed with Sambhu, negotiations were on for a very good match, but when leaving to go to see the groom, her father stumbled on the threshold. The night before the day her first son died in her womb, an owl screeching in the mango tree at the back of their bedroom had her half-dead with fear. Suddenly she stiffens. A gecko on the fence is clicking now. Oh dear, who knows what's written on Sarala's forehead!

Waking up in the afternoon, splashing water on his face and recalling the pleasure of smoking a prepared hookah after lunch, Sambhu says, 'Make me a chillum of tobacco, will you?'

'Make it yourself,' replies Sarala.

Sambhu feels profoundly magnanimous, as if he were a jailed prisoner who has just woken up from his first sleep after a long time on his three-generation-old family bedstead. Preparing the hookah himself, he goes and opens his shop and sits on the wooden squat stool smoking. The poor young widow of the neighbourhood comes in and leaves after washing the utensils, filling the water containers, cleaning and wiping the kitchen floor. The other household soon begins waking up after the midday lull. The afternoon ends and evening sets in. Sarala doesn't take her afternoon wash, she doesn't light the stove to cook supper, restlessly she spends some time inside, and some time standing behind the shop shelves watching the proceedings there. Dinanath stops by the shop on his way home from work. After the last customer has left, he asks Sambhu: 'Got the money?'

'Yes. You go home, I'll be there.'

'Why don't we sit here and talk?'

'No. No. Not here. She hides and listens to everything.'

Transferring the files from under one arm to the other, Dinanath says: 'The children make too much noise for us to talk at home. If she comes near here, wouldn't the sound of her anklets . . . ?'

When Sambhu explains that her anklets don't always ring, Dinanath goes home with some remark about the kind of father whose daughter she is. After some time, Sambhu closes the shop, puts out the light and comes inside. Under the sacred tulsi that Sarala herself planted a year ago in a corner of the porch, there's an oil lamp now about to go out. There's no other light in this house. Only a little light on the bedroom ceiling coming from the lamp lighted in the other house across the fence. Coming in, he strikes a matchstick in the flame of which he notes that Sarala is lying down in bed. He lights a bidi. Then after calling her once, and getting no response, he leaves for the other household in a relieved mood.

Then Sarala sits up. She takes off for the first time the anklets she has worn constantly for a year now, walking like a queen. Her feet feel strangely light. Lightfootedly she steps out on the porch. Through the holes in the fence she finds that the only sooty lantern in that house is inside the big room, which must be where the three brothers are conferring, with Kali sitting near the door and her mother-in-law sitting inside, invisible in the background except for her hand turning the beads. Shunning her usual shortcut to the other yard along the side of her kitchen shed, she goes straight for the thicket at the back of the shed and Khenti's room next to it. It's terribly dark here. Her heart pounds in fright. When crossing the dump of refuse and kitchen scraps, a fishbone pricks her bare foot. But what can Sarala do? How can she afford to be deterred by fear or a fishbone prick? A lone woman, with so many people conspiring against her, setting a trap she knows nothing of! What's fear now or the pricking of a fishbone! She doesn't care what else she encounters; she only hopes that no evil thing catches hold of her while she walks like this in the scrub and refuse dump in the dark, that the son in her womb doesn't die this time too before birth. She didn't venture out with her hair loose, though; before stepping out into the yard, she took the precaution of gathering her hair up in a tight bun, tearing off a strand and casting it away, and then biting off a bit of the nail from her left hand's little finger. This is all that she has working for her by way of protection.

At the back of the big room are several banana plants. The two windows in the room also face this side. But the room sits on a high foundation and the windows are well above the fence. After taking so much trouble to come this far, she is close to tears at finding the windows too high for her to look in through. However, the three brothers must be sitting on the cot next to one of the windows, for she can hear them quite clearly; only the remarks by Punti, Kali and her mother-in-law can't be made out. Checking her tears and the urge to see the scene inside, Sarala puts her ears to work.

Sambhu's voice: 'So many times I've told you, Baidyi, yet this simple account doesn't get into your head? The stationery still left in my shop is worth over one hundred approximately. By not restocking the goods, I've saved up one hundred and a few rupees more—let's suppose one hundred. And my father-in-law has given me three hundred. That makes five hundred rupees—that's my share. If you and dada contribute five hundred each, then the total will be fifteen hundred. The store can be started with one thousand, and five hundred we'll hold in cash.'

The sound of the youngest wife's giggle, muffled by her stuffing some of her sari into her mouth, is followed by Dinanath's stern rebuke—'Bou-ma! Stop acting shamelessly!' He then says, 'The problem, you know Sambhu, is that even if I somehow manage to raise five hundred scraping everything together and selling your bou-di's jewellery, how's Baidyi going to find so much money? Selling his wife's jewellery can't bring so much.'

Baidyanath's voice: 'Three hundred at the most. But if I sell my wedding ring . . . .'

Sambhu's voice: 'Why don't you shut up, you're always acting the clown.'

Dinanath's voice: 'Baidyi! Your nature is becoming as impossible as your wife's.'

Sambhu's voice: 'Enough. Let's talk business. Let Baidyi then contribute two hundred and fifty, he'll get half as much as each of us gets from the profit. The reason I want to settle everything about this division beforehand is because otherwise there may be trouble in future. It's simple, each gets a share of the profit proportionate to the capital he puts in; that settles all problems.'

After a short silence, Dinanath's voice says, 'In that case Sambhu, I too would like to say something clearly. The five hundred you're promising . . . .'

Sambhu's voice: 'Five hundred not in cash. One hundred in goods, four hundred in cash.'

Dinanath's voice: 'All right, show us just once the four hundred in cash. I don't want to be told of problems after I've sold all the jewellery.'

Sambhu's voice is now angry. 'You don't' trust me, is that it? You think I'm bluffing to . . . .'

Four or five voices express objections in various ways. Sambhu's voice gets angrier. 'Because I offered to make you equal partners, you suspect me! As if I couldn't open a store on my own! If I start a store with five hundred, I'll make a thousand in profit in one year. If you don't want to come along, don't! I don't need your money.'

Shouts and angry words are followed by mild voices trying to mollify the angered ones. After some silence, the conversation resumes on personal matters. Again, a quarrel nearly breaks out.

Then comes Sambhu's voice. 'Very well, tomorrow morning I'll show you my cash.'

Dinanath's conciliatory voice follows. 'I've already spoken to Gajen the goldsmith, he has offered a rate of twenty-nine-and-a-half. Tomorrow I'll skip going to office and finish this business. What a loss! It's not like selling a lump of gold, there's nothing more punishing than having to sell jewellery . . . Looks like bou-ma over there hasn't lighted the stove tonight, has she, Sambhu? Then have your meal here before you go back. Oh Punti, go set the places for our supper now!'

Where did the money go, the money that he put in the box the day before! With grief for the money and the loss of face before everyone in the other house, Sambhu starts tearing his hair like a lunatic.

Consoling him, Sarala says, 'What can you do? One has no control over one's fate! I was sleeping, the door was open, and you went over there and stayed till ten at night! And the box! Maybe it broke with just a little prying with a pick. I too fell into such a sleep that I knew nothing!'

Eyes filled with suspicion, he glares at her and says, 'Whether or not you knew nothing . . . . '

Sarala quickly interrupts, 'Don't be so desperate, dear. Just go on running the shop here a little longer, the way you did, until I talk my father into giving you some more money . . . .'

'Your father isn't going to give me any money again!'

'He won't easily. But if I cry and fuss, maybe . . . .'

Jingling the anklets, she goes and brings him a bowl of puffed rice with some molasses, and says lovingly, 'Eat. Staying hungry will not bring back your money. If my father doesn't give the money—he will, of course, but *if* he doesn't—I'll get you the money by selling my jewellery.'

The Spirited Wife*

An unsubmissive spirit was Sumati's one major flaw. She was a decent-looking young woman, not lacking in the skills of housework either; if needed, she could work from sunrise to sunset without a word in complaint. Her capacity for loving, caring, and attending to others' needs was in no way less than that of an average young Bengali woman. Her only fault was her abnormally tough spirit. She couldn't tolerate the slightest unjust or excessive conduct; to forgive even a minor lapse was something she considered utterly humiliating. She met all the wishes of those having a right to give her orders—but only until they were expressed as orders. The louder the order came the more defiantly she reacted.

The most hazardous thing was that not only could she not bear anyone's overreaction, she would go out of her way to criticize it spiritedly. For a young wife in a Bengali family, unbalanced criticism invariably means insulting her elders, fighting with her peers, and scolding the hell out of the little ones or hitting them.

Unfortunately, overreaction is quite a common thing in life. Is there anyone who doesn't feel deprived in life in some way? To resist trying to make up for the deprivations in some areas of life by behaving excessively in others requires dedicated cultivation of the habit. Sages and mahatmas would have us believe that most people do care to cultivate such a dedication or that they could only if they wanted to, but that is not quite true.

Sumati is faced with peril at every step. Even if it is possible to scrape through life before marriage constantly getting into trouble for disrespecting elders, fighting peers, and scolding the little ones, how could all this continue after marriage, at the in-laws' home? The first couple of years after her marriage, Sumati kept her spiritedness in check with an extreme effort of will and produced nothing worse than a couple of roiling incidents. In the constant tussle between her artificial restraint under duress and her inborn defiance, as the restraint gradually wore out and ran thin, she got into trouble. She even provoked her mother-in-law to raise

---

* The Bengali title is *Tejee Bou*.

the rolling pin at her one day. Only because it was the first time, she stopped at merely brandishing the rolling pin. But how long could she be expected to hold back from hitting? Being a woman, and a mother-in-law at that, the limit of her tolerance was quite naturally small.

It's hard to say from where Sumati got such a spirited temperament. Her father Sadananda is a bovinely timid and harmless man—perpetually worrying about offending someone or the other. Her mother has been sick all her life, and her temper has gone awry because of her endless illness. Every now and then she is given to fits of temper, tears and head banging. But this is not symptomatic of a strong spirit; she's in fact a very fearful woman. Sumati's two elder brothers have been petty clerks from the time they were twenty or twenty-two—no question of their being spirited. Her sisters are imbued with inordinate amounts of bashfulness and sentimentality; armoured with superhuman tolerance, all four of them have dedicated their lives to serving their husbands and sons.

By what rule of nature Sumati came into existence in their midst is hard to tell. It is also hard to tell exactly which rule she's an exception to. The phenomenon is an impenetrable mystery from start to finish. Being a bit short on bashful modesty and sentimentality wouldn't be surprising, even a little impatience is understandable; but holding such strength of spirit while dedicating one's life merely to the service of husband and sons seems as incongruous as it is unimaginable.

Sumati has just one son, not yet two years of age. She is expecting another baby in a few months, and it would not be possible to tell wether it is a son or a daughter until then. However, she hopes it'll be a boy, because if she can have a daughter after two sons, then one day she would be able to combine a lot of pride with the joy of motherhood.

But that's all in the future. Meanwhile, serious trouble arises as she increasingly desires to be at her parents' place for the birth of the second child as was the case with the first.

Her mother-in-law shakes her head and says, 'No, you can't go to your parents' place now. Didn't you just come back from there?'

Sumati argues: 'That was for my brother's wedding, and I couldn't stay for even a week.'

Her mother-in-law was not well disposed towards her that day. In the morning, when her little boy cried a lot as Sumati spoonfed him, her mother-in-law, though not particularly dissatisfied or annoyed with it, remarked, perhaps only to assert herself, 'Can't you even feed him his milk without making him cry, my dear?'

Earlier, Sumati would have kept quiet. But with her self-restraint worn down these days, she looked up and said, 'Babies cry a little when being fed.'

'Rubbish! You're talking back too much these days, daughter-in-law.'

'Not a question of talking back. What I said isn't untrue.'

'So, is what I said untrue? Do I lie? You are calling me a liar!'

Anger choked the mother-in-law's voice for a second. She would have said a lot more but she caught sight of Sumati's expression, one that she had not seen before—the sharp look in her eyes and her unperturbed manner—and somehow it held her voice back. Sumati stopped feeding the baby, got up calmly, quietened him unhurriedly, and held him to her mother-in-law, saying, 'I did not call you a liar. All I said was that babies sometimes cry when being fed milk with a spoon. Why don't you show me how you can feed him without making him cry at all.'

Taken aback, her mother-in-law said, 'Is that an order from you?' Then she raised such an uproar that Mohanlal responded by coming down heavily on Sumati.

Hurt by her husband's unjustified rebuke, Sumati has not eaten the whole day, but still her mother-in-law is in a rotten mood. Had she tried, even once, to defend herself, or cried a little when taking her husband's undue scolding, perhaps her mother-in-law's mood wouldn't have remained so bad. Taking a husband's scolding silently after indignantly responding to one's mother-in-law is not something a mother-in-law can be expected to like. She is sullen.

'You arguing back again?' she now snarls. 'I said there's no need to go to your parents' place now. Why can't you let it rest at that, why do you argue so much? Went for only a week, indeed. That I let you go for a week is lucky for fourteen generations of your ancestors, keep that in mind.'

Sumati's nostrils flare. She says, 'Mother, is it proper for the respectable elderly to insult someone's ancestry?'

'Respectable elderly! As if you treat me as a respectable elder! I can't keep talking and arguing with you, I'm telling you for the last time—you can't go, you can't, you can't.'

At night, Sumati eats her full meal and comes into her bedroom. Mohanlal was hoping that Sumati would cry a little. Sitting close by him, letting her body touch his, she says with a smile, 'See how unreasonable it is of mother! Who doesn't know that at this time a woman needs to be with her parents? My father wrote asking for permission to take me, and your mother said she wouldn't let me go. The reply to that letter must go tomorrow—try to reason a little with her in the morning, will you?' She says this in a tone of forgiveness for her mother-in-law's childishness despite feeling annoyed.

Had Sumati cried a little, had she placed her head on his chest, if not at his feet, to express her eagerness to go to her parents' place, Mohanlal would have complied. He would not just have reasoned with his mother, he'd in fact have categorically asserted that Sumati should be sent home.

But seeing the toughness of Sumati's spirit, he replies angrily, 'I'm not going to do any such thing.'

'You won't? Fine.'

'What do you mean by that? Are we to let you go to your parents' as and when you want?'

Moving away from him, Sumati sits up straight and retorts, 'When did I ever go to my parents' place as and when I wanted?'

Getting angrier, Mohanlal says, 'Are you the boss here to decide when you're to go to your parents' place? You'll go when you're sent, and keep quiet when you aren't. What gives you the right to show so much temper? Aren't you the wife in this household?'

'Does one suffer this fate unless one is a wife! You won't let me go?'

'No!'

'Why not?'

'That's my prerogative.'

Sumati has restrained her righteous spirit so far. She cannot any longer. Her nostrils keep flaring. 'Even the cobblers and sweepers don't exercise prerogatives with their wives so arbitrarily, even they have some compassion and love. You, because you're gentlefolk . . . .'

She flings herself down by her sleeping child, and with her eyes closed, finishes with very different words, in the solemn tone of a resolution, 'I'll definitely go this time.'

Ablaze with fury Mohanlal says, 'Even if mother lets you go to your parents, I'll not. A shameless, ill-mannered broad like you deserves to be whipped.'

Sumati opens her eyes wide and says, 'If I don't manage to go to my parents within a month, why bother to get a whip, you can beat me up with your shoe.'

There was no need for so much to have happened. Had Sumati behaved a little modestly with her mother-in-law, had she lowered her head and tugged at her heart with entreaties, then even if reluctant at first, she would have agreed in the end. Had she shed a little tear before Mohanlal, her purpose would have been accomplished. On the other hand, if her mother-in-law had said just a little nicely that it would be better if she did not go to her parents' place this time, then however upset, Sumati wouldn't have turned so desperate for it. Even after the argument with her mother-in-law, when she came into the bedroom, had Mohanlal just said, 'As mother seems to be so much against your going this time, why don't you drop it?'—then she'd perhaps have wept a bit in disappointment but finally agreed. This pointless dispute about her going to her parents' place would've been solved nicely. It is all a mess now because of Sumati's spirited attitude.

From the authorities on this side a letter goes to her father, telling him they couldn't send her this time as there are problems. Sumati also writes to her father on her own, asking him to send someone as soon as possible to accompany her to their place.

Sadananda writes a long letter to his daughter, taking pains to reason with her, telling her that when they are all against sending her, would it not be improper for her to insist?

The reply Sumati sends to this letter is of such a nature that the poor gentleman takes three days' leave from his office and hurries to his daughter's in-laws' place. His heart beats fearfully, his face is wilted. Close to tears, he pleads and begs at length for permission to take his daughter with him. But Sumati's mother-in-law wouldn't budge. Shaking her head, she firmly says, 'No, my son's father-in-law, no. We can't send her this time.'

He stops fearfully when he sees that the mother-in-law, instead of softening at his tearful entreaties, is about to get angry. At another time his coming here himself and begging like this might have moved the mother-in-law; she might no longer have remembered her initial arguments with Sumati regarding this visit, but Sumati has meanwhile spiritedly argued back several times. Not just a little spiritedly, but in a manner that scathes, singes, sets a person on fire.

Sumati tells her father, 'I must go with you right now, Father. You have to take me.'

He tries to reason with his daughter. He does not leave untried any of the ways in which it might be possible to persuade her. But it is a matter not of reasoning or persuasion, but of the unyielding nature of her defiant spirit.

Finally, even the harmless, bovinely timid Sadananda gets annoyed and scolds her. 'How's it possible that you'll go when they'll not let you go? I can't take you. If you can persuade them, then write to me and I'll come and take you. And why're you so crazy about going? You can go later.'

Sadananda goes back. Now Sumati keeps burning in the fire of her spirit. Her physical condition cannot bear so much mental heat; the more peace and quiet the mind has in this condition, the better it is. Very soon, her limbs become thin like sticks and in her thin, wan face only her eyes glow as if in a fever. She talks less, eats less, rests less—she keeps to herself, works as much as possible at essential and inessential tasks, and agitates as much as possible when there's no work. Then as a month nears its end, the period after which she has offered to take her husband's beating with a shoe instead of a whip—she leaves before dawn one day, alone, with a few rupees knotted in her sari.

It's a small town. Her father's place is in another small town. But, as there is no direct connection, the journey takes a little time via Calcutta.

It takes Sumati a lot longer. Because by the time she reaches Calcutta, instead of taking the train to her parents' place, she's in a hospital's obstetric ward. Upon being informed, Sadananda comes, Mohanlal comes too, and without a word of objection, gives Sadananda permission to take her with him. But the hospital doctor doesn't permit her to leave before a month.

After one month, she goes to her parents' place and, after spending three months there and recovering only partially, she returns to her husband's place. Whatever other change may or may not have taken place in Sumati, one change becomes quite obvious. Her defiant spirit seems to have totally evaporated—like a lump of camphor left out in the open.

The Clerk's Wife*

Sarasi's face is not exactly pretty! The nose is snub, the forehead unevenly wavy, the eyes small and pale. Her complexion is very fair, but somehow lacks lustre; it reminds you of a damp cement floor.

But Sarasi's figure is striking. For daughters of ordinary Bengali families brought up on rice with a bit of lentil and pumpkin curried in very little oil, the body gets a faint touch of youth only at a certain age; for the rest of their lives their body and age remain mismatched. By this standard, Sarasi is indeed extraordinary. You don't usually come across a figure like hers. With her face veiled, she could easily have enchanted a poet. And it shouldn't be surprising if a low-grade ascetic was moved to fancy lifting the veil and taking a look at her face.

The trait is inherited from the mother's side. Sarasi's mother is not young, no less than forty. But even now the construction of her figure astonishes all and embarrasses her.

At the age of thirteen Sarasi senses that she not merely has a fair complexion she can boast of, but her real beauty lies in the arrangement of her bones and flesh. After she realizes this, the change in her manner of wearing the sari stuns everyone.

'What's this, girl? What sort of showing off is this?'

'Where am I showing off?'

'Why are you wearing your sari like this? Dressed as if for some fancy show?'

'I like it. What's it to you?'

'Set fire to the girl's mouth that talks like this! Don't, Sori, I'm telling you, don't go out in the neighbourhood striking poses dressed like this. Or I'll beat the skin off your back.'

Sarasi's desire for outings in the neighbourhood come to an end by itself.

Coming back home one day, she clasps her mother and breaks down in tears!

'What's the matter?'

---

* The Bengali title is *Keraneer Bou.*

Sarasi is unable to describe it in words; with much effort she hints at what has happened. The rest her mother herself figures out by cross-examining her.

After figuring it out, Sarasi's mother feels as if she has been hit by a thunderbolt. What a disaster!

In the heat of anger, she pummels her daughter's back a good many times, saying, 'I warned you then—don't go out, Sori, don't stay out the whole afternoon, stop your trips around the neighbourhood. Are you satisfied now? Are you the kind of girl to stop at anything short of smearing the lime-and-soot of disgrace on our faces!'

Sarasi cries a lot. She doesn't eat her rice that night, because her injured feelings kept her questioning: Why did mother hit me? What was my fault?

She is acquainted with unfairness and injustice in life, but this seems excessively harsh to her. She isn't the guilty one at all; the moment she guessed Subal-da's intention, she had bitten his hand and run away, that good a girl she had been. Yet she is the one who gets the beating. The attitude of everyone in her family tells her that this is a terribly shameful thing she has got herself into and the fault all along has been hers alone!

She waits eagerly to see what penalty Subal would get, but nothing happens to him. Even the proposal to inform Subal's father of the incident is rejected after considering the reasons her mother gives. Keeping a tight watch on Sarasi remains the only target of their endless efforts. Each time a close relative comes on a visit, the history of the incident is recounted before all to shame her. Whenever she sees any two people in the house talking in a low voice, she at once knows they are talking about her. In a few days she is choking, tied down by the terrible discipline.

In time the discipline slackens a bit, and Sarasi grows accustomed to it too, but she becomes unspeakably timid in her mind. She begins to feel fearful about talking to even the boys who come to their house, whom she has known from infancy. People might find fault with her and think she perhaps has some design on them! She loses the courage to go alone even to the house next door. She spends the afternoons lying next to her mother, even when she is not feeling sleepy and wishes to be alone for a while in another room. For suppose she is asked where she was and she said she was only in the next room, her mother might not believe her.

She's not like all the other girls, she doesn't have their determination to preserve her virginity, she doesn't make enough of a life-and-death effort. Sarasi knows that some such idea has struck root in all minds, so she consciously controls her movements day and night.

In the game of stealing and spying that everyone has got into playing, the poor girl is made to play the role of the thief without her having stolen anything.

She is given a lot of advice. 'What is a woman's responsibility in life, daughter? The male ruffians are waiting all around with gaping mouths. Just avoid slipping and falling into their jaws—that's all that needs taking care of.'

She hears sayings like, 'A girl's cremation over, her ashes flew; only then we sang of her virtue!'

Hearing such things constantly, her fearfulness grows. By then, she has more or less understood the rules of society concerning women. It is assumed that every girl is by nature inclined to be bad; not being bad in action is what makes a girl amazing. And accomplishing this amazing feat is the only vocation in a woman's life.

In her effort to be cautious all the time, Sarasi gradually becomes too cautious. Moral conduct no longer seems to her to be part of her personal judgement of what's good and what's bad. She sets out to train herself to pursue this womanly vocation for the sole reason that everyone wants her to do just that.

Then, a few months before she turned sixteen, Sarasi is married off to Rasbehari.

Needless to say, Rasbehari is an office clerk.

Needless to say, because Sarasi is the daughter of a family of modest means, because she's partly rustic from living in a rural area and partly citified from secretly reading novels after an education at the level of the first book of words and because she's considered merely healthy for her uncommon shapeliness and somewhat valuable for her fair complexion. Girls fitting this description can't get husbands other than office clerks. That Rasbehari's monthly salary is now one hundred rupees and likely to go up to two hundred some day is due solely to Sarasi's fair skin.

Rasbehari has an ordinary physique, medium looks, modest education, moderate intelligence. Exactly the sort that is called middling. He loves Sarasi in a moderate sort of way, sometimes worshipping her, sometimes holding her to his chest, sometimes keeping her under his foot. In two years of marriage, while he doesn't refrain from giving her a few slaps and cuffs, he also brings her a nice sari every now and then and a necklace of ten and a half grams of gold.

Rasbehari and his elder brother Banbehari lived in the same household. On the first of each month Rasbehari always handed over to his elder brother two-thirds of his salary. When after about two years of his marriage, he reduces this by half, Banbehari asks him to set up a separate household.

Rasbehari arranges to move out to a rented unit, consisting of one room, kitchen and a small veranda on the first floor of a house in the crowded Patoldanga area.

'Can you manage with it?' he asks Sarasi.

'Why do you ask! Of course I can.'

Saying this with a smile, she puts her arms around his neck, and kisses him on her own for the first time after their marriage.

In her craving for independence—not a lot of it, just a little—Sarasi's happiness knows no bounds. Isn't her husband going to leave for his office? She'll be staying home all by herself! Absolutely alone! No one would question her about taking a bath when the servant is looking, no one would know if she visited a next-door neighbour twice a day, no one would bother to impute some ill meaning to her standing at an open window, watching the people on the street and letting herself be seen by all those unknown, unfamiliar, dangerous and mysterious men.

Banbehari's wife is withered and stick-thin from bearing four children and chewing unlimited quantities of tobacco-spiked betel; on the day Rasbehari is to move out, she says to her husband, 'Whatever you may think, I'm relieved.'

And at a suitable moment, she takes Rasbehari aside and says, 'I'm telling you this only for your own good.'

When he seems curious, she looks about her and says in a lowered voice, 'Keep an eye on your wife.'

'Why do you say that?'

'Her modesty is so excessive. The other day Rakhal came for a visit, you know, and I went downstairs to make some snacks and stuff for him to eat, so I said to her, "O little sister-in-law, we've a visitor, why don't you say a few words to him so he doesn't have to sit here alone?" You know the answer she gave? "I can't, sister, I feel shy." My brother, god knows, isn't even eighteen yet. Why should she feel shy before him?'

'I don't know.'

'Yet there's no letup in her watching on the sly. And what watching, it's like devouring!'

'So what's wrong with her looking at your brother?'

Banbehari's wife smiles a little. Perhaps with all that chewing of betel and tobacco, even the smile on her face seems pungent.

'Listen to this then. Whenever I ask her to hang the clothes to dry on the roof, she says, "Men stare from all sides, sister, I can't go." I kill myself climbing those stairs and thinking, poor young thing, it's all right if she doesn't want to, and really, the men in the neighbourhood are such rogues But, oh no, in the afternoon as soon I lie down, before I've even closed my eyes, she loses no time getting up on the roof!'

'What does she do on the roof?' Rasbehari asks.

'Who knows, dear, what she does there? Who goes up to check? Just one day I noticed the empress walking about, her head uncovered and her hair let down.'

'Maybe she was drying her hair.'

'Maybe she was. But what's the need to sneak up! And the need to whine about feeling shy and not wanting to go up!'

Sarasi's curiosity is intense. There's no way anything can occur anywhere in the household without her knowing it. How long Banbehari smokes his hookah at night, what her older sister-in-law tells him or doesn't tell him, the things they argue about from time to time, Sarasi knows everything. Hiding herself, she doesn't miss hearing what her older sister-in-law just said. For the time being she shows no reaction. When her sister-in-law offers to do her hair, she lets her do it; when it's done and she puts vermilion in the parting of her hair, Sarasi even touches her feet according to custom. Their belongings were mostly moved in the morning. In the afternoon when Rasbehari brings a carriage, piles the remaining things in it and waits for Sarasi to come out, she confronts her sister-in-law with a fiercely grim face: 'What were you telling him this morning?'

'Whom? My brother-in-law? Why, I didn't tell him anything!'

'You'll get leprosy in your mouth.'

'What did you say?'

'I said you'll get leprosy in the mouth. Don't you know what leprosy is, the disease?'

'God decides who gets leprosy in the mouth. I'm your elder, and you talking to me . . . .'

'Oh, what an elder! Stick fire in the mouth of an elder of your sort! You think nothing of loading up my husband's mind with made-up things! You'll get it, you'll get rewarded for it. The mouth that told him lies against me, if it doesn't get worms, then the sun and the moon will stop rising, God's creation will come to an end. If I'm a chaste sati, then . . . .' Sarasi bursts into tears from the force of her sentiment, but doesn't let it stop her from finishing, '. . . if I'm a sati, then the harm you've done me will return to you doubled by God. Your limbs will fall off, sister-in-law, they'll rot and ooze—your husband will kick you out of his house!'

The older sister-in-law had no idea Sarasi could talk like this. She's so surprised to see a venomless snake hiss like a cobra that she isn't even able to serve a decent return. Wiping her tears, Sarasi gets into the carriage and leaves filled with the pride of victory. Having been able to make these words issue from her lips in a torrent, she sees herself as a topnotch, ideal wife.

After coming to the new rented place, Sarasi gets busy setting up her household. The bedroom is right by the street, its inside is visible from the house across. She puts up a curtain covering the entire window. Earnestly she tells Rasbehari, 'Don't part the curtain, dear, they can see everything in here from that house. This makes the room a little dark—but what can I do!'

His sister-in-law did have a point, he concludes, Sarasi does seem excessively modest.

The night before, they ate cooked rice and stuff brought from an eatery. This morning too, in the flurry of arranging things around the room and fixing the curtain, Sarasi is unable to cook. When it's time for Rasbehari to leave for the office, Sarasi says, 'Have a meal at the eatery on your way to the office. I'll find some time later to boil some rice for myself.'

Rasbehari gets dressed feeling irritated. It's hard to constantly digest this profound sort of chastity that makes a wife ignore her husband's food requirements for fear of a slight gap in the wall.

Before leaving Rasbehari again says to her, 'Don't go up on the roof.'

'No, I won't.' Then Sarasi asks, 'But where shall I dry the clothes?'

'Okay, you may go for just that, hang the clothes quickly and get back.'

'All right.'

This kind of insult doesn't bother Sarasi. She has grown used to it. An uncovered roof has temptations, surprises and mysteries all around. Of course a husband will forbid his wife going there. Not because he thinks ill of her, but out of concern for her own good.

Within five minutes of Rasbehari's leaving, Sarasi goes up on the roof. She decides she'll go for a minute, just for a quick look around.

But looking around is not something that can be done in a minute.

People have made this city by putting together piles of bricks; wherever you look are homes of people—countless, endless nests with no break allowed on any side, not the tiniest gap anywhere; the mutual embrace of those nests is astonishingly energetic, the joining of the roofs through parapets and cornices unbelievably intimate. It takes Sarasi half an hour just to feel the amazement that is in store for her in this immensity; she has little opportunity in that time to look at any particular house with any particular interest; yet this city is not new to her; from the roof of the other house, she has, unknown to all—no, not unknown to her sister-in-law despite so much precaution—looked at this city. But looking from the unfamiliar roof of her new home, looking without fear and anxiety, striding to all sides to look, letting the pallu of her sari trail at her feet in the dust from the dry moss on the ground—all this is absolutely new today.

The sun overhead is pouring fire; there must be a piece of broken glass somewhere on the roof, Sarasi's foot bleeds from a cut. Her sari is barely tucked in around her waist; it has come entirely off the upper part of her body and she's not even aware of it. The sound of the anguished cry of a lone hawk in the sky sends a shiver through her body. In her heart rushes a flash-flood of joy and excitement; she's a mad woman today. In her feeble heart, walled-in for so long, this pathetic daring on the open roof, this first brief sensation of not being afraid of people, this frenzied delight of letting the skin of her chest and of her back feel the hot air from the earth and the harsh sun from the sky seems almost unbearable. She wants to remove the restriction of mere cotton still on half her body, and run all over the roof for some time like a lunatic.

And shout. Let out a throat-splitting shout, as if her life's at stake. Forgetting all about the fact that she's a wife whose place is inside a home—a mute, fearful, helpless woman—she wants to spew and scatter all the sound that has collected within her. Or perhaps jump over the parapet.

And yes, in the little time it would take to fall through the air, she would like to fling her arms and legs in crazed joy and crash preferably on the hard cement of that front porch right by the street. Her head will get smashed, but her body will be intact. This golden yellow body of hers will be splattered in places with blood. The people on the street will crowd around and stare at the stunning, unnatural death of her beautiful body.

There will be no more shame and embarrassment! Who would even imagine that the creature who dwelled in this body spent her days constantly hiding herself, felt paralyzed with fear before a boy of eighteen, never dared even to look at the face of any man other than her husband? Who would be able to guess that she committed this atrocity because she had no alternative way of revealing herself before all, as the fear of dying before everyone's eyes was for her a greater obstacle to overcome than even her fear of injury and an unnatural death? That this was only a desperate shrill protest on her part against her own unfathomable weakness, this was her ultimate revenge on herself.

And would it occur to anyone even once that she gave herself this terrible punishment because she had known herself to be a contemptible creature who could never have stayed pure without the help of her husband, without the whip of society?

Sarasi now mutters to herself, her hands clenched in two tight fists and a fine foam gathering at the corners of her mouth. Her knees suddenly give way, and she kneels on the floor of the roof. Scraping her palms hard against the rough concrete, she loudly declares: 'Yes, yes, yes! I'll do as I want! As I want, as-I-want!'

Then, flaring up at the empty space, she addresses the same empty space again: 'Hear that?'

The world surrounding her now starts making a buzzing noise—the whole universe castigates her in one voice. Nobody will hear her case, nobody will give her credit for even a moment of self-conquest in any form. Keeping her pinned down and in restraints, they will steam her in the sweat of her own fair skin over the heat of her own youthfulness.

Tears roll down from her eyes. Picking up the trailing end of her sari, she covers herself. Rubbing the tears dry, she gets up and stands facing north leaning against the parapet. As after a fit of hysteria the whole world seems absolutely still and a metallic taste clings to the mouth, in the same manner the crashing sound of her blood in Sarasi's ears suddenly stops and her tongue has a bitter taste on it.

Sarasi no longer feels any kind of excitement. She's a little bewildered, feels as if she has let herself do something that no proper young woman ever does. Something shameful, illegitimate.

She's not remorseful for disobeying her husband's instruction not to linger on the roof; one has to disregard some minor, even major instructions of a husband; otherwise it's impossible to live. But hasn't she done something over and above just disobeying? Why else does she feel tainted, impure?

Still trying to understand this feeling, Sarasi starts climbing down the stairs. As soon as she reaches the shade under the roof, her mortification seems half gone. The daylight inside the room is dimmed by the curtain drawn across the window, the slight dampness in its air has still not dried off. Bit by bit calmness seeps in and floods Sarasi's eyes, her face, her entire body.

The unfinished tasks in the room look as if they're waiting just for her with their arms held out. Standing in the middle of the room, Sarasi looks around with affection. So many things she must take care of, so many tasks, endless duties! Does she have time to pause and bother about what's possible in life and what's not? Her husband has gone to office on an eatery meal; she must finish arranging things by the afternoon. It won't do if she can't give him a home-cooked meal in the evening. Is it to live on eatery meals that he supports her with food and clothing?

Wanting to waste no more time, Sarasi gets busy. She picks up the spice-grinding pestle, uses it to hammer two nails in adjoining walls, fixes a cord diagonally and arranges neatly, one at a time, the clothes for daily use. Then she covers the shelf with a sheet of newspaper and arranges there the bottle of hairoil, shoe brush, Rasbehari's shaving stuff, and her toiletry—face powder, vermilion, a bottle of red lac-dye to edge the feet.

While arranging the hair grooming things, she smiles a little and says to herself: Will I have the time to do my hair before he's back. As soon as I finish cooking, I must have a quick wash with soap and do the hair—he saw me so untidy, ungroomed when he left.

As her hair keeps coming over her face, she gathers it with both hands and, lifting her arms in an exquisite pose that is both unnecessary and wasted in the empty room, makes a loose bun at the nape of her neck.

Now, what must she tackle next?

The trunks can't be there, they must be moved to this side, where the clay water pot is.

The clay water pot! Sarasi's eyes glisten at the sight of it. She's thirsty!

There's a glass within reach, but she doesn't notice it. Squatting by the water pot, she lifts it up with both hands and pours water down her upheld open mouth. Some goes down her throat, the rest wets the clothing over her chest.

How very, very thirsty Sarasi must have been!

The Writer's Wife[*]

A novelist? Was she really to be married to a novelist of countrywide fame? It isn't easy to say exactly how long the amazement kept Amala overwhelmed before her marriage. Perhaps for about three months. Because, about three months after it was arranged, the 'auspicious wedding' between her and the renowned novelist Suryakanta took place.

Amala was one of those girls who, after attending school upto the fourth grade, grew up under the careful watch and careless nurture of family and relatives, and staying at home, learnt a little of everything—reading, singing, sewing, housework, quarrelling techniques and so on. Needless to say, therefore, she became fairly familiar with Bengali literature through the neighbourhood lending library. Starting out secretly, then openly once old enough to seek the seclusion of a corner of her home, she regularly read three to four novels and story collections a week and three to four issues of monthly magazines a month. Actually, ever since she was taken off school, this has been her only form of reading, and writing letters her only form of writing. She had read five novels and three plays by Suryakanta well before her marriage was fixed with that gentleman. Little did she know then that the creator of those accounts that kept the heart overflowing so delectably with intense sentiments, making one cry one moment and smile the next, would himself appear one day, accompanied by three friends, to view her as his potential bride, and after checking her out, give his consent!

This matter struck Amala as highly incongruous. So even novelists, especially those like Suryakanta, chose a life companion just like any ordinary man? And picked an ordinary stay-home girl like her? (Of course, she wasn't ordinary, but how would he know that from just looking at her briefly one day, asking her a few questions, checking some of her sewing samples, and hearing her sing a quarter of a song? Weren't writers the ones who virtually brought about romance between men and women, and whether they ended up united or separated, didn't reading about the course of the love affairs they created move people's minds? Except a few

---

*   The Bengali title is *Sahityiker Bou.*

short stories, was there a single piece of Suryakanta's writing she had read in which the complex relationship between two persons, a man and a woman, did not keep her distracted, tossed by anxiety, emotion, and sympathy? That Suryakanta, what's this he was about to do? Shouldn't he have fallen in love, at least in a plain sort of way, before marrying her? Even if there was to be no first meeting amidst breathtaking, extraordinary events and the birth of love through some complex and startling circumstances? Instead, what sort of logic made him take an unknown, unfamiliar girl as his wife? How was he going to live with such an anomaly in his own life? In his books, so many married couples had been unable to love each other, and their lives laid to waste. Did Suryakanta have no fear that something like that might happen in his own case too?

Amala had three months' time to mull over these deep problems. How much wondering and imagining a girl of nineteen can pack into her head, how much tingling romance she can feel in three months, that only nineteen-year-old girls know. One thing Amala thought particularly about. If some immense experience of love had not occurred in Suryakanta's life, then how could he gain such deep and perfect knowledge of that subject, and if some such thing had occurred, then how could he acquire a taste for such an ordinary marriage? Sometimes it seemed to her that if Suryakanta could forget the thrilling history of his own heartbreak, if the constancy of his love was so flimsy that his broken heart could mend meanwhile, then maybe the man was unworthy of respect! Wasn't that terrible, an awful shame, that she was fated to end up with a husband who could fall in love and then forget about it? Other times it seemed to her that perhaps his heart never had an imprint of love, maybe the man actually possessed so much knowledge and insight that simply by observing events and mental turmoil in other people's lives, by using imagination and inference, he gained all his knowledge of the hearts of men and women. Perhaps knowing that the chance of getting hurt is inevitably greater with falling in love, he decided it would be better to marry without falling in love? In that case too, Amala thought, she couldn't respect him. Not falling in love out of fear of getting hurt? Such a person was not quite a human being, but an absolutely worthless creature! At times again she thought, perhaps it was the unforgettable memory of his own love's cruel ending that drove him through unbearable pain to do such an absurd thing! Didn't Amala know the strange things so many do in that condition? Some drink their way to oblivion (as in Suryakanta's *Daydream, The Path Away from Home* and so on), some become renouncers, some take to ruining thousands of people for money and fame, some even kill themselves (oh god!). If Suryakanta decided merely to get married, can it be called an excessive reaction? Considering this, Amala felt compassion for her would-be husband. Sighing, she said to herself, Poor man! Will I be able to bring him a little peace and happiness?

No matter how much haphazard, volatile imagining gripped Amala's mind, one thing she never lost track of. That she was going to be married not to the usual lawyer, clerk, doctor, official, businessman or some such type, that the husband she was getting was uncommon, one whose name everyone in the country knew, whose writing moved them all to tears and to smiles.

Suryakanta was nearly thirty. Even if not exactly a handsome man, his appearance bore the stamp of a personality that was not commonplace, he was a surprisingly attractive man. In the way he talked and moved, he was rather quiet and considerate—a lot like the head of a large family who was upto his neck in practical affairs. When talking with someone, his smile was neutral and unexcited, as if he had already known many others like the speaker and heard countless times the stuff the man was saying. Not just people, everything in the world seemed to strike Suryakanta as unoriginal, nothing quite surprised him, everything—people, events, objects, surroundings, details of life imagined or real—fitted his experience comfortably like a pair of used shoes, so that there was not even a faint crunch of leather flexing, let alone blisters on the feet. Whatever life held had already been assessed and evaluated—hopes, desires, sorrows, joys, excitement, emotions, imagination, all seemed well-regulated to him; nothing to feel either discontented or grateful about. It would seem as if the only point he saw in living was to enjoy a sense of ease and normalcy. Like a skilled swimmer he swam in life's ocean, smoothly, with natural ease—no foamy whirls with frantic flinging of arms and legs.

Life's ocean? Amala was downright perplexed to find a windless unruffled pond! So calm and composed the man was. Where was the emotion, the eagerness, the effusiveness? Being distracted, childish, moody, those small and large signs of a mysterious nature—where did they go? Not once in all day and night did he give any indication that he was an extraordinary man. Even the little distinctions of nature and originalities of character that ordinary men have seemed absent in him. He seemed to be uncommon only in being more common than most common men. Neither very quiet, nor voluble. Dressed neither fastidiously, nor negligently. If comfort and convenience fell short of the expected quota he wanted to know the reason; if he got more, he showed pleasure. Acted neither too generously, nor too selfishly. Ate when hungry, slept when sleepy, showed anger when angry and pain when hurt, laughed when amused, engaged in conversation—was · this the absent-minded, mysterious man of Amala's imagination? Not just that, he even laughed and chitchatted with his new wife, teased her for fun, caressed her to show affection—in a common fashion, no different from other trashy men; as if no uncommon, exquisite relation needed to be created between them: the kind that produced a mutual shiver at the touch of a finger, revealed new facets with every look into each other's eyes, endlessly gushed with excitement.

One of Amala's initial observations stayed with her—as nothing else till then had given her so clear a glimpse of her husband's nature. The distressed editor of some magazine came one afternoon with an urgent demand, and all evening Suryakanta sat in their bedroom writing. The house was full of people: many of the relatives who had come for the wedding had not gone yet. Countless interruptions kept barging in on his writing. One called him for some trivial reason, another asked him something important, the children made noises in the veranda facing the room, the smell from the kitchen of chilli pepper pods singed in oil to flavour the boiled lentil got him into a sneezing bout. Even though she couldn't come into the room, she sensed that her husband was writing. She felt restless to go up to the room and take a look at the famous writer Suryakanta creating, and resentful that the noise in the house was not letting him write a line. Really, didn't his folks have any sense? If she had the power, she would've straightened them up. The house is to fall silent when Suryakanta sits down to write, they should all be walking on tiptoe, talking in whispers. They should skip frying dry chilli peppers for the lentil. Instead, the noise in that house seemed to increase that day—what a shame they were so inconsiderate!

At ten-thirty that night when she finally came into the room, Suryakanta was still writing. Amala was astonished to see seven or eight sheets of written pages on the table. So he could write amidst all that interruption and noise? Besides, although she had tiptoed into the room so carefully, he was aware of her even as he wrote! Amala then felt resentful towards Suryakanta himself.

'That's all for today,' he said, putting the pen down, stretching his arms, and yawning in an ungainly manner. Then with a smiling face he asked her to come closer. With a sad face Amala stood by his table and asked, 'Tell me, how do you manage to write?'

There was so little curiosity in her voice and so much slight in her tone that she seemed to be asking how it was possible that a man like him could write. It's hard to tell if he sensed it; turning his chair around, he took Amala's hand and then made her sit beside him on his chair. He did that not because he was a novelist. Can a husband's silent response come in any other way when his new bride asks such a question standing so close to his desk? Then he tried to smile and said, 'Exactly the same way you write, with pen on paper. But, Amala-rani, how much longer are you going to address me in that formal aapni?'

Amala faintly said, 'You never asked me not to.'

'You know why I didn't? I wanted to see if you would on your own. Tell me why you didn't.'

'Don't you know that I felt shy? And hurt, that you didn't ask me?' She used the informal form of address, tumi, this time.

So, as soon as she was granted the right her husband had held off for a week, she was left with neither shyness nor hurt feeling. Her only thought: Did I give the right answer! Is this the sort of answer expected in such a situation? Should I have said something else? Well, I could say: How would you know how deeply it hurt because you didn't ask me to use tumi? But he's looking steadily at my face. Maybe it's better now to lower my face without saying anything more.

Indeed, for a few moments Suryakanta was looking sharply at Amala, as if trying to gauge her lajja (modesty) and abhiman (pride) from her slightly flushed face. No matter how great a psychologist he was when writing his books, he was not quite able to figure her out. He could sense little by little Amala's desire to get close to her husband, but he also sensed that getting close was not the cause or the goal of her eagerness. It was not quite sentimentality; Amala seemed to be trying to find out something about him, always expecting some sort of surprise from him. She talked in such a melodramatic tone! Yet there was nothing really dramatic in her words. A curious combination of sentimentality and reasoning seemed to produce her gestures and words. His new wife was giving Suryakanta a taste both sweet and sour like a mild-tasting green mango. It was not his fault. For that was just how she was behaving with him. Hadn't she contemplated for three months the various reasons an uncommon man like Suryakanta could go for a commonplace marriage with a girl like her? Now, after that marriage, wouldn't she try to find out which of those reasons applied? Should her three months of in-depth research go in vain?

However, her desire to gain knowledge on the subject was gradually slackening. She began to think that no matter how much turmoil had taken place in Suryakanta's heart in the past, it was better not to think of it now. Let a new chapter in his life begin with her. He waited to see if on her own she would start using the intimate you. Could it be that he was also waiting to see if she'd start loving him on her own? Oh you, Amala's poor husband, you're so ignorant in this! How can Amala not love you, the great writer that you are? Soon she began to see herself and him as the newly married couple in a novel by him. The couple, Sankar and Saraju, got married only in the last chapter, and that too, after three long years of misunderstanding, conflicts and obstacles; but that did not matter. Can it be too difficult to imagine that they too are united now after three eventful years? It couldn't be for him; he wrote it.

Amala (now as Saraju) slowly put her arms around the neck of Suryakanta (now Sankar), and her half-closed eyes heavy with 'dreams of indescribable ecstasy mixed with memories of pain,' she said in a voice that 'for three years carried a sad tune of hidden tears and now took on an enchanting hint of happiness': 'Tell me, darling, could you ever imagine that you and I would come so close to each other?'

Noticing a pair of bracelets on her in addition to the jewellery that was promised, Suryakanta was going to ask her who gave them. Instead, he asked in bewilderment, 'What does that mean?'

Amala said, 'Seems as if fate forcibly kept us apart for so long. If our marriage was delayed another year or two, then perhaps I . . . .'

Amala stopped, noticing the look on Suryakanta's face. This was no acting, her heart really pounded, and her breathing grew shallow from the pressure of emotion! For an inexperienced, tender-hearted girl from a family of modest means, acting like a seasoned lover for the first time in her life involved much more than book knowledge! The emotion, the excitement, the sentiment, and the bashfulness that now overcame Amala, making her want to hide her face in his chest and never say another word in her life, none of it was put on.

Frowning at her, Suryakanta asked, 'Tell me, how old are you?'

'Nineteen.'

'Before marriage I was told you're only sixteen, just in that fast growing phase.'

What unthinkable injury! The autumn night, the sky perhaps moonlit, the room's air scented by a bunch of flowers brought yesterday by the wife of one of Suryakanta's friends. There was also that last sentence of Suryakanta's unfinished story on the pad—Amala has already read it from a corner of her eye. It is about a certain Abani stunned to discover the disguised love of a certain Anupama; it describes how his face turns pale and how Anupama's incomparable eyes blaze defiantly against custom, against weakness, against who knows what else! Fresh from writing of those exciting moments between Abani and Anupama, and holding his own wife to his chest, what sort of rude matter-of-fact remark was it that he just made! If her parents understated her age by a couple of years when arranging the marriage, was this the right time to bring it up?

Amala later read that story of Abani and Anupama many times. She read it from the beginning upto the point where Suryakanta had stopped that night, and every time her blood pumped faster. And Suryakanta on that night, after writing upto that point, how could he behave as placidly, unexcitedly as he did? What a deceiver!

Amala these days is learning to look at her husband's deception as a form of self-discipline. She has also sensed that however common Suryakanta appears in all aspects of life, the man has something in him, something uncommon and fascinating, which can't quite be identified, proved, or even taken for granted. The same way the talent of the talented is not evident prior to success despite its being there, her husband does and yet does not possess an immense undisclosed personality. At least that's how it seems to Amala. Hence, from time to time she feels so full of modesty that she wishes to keep her head down before him, to become his pet—she doesn't know why. Her husband breaks up her dream, blocks the flow of her imagination, leaves her fond hopes unfulfilled, doesn't properly love her or let her love him—and yet!

These days—meaning about eight months after her marriage—as spring ends and summer begins, the heat makes Amala frequently thirsty; that's natural. But her unsatisfied thirst for Suryakanta's love, an unreal, poetic love, is not due to the summer heat, nor is it natural. If only he would become undisciplined—even if it were just for a day—and tell Amala a few senseless things, act strangely emotional, love her like a lunatic or a drunk—so the reality would briefly be covered by a screen tinted with romantic love! But he doesn't seem to know how to forget to be himself even for a moment. Even if she becomes a little exuberant, and tries to create an environment of poetic illusion, he cuts her off crossly, saying, 'Where did you learn such shallow talk?'

In the heat of her anger Amala says, 'From you. From your books.'

Suryakanta says, 'When I came to see you before the marriage was fixed, I thought you were a simple girl—innocent of this sort of precocity. What you've learned, Amal, is not in any of my books. If I ever wrote such things, it was in sarcasm, to show that those who go for this sort of poetic melodrama have some kind of brain disease.'

The critics of Suryakanta's writings, if they had heard this, would have called him a liar. Amala only says breathlessly, 'Is love a brain disease?'

'What do you think you know of love?'

Amala is speechless. A shock of anger and humiliation at first makes death seem preferable to this. He questions her knowledge of love? All right, let love go to hell! She doesn't want to know. But doesn't Suryakanta know what she wants? Even if all this is shallow talk, what's wrong with it, what's the harm in it? If he joined her a little in such shallow talk, would it bring the roof down or make the police put them behind bars? Not only was there no harm in it, there was in fact, a lot to gain—all this clash of their minds and pain could be avoided. Why does he act this way with her for no reason? What happiness does he find in hurting his wife like this? She sheds tears while doing little things in the room like moving the water jug, organizing the writing desk, rearranging the books and papers. Suryakanta sees her tears, but Amala doubts if he does.

'Give me a glass of water,' he says to her.

When Amala hands him the glass of water, he takes a sip and says with a laugh, 'When you give me water, I should feel as if I'm drinking nectar, not water, right Amala?'

Joking! Teasing her so cruelly even when he sees her crying! Amala now throws herself on the bed and sobs. As she does so, she knocks the glass of water off his hand and wets the bed. After putting the glass away, it seems to him that the bed got so wet with just her tears.

Upset, he says, 'I can't deal with it, Amal, the way you're constantly bringing distortions into a simple and easy life. How did you get such a problem at this early age? Why do you pointlessly manufacture pain? What disaster has hit you, has your son died or your husband left you? Are you not getting food and clothing? Does my family give you too much trouble? You should be spending your days at ease, smiling, playing, having fun; instead, you constantly suffer artificial pain. If you were in love with someone before our marriage, then I could make some sense of it. But all your suffering revolves around me. Why? Do I neglect you, not give you care and affection? Tonight I tried so much to make you laugh, you didn't laugh, I tried to make you angry, you didn't get angry, I said let's play a round of bagatelle, and instead you . . . .'

Trembling in agitation, Amala sits up and thrusts her tear-streaming face at her husband's feet saying, 'Forgive me. I don't deserve you.'

'See what I mean!' says Suryakanta. 'What're you up to now!'

When this kind of conjugal exchange finally ends and the agitation subsides, of the many feelings that growl and moan in Amala's mind, the one that stays uppermost is disappointment. The sleep fairies get thoroughly exhausted trying to lull her restless hurt feelings to sleep. In the morning, she's sad. Absently she does her share of the household chores. Her husband's elder brother's wife, two sisters, two brothers and the others in the household watch Amala's face with examiners' eyes; the women discuss her in whispers. Once Suryakanta leaves for his office, she acts, unknown to herself, as if there's no one else in the house, it's empty.

Chandrakanta, his younger brother, comes to the door to check: 'Got a headache, Bou-di?'

'No. Why?'

'Instead of lying down, will you then please go downstairs and see why big sister's calling you? Is this any time to stay in bed!'

Amala then remembers that today it is her turn to cook, but she hasn't done much. Someone else must be having to mind the kitchen on her behalf this morning. A husband who insults her at each step ridiculed her today for saying 'How'll I spend the whole day?' in a trembling voice while buttoning his shirt as he started for office, and thereby made her take to bed at ten in the morning, staying there upto one in the afternoon thinking, eyes closed, of none other than him. What can she do now? What excuse can she give for lying in bed?

In an afflicted voice she suddenly says, 'I'm not feeling well, I'll not eat today.'

The rampage in her starved heart keeps Amala fasting the whole day. Getting increasingly worked up as the afternoon passes she becomes explosive like a bomb. The moment Suryakanta comes home, she says to him, 'Listen, darling, come closer and listen. Take a month's leave and take me somewhere. Anywhere, let's go wherever our eyes take us, just the two of us. Will you go? Standing before the Taj Mahal, I'll finally ask you just like Aparna . . . .'

Suryakanta, back from office sweaty and hot, slowly removes Amala's clutching arms off his neck. Then he takes off his sweat-soaked shirt.

'Who is Aparna?'

'Oh, you have forgotten? Your Aparna, my darling!'

'My Aparna?'

'The one in your *Rainbow*, the one who said, "The motto of a woman's life should be to love one man, no matter if he is a king or a street beggar . . . ."'

'Oh, that Aparna.' After taking off his shoes and his shirt, he sits in a chair away from her. With an unsmiling, anxious face, he watches the expression on Amala's face, and says, 'I'll take leave this Saturday and take you to your parents' place, you'll stay there for some time.'

Stunned, Amala asks, 'Why?'

'You'll go off your head if you stay here.'

At this blow, her bomb of passion explodes in tears. Suryakanta is not cruel; within a minute Amala's tears make his sweaty chest wetter and his face looks awfully gloomy.

Instead of having his wife treated with a nerve tonic here, Suryakanta decides it's better to leave her at her parents' place for some time. Amala hasn't seen her parents for a long time. Being back in her pre-marriage environment might help her acquire some of the skills needed to live a married life. Nineteen years she spent there; maybe she hasn't been able to bring all of those years with her, and that's why she does these childish things. Besides, a little separation might do them good. The virus that caused her love's abnormality might weaken from the temperature of the pain of separation.

Although Amala finally agrees to go, she fusses not a little. After sulking a long time that night, she asks him, 'You aren't sending me away because you can't stand being with me?'

'No, darling, no.'

'Will you miss me?'

'Won't I? You think I don't love you? I'll be miserable alone, Amal.'

'You'll only be miserable! I'll die without you,' she says emphatically.

After spending a month at her parents' place, Amala comes back. She could indeed have died, because she was sick with fever for about seven days there. A strange sort of fever it was for as soon as her temperature got to one hundred and one degrees, she started to mutter deliriously and confided to the youngest of her four elder brothers' wives that her life was ruined. Her youngest sister-in-law told Amala's brother and two elder sisters. The entire family felt desperately anxious after hearing in the seven days she was down with fever, seven different accounts, all difficult to follow, of their beloved youngest daughter's failed life. After she recovered from the fever, her eldest brother's wife asked Amala some questions as the family's representative. Are the folks at her in-laws' place not nice people? What exactly do they do to her? Do they reproach her? Chide and harass her? Don't feed her well? Work her to death? Do they beat her up? If none of these, then is Suryakanta perhaps . . . .

After hearing her answers to the questions, her family's anxiety turns into bewilderment. Why exactly did she feel her life was ruined? After so much searching they had found Amala a husband like Suryakanta! They had given him sixteen hundred rupees in cash dowry alone! When a newly married girl's entire family is puzzled and worried about such a major complaint as her life being ruined, she can't but start feeling troubled herself. She wonders if she herself is mistaken then. Is it really the case that her hopes, desires and fantasies are no more than a bizarre kind of mental sickness?

Her obstructed excitement, her unmet desire for a garden of sky-flowers on earth, and her very real experience of married life—all start acting on her mind within a few days of her being away from Suryakanta. Besides, if books exert an influence on an imagination-prone mind innocent of actual experience, don't the writers of those books also exert an influence? The regret Amala had about her husband seeming to be like an ordinary man, hardly recognizable as the famous novelist, slowly evaporates while she is there, except for the seven days in fever. She starts thinking: Doesn't everyone have that sort of ordinariness? Wasn't she killing herself looking in the wrong places for exceptional qualities? Of course, he was exceptional in many ways! His sharp intelligence, heaps of knowledge, ability to judge people's conduct as good or bad on the basis of intention, creating all those beautiful stories and novels, while staying within the mundane reality of a noisy household—weren't these exceptional qualities? After working all day at the office, and staying up till ten or eleven writing, didn't he look very tired some nights? Didn't she sometimes mistake the tiredness for neglect, at other times for preoccupation with family matters, at still others for lack of enthusiasm, and pile up a mountain of her own anger, sadness and disappointment? Wanting to play at thrilling romantic love, didn't she end up crying in pain? When a man who creates hundreds of women like *Ramdhanu's* Aparna feels tired at day's end, how can he be expected to take his wife on the rooftop simply because the night happens to be moonlit, and act overwhelmed with fascination? Instead of letting him go to sleep, she kept him up until two in the morning talking, getting upset with him and crying!

Many such thoughts Amala has had over this month. Suryakanta's personality, the practical ease of his conduct and his advice were covertly working on her, and the tonic she was taking after the illness was calming her nerves. Who doesn't crave a bit of peace and quiet after a bout of fever! Thus, Amala returns to her husband's home a little changed, not just with the outward quietude of the convalescent.

'You've become so thin!' Suryakanta says to her.

'Because I had a fever.'

Her answer sounds incongruous to him. He was expecting something like, 'Wouldn't I? Being away from you for a month . . . .' Anyway, if Amala has learnt to give a direct answer to a simple question, that's good. Nothing to be offended about.

'You too have become thin,' she says to him.

'Wouldn't I? One month I lived alone without you.'

His answer sounds incongruous to her. She was expecting something like, 'Have I? Oh, the amount of work I had to finish in the past few days, Amala!' Anyway, if Suryakanta has learnt to give a sweet answer to a plain remark, that's good. Nothing to be thrilled about.

This was their first meeting after her return. It was in the afternoon and brief. At night when they are together again, the moon is sending its beams elsewhere on earth. Suryakanta has been pacing up and down in their bedroom, a little agitated and distracted. The skyful of clouds has produced so much still, humid heat that the electric fan, even at full speed, is not making any airflow, only agitating the pages of the writing pad that lies open on the table.

Amala complains of the weather: 'So clouded all evening, and still no sign of rain. When it comes, it'll bring some relief.'

'Is the sky clouded?' Suryakanta asks.

'Haven't you noticed? The rapid lightning and thunder?'

Suryakanta watches Amala with a different look in his eyes, the look with which boys at an exam skim through a question sheet the first time. Then, with the look of the boy who finds he knows the answer to none of the questions, he says, 'I've been trying to write a story, Amal, all evening.'

'Really? A new story! Let me see how far you've got.' Amala promptly goes to the table, and is surprised to see not a single written page under the paperweight. The top page of the pad has just a heading, his name and barely five or six lines.

'Wrote just this the whole evening!'

Suryakanta slumps on the bed, saying, 'No. I wrote a lot of pages. You'll find them in the wastepaper basket.'

She's astounded. 'Oh, it's full of torn pages! All this you wrote this evening and tore up?'

He nods and yawns. Is he very tired? Amala goes to him with concern and asks, 'Sleepy? Go to sleep then. Let me fix the pillow.'

'No. I won't sleep,' he replies. 'I couldn't write a line this one month—how can I sleep! Not just tonight. So many nights I filled the wastepaper basket like this, I lost count. What you did to me before leaving only you know. I don't even feel like sitting down to write any more. What I force myself to write I tear up. Couldn't even supply this month's instalment of the novel.'

His wan face is too painful to watch. Amala's heartbeat quickens, she stares at him with dilated eyes. Being back in this familiar environment of her married life is depleting the mood of ease and calm she collected at her parents' place and brought along. Her body and mind start reabsorbing the electricity she had all by herself packed into this room's air before going away. Still, she could perhaps have restrained herself this time and tried to be the way he wanted her to be—if only he himself would not act and talk in this strange way tonight. He seems to have become exactly as she had fantasized him in the months of her prolonged virginity! The anguished running of fingers through the hair makes him look so wild tonight! The look in his eyes mingles desperation with rebellion, the tone of his talk was the complaint of a spirit in defeat and despair, the manner of his sitting indicates a readiness to spring any moment and do something terribly daring. Besides, isn't it because of her absence that Suryakanta hasn't been able to write at all for one month! With the first long separation, her husband realized how madly he had fallen in love with his wife! Amala shivers in ecstasy. Her voice is overwhelmed. 'For me? You couldn't write in a month because of me?'

Suryakanta squeezes her hand so hard that her gold bangles almost dig into her wrist. Voice quavering with emotion, he replies, 'What else? You've made me crazy, Amal, turned my head completely. So many times I felt like running to see you a little. You know why I didn't? To feel how intense the pain of separation can be. Remember Aparna of my *Rainbow*, how from time to time she herself created a distance to heighten the sensation of love? I too thought . . . .'

It is as if a drama is being enacted in their room, upto two in the morning, with just these two characters, a voluble hero and an almost mute heroine. Before the first act is over, Amala's excitement is all gone, fear has taken its place and her face is pale. What's happening? Has Suryakanta really lost his mind? Why's he talking and acting so strangely? After some time Amala grows tired, she wants to sleep. But she can't. Her husband is giving her back her eight months of obstructed effusion, he's returning both principal and interest—does she have the choice not to take it? He's bringing on tides of love, now strong and hard, now gentle and soft, just what she has been wanting from him. How would it do if she doesn't let herself go in this flood tonight? Oh dear, why did Suryakanta become like this, what brought this frightful change in him?

Perhaps it's the expression on her face that finally moves him to pity at two in the morning. Suddenly, he brings himself to a stop the way you apply brakes to a car. Amala seeks his reassurance. 'Now that I'm back, will you be able to write again?' she asks solicitously.

Absently he replies, 'I'm thinking, Amal, don't talk now. I'm thinking of you. You're lying next to me, yet you're so far away, behind a mist, beyond many oceans and deserts, and I'm out with a heavy heart searching for you. Don't interrupt, don't say a word.'

They say the antidote for one poison is another poison. Even so, it's hard to approve of Suryakanta's use of this unconventional method of treatment for the slightly abnormal immaturity of his wife's mind. The truth is that his own mind is no less at fault. Most teenage boys and girls are more or less possessed with sentimentality, an excessive thirst for things romantically poetic. But Suryakanta here has grown quite old. Mentally, even if not in years. He has piled up experience not just from his own life but also through mentally identifying with others' experience. When writing, he has countless times savoured in various forms the intimate feelings felt not only of men but also women. You can say that Suryakanta has been married many times already, as wife in some cases, as husband in others; he has himself created couples and lived many kinds of conjugal life. It's hard to say what number Amala is as his wife. Yet, to this day he carries in him a craving to stun with adolescent fantasy even the imagination of a girl like Amala, to make life seem heady like poetry and drama—a thirst, in other words, for induced turmoils in the emotional world that are the opposite of summer storms and spring breezes in the natural world. But he also hides this thirst, this desire, along with his incapacity to engage any real-life woman of flesh and blood in it. People need a dose of fiction in their lives; in writing his novels and stories Suryakanta takes many times that dose. That's why, except when he's writing, his feelings are dulled, he wants only peace and quiet and an easy, ordinary life. I don't know if the very talented writers are like this, but the writers whose books make the hearts of girls like Amala race uncontrollably are exactly like this or a variation of the same type of mentality.

He carries out the regular tasks of life in a systematic manner, and he tries to solve common problems using his common sense, which works well. If Amala were running a temperature, he'd no doubt have called a doctor, but fever is a familiar ailment. The abnormally high temperature of her heart is not exactly fever. In arranging for its treatment, his common sense is confounded. He forgets that even if poison can be neutralized with poison, hysteria can't be treated with hysteria—because hysteria does not work like poison.

In a few days, Amala starts wilting. It's not the same thing as reading books, imagining, daydreaming, or somehow ventilating one's effusive sentimentality. It's the weight of carrying another person's heart—imbibing romantic stimulation like alcohol every night and passing out inebriated. The first night Amala was alarmed by her husband's unexpected attack. She no longer feels alarm, only her chest hurts as if it's about to burst, her head reels in a swirl of confusion, things grow blurred before her eyes. From time to time she wants to laugh aloud, or cry. Sometimes she feels an irrepressible urge to smash and wreck the room's things or scratch Suryakanta's chest bloody. His caresses make her feel as if she's choking, his words produce a ringing in her ears, and when suddenly he stops talking, the silence around her keeps crashing like breakers against her heated mind.

'Turn off the light! Turn off the light!' she whispers.

'Light? Don't take moonbeams for electric light, Amal,' Suryakanta protests.

Amala dozes a little. 'Aren't you going to write tonight?' she says after some time.

Suryakanta smiles and says, 'Write? For whom, Amal? I'm writing on the pages of my mind and reading it out to you. Is there any need to write on paper any more?'

'My head reels, I feel sick.'

In a blink Suryakanta becomes the Suryakanta he used to be. Brings her a glass of water, wipes her forehead and the back of her neck with wetted fingers and says in a quiet tone, 'Lie down.' Then he turns off the light, lies down himself, and enquires: 'What kind of sick feeling?'

'I don't know, I don't understand.'

There are many things she can't understand—not just her feeling of sickness. Why did Suryakanta suddenly go out like a firework that has run out of powder? How could a passionate, complicated love like Mohit's in *Ramdhanu* turn in an instant into such gentle affection? Amala feels deeply sad and exhausted, but sleep eludes her. At one point he calls her in a low voice. She does not answer, pretends to be asleep. Joking? Is Suryakanta playing a joke on her? He's not the kind of man to go on teasing for so long! Besides, can mere teasing move anyone like this? The first day or two her husband's transformation had seemed incongruous to her; even now it sounds off tune sometimes, artificial. But the rest of the time? The amazing eagerness he shows, the expression his eyes and his face reveal, never seen before, how can it all be pretended? Sometimes he stops talking in the middle and just gazes into a distance thinking absently. Then the merest touch of her hands startles him and, bewildered like the spellbound, he clasps her like a scared child. How can anyone think he's acting even then! On the other hand, she has caught him in a big lie. He had said that when she went to her parents' place he was unable to write even the monthly magazine instalment of his novel. A few days ago, after he left for office, the magazine came by the noontime mail. It had a ten-page instalment of the novel! He, of course, explained that he meant the coming month's instalment, not this month's, which he said he wrote long ago, before Amala went away. 'A piece must go in at least two months ahead, Amal. How else will they have the time to print it?'

But her suspicion doesn't leave her. Written two months ahead or four months, which piece hasn't she managed to read before he sent it off? When did he write this piece?

'I wrote it in the office. For ten or twelve days there wasn't much work; I wrote it then. The editor was at my back, that's why I couldn't give it to you to read.'

Still, the web of these explanations didn't cover the lie completely. Her mind's objection, unstilled, nests in her to this day, transformed into a distasteful sort of pain. Nests secretly, deep in there. Where éven the current new-style love of Suryakanta has no right of entry!

Suryakanta has indeed stopped writing. He doesn't write at home, he doesn't write in the office. Amala has robbed him of his writing ability not by going away to her parents' place, but by coming back. In the factory of passion he has set up within himself to lavish on Amala, he now hires as labourers the suppressed lunacies of his own mind. Pacified until now with the artificial food of novel writing, they don't always stay under his control. If he attempts to make them work on something other than producing for Amala, they go on strike; if he thinks of closing down the factory, they start rioting and making trouble. His condition has become like those who, starting to drink occasionally for special needs, become slaves to it. Nothing interests him other than Amala's company—not relatives, not friends, nor his routine duties. Outside his bedroom, he is even more reserved than before, his contact with people even more casual and brief. He seems to be struggling constantly to keep himself under control, and feeling very uncomfortable for that reason. His writer friends want to know if he's working on his number one epic, the editors indirectly let him know his persistent defaults can't be tolerated, his non-writer friends advise him to go on a vacation, the folks at home try giving more attention, love, care and sympathy. Trying to do at thirty what should have been done at twenty-two, Suryakanta brings chaos all around him. Gradually it dawns on him that he is not treating Amala, but using her abnormality as an excuse to give full expression to his own suppressed mental disorder. He was not curing Amala's sentimental lunacy, he was satisfying his own desire for it. Otherwise, wouldn't he have stopped at least on seeing that she was unable to take it? Wouldn't he have moved on towards ease and normalcy during their times together? He had no intention to torment her like this! He only wanted to make her see how trivial, trite, and laughable the melodramatic love she wanted was! He wanted to do theatre for a few days, only an educational play based on Amala's confused imagination, staged on his own room's cement floor, with real life for a backdrop. Now the acting has become such an enormous truth for him that he somehow just can't ring the curtain down.

Days pass. Suryakanta takes a month's leave. Office seems too bothersome. The dark circles under Amala's eyes deepen. There's housework for her, and interaction with family members in the joys and pains of daily life. All this she carries on in a tired, sad, and absent manner. Even when cooking in the kitchen, she behaves as if she were in her bedroom; at the sewing-machine making an outfit for her husband's third sister's baby boy, she's nestled against Suryakanta's neck. Amala had a bit of quietly pleasant beauty, and a bit of dull grace as of an oiled stone bowl. Now the sharp, spirited expression on her face has made her beauty eye-catching and unusual, changed her grace into the glint of a just-sharpened knife made of lead. Her temper, sensibility, self-control, her thought and imagination, good nightly sleep—all have become terribly disobedient to her. Even a slight reason suddenly makes her temper flare so badly that if she had been a wife of at least one more year's standing, she would never have gotten away without raising a storm in the household. She merely lies in bed, instead, without food. Her thoughts are in such a disarray that she doesn't always understand what she's thinking of. The steamer trip to Dhaka she had once made, Suryakanta's third sister feeding her own son her eldest sister-in-law's son's share of milk, the account Suryakanta gave her the night before last of a mistake he made when he was nineteen, and . . . . Even if it were no big deal to lose the main thread of thought in such a jumble, still what sort of whim is it that makes her wish to empty a pitcher of water over the head of the maid taking an afternoon nap on part of her sari spread on the veranda floor? And to sleep tonight in her husband's widowed elder sister's bed? Or slip out, sneaking open the front door, and run away? Or put her finger under the sewing-machine needle, setting the household in commotion? Well, yesterday when her foot slipped coming down the staircase, what would have happened if she hadn't steadied herself by clutching the banister? Would it have been too much if she rolled down, broke her bones, her skull? If she lost consciousness entirely? What would all of them have done? . . . Oh no, she has sewn in a wrong place the top she's making for her husband's third sister's baby boy! Why doesn't her husband's third sister just die!

Suryakanta has taken a month's leave, but Amala no longer goes to the bedroom in the afternoons—he doesn't send for her either. He enjoys the laziness of skipping office mixed with the freedom from Amala's too close proximity. He suffers heartburns from the big late lunches. With eyes he watches the ceiling joists, with ears he listens to the faint sound of Amala working at the sewing-machine in another room, his heart droops with a curious sort of dull misery, and his brain thinks of drawing three hundred rupees from the post office savings account and catching any train this afternoon to go on a trip somewhere. A train in the afternoon, at least before nine in the evening, that will leave before Amala comes in. Which Amala? The one in his imagination, or the one who is turning the sewing-machine's handle in that room, making a top for her husband's third sister's son, the one whose coming in will thicken the air of this little room with a million springs and a million lovers' moment of union? He can't quite figure it out. It's possible to take off in an afternoon train in the company of the Amala of his imagination, but will that lessen his longing for the Amala in the other room?

One afternoon four or five days into his leave, Suryakanta attempts to write a letter, but halfway through he tears it up and gets up as if furious with someone. If he has lost the ability to write a letter in simple words about an essential matter, it's time to do something about it. As he gets dressed to go out, his anger subsides. With whom can he be angry? If on sitting down to write a letter he starts thinking of how to launch a novel kind of sweet quarrel with Amala as soon as she comes in tonight, then how can he write a letter on a serious practical matter? Dressed and in shoes, he comes out of his room. In the veranda a kerosene stove has been lit and afternoon tea and snacks are being prepared. Amala in a cloud-gray sari is rolling out dough for deep-frying. The touch of natural unrestraint in Amala's manner among the family's young women and kids seems so laden with mystery! He pauses. His third sister says, 'Going out, Dada? Have something before you go, I'll make you a cup of tea. Bring me some water, Bou-di, what's fried will do for him.'

'I don't want anything now. I'm not hungry, I've no time.'

Amala gets up then and goes into their room. She wants to talk to him. In this household, the custom for semi-new wives is first to move out of others' sight and then sign to her husband to come over for a word. But signing is superfluous now. Suryakanta follows her into their room.

'Don't have tea outside,' she says. 'I too won't have tea now. When you're back, I'll make a cup of tea myself, then we'll drink from the same cup, all right? We'll drink like this . . . . '

Not a bad idea. Sipping tea from the same cup cheek to cheek, perhaps they can try that. But why? What's the harm in keeping tea drinking and cheek touching separate?

'I'm not going to be back tonight, Amal.'

Not coming back! Not coming back for the night! Where will Suryakanta be the whole night? In a friend's place? Why? Because he's been invited and it'll be late when the meal is over? Even so, he must return, take a taxi. Let a couple of rupees go in taxifare this once! The unnatural intensity of Amala's gaze keeps piercing his eyes, his head spins. 'Then I won't go Amal,' he says.

'That's better. What good can come of going out to keep an invitation for merely a dinner?'

Indeed! Sipping tea with Amala from the same cup can be far more enjoyable. But how would he start that sweet quarrel with her tonight? With what move will he initiate another variation in their love drama? If it's too complex, too artistic, it goes over her head, makes her cry and say that she's not upto his standard as a wife, that she should better die. Amala likes it frothy, just the froth, the froth that a common half-educated girl raised in the confines of home can grasp, feel and enjoy. He has to turn water into seltzer for her, a desi sweet drink of cannabis bubbly like champagne. Otherwise, their drama doesn't take hold. And if their drama doesn't take hold, then to him too, as to Amala, it seems as if life's all wasted with no meaning left in living.

That evening Suryakanta doesn't go out for his friend's dinner; next evening he goes to the theatre. Amala accompanies him, of course, along with other young women in the family. So, at the theatre nothing much transpires between them except exchange of glances. Back home at three in the morning, they fall asleep with barely a few words. The evening after, Suryakanta stays home, but perhaps due to the previous night's experience of professional drama, their amateur bedroom drama doesn't quite get going, and both sleep fitfully, with an awful feeling of discomfort. The next day Suryakanta leaves for Patna to reach his visiting third sister and her baby to her husband.

This duty could have been rendered by his younger brother—in fact, that's what had been decided earlier, and it would only have meant his missing college classes for three days. Amala feels mortally wounded at the thought that Suryakanta is more concerned about his brother missing classes than about being away from her for three days. Besides, he could have sent his third sister with his nephew, or he could have written to his third sister's husband asking him to come for his wife. Of course, the nephew is a little too young, and his third sister's husband has been unable to get leave despite trying. But does hurt feeling ever listen to this sort of reason! Then, after three days, when a brief letter comes from Suryakanta for his brother, instead of for Amala, saying that his return will be delayed because he'll travel around a little, then the world turns all dark in Amala's eyes. She knows she has been deserted by her husband. Just as once he abandoned her by abruptly sending her off to her parents' place, so this time he has done it by going away on the pretext of reaching his sister to her husband. With only this difference: the last time she got her husband back on her return; this time even when he returns she won't get him back. If his intention was not to shed an unsuitable wife from his life, why would he volunteer to go to Patna, ignoring the plea in her tearful eyes? Alas, he hasn't bothered even to write to Amala!

After just a few days, a letter does come for her from Agra, a long letter in fact, nearly one whole foolscap page. From one look at the paper and the form of address, 'Kalyaniyashi,' Amala knows it's not a husband's letter at all, only a gesture of politeness towards a discarded wife. What has Suryakanta written? Nothing really! He has sent her a travelogue. Only at the beginning he has provided some meaningless excuse as to why he suddenly felt an urge to travel and at the end he has written that Amala must eat well and take care of herself adding that he would be very happy to see her a little filled out on his return. That's all he has to say! Then the letter ends with love and a false declaration that he is Amala's very own.

Amala bars her bedroom door to read the letter, she unbars it after five hours. Her drained face and red eyes convince them all of the truth in her claim that she is 'feeling unwell'. Only her youngest sister-in-law, the one approaching marriageable age and whose heart pounds on reading novels by writers like Suryakanta, asks, 'Lovelorn, sister-in-law? The letter that came today—you spent the whole day reading it, didn't eat, didn't do anything, must be feeling heartsick. Sweet sister-in-law, won't you give me the letter, let me see what big brother wrote you?' Amala can no longer feel that sort of gentle, insignificant pain. Is she left with any doubt that Suryakanta's sudden decision to go to Patna and delay the return is only a prelude to dropping her? For a reason that is the exact opposite of why Aparna of *Rainbow* was left by that ordinary, inadequate husband of hers. Amala fits small and big events taken selectively from her married life into this conclusion. He married her on a fleeting impulse; that's why he didn't feel any love for her until the time he sent her away to her parents' place, or make any attempt to encourage her love, which he thwarted instead. He didn't want Amala's love then, as his heart cherished the memory of another (who knows if she's the same one he named in his account of the mistake he made at nineteen!), and did not open himself to her. Yet, he was waiting to see if Amala would prove worthy of him by winning him over. If she couldn't rouse passion in his heart in spite of being with him all the time, how could she qualify to be the wife of a renowned writer like him? Then, after throwing her out in the name of sending her for a visit to her family, he perhaps felt pity for her and decided he'd make one last try by giving himself to her in every way to see if she could captivate him. When she couldn't do even that, what other option did he have except leave her on the pretext of going to Patna on family duty?

In rejecting her, he would perhaps not send her away. He might let her live here as before, maintaining a distance built of reserve and plain conduct. She might get a little mild affection from him, nothing else. Not another night will come in Amala's life when she would be able to reach her husband, when he would love her.

Such thoughts might have entered her mind earlier, before she returned from her parents' place, but it had come only in a chariot of fantasy. No matter how upset she might have felt then, the unalterable natural inclination of her woman's brain—to go by reality and practical consideration of gain and loss—would never have let her forget that this sort of absurd analysis went against all custom and practice, that it was insane, because not one of the essential forms of success in her life as a woman would be obstructed by reasons of this sort. On the contrary, she might have used this episode to tie her husband down even more firmly by singing a special piece on hurt feelings in need of soothing. But before leaving he had rendered useless this natural defence, ultimate and unbearable, against abnormal and dangerous sentimentality. What was mere effusion of fantasy and sentimentality would soon have drowned under thoughts and preoccupations that would become far more important and dearer to her. But with his own temporary sentimental immoderation, he had given it the place of truth and reality in Amala's mind. Precisely because she knew that real life did not have the atmosphere of novels, she grew an irrepressible thirst for a bit of fiction in her life, especially when she saw in her marriage to a famed romance writer like Suryakanta a rare opportunity to make life imitate fiction. An opportunity to bring a little poetry into life, not to base life on poetry. It's this instinctive knowledge of the difference between life and poetry that enables even a poet, let alone a simple young woman like Amala, carry on with life in this world. But Suryakanta has totally messed up this instinct in her case. Earlier, when her attempts to make things poetic met with her husband's rebuff, she cried and found some pleasure in the crying, because even that was a kind of poetry. Overstimulated imagination, on being frustrated, brought superficial pain and made Amala's life juicy. Now that sense of superfluity is gone, the juice has become toxic. If only he had sought a clear understanding with her before leaving, if only he had left her with some new food for thought! If somehow she could forget that when he started bringing her nectar from heaven in unlimited quantities, she couldn't stand him, she feared having to go near him. Oh god, no wonder her husband gave up on her and fled.

No more timely bathing and eating, no more sleeping well at night; the very root of life seemed to have come loose for her. Even talking seems painful, anyone coming near her produces only irritation in her. Let her be. No one dares to tell her anything—who'd bother this forlorn madwoman? Amala stays by herself and uses with ample liberty the distortions of her own mind. From time to time, Suryakanta's letter comes from one city or another, some addressed to Amala some to another member of the family. Each letter deals Amala yet another blow. Not one word on anything that has value in her morbid world, only trivial talk about irrelevant things. The letters only prove Amala's utter insignificance to Suryakanta, they only stir up a storm of self-torment in her mind. Amala stays up almost through one whole night writing him a letter, asking him to give her another chance, just one more, and if this time Amala can't prove adequate as Suryakanta's lifemate, then she herself will leave by taking poison or by hanging, so on and so forth. After ten days, the answer to this letter comes from Madras. It says how happy Suryakanta is to have Amala's letter at last, though all those crazy thoughts were quite out of order, a shame really. It says how bewildered he feels, sitting in a hotel room in faraway Madras, wondering what possibly could have given her the idea that she wasn't adequate as his lifemate . . . .

Meanwhile, Suryakanta has applied for another month's leave. He'll travel around a bit longer before returning. Until then, Amala must take good care of herself, all right?

Amala is choking, apparently in the throes of laughter. Her mouth starts foaming, and the way her arms and legs are flung about makes one fear that her limbs will come off any moment and scatter in all directions. 'How long will he keep running away, little sister-in-law?' she says and laughs.

And as she laughs, her body bends back like a bow. Furious with the snapping buttons of her blouse, she tears it off. She seems to find even the loose cover of her sari unbearable. Her elder sister-in-law screams, her husband's young unmarried sister cries, his young brother empties pitcherfuls of water on her head, the aunt calls the names of various gods and goddesses and says things that are incomprehensible, and the rest of the household start doing and saying things that make no sense at all. Finally they join forces to hold Amala still; Amala in turn bites her elder sister-in-law's hand, making it bleed. When with much effort they manage to extract the hand, the two rows of her teeth clamp with such force that it seems to take away all trace of strength from the rest of her body, and her entire body goes limp.

That was the first attack. The second one comes as soon as Suryakanta returns home after getting the urgent telegram. But this time it starts not with laughter, but with angry words. Asking him at whose instance he has come back, Amala soon starts screaming, shouting abuses, frothing at the corners of her mouth. With a frenzied flinging of arms and legs, her body bends back like a bow. Then her teeth clamp shut, and the rest of her body goes limp.

This time all of them are less concerned. Splashing water on Amala's face, the elder sister-in-law even speaks ill of Amala's father and brother for thrusting her on this household. Suryakanta remarks: 'If they could lie about her age by three years, it's no surprise that they would hide this disease. The surprising thing is why it took so long to show up.'

These words Amala, of course, can't hear. That's why in bed at night she whispers eagerly, 'Is it the truth, what you told me? You really felt miserable away from me? Then why did you leave me and run away? Why didn't you come right back from Patna?'

But what difference does it make if her words sound merely sentimental. Hysteria is not sentimentality, it's a disease.

The Widower's Second Wife[*]

Protima's father is not exactly poor, nor can Protima be described as plain looking. Had they searched a bit longer, a bachelor could certainly have been procured for her. Yet her parents decided in favour of giving her into the hands of Ramesh, a widower. Ramesh seemed to them peerless as a groom except for the little blemish that he had been married once and had a six-year-old son. Only thirty-one and strikingly handsome, he holds a government job with a monthly salary of three hundred rupees. He lacks nothing in terms of education, behaviour and family background. Who would let go of such a matrimonial prospect?

Ramesh came to look at the prospective bride, and thus Protima too got a chance to see him before the wedding. The aversion Protima felt towards her groom-to-be, ever since she heard that this was to be his second marriage, should have diminished a little on seeing his handsome looks. But it did not, it only seemed to intensify. Till then, it had concerned an imaginary person, and for that reason it had not become very strong. After seeing Ramesh, precisely because he was so uncommonly handsome, the idea that he had belonged to another woman for four or five years struck Protima's mind as terribly obscene. The reason for this was complex. She still had no knowledge of any aspect of Ramesh as a person, she saw only his external appearance. It was not possible for her to imagine his relationship with his earlier wife except in terms of his physical looks. The moment she tried to think of her husband-to-be, the man came to her mind in the embrace of a slightly plump woman who looked like an embodiment of flaming lust. Protima's virgin body bristled with revulsion.

This sense of impurity Protima felt about her husband was largely gone when she came to his home and saw an enlarged photograph of his dead wife. Anyone could tell at a glance that she did not at all look like someone who knew only to hold her husband day and night in her arms, filthy with lust. A round smiling face, a simple, quiet look in the wide eyes, a little boy of about two in her arms—the face in the photograph

* The Bengali title is *Bipatniker Bou.*

seemed slightly blurred from movement. The way she wore her sari, the way she stood, everything showed that she was rather simple, artless like a cow. It seemed almost impossible to imagine her as Ramesh's wife.

The second time Protima sees the picture is around noon the day she returns from her parents' before she sees Ramesh at night. On the few occasions they saw each other during the first phase after the wedding, the situation was saved by his making no attempt to come near her. With the intense contempt she then felt for her handsome husband, she might have reacted terribly if he had. This time, with her mind a little eased after seeing Manosi's photograph, she does not keep from answering a question or two when he tries to have a conversation with her at night. Ramesh's mild voice, quiet manners, and detached way of talking seem rather pleasant to Protima. Who knows what the man is really thinking? Seems distracted! Is he capable of thinking? The burnished dandy look is not all he has? What's that mark on his cheek? Got quite a cut when shaving, poor fellow!

The night advances, Protima grows sleepy, Ramesh says nothing about going to sleep. They keep sitting, he at one end of the bedstead, she at the other, their legs dangling. What sort of a man is he? Not quite the type she had thought! There seems to be a slight veil of mystery around him. At one point he remarks, 'It's better to talk these things over beforehand don't you think? Then you'll be able to understand me, and I'll be able to understand you too.'

Talk over what things? Protima can't make anything out. But she gives a nod in agreement. Why not find out how her husband's first words of love sound!

'Let me tell you why I married again,' Ramesh starts. 'I didn't do it easily. After having lived with one person for five years, to start again with another—you must be feeling utter disrespect for me. Aren't you?'

'No. Why should I?' Protima replies politely.

'I'm sure you are. But when you hear everything, you'll feel only pity for me. When she died suddenly after a three-day fever, the grief turned me strange. Never in my life had I imagined such a blow. Time would do the healing, I thought, but it did not. I couldn't concentrate on anything, couldn't stand anyone's company; even the barest of duties seemed so unbearably difficult. You'll gradually see how many kinds of responsibilities I have on different fronts, and I don't even have the option to leave those to someone else; if I don't look after them, there'll be ruin on all sides. Yet the state of my mind was such that I'd rather have drifted away without moving an arm or a leg. Earlier, the people at home were happy and smiling. With me so depressed, nobody would laugh openly any more, a shadow of sadness fell over the house. My temper also turned sour; for the slightest reason I'd start shouting, and everyone in the family lived in fear of it. Even the boy didn't come near me easily any more. At first I didn't pay much attention, then some time ago I became aware that the beautiful life I'd built up with friends and relatives was about to collapse due to my neglect. I felt so remorseful. It was not right to let my grief shadow others' lives. It would have been different if I didn't have any responsibility in the family and no one was affected by my state of mind. I had to shake off my grief and sorrow and get up. So after much thought, I decided to start again with you . . . .'

Even a child can understand something explained so well. Protima knows that the fashionable haircut and the clean shave he got for the wedding don't really mean a thing. Though he looks like a college student in that tight-fitting short-sleeved shirt, the mind behind it is practical, cautious, sober, and packed with consideration, instead of sentimentality, ardour or fantasy. He has married again not because he wants to forget his first wife, but because it's necessary that he forgets. His ardent desire is to spend the rest of his life grieving for the woman he set up home with for five years, but what can he do, his consideration for other family members has made it his unavoidable duty to control personal grief. And who doesn't know that Ramesh is a particularly dutiful man!

But what is she supposed to do? With juicy ripe love she has to wipe from her husband's mind the lines of memory, like wiping a written-over slate with a wet rag. Protima's sleepiness disappears. Glancing at Ramesh's sombre sad face, she wonders why he is telling her all this. What sort of mutual understanding is this! Did she leave behind at her parent's place a part of her youth, her beauty and ability to enchant a man? When the person had come and presented herself in entirety, she wasn't going to stop him from putting her to whatever use he wanted. Who knows, maybe Ramesh is of the opinion that women have a secret reserve fund of love, affection, and the ability to sweeten life so that, given advance notice, they can draw from there as needed to dispel a special man's penance of grief in a special situation. This is a much worse indication of mental weakness than marrying for the second time out of the need for a wife!

Ramesh goes on talking about many other things that night and they do not sleep before three in the morning. The family members feel very happy sensing this. Until then they had been worried that he had not even talked nicely to his new wife.

The house has many people in it, much activity and variety. All kinds of love traps are laid in the various hearts. No one neglects trying to capture Protima. She had no idea that so much nice treatment could await a new bride in any family. She seems infinitely valuable to everyone. Not given any household chore, and kept at a distance from the troubles of daily life, Protima seems to have no duty other than a bit of luxurious tending of Ramesh. Young and old, they seem to be killing themselves conspiring to create opportunities for her to see her husband all the time, day and night. Protima fully understands what they want. She'll have to quickly remove from this home the wife whose presence remains undiminished even a year after her death, immortalised in its inanimate objects and consciousness. The huge gaping hole she left must be filled soon. Protima need not waste a drop of herself on such insignificant daily needs of living as cooking and eating. Let her singlemindedly spend all she has in making preparations to install herself in the empty throne of her dead co-wife. Let her overflow with smiles, songs, and happy talk, to carry Ramesh away, to let his broken heart mend and find happiness, enthusiasm, an abundance of love. More smiles are needed. Plenty of fresh, unwilted smiles! Her co-wife was such an incredible person, so great an empress of this family's small world, that she's remembered the first thing each morning. So totally has she occupied everyone's mind, from Ramesh down to the housemaid. So unbearable is the pain she left behind that the entire family is this desperate to become free of its pressure. The more eagerly they convey to Protima their silent prayers to make them forget her, the more they draw her attention to her co-wife's value to them. What spell did the enchantress possess, that simple-looking, round-faced wife!

Her sister-in-law Nanda expresses concern: 'Why the sad face, dear sister-in-law? Missing your parents' home? Just tell me, we'll arrange for you to go for a visit today; come back feeling happy. Your sad face reminds us of her, sister-in-law! We didn't allow her to go even after hearing of her father's illness, she wept for two days. That's why she left, punishing us so!'

This is another aspect of the problem. When Protima's face shows sadness, they are reminded of her; if she smiles, they remark with astonishment, 'Oh, isn't this exactly the smile of that unfortunate girl?' Different people keep discovering different aspects of Protima's similarity with her dead co-wife. The youngest daughter-in-law, Bimala, has discovered how similar their walk is when seen from behind. How amazingly perfect her bangles look on Protima's wrists, is the finding of her sister-in-law Nanda. The widowed aunt who lives in the household makes a more serious and far-reaching discovery. Studying every limb of Protima with a sharp gaze, she says, 'O Manda, O Nanda, come here, take a look at this. Look at the chin of the new wife, her neck, and her pointed elbow. Bend your arm, will you, new wife? You see that, Nanda, see that, Manda?'

The curve of her waist, the heels of her red-lined feet, the space between her eyebrows and ear, all seem to be features she has borrowed from that one! Seen altogether, of course, Protima looks very different. She was plump, regally full-figured, and Protima is slight, slim. Yet, with hawk eyes like the aunt's, they all divide Protima's body into various sections and compare it with the image of that poor girl so indelibly imprinted in their memory! Is it for nothing that Ramesh picked her from among so many prospective brides! It's for just this resemblance, they conclude.

One day, when taking the dressed betel from her hand, Ramesh remarks, 'Do you know, new wife, that your fingers are exactly like hers?'

Even her fingers? Protima's mind is scorched with anger. To deal a rude blow to Ramesh's emotions steeped in nostalgia, she pretends not to understand, and asks, 'Like whose, darling? Do you have someone else, one you're in love with?'

Startled, Ramesh says, 'What're you saying? Don't! I'm talking of your elder sister.'

'Where did you see my elder sister? She didn't come to the wedding!'

'Not her . . . Manosi. The way your nails are wavy at the tip, Manosi's were like this.'

She now wipes the amused look off her face. 'Your first wife? Manosi was her name?' she says.

'Didn't you know? You've been here so long and you have not known even her name?'

Protima answers with a sad face, 'Who would tell me? No one tells me anything about her.'

Eagerly Ramesh says, 'You want to hear, new wife, you want to know about her?'

'Yes. Tell me.'

Ramesh's voice chokes when talking about Manosi. Protima feels acutely jealous. It seems as if everyone in this family is engaged in an amazing farce. Having brought her here on the pretext of wanting to forget Manosi, they're constantly looking for Manosi in her. Her originality is unacceptable in this family, for she's only a new form of Manosi—like an image of the inconceivable, inexpressible deity, she's a living image of their disembodied, all-pervasive grief. Despite being different from Manosi in all respects, she's therefore endlessly similar to her. They've set her up as Manosi's representative before whom to place their offerings of sorrow.

One day Protima asks her husband, 'Where's the boy?'

'At burra-pishi's place.'

'Don't you want to bring him back?'

'I will as soon as you ask me to!'

Genuinely surprised now, Protima says, 'Have you been waiting for me to ask? I'm really amazed by the conduct of all of you. In all this time

I've been here, I heard no one mention the boy even once. I don't understand.'

'I asked them not to, new wife. Only after you feel mentally settled here . . . .'

'And then I'll find time to think of the boy? How well you understand the human mind!'

Two days later, the boy arrives. A healthy, good-sized boy, not easy to pick up. Yet, seeing the eager look in everyone's eyes, Protima somehow picks him up in her arms. She feels embarrassed. Even without giving birth to him, she's the mother of this big child? The boy too stays stiff in the stranger's arms. If she had had a chance to befriend him the way one does any kid from another family, then perhaps the first mother-son meeting wouldn't have been so uncomfortable. But as she's the new wife and the kid's new mother, she's left without recourse to the usual process of gradual intimacy through smiles and jokes. She has to hug him as soon as he comes near and kiss him from behind the veil over her face before all those watching eyes.

At least the boy is back, she even feels a little attached to him, but coping with a co-wife's son is not a little tricky, it's a difficult problem. The amount of love and care must all be weighed carefully beforehand; if it's too little, they'd think she neglects her co-wife's son; if it's too much, they'd think it's all a show. It's hard for an eighteen-year-old girl's emotional mind to maintain such caution in day-to-day life. The calculations aren't always correct either. How would she have the presence of mind to act precisely at each step in daily life? While attending to the child's meals, if she becomes a little absent-minded, she looks around with a start, fearful that someone might have caught her like that. The boy's countless childish demands pose countless problems for her. She does not know how to respond. If she yields to his demands, she's criticized. If she doesn't, the boy cries and then too she's criticized. After a meal if she gives him a sweet, she hears her mother-in-law sigh and remark, 'How can she have the kind of judgement you're talking about, Nanda? There's no blood tie here.' When he cries for a sweet after the meal next day, she doesn't comply and lets him cry. Then the aunt comes, picks him up, hands him a sweet from the pantry, and leaves the place without a word. Protima goes red in the face.

In various contexts involving the boy, Protima slowly becomes aware that underneath the excessive care and love shown to her they're also resentful of her. As long as the hearts in this family can use Protima as a tonic, they are grateful and affectionate, but whenever anyone becomes conscious of some distinction in her existence, something that no one in this family can use, they strike out at her. They're then Protima's critics.

Days pass, but still there's not much change in the way things are. Protima's head is covered less and less, her movement gains more freedom, some extra arrangements are made for her convenience, their enthusiasm to find similarities between her and Manosi subsides, yet Protima's conduct does not shed its artificial stance, nor does anyone allow her a natural, spontaneous life, to be her own self. The fact that another woman was in her place, and her preoccupation with the curious vocation of being the family's wife, relentlessly constrains Protima's life. She goes away for a month to her parents' place. But the whole month she spends worrying if she should have brought the boy with her. She's unable to mix freely even with her own family. To savour a curious blistering sort of pleasure, she reviles her in-laws with a do-or-die zeal, mixing truth and falsity, and becomes sad and distracted for that very reason. The habit of acting on the basis of calculating what others might think has become almost a permanent trait in her. Her conduct, even at her parents' place, is now mostly a reaction to her perception of others' thoughts. They readily agree that she has changed after marriage and grown distant from them, as they all do. She's no longer the same Protima she used to be!

Protima could bear all this if she could love Ramesh. The revulsion she had felt at first was erased long ago; it didn't take her long to begin respecting him. The man is uncommonly endowed with good looks and good qualities, his conduct is simple and natural, and behind the grave appearance he's very affectionate, strict but considerate—the kind of man whose company women find most pleasant, whose slaves they willingly become. He can't be said to have defaulted much in his duties towards his wife either, yet her inexpressible jealousy for her dead co-wife pricks her like thorns in the path of her enjoying even the pleasures readily available in conjugal life. Forgetting Manosi is not yet possible for Ramesh; sometimes he's still distracted thinking of her, sometimes he still reaches beyond Protima to embrace the one who is not there. Sometimes even his kiss is incomplete. Protima clearly feels her husband's embrace slacken, like a string snapping, and the passion go out of his kiss. But even this she could have ignored. Perhaps it could even motivate her to a greater determination to conquer her husband's mind. At her age a woman doesn't take the insult of defeat to a dead woman. But her problem is with the goal itself, of conquering his heart, from too many obstacles of pain and shame. Whenever Ramesh is fascinated with her and his eyes are turned away from the past, his love-filled words and look bring her shame instead of happiness. She feels: these words have been spoken before, this look is a used one. The words he spoke to Manosi, the eyes with which he looked at her, the same language, the same look he's now offering Protima. This is old acting, practised lovemaking. It's all taken place many times in the depth of many a night in Ramesh's life. Repetitions and echoes. Nothing else.

Then she no longer feels any desire to conquer him and turns away, offending him. Someone inside her seems to hang her head in shame. Anger brings tears to her eyes, and she's overcome with jealousy towards a woman seen in a picture. She had desired so much, fantasized so much, and now it was all reduced to merely a troubled, distasteful engaging of herself—not in duty, nor in play, but in the cumbersome needs of living.

In such moments even her initial revulsion towards her husband comes back for a while. If his love for Manosi is so unforgettable, then what sort of worthless fellow is he to be capable of developing even a temporary liking for her? What's there to respect in a man who even while lost in honouring one woman's memory, can be fascinated with another?

'Why hasn't your mind settled here?' Ramesh asks Protima.

'Who told you about what goes on in my mind?' she retorts.

'Does anyone need to tell me, can't I sense it? Seems you're not happy, not able to mix freely. Does anyone say anything that bothers you? Don't they look after you?'

'Oh my! Don't they!' Protima laughs. 'I'm quite overwhelmed with all their caring. They're all so preoccupied with me.'

'It'd have been nice if you too could feel the same way with them,' he says, 'I wanted just that.'

She feels like asking, 'Why talk about my mind not settling here, why don't you tell me why your mind doesn't settle on me? Instead of just being polite, why not try loving me and then see if my mind sticks!'

Manosi's memorabilia strewn all over the house irks Protima. No fewer than three framed pictures of her, one in Protima's bedroom, one in the room where Ramesh works and one in her mother-in-law's room. In the photographs, Manosi doesn't strike her as of a fashionable or fanciful disposition. Yet the amount of craftwork she has left behind is astounding. How did she get the time for so much junk work between all the essential work in a span of just five years? More than half the furniture in the house, they say, is her selection. She didn't know how to sing, yet she was enthusiastic to purchase an organ and Protima now has to sing with it. Manosi's dressing-table now holds her toiletries, a selection of Manosi's jewellery decorates her body, Manosi's bed is where she sleeps. The house is full of trunks and cases packed with Manosi's clothes. And the countless little things she has left behind.

As her new-bride status wears out, Protima takes off the pieces of jewellery that were Manosi's. They don't fail to notice it; her mother-in-law grumbles, but no one really objects. But what can taking off inherited jewellery accomplish? Who'll keep all the usable and unusable stuff she left behind from having such prominence? Memories preserved internally and mementos displayed externally have given that dead woman immortality in this house.

'Do you know, sister-in-law, that almirah you're clearing out and putting other stuff into was her special favourite?' Nanda says to her. 'She kept images of gods and goddesses arranged on the top shelf and she did pranam there every morning on getting up.'

'Where did the gods and goddesses go, dear?'

'Who knows where big brother moved them! Got mad at them when she left for heaven.'

'Is it since then that your big brother has become hot-tempered, dear?'

'Why do you say that, does he get angry with you?'

Protima smiles and squeezes her cheeks, saying, 'When you're married, you'll realize how sweet it can be when the husband gets mad—sweeter than when he acts sweetly. If he doesn't get angry even once, you can be sure there's something wrong with him.'

It's not surprising that Protima believed without a doubt that whatever was wrong in her husband's mind on account of the dead woman was permanent. A chaste young woman in whose life no man other than her husband has ever entered is innocent to a fault; she is a sincere believer. She believes the husband's first expression of love right after marriage to be his ultimate expression, so that the subsequent advances in his love must seem endlessly baffling. Seeing Ramesh distracted by Manosi's memory, on the basis of what knowledge and experience could Protima reason that death is final, memory has the evaporative quality of camphor, that in life the strongest attraction is the one between living men and women, and no one wants to preserve forever a painful memory? The petals of her mind that Protima kept from opening up to Ramesh, due to the pain of envy, remain for him veiled in mystery. As the smaller and larger expressions of her personality make Ramesh aware of her, this mystery starts working as an antidote to whatever it was that had gone awry in his mind.

By the end of the first year, so many new habits have been formed, so many novelties of delicious feeling tasted. Even if her coming here was to fill the gap left by Manosi in the first place, still it was her own world that Protima brought with her. It is impossible to fit her into Manosi's mould! In places Protima is too large, in places too small. The ways in which she's different from, even the opposite of, Manosi become increasingly clear. The novelty of the irritation and the affection produced by her faults and her qualities gradually wears out its ability to upset her in-laws, they find themselves accepting Protima's faults and merits as her own. Besides, no one is able to have Protima by wanting her as Manosi, and not having a person one wants to have is not a pleasant feeling. And when Ramesh goes to Protima acknowledging the attraction he feels for her as her husband, he comes in touch with a very lovely heart.

In exactly the same way in which inseverable ties grew between Manosi and them, Protima keeps tying them and getting tied to them. The boy's addressing her as 'mother' no longer produces in her a dreadful discomfort; she sort of likes it, though the attachment she feels to the boy is not exactly maternal love. And where her relationships as the wife of the family with her mother-in-law and sisters-in-law are concerned, she's able to maintain as much as can be decently maintained with half one's attention.

Everything becomes sort of easy and natural; only Protima is unable to adjust herself to Ramesh. The first time she realizes that the grief for Manosi is lifting off his mind like winter fog, a deep sadness overcomes her envious mind instead of gladness. Somehow she feels embarrassed. As if an unholy vow she observed for so long has reached its day of consummation.

Yet that's not what she had done, was it? So many times, standing before Manosi's photograph and burning with jealousy, she felt like throwing it out the window, and smashing to bits all the mementos of the enchantress that are everywhere. But on her own initiative had she really attempted to drive Manosi out of Ramesh's mind?

Protima's wedding had taken place in the fortnight of the full moon for the worship of Durga; that night returns. Ramesh secretly brings home flowers and a gift of gold. The sober, reticent man's deep current of excitement and eager expectation to make this special night enjoyable does not escape her. But she doesn't feel happy. She feels mild surprise, and a sickening discomfort.

Thinking of something, she picks up one of the garlands Ramesh has brought and puts it around Manosi's picture. In Protima's mind she has been permanently singed by the sharp heat of resentment applied for a long time. Thinking of her constantly has so conditioned Protima that she has no way of forgetting her even on her own wedding night. In an amazing coincidence, as soon as Ramesh raises his head from kissing Protima, his eyes land on Manosi's picture.

'You put a garland on her picture?' he says ecstatically.

The embracing arms that only a few months ago would slacken at Manosi's memory, like a taut rope snipped with a sharp knife, now tighten like two live snakes round her neck. The kiss that used to be only the touching of lips grows indescribably passionate.

Suddenly feeling sick, Protima cries out, 'Let go, let go of me now, quick!'

'What happened?' Ramesh asks in a stricken voice.

'I can't breathe. Let go.'

Pushing her husband away, Protima gets off the bed. She does not even stay in the room. The electric light reflected on the glass on Manosi's photograph hurts her eyes; it seems like the glare of Manosi's reproachful look.

She flees to the terrace. There's hardly another place for young wives to escape to. Over the terrace is the unchangeable sky, and the unwavering darkness of night blended uniformly with starlight. Protima wants to cry from the sorrow she now feels. He has forgotten her! Her husband's heart is such that he has already forgotten Manosi, who used to be the omnipresent empress of his world within.

An Elderly Man's Childbride*

The biggest proof of Rasik's having become an elderly man is his fear of death. It is the age when, with the weakening of the arrogant spirit that refused to listen till now to the incessant 'I'm coming, I'm coming' hum of death, even while hearing it well, a man for the first time becomes aware of it from its change of tone. Becomes aware that death is now calling from a distance reassuringly, saying, 'It's not time yet, wait a bit longer.' An old man, already in the process of tasting death, thinks: It's far off, it's still far off. And an elderly man, having lost the taste for life, thinks: Alas, my days are ending.

So Rasik thought it wouldn't be right to bring a young girl home as a wife for just a few days. Not just that. Rasik felt terribly uncomfortable just imagining how immaturely a young wife would behave and what sort of immature acting she would expect from him. Wasn't he past that age? Was it possible for him to even grin and bear the endless frivolity of a childbride, let alone return any of it? The departed wife was a mother and a housemistress, the new wife will be a restless girl. How could Rasik possibly get along with her as wife?

There was no need for it, there was no desire either, yet one day Rasik remarried.

Calling him into the house at an unusual hour, Sulochana one day said to him, 'Would you take a look at this girl, brother-in-law? Her name is Sudharani.'

Taken aback, Rasik said, 'Is that so? That's nice.'

Not a little girl—she was fairly grown. With an unsmiling face and a definite self-assurance in her manner of sitting ladylike on the floor. Rasik, of course, had no idea it was Sulochana who had dressed Sudharani in that black-bordered plain white sari, taken off her little girl's earrings, slipped on the thick bangles and armlets, undone the tangle in her hair and, parting it in the middle, pulled it into a tight bun at the back, and instructed her, 'Sit here with a glum face, dear. When you see my brother-in-law, if you act even a little shy, if you fidget even a little,

---

*   The Bengali title is *Prowrher Bou.*

then . . . .' Maybe that's why Sudharani did not seem so distasteful to Rasik.

Afterwards he heard, again from Sulochana, that the girl was quite grown up, her poor father could not get her married and so she was now an old maid past twenty . . . . 'If married off in time, she'd have been a mother of three sons, you know, brother-in-law.'

Requests and pleas to get remarried had been coming from all quarters; but now, perhaps at Sulochana's initiative, it turned virtually into an offensive. Conceding defeat, Rasik said, 'Let it be, then.'

It is hard to say how far his willingness to concede defeat came from seeing Sudharani.

But as Sudharani's luck would have it, she irritated him with the very first word she spoke in her first conversation with him. At the time Rasik was having quite a whirl of regret and self-justification, hesitation and curiosity in his mind, producing sadness sometimes, and the pleasure of anticipation at others. He was rather preoccupied with himself.

Around eleven one night, when he was in his outer room on the pretext of work but thinking of things ranging between heaven and hell, Sulochana came in quietly and said to him, 'Is it true, brother-in-law, that you haven't said a single word to your new wife? You stay here working upto one or two in the morning? That's a shame, brother-in-law. Does one hurt the feelings of a young girl like that? She was secretly crying today.'

Sulochana made this up with all good intention, but the result was just the opposite. Rasik thought: Young girl? Crying? That's disaster! What sort of understanding could he expect from someone who did not have the slightest patience?

Still, deciding it was better not to hurt the girl's feelings as he had married her, for the first time tonight he went into the bedroom before one in the morning without giving her time to fall fast asleep. The idea he had was to explain to her that none of his actions indicated neglect, that she would not suffer from lack of love, care, affection; however, as Rasik was getting on in age, she must understand that for adjusting to him she would have to be a little calm and quiet, otherwise it would not do.

Sudharani was sitting on one side of the bed, slowly swinging her feet. Perhaps absentmindedly, perhaps out of habit. Quite clearly she looked like she was waiting for someone. Moreover she was sitting exactly the way his eldest daughter sat, palms planted on two sides and feet dangling playfully. The sight was quite disheartening for Rasik. Perhaps Sulochana had informed her that her husband would be coming in any moment, but why must she wait so eagerly, dressed like this, waiting as if for a lover? And dangling her feet in the way a ten-year-old girl would, restless as a doe?

Seeing him, Sudharani gathered herself a little—only a little. Sulochana had asked her not to show too much shyness. Face stern, Rasik sat a yard away from her, in the pompous manner of one taking his designated seat in a gathering.

With what was he to begin? Rasik possessed so much knowledge, intelligence and experience and a nature so calm, quiet and unperturbed—why were beads of sweat forming on his forehead as he tried to talk to an adolescent girl? What a fate! Seventeen years ago, he didn't have to search for words to talk to Promila on the wedding night itself. As soon as the room became empty, he found himself spontaneously uttering in a hushed voice, in a caressing tone, with the rhythm of epic poetry, 'How does it feel? To know that from now on you are mine?'

Rubbing his chin with a finger like a man troubled by uncertainty, Rasik finally said, 'I wanted to tell you a few things, Sudha.' Sudha said nothing at all. Rasik continued: 'I'm getting on in age, perhaps I'm not exactly to your liking . . . .'

Hearing this, a mischievous smile stole into the put-on glum expression on her face. As she quickly lowered her face, a flash of light reflected from her earrings and she gave him a sharp, quick, stunning glance! And she said just one word under her breath. 'Bosh!'

Silently Rasik returned to his office room, he did not come even when he knew Sudharani would be asleep. He lay down there for the night. Even in Promila's time a bed was kept ready for him in this room, though he rarely slept in it then.

Of course, he couldn't make a permanent arrangement of sleeping in his office. What would people say? It was possible to stay on till late at night on the pretext of work, even to spend an occasional night or two in the name of special work, but simply because a frivolous girl had come in as his wife and occupied Promila's bedroom, he couldn't cut that room off his life. It wasn't possible for the elderly Rasik to behave so childishly.

It wasn't possible for him to spend his days without the frivolous girl either. Especially with Sulochana so busily at work behind his back. She sent Sudharani to him on all sorts of excuses, or created conditions so that there was no way of meeting the many small needs of Rasik's daily life without Sudharani's help. As a result, Rasik got somewhat used to Sudharani's presence; out of these small occasions for contact, an easy though superficial relationship grew between then. Even some conversation occurred by way of questions and answers in the context of various major and minor matters. But nothing more than that. When did a couple ever get in touch with each other's minds through the efforts of a mediator, except those eternal mediators like moonlight, floral scent, spring breeze, and the poetry of the needless talk of sleepless nights.

Sulochana asked Rasik, 'What's the problem, brother-in-law? Sudha not to your liking?'

'The question of liking or disliking is irrelevant at my age,' he said.

'Still, why don't you tell me. It'll do no harm.'

'Sudha is very frivolous, sister-in-law! Am I at an age to take the flippancy of a silly girl, when in a few days I'll be closing my eyes?'

Now Sulochana was irritated. 'Frivolous! Sudha's frivolous! Would you have been happy with a mother of seven sons? Even a mother of seven sons acts a little frivolous from time to time, like most normal people. Not everyone is like the elephant-headed Ganesh that you are.'

Sulochana's irritation increased the disquiet in Rasik's mind. Sometimes he did wish he could love Sudharani like a wife, but the very thought of starting all over again that childish play of long ago with Promila, of which he had but a faded memory, produced fear in his mind. It felt distasteful. He'd have to dress like a joker and act ridiculously to be close to a childbride who turned sad if he sat apart, smiled mischievously if he brought up the serious topic of their relationship, who unbearably affected modesty, shyness, timidity if he sat near her, and tried day and night to charm him with the loveliness of her body, words from her lips, and glances from her eyes rather than with the tending and caring of her unskilled hands. Sudharani would not be satisfied with anything else, she would not understand any other game. She had no idea of the depth, sobriety and sweetness of the play between him and Promila towards the end. If he tried telling her that discussing life's problems could be more satisfying than lovers' cooing, she smiled. That same irritating smile Promila had in the early years that couldn't be wiped off except with kisses.

Thus, no matter how hard Sulochana tried, Rasik couldn't overcome his aversion towards drawing close to his new bride. Days passed in this manner. The expression of surprise and sadness on Sudharani's face was gradually eclipsed by an inscrutable dark shadow.

Initially Rasik found it difficult to stay up in his study upto one in the morning. Sometimes while lying down in bed working, he fell asleep without being aware of it. Then somehow that natural sleepiness passed; he couldn't fall asleep any more, even when he wanted to sleep. He didn't have to make any effort to stay awake. Midnight passed at some point, the house and the neighbourhood slowly grew still, only Rasik in his room stayed awake. He felt a mild pain in his head, and a burning in his eyes, but sleep eluded him. While the world around him slowly fell asleep, the world of his own thought and imagination grew clearer and brighter.

Rasik then missed Promila terribly; like an inconsolate child his mind wanted Promila back. As an irrational, angry resentment rose up in his mind against the whole world, he kept thinking, if Promila had been here she'd never have let him stay up this late, she'd have made him lie down in bed and brought sleep to his eyes by simply stroking his forehead.

Going to the bedroom and seeing Sudharani asleep would then set him on fire. He'd feel like kicking her awake and throwing her out of the room. What kind of a woman was she, what kind of a wife, if she could fall asleep before her husband, and did not even know how to put her husband to sleep?

One evening at ten o'clock, Rasik was with a neighbour who had come for a chat. Surprised to see him yawn, holding a hand to his mouth, Rasik asked, 'Are you feeling unwell?'

'No, I didn't have an afternoon nap, I'm sleepy.'

A little later, after yawning once more, he left. Rasik sat wondering if he could, on some pretext, keep the man here till late in the night; then he could have watched him fight sleep. Wouldn't it be amusing to watch with sleepless eyes how he manoeuvred to stay awake? Besides, sleep could be infectious. Perhaps a touch of sleep would come to him from just seeing someone's body and mind grow limp with sleep.

No, it wouldn't. Had he once felt sleepy on seeing Sudharani knocked out in sleep?

He was unable to return to work, his concentration was ruined. Pushing the chair back a little, Rasik reclined and put his feet up. Right in front of him was a large photograph on the wall, a full-length of Promila, standing simply dressed, with a smile of mischievous satisfaction on her lips, in an expensive frame. The wall on this side was completely blank, except for several nail marks here and there. Clearly, a few other pictures or photographs used to hang on this wall which had been removed.

Putting the pipe of his hubble-bubble to his lips, Rasik became aware of something new around Promila's picture that had not existed till yesterday—a garland of fresh flowers. Coming into the room this evening he got a mild scent of flowers—this must be it. Then the smell of tobacco covered up the scent and the air from the fan dispersed it.

But who had suddenly put a fresh garland around Promila's photograph, who had had this idea? The first few months he himself, on his way home from his afternoon walk, bought a garland from the shop at the street crossing and put it around the photograph. And then one day while taking the old garland off to put a new one on, it suddenly occurred to him that nothing could be more childish than trying to maintain the sanctity of memory with the bribe of a garland of flowers. He didn't know why this occurred to him, but from that day he brought no more garlands. After all this time, who was paying homage to Promila's memory again with a garland of fresh flowers?

The servant, Nikhil, opened the door slightly, looked in once and went back. Every evening around this time he looked in like this and went back. In a few minutes Sudharani would come into the room softly, stand near his table, and ask in a quiet voice, 'Won't you come to eat?' Tonight also she came in, and putting her hand on the table near Rasik's feet, raised her eyes upto his chin in an effort to look naturally at his face and said, 'Won't you come to eat?'

Putting his feet down, Rasik sat up straight.

He knew all this was Sulochana's design. When it was time to eat, Nikhil, at Sulochana's bidding, came to check if anyone from the outside was still here, and then again at her bidding, Sudharani came to call him. He could also see Sulochana's training and advice in her pathetic attempt to forget that she was a new bride and act like a matter-of-fact housemistress. Sometimes he felt amused, sometimes affectionate. But tonight his mind felt soured.

'You put that garland there?'

Sudharani's face turned pale—not at the question, but at the tone of his voice. She'd always been rather timid; on top of that, after becoming the wife of this elderly widower at the close of her adolescent life, her days were being spent in a rather odd and unnatural manner.

'Where did you learn such posturing? Wherever you learnt it, I don't like this sort of stuff. Do you understand?'

Wordlessly Sudharani kept wrapping the corner of her sari around her finger and Rasik, now annoyed with himself, wondered why he had said such harsh words to the poor thing when he really wasn't angry. He had no wish to say any of this. He only wanted to ask her not to put garlands and stuff on Promila's photograph any more. What was he going to do if she burst into tears now?

But Sudharani didn't cry, her face didn't seem even a little tearful. Pressing her lower lip with her teeth with an offended look, she stood there a little and then proceeded to leave. Then, prompted by suspicion, he called her back, 'Don't go, listen. Did the elder sister-in-law ask you to place the garland there?'

'I don't know. What'll you do if I say I put it on my own? Will you hit me or something?'

Her words, the manner in which she gave the answer, her tone, everything was unexpected. Rasik was amazed. It seemed incredible that even Sudharani could feel so hurt and express such an angry objection to unfair chastisement. Until now he hadn't heard her talk like this even once. Perhaps because he hadn't given her a chance; if given the chance, she would perhaps have hissed like this even earlier and proved that even if a new bride, she was no whiny thirteen-year-old wrapped in frilly clothing. It seemed to Rasik as if he was feeling Sudharani's existence for the first time now. As if though she was around, she had not really been there all this time.

Thus, for a few seconds he almost forgot that Sudharani was not Promila. Just as he used to mollify Promila when she got angry with him, he attempted to pacify Sudharani with an elaborate prelude. But he didn't get very far. Soon after holding her hand and saying a few of his standard endearments, he looked up and saw drops of tears running down her cheeks.

Promila would not have cried. Even if she had been crying earlier, she would have stopped crying now. It would perhaps take a long time for a smile to replace the cloud on her face but she would never have engaged in the affectation of shedding big tears.

Sudharani's childlike tears made Rasik self-conscious; he felt awkward and stopped. Interrupting his words of endearment, he said politely, 'I'm hungry. Isn't the cooking done yet?'

Wiping her tears, Sudharani said, 'Yes, it's done. Are you angry with me?'

Rasik did not answer. A few days ago, when he abruptly stopped uttering endearments while consoling his crying daughter, she too had asked apprehensively, just like this, 'Are you angry with me, Father?' And with that she had stopped crying for fear of annoying her father.

The Wife of a King[*]

From the age of twenty, Jamini has been a queen.

The kingdom of Jamini's husband Bhupati is, however, only a large estate. It brings an annual income of no more than Rs 150,000. Bhupati is a king only by title. Jamini therefore isn't strictly a queen. She is a queen by title, a king's wife.

Bhupati is the third in a dynasty only three generations long.

In one of the many narrow lanes of Calcutta, in a medium-sized two-storeyed red-plastered house, lives a man named Bhabashankar Ray, who somehow supports a large family on a monthly income of two hundred and fifty rupees. In the evening, during card-playing sessions with friends, he is often heard talking about his ancestors' estate, which, from his words, would seem to have been almost the size of India. The til of an estate in that taal-size exaggeration of the story constituted Bhupati's kingdom.

It happened at the time of Bhupati's great-grandfather, Mahipati. Mahipati was the chief collector of Bhabashankar's landlord ancestor. He used to call himself the finance minister, but the landlord used to call him Mr Collector, Nayeb-moshai. It's hard to determine whether his resentment of this was the motivating factor, but the conspiracy he hatched against the landlord caused half the estate to be sold off and the other half to come under his ownership. By the time of Bhupati's grandfather Jadupati, the sold half had also come to him, the estate had gained hugely in prosperity, and three years before his death he got himself known as Raja Jadupati Ray-chaudhuri (Sarkar), Abantipur Royal Estate.

His son Ganapati, towards the end of his life, developed a strong urge to be not just a raja, but a maharaja. Maybe he was inspired by a sense of duty arising from the notion that each generation must accomplish some advancement. The income from the estate was quite large then. He poured so much money into his unsuccessful attempts to become a maharaja that had he spent it instead on buying up faltering estates, he could have left his son a smallish kingdom truly befitting a king. But instead of enlarging

---

[*]   The Bengali title is *Rajar Bou.*

his kingdom, he left it a lot reduced in size.

Bhupati now has a little difficulty as a result of this. It is not easy to sit back maintaining the appearance of being a king with the income of an estate. The worry of balancing expenditure against income has produced a bald spot on Bhupati's head even though he is only thirty-two.

At the time of Jamini's wedding, however, it was Ganapati who was bald. Bhupati was then a young man of twenty-three. With the help of a male attendant he used to carefully groom his full head of black hair in a side-parted style.

Jamini is beautiful. She is beautiful not because she is a king's wife, she is a king's wife because she's beautiful.

Like all beauty, Jamini's also has a history. A family that was poor four generations ago, and in which every one of the male and female members was as dark-complexioned as the Santhal tribals and as blunt-featured as Chinamen, would appear to have acquired after only four generations with wealth piled in its safe, heaps of beauty and grace, totally rid of all shabby spots in its heredity. Jamini is not a king's daughter, but an aristocratic family's daughter, with plenty in the safe for generations. The beauty collected over those generations has made Jamini a real-life image of the fairy-tale princess. Like an earthly Tilottama, the beauty of various beauties has accumulated in her over a very long period of time. From her arched eyebrows to her rosy pink toenails, derivatives of a variety of wondrous beauties and lovely skin complexions can be found arranged together in her.

Before her marriage, Jamini had often heard the common blessing uttered for her, 'May you become a queen.' But due to lack of exact knowledge of the kind of existence that comes with life as a queen, she neither dreamed of being one, nor thought she might have to be one. Hence she was somewhat bewildered and apprehensive the first year after becoming a prince's wife.

She lacked nothing in her education in dressing and grooming, conduct and manners. The training to properly weave the complexities of life with the hauteur of aristocracy was hers from the moment of birth. But in spite of being the daughter of an aristocratic family, there was always in her a slight doubt as to whether people of flesh and blood lived in the households of kings and the like. The kings in her life before marriage all belonged to fables, to the *Ramayana* and the *Mahabharata*, and to history books. The day she heard that a proposal for her marriage with the prince of Abantipur estate was under way, mystery-laden marble palaces came floating in her imagination, with flower gardens filled with peacocks and deer, a golden throne attended by fly-whisk wavers and an array of brightly attired men and women, their faces solemn and heads held high.

And a prince wearing a sword at his belt, a diadem on his head, and riding a noble horse!

After coming to Abantipur, she stored away these images as those belonging to the realm of fantasy, but a shade of fear still clung to her mind. What was the rank of a king's daughter-in-law, what was she supposed to say and how was she supposed to act by her rank, when was she to draw a line of innocence and when was she to act a part—not knowing the protocol did put her through a bit of anxiety in that first year.

She kept asking her husband, 'Am I making mistakes? Is anything wrong in my conduct?'

Bhupati reassured her, 'No, darling, no. You're making no mistake, you're doing nothing wrong. Everyone is full of praise for you.'

'Do tell me if there is a lapse. Correct me. Teach me.'

'You've nothing left to be taught, Mini.'

Jamini thought, perhaps that was really so, what he said could not be untrue, perhaps she was just worrying unduly. Her nights were spent enjoying a feeling of self-satisfaction. But the next day she would again start feeling uneasy in the disorderly pomp of the life surrounding her.

But there was no bitter expression of this discomfort. She expressed it as if it were an aspect of her charming modesty. Jamini grew up among non-aristocratic young women. Unknown to herself, a form of conceit had developed as a result in her mind. Unintentionally she often ended up hurting the feelings of the girls from non-aristocratic families. When she could sense their hurt feeling, she'd smile and say to herself: small minds attribute worse meanings first; I'd die of shame before I lower myself by being upset about it. This bit of arrogance in her words and her conduct escaped none except her own family members. True, it got buried under the new bride's shyness and modesty after coming to Abantipur; but the mere drowning of arrogance does not produce a store of polished, smooth grace in human nature. If just this bit of flaw in her nature had been reformed, her beauty would have stunned all, her qualities earned praise, and she herself would have enjoyed the love she truly deserved. However, what she would have got then is not the same as what she actually got. In her mild timidity she seemed so sweet that without any effort at self-reform she won hearts to an extent well above the ordinary. Jamini got used to the rare pleasure of rousing an exquisite love in other's minds merely by displaying respect for one word, king, when she came to live in a house only slightly bigger than her own with a family only slightly richer than hers.

Of the conquered hearts, the toughest was that of Ganapati's wife Nagendrabala. She was big and pungent, a ruthlessly powerful woman like Queen Elizabeth. She liked to keep her husband and son under her control. Over the servants and maids, relatives and dependents, her control was unlimited. She could feel no pleasure without having the entire household revolve around her. Stretching the limits of her power in her domain, she got herself so big that anyone there could get away with any wrongdoing by just massaging her feet and getting her support.

Nagendrabala was a little peeved at first by her daughter-in-law's beauty. She didn't refrain from acting out her envious antagonism. Most of the occasions for trouble arose in connection with the worship of deities. Her devotion for the deities of the house had become overpowering in her old age, perhaps because lording it over all her life had left unsatisfied the eternal desire in her woman's heart to bow down before a more powerful force. Arranging the food offerings and the lamp wavings before the deity had become the grandest events in life as far as she was concerned. Now she dragged the new bride into this. Jamini really got into trouble. In her father's house too, seasonal religious celebrations like Dol and Durga-puja were held, but there was no custom of elaborate daily worship of house deities. She was more familiar with the festive aspects of worship; about worship itself she knew little more than that it required flowers and bael leaves, a pair of large-and-small copper boats, ritually arranged offerings of uncooked food items, and chanting of mantras with the sounding of a bell and a gong. But Nagendrabala was relentless in her demands. If the bride of this family, and future queen, hasn't learnt to worship house deities, then all other education in her life is useless. No, she wasn't going to tolerate any of that atheism in the royal family of Abantipur.

'That's incredible, daughter-in-law. What's this you're saying? How'll a woman learn to serve her husband without first learning to serve the deity? Haven't you even learnt, my dear, on which side of the priest's seat the copper boats should go? Don't you know how to do the soaked-rice base for the offering layout, don't you even know it isn't done in a flat-top mound like that?'

Nagendrabala talked to her like that, hurting and shaming her.

She went on to lecture her. 'This work is not for hired people. Showing off your wealth won't do with the gods. You can't serve your husband through others, how can you serve the deities through others! You've to do everything with your own hands, even washing the floor.'

Jamini felt afraid, tears came to her eyes. Nagendrabala felt satisfaction.

But if the timid obedience of someone superior in beauty and quality is genuine, if tears can be brought to her eyes by shouting at her, then a certain affection gradually develops for her as for any valuable property that is one's own. Ineptitude in worship was a serious offence to Nagendrabala. But Jamini lightened even this offence by making herself a fearful pupil and an eager disciple of her mother-in-law.

Nagendrabala soon became unable to shout at her, she came to love her daughter-in-law.

The relationship Jamini came to have with her husband was incomparable. Bhupati embraced Jamini with the intense desire of his robust nature. He loved Jamini with inordinate passion, with all the propensities there are in a man's body and mind to love a woman. He gave up his studies. Ganapati said nothing when he gave up even the one bottle of champagne he had a month. Nagendrabala was envious, but even she didn't object to her son's dropping his studies for his wife. Let it be, she thought, let him get through this age without trouble, occupied with his wife.

When Jamini came to Abantipur for her first long stay with her husband, it was autumn. On autumn nights around the full moon, such a light pours forth from that old moon and floods the earth that human hearts feel strangely moved. Late in the night thus lit up by the moon, Jamini and Bhupati crossed the nocturnal mysteriousness of the sleeping royal household and went up to the terrace-roof. Standing by the parapet, they watched the world. The half-city, half-village world on one side would be motionlessly asleep, with maybe one solitary light visible through a partly closed window. Jamini thought, there too perhaps a wakeful love like theirs kept the light on. The pond on the other side held startled flickerings in gold. The deserted, tree-lined path along the other side of the pond led somewhere far away.

Jamini nestled against her husband's chest, she tied herself with her husband's arms, wistfully wondering whether it was possible to follow that still path away from this world to some other world of stars and planets.

'Tell me, when was the world made like this?' Jamini wanted to know how long the world had been this beautiful and unearthly. On such luminously mellow moonlit nights, feeling Bhupati's expansive love, she often asked questions like this.

He whispered in her ears, 'Long ago, my darling, very long ago, ten million years ago. All was dark at first, then God said, let there be light, and there was light. Then He created the universe.' Jamini felt so childlike listening to his voice that she then asked helplessly, 'Tell me, is there really a god?'

A rug would have been left there by a servant in the afternoon. Bhupati would unroll it and sit down. Jamini would lie down with her head on his lap. Upon her face would be the streaming moonlight; behind his face the background of sky. They would look at each other with searching, eager eyes. As if there was no end to their getting to know each other, as if it was a mystery that they would never figure out. Jamini had her hair done in a leaf-like curve around her face; Bhupati moved that drape of hair to explore the usually covered part of her cheek. Jamini lifted her husband's face by the chin towards the moonlight. When she became sleepy, he kissed the fathomless mystery in her half-closed eyes, and she clasped his hand to her breast.

A tender girl of eighteen, she'd say to him, 'I can easily die now, you know.' They didn't indulge much in laughter or light-hearted quarrels. They played very little. Not that he never undid her hair suddenly, nor that she never put a large dot of vermilion on his forehead while he slept. But Jamini never responded to his unmaking of her bun by messing his hair, and on waking up, he never attempted to wipe the vermilion on his forehead with her sari. Their laughter died a premature death. They never even knew when they were enveloped, overwhelmed by a deep, almost spiritual passion. At the age when love seeks the shelter of outside props, when two people play meaningless games with love like children, when dodging and running is more fun than getting caught, at that age these two acted like mature adults at something as dangerous as the love that pulls and sways like the bottomless depths of an ocean.

It was also dangerous for this reason. Neither had yet gained maturity of mind, they were just adolescents with very little of the heaped up experience which fertilizes the mind and makes it capable of holding powerful emotions. The heart has to be strong to bear the painful extremes in passionate love, it has to acquire that strength. Their minds had neither the scope to grow strong like that, nor the unborn capacity. Yet one of them was a king's only son, the other a blue-blooded aristocratic family's daughter. Even at that young age they knew how to be solemn, regarded life as a matter of serious responsibility, and hence appeared precocious.

No matter how passionately spiritual their love became on the open terrace in moonlit nights, it was much beyond their age. But they had no other way! Life had not taught them to feel light, nor had it equipped them to carry any of life's weighty happiness or sorrow. That's why, when they should have brought laughter to each other's lips, they listened in silent wonder for the unspoken language on each other's lips; when they should have played hide-and-seek, they drew closer to each other from the pain and ecstasy of self-immersion.

Two lyric poems supported each other and aspired to become an epic. And that is an incongruity, an aberration in the strict rhythm and the rule-structured verse form of the poetry of life.

Three years after Jamini's marriage, two significant events occurred in the royal mansion of Abantipur: Ganapati's death and the birth of Bhupati's son. In the span of a month, Nagendrabala became the queen mother, Bhupati the king, and Jamini the queen and mother of a baby boy.

The queenship Jamini got free, but the son did not come so easily. Things took such a turn that neither she nor her son were expected to live. Three reputed Calcutta doctors used some exceptional method to save both lives. But they also told her that this first one was to be her last; she would have no more children.

So be it; at least the dynasty was saved. If the boy lived, Bhupati would not have to remarry.

The consolation that the dynasty was saved was Nagendrabala's and all the others', the assurance that Bhupati did not have to remarry was Jamini's own creation, it did not come from anyone.

There was no way of clearly knowing Bhupati's position. Even before he became the king, he had begun changing bit by bit. Now he was changing a lot more rapidly.

No, it was not champagne or women. There is no rule that those vices take hold as soon as one becomes king. Bhupati's transformation was the revenge of poetry.

No one can go on living with recourse only to the heart. Bhupati was exhausted playing the game of limitless love. He was looking for something outside of it. He didn't lack other responsibilities; indeed he had been avoiding it on Jamini's account. Having a wife like Jamini satisfies many of the heart's needs, but life doesn't stop making demands. It demanded much from Bhupati. The royal mansion, with over a hundred male and female members, and the future responsibilities of the estate, with Rs 150,000 in yield, had from the moment of his birth claimed him as their bearer. From childhood his life had been weighted down by the demands of external grandeur—and there never was any letup in that area of life.

The temporary gap in the relationship between him and Jamini with the birth of their child offered Bhupati an opportunity; he used it to fashion a separate world for himself. Owing to his unavoidable responsibility for the estate after Ganapati's death, this world became a permanent one for him. There was not even the need to produce an excuse to give Jamini.

With unnecessary enthusiasm he went about overseeing his estate. One day he went on a hunt with a friend, next day he opened a fair in some village, the day after there was a grand banquet to attend in honour of some high-ranking royal officer. Being of a new generation he also showed plenty of enthusiasm for familial and social reforms of many kinds.

In the shock of the brush with death and in the pleasure of having a son, Jamini easily remained unmindful of all this at first. For a while she really had little need of Bhupati and didn't miss him. She too was out of breath tending a mature love in an immature heart, and looking for another shelter. The physical weakness and the joy of becoming a mother provided her that support.

But not for long. In six months her health recovered and motherhood's novelty diminished. In a sense the baby, right from birth, did not quite belong to her. He was a king's son, a prince. A strong, healthy wet-nurse was hired for him, and attendants to serenade the sleep-giver aunts. If Jamini picked up the baby in her arms sometimes, that was a superfluity, not a necessity.

So it was and she didn't particularly regret it. She was not a pen-pushing clerk's wife that she would have to put up with the troubles of bringing up a baby and scratch together her own heaven out of its very irritations. Rich people's children were raised just this way. She approved of the custom. Besides, if she wished to be preoccupied with her son all day, if she desired to pour herself out after her son, no one would have stopped her. Nagendrabala would have grumbled a bit, Bhupati would have been a little annoyed, but if she needed to cling to her son to go on living, they couldn't have stopped her. It was not her son she desired in that way. She desired Bhupati.

It took Jamini a while to realize that Bhupati had distanced himself enough to bring her days to a standstill. But she realized it very well, for she had no life-support other than in love, the unbearable love to escape which Bhupati kept himself busy with his work and nearly useless activities.

Her heart would grow tired and droopy from bearing that love in all its restless eagerness; she would sometimes feel like running away unable to bear being close to Bhupati, she would stay lifeless the whole day the way the poet does after writing a poem; yet she wouldn't let Bhupati go away from her, out of her sight. She was a woman, she was a prisoner of love, there was no escape for her; any evolution of her desire had forever been rendered impossible. She had loved once; until the breath went out of her, she would go on loving without a moment's respite.

Yet by ordinary standards it couldn't be said that Bhupati started neglecting her in any significant way. Bhupati was showing no more than the natural degree of indifference that any happy couple settle into once the initial ardour in union subsides. When home and not busy, it was Jamini's company he sought. When taking leave of her, if she asked him to stay a bit longer, he happily stayed longer. At Jamini's request, he would not even hesitate to neglect essential duties sometimes. He did not invariably stay up through the nights with the sleepless Jamini, but by ten in the evening he came to their room, chatted with her, caressed her, expressed his love for her. All this was perhaps more than any quiet husband would do in the case of an average peaceloving, happy couple.

But because their relationship at the beginning had not been that of an average happy couple, Bhupati seemed to Jamini thoroughly unmoving, absent and distant. Her heart smarted with pain, tears came to her eyes. Listening intently to the sound of her husband's breathing, she shivered with horror and prayed for her own death.

And so unalterable is the rotation of the earth and of the stars and planets in the sky that full moon nights came and several nights before and after were lit with moonbeams. Abantipur Royal Estate's queen would then sit up in bed and puzzle over this in anguish: 'I have everything, but not one thing.'

Her life was nicely arrayed in layers, she had the kingdom, the king, the lover, the son, the love of a hundred hearts, she had a past and all future, even the life hereafter. Still, what was it she wanted? Did she want to wake her husband and go up on the roof one more time? Did she desire only this? Would her restless craving be satisfied as soon as she got this?

Jamini placed her hand on his body, but couldn't push him to awaken him. Tears overwhelmed her. She trembled as she wept, the passion of it so like her endless, unbearable love.

In the morning she said to him, 'Last night there was such beautiful moonlight.'

Bhupati said, 'I too saw it. I came out of sleep once in the night.'

Jamini then yawned and said, 'You know last night I didn't sleep well at all?'

'Why didn't you call me? I'd have put you to sleep by talking to you?'

She thought: 'Talking? O God, staying up all night and talking!'

A king's wife had to fulfil not a few duties in daily life. Jamini too had a lot of work. After Ganapati's death, Nagendrabala was by degrees shifting the load of queenship on to her daughter-in-law's shoulders. Perhaps her wish to lord it over in this world was fulfilled, and now she just wanted to think of taking command of the other world. After spending a couple of years trying to do that, she departed there. Jamini's work became endless.

Her work was curious. Except for preparing the offerings for the deity, there was almost nothing she had to do with her own hands, she only had to supervise, give orders, and listen to this one's complaint, that one's homage, and the other's plea. Just as it would not do for a throne to be kingless for even a day, so the inner quarter of a royal palace must also constantly have its centre. Jamini didn't enjoy any of it, but she had no choice. The royal household kept turning to and around her out of its own needs, not out of consideration for her preferences or her innermost likes and dislikes.

Then there was her toilette. Even with the help of two maids, it took a lot of Jamini's time every day to apply cosmetics. It was not enough just to do the hairbun with perfumed oil; the oil had to be applied bit by bit, all the while minding that the amount of oil that went into her hair was neither too much nor too little. The task of kohl-application to the eyes was so delicate that she didn't lift the brush without a lengthy prelude. By the time she finished washing her face four or five times in water mixed with skimmed milk, applying sandalwood paste on the arms and wiping it off, applying red lac dye to the edges of her feet, and many other such chores, the sun had climbed off the mid-sky, ready to drop behind the line of trees! All this was a custom, a system. Jamini was used to it too. But now she felt irritated. Why did there have to be so much show when one was burning inside?

Now the boy had grown a little. The circle of wetnurses and lullaby singers around him had largely broken up. Jamini's son was gradually coming close to her again. He kept demanding the 'mother' he associated with all his laughter and tears. He would not play with his many toys and dolls, unless Jamini joined in. When tired with the playing, he would sit only in Jamini's lap and looking at the dolls with a solemn face and indifferent eyes he would slowly nod off to sleep. He'd not run around in the garden unless his mother was watching. It was his mother's back, no other's, that he jumped on to startle her, no one could persuade him to drink milk except his mother. When he woke up at night and cried, he would not stop until Jamini got up and came to him. No other creatures in the world are more selfish than children. They are unerring in their valuation of people. Without waiting for anyone to tell him the boy had decided who was more valuable to him than all the others.

Jamini quite liked it, she tried to like it even more. But it was too late. The intense, insatiable hunger for the billowy, deep love of her husband had become a separate and autonomous attribute of her nature. It was no longer possible to alter, modify or distort it. It might even do to feel in her imagination her husband's touch which was out of reach, but the desire for that could not be satisfied by embracing her little boy instead.

Jamini started using her imagination with amazing adroitness. It was as if she had divided herself in two parts. With one part she went on living her regular life, acting the part of the king's wife, carrying out her duties as wife and mother, taking her personal share of the small and large joys and sorrows of daily life. With the other part she wove fantasies. Creating a space of free time hidden behind the rule-bound mobility of life, she animated in her mind the immobilised side of her life. Her whole body would heat up, her eyes shine with a bright, unearthly light, the flow of her blood grow restless with a keen exhilaration. The royal palace and the king and prince were left far behind as she relived again and again the first year of her marriage in the minutely created world of imagination in those lonely, heartsick moments day after day.

On moonlit nights, Jamini went up to the roof, all by herself.

At first she just stood still, leaning against the parapet. Her eyes sometimes filled with tears. Just come away from her sleeping husband and her dulled real life, she could not turn on her imagination full steam all of a sudden. She stood and thought haphazardly of all sorts of things. In that sweetly aching world of her yearnings only a lone banyan tree nearby, a light in the distance and the solitary moon in the sky stayed awake. Even now the deserted path between the two dark rows of trees went somewhere far into the unknown. Some nights even the symbol of that path attained the clarity of language. She let her gaze slowly move from the beginning of the path into the indistinct distance. There it stopped, and paused for a long time wavering in fearful doubt.

Then her imagination started working. The ceaseless, close embrace of Bhupati settled around her, and feeling the breathtaking rush of his love, her heart throbbed with eager longing.

As already mentioned, Bhupati developed a little bald spot on his head at the age of thirty-two. Not just that. Around this time he also started having some chronic pain in his head. The doctor advised him six months rest in Darjeeling.

Bhupati did not like a cold place, he preferred a mild outdoor warmth. He decided to go to Bombay instead. Bombay was farther away, and Bhupati wanted to go far away.

He was not keen on taking Jamini along.

He was still afraid of her, he hadn't forgotten the primal turbulence in him that was triggered by her.

But Jamini said, 'I'll go too.'

'What'll you do there?' Bhupati objected.

'I'll be with you, I'll die if you leave me behind.'

That amazed him. It seemed as if some forgotten mystery of life had escaped the realm of morning mist and made its appearance in the glare of the midday sky.

Within a short while of his going to Bombay, his heavy head began to feel lighter. The days here were lazy, with little variation. No lawyer and attorney here, no task of estate expansion, no ruling over tenants. Exercise of authority was limited here, irritations few, variety scarce. The distance between him and Jamini was narrower. As long as the boy was with them, he could be kept standing between them as a sort of buffer. But he was older now. He attended a boarding school at Namkum. They could not hold on to him for very long and harm his education for their own needs.

Bhupati became shelterless, helpless.

So one day he said to her, 'You are still just as you were, Mini.'

'No one remains the same, I've changed so much.'

They looked into each other's eyes, but they couldn't find each other any more.

Not cold, nor hot, Bombay's climate felt non-fanatical, indifferent. In the streets of Bombay were people of all religions. The city slept and woke up; the moon rose in the sky. Without the outer layers of life as the king of Abantipur that he had left back at home, other layers that had stayed buried slowly revived, like the yellowing wilted grass exposed to sunlight after having been buried under a pile of bricks.

Bhupati felt afraid, he wanted to smother these powerful desires under the weight of will-power. He thought of returning to Abantipur. But something that was stronger in its claim than even death could not be resisted. It was possible to drown wakefulness in sleep, but when sleep is ready to leave it was no longer possible to avoid waking.

At first Bhupati had thought Jamini was still the same. Once he was wide awake and able to look carefully, his error was dispelled. Even now he could have her whenever he wanted, but something seemed to be missing from it. Just as one day he seemed unstirred, distant and absent to Jamini even as she was in his embrace, in the same way Jamini today seemed to him unstirred, asleep.

Jamini couldn't take her husband's newly reawakened love. She spent her days with her imagination. When Bhupati's eager gaze searched her half-closed eyes for the mystery he had once known, she dreamed of another Bhupati and sought the fervence of that Bhupati's eager gaze.

In the depth of night, sleepless, Bhupati sat up in bed. Jamini slept, breathing gently.

'Couldn't sleep well last night, Mini,' Bhupati told in her the morning.

'Was it a headache? Why didn't you wake me? Start taking the medicine again today.'

One afternoon they took a trip to the Vehar lake, which supplied water to Bombay's people. The scenery was lovely. Many went there for a picnic.

Sitting beside Bhupati, Jamini had forgotten him. She preferred to look at the scene around, rather than feel his proximity. The trees and the shrubs around, she didn't even know all their names. Several palm trees nearby were visible all the way from the base to the tip, but farther away, close to the water, eight or ten trees were mired in green mystery. Those trees and the lake's bank stood at a lower level, the water was pushing inland. Four or five mute animals trudged there to drink. On the other side were reclining hills, the water touching their base.

All of a sudden Bhupati grasped one of Jamini's hands tightly in both his hands. So tightly that it couldn't but hurt Jamini.

Surprised, she turned her face to him, 'What's wrong? My hand hurts.'

But there had been a time when it did not hurt. Bhupati let go of her hand. Jamini should have sensed everything from the look on his face, but she sensed nothing at all. Brushing aside a slight suspicion she asked him again with much affection and concern, 'What happened? Are you feeling unwell?'

'No. Not unwell.'

She moved a little closer to him, put her distressed hand on his shamed hand, and kept looking at the hills in the distance. She held within her what Bhupati wanted, that indescribable love of theirs, which was still unsatiated. But he was unable to reach it. Perhaps one day she would find the wheels of her recall stopped, perhaps in the dark of this very night she would fervently long for the real-life Bhupati of this moment, but perhaps he would not be awake then. Again, the night after, when he would switch on the light and gaze at her face with unblinking eyes, she would perhaps be asleep. There were many obstacles today to their being able to demand and receive each other in the same way at exactly the same time.

The Gambler's Wife[*]

Virtually from his childhood Makhan had a propensity to gamble. No one could, of course, have seen in the whims and games of his early age the beginnings of such a severe mental disorder in his later life. Who doesn't bet and buy lottery tickets, who goes to a fair and doesn't place a few coins on the table marked with numbers and throw darts at the numbers on a rotating wheel? These are games—only games. Makhan played a bit excessively, though. He betted with one and all; for the money to buy lottery tickets he bothered adults to the point of getting a beating; at a fair he lost all the money he had for buying other things on a dart game. It occurred to no one that this trivial childish craze would one day turn into a deadly addiction.

The real gambling started on the racecourse. Makhan had then passed through two levels of college exams. Nalini's elder brother, Suresh, was his best friend; he was the one who took him to the races.

'Come, Makhan, we'll bet a little at the races today.'

'Races? I've only ten rupees with me.'

'How much more do you want? I'll give you more if you need more—come along.'

The thrill the two of them felt on winning seven rupees that day! After going to an Anglo-style restaurant, devouring prawn heads and chicken, and paying seven times their regular price, and seeing a movie, Suresh went home and Makhan returned to his boarding house. After returning to the racing fields a couple of times more, though Suresh sort of stopped, annoyed with having lost a few rupees, Makhan began to get restless if he could not go even for a day. As a result, he frequently borrowed money from Suresh.

While doing his accounts one day after he had somehow scraped through the third-level college exams, Makhan discovered he owed Suresh a lot a money. The money in Suresh's post office savings account had nearly been wiped clean as a result of lending Makhan small amounts so often.

---

[*]   The Bengali title is *Juareer Bou.*

'This time when I go home for a visit,' Makhan said to him, 'I'll bring back the money I owe you.'

It wasn't easy for Makhan's father to shell out that much money. Still, what choice did he have but give the money to a son who, after passing all three levels of college exams, wanted to try his hand at business in partnership with a friend before he tried looking for a job. And wanted it with such fierce eagerness that it seemed he might do something drastic if he was not given the opportunity.

With the money to return to his friend, Makhan came back to Calcutta at ten in the morning on a Saturday. All the way he had been thinking that he had lost all this time because he bet on small sums. The chance of winning was greater if he bet on a large sum. Was it really necessary to repay his debt to his friend all at once? If he put some bit of the money on Tiger Jump today—no doubt Tiger Jump would win today—then he was bound to get at least three times as much even though that horse was everyone's favourite bet. What harm could there be in making a little profit with the money before giving it back to Suresh? Not all of it—just half. No matter whether he won or lost, the other half of the money he would not touch, it was going to stay in his pocket for immediate payment.

Before that evening, at the end of the last round of the race, Makhan came out of the enclosure with his pocket all empty.

Late next day he went to Suresh's house with a depressed face. Nalini opened the door. She always greeted him with a smile, but today her face looked rather severe.

'I was on the roof drying my hair. I saw you coming and came down.'

Makhan tried to smile a little to compensate for the absence of a smile on Nalini's face, and said, 'That's nice. Where's Suresh?'

'Dada is coming. Have you brought his money?'

Flustered, Makhan said, 'Money? O, yes, money. How did you know about the money?'

'Not just me, everyone knows. Father's so angry he's ready to blow up. You haven't brought it, right? Why should you do such a thing!' Nalini went inside, the grim look on her face darkened further.

When Suresh came, their talk about the money began in the oddest possible manner. Makhan said to him, 'I can't pay your money back, Suresh. Settle it this way, let me have that money as dowry and I'll marry Nalini.'

It was agreed that the matter would be kept secret, but in the end it did not remain so. His family members were all quite upset about his marrying his friend's sister without a dowry—Nalini wasn't that goodlooking either. Criticisms were aired in various ways—a bit too bitterly. They all expressed surprise that Nalini could charm Makhan. A girl of this day and age, and the daughter of a tricky father, perhaps everything was possible for her kind. Well, as Nalini's father didn't give any money in dowry, shouldn't he have given a bit more in jewellery?

Hearing these complaints constantly, Nalini one day was beside herself with anger. If the comment was from some respectable elder, she probably would have kept quiet, but the comment that day was made by his young sister Bidhu. As she had meanwhile grown somewhat friendly with her, Nalini blurted out, 'What do you mean by saying no dowry was paid? He was paid the dowry well before the marriage.'

Then everything came out. At first no one wanted to believe any of it, but what choice was there but to believe a true statement! And when asked, Makhan confessed.

At night Makhan berated her, 'Didn't I ask you not to say anything about the money? Why did you tell them?'

'Why didn't you tell me that you took money from your father to repay my brother on the pretext of starting a business? Didn't you know that would upset me?'

'Hm, so when upset you'll take revenge by saying bad things of me to anyone and everyone? I can see that you're not just a little wicked!'

They had a terrible fight, and didn't speak to each other for three days. When they started talking again, within ten minutes Nalini asked, 'Well, what did you do with all that money? You took some from my brother, some from your father—it was not a small amount in all!'

The explanation he gave did not quite get into her head at first. Makhan had been secretly doing business with someone, and they had gone bankrupt. Then she sensed that Makhan was lying. She felt sad. Her husband was not petty-minded; on the contrary, in matters of money he was excessively generous. Why did he have to lie to her, and that too on a matter of money?

With the efforts of his father and his father-in-law, Makhan has now landed a decent job. In five years his monthly salary has increased to almost three hundred. By this time Nalini has had a son and a daughter and, partly because of her husband's job, rapid promotion to the position of mistress in her husband's household. There's not much trouble in the household, not much sickness or grief, not too much scarcity—there's no great sadness in Nalini's mind either. Only a strange, odd sort of residue of the sorrow she felt when Makhan lied to her that time, after three days of their not talking to each other, has stayed on in the form of a permanent unease, like the discomfort of a mild dread. Nalini has not committed any sin, yet her mind carries some incomprehensible weight just like that of an old sin metamorphosed into fear.

Makhan's addiction to gambling has not left him. As with addiction to lovemaking, the phase of uncontrollable recklessness and unbearable eagerness has been replaced by a quiet, calculated habit. Like an old lover's practised lovemaking, his gambling has turned into a matter largely of routine. Of course, no money gets saved, most desires don't get met, and from time to time when there's an urgent need for money they are in serious trouble temporarily. Still, the household somehow pulls through. Keeps running the way it would have run if Makhan's salary was only a hundred rupees. Much of the trouble could, of course, be settled by assuming that his salary was indeed one hundred, but the problem is that in the case of one who draws a salary of three hundred, even if two hundred out of the three come to no use at all, it's impossible both for oneself and one's relatives and friends to assume that one's salary is no more than a hundred.

Although the relatives' and friends' resentment and irritation on the one hand, and advice, pleas and criticism on the other have continued, Nalini says almost nothing about it. She knows there's no treatment for the disease. She also knows that if there is an urgent need, Makhan will reduce his spending on gambling, but it has to be a real need. An absolute need like feeding the stomachs, clothing the bodies, paying the doctor's fee or buying medicine when there's illness. His addiction to gambling makes room only for his hard-core sense of responsibility towards meeting these sort of genuine, proven necessities.

So many assumed needs Nalini has tried to affect! So many times she has tried to convince her husband that the household needs this, it needs that. He always responded with a cursory 'Yes, yes, it'll be done,' but in the end almost nothing was done.

She has tried to persuade him to move to another rented place, and announced, 'I won't stay in this house. Move to a better place.' With this, she even left for her parent's place. Then, of course, Makhan moved them to a nice place at a higher rent, but it proved disastrous for Nalini. For Makhan didn't reduce his gambling expenditure by one paisa and the squeeze fell on essential household expenses. And they had to move again, to a place with a lower rent.

Nalini has tried insisting, 'I want a pair of new bangles for the wrists.' Makhan has said, 'All right.'

But in the two years since then not even a pair of earrings was ordered at the goldsmiths. Because Nalini has bangles from her wedding, and a pair of earrings.

However within a month of her saying, 'Won't you even get a life insurance?' he took out a life insurance for ten thousand rupees, and while he has paid the premium regularly so far, Nalini has not had to suffer the consequence of moving to a better place on a higher rent.

In matters of money, she has reached a kind of mutual understanding with her husband. Yet the torment of the mysterious mild terror has not decreased one bit. She feels as if a disaster is waiting to take place—it will, too, and very soon. But what could possibly happen? Makhan will lose everything in gambling one day? But Makhan has his three-hundred-rupee job that's his everything; no matter how unwise he is in wasting the money he earns on gambling, he's not one to ruin his job. Nalini is confident of that. What is it then? Is it just a reaction to the discontent of having to live like the very poor, barely getting by on food and clothing, all because of her husband's addiction, despite having the means to live at a much greater level of comfort and happiness?

But what exactly is the nature of this chafing discontent, if that's what it is? She does wish Makhan would arrange things so that she could live like a queen, she wants it as an expression of his love, but she's not particularly distressed or disappointed about not getting it.

Nalini therefore doesn't say anything any more. She has more or less given up on him in all matters, even in her efforts to induce a bit of romance in Makhan's plain and mundane lovemaking. A familiar man became her husband; how could she expect a dramatic falling in love? She had tried so long because she was immature; before the marriage she had very little knowledge of these things and thought he would perhaps change afterwards. But a man whose mind's tide and ebb come from the excitement and exhaustion of gambling, does such a man ever think romantically of his wife, does he ever have the time for being even a little crazy about her!

When deep in such thoughts, a shade of intangible dreams produces in Nalini's plain smallish eyes such a wondrous scrim of emotional absorption that seems impossible even in the most beautiful eyes in the world. Perhaps she has a little free time after lunch to lie down briefly on a part of her sari spread on the floor. Of her two children one is playing, the other is fast asleep. Closing her eyes aggravates the pain of disappointment; so Nalini dreams with her eyes open—the dream of her virgin life: how Makhan would have acted if he loved her with a self-losing passion. So many things she thinks of then, things possible and things impossible.

Then as her dreaming ends in moderate discomfort, from the pressure of that vague fear, her eyes look very plain again. Is dreaming about these things any good for a woman with two children, could such fantasy come true any more! Even when something does happen, it's like an amazing fractional realization of the dream; and in a short while the possibility of even that happening will disappear. She's going to have a baby again, soon it'll all be over. Will she herself not feel embarrassed even to think of inducing the excitement of lovemaking in the dull indifference of Makhan's mind? And with what will she induce such excitement?

It's not yet known to anyone, but will be in a short while. Makhan will perhaps be glad, give her a bit more care and concern, and say, 'Have some milk—you need milk and stuff at this time.' But after that? He will become even more exhausted, grow even more droopy. Nalini would not manage to wake him up even if she were to beat her own head to death. The shadow of a terror deeper than of death falls across her narrow eyes, her eyebrows squeeze into a frown, and beads of sweat appear on her forehead even on that winter afternoon.

Is there no way? No way at all? Even if it means losing all she has, still the small chance of success would be enough to tempt her to try it. But is there even such an extreme course, one that might bring her either total ruin or Makhan's love?

Precisely at this moment, he is leaning over the railing of the racecourse, watching with trembling heart and tense eagerness, the progress of one of the eleven horses, and thinking: he will be in real trouble if he doesn't win even this time, but then if he does . . . .

After dusk, a tired, drained Makhan returns from the racecourse with his friend Abani. Abani is now his most intimate friend in the same way Suresh used to be. Abani is a short and thin man, a shy and timid man. It's doubtful if anyone ever saw him excited. When the horses are running, while Makhan chews his thumb, Abani calmly puffs at his bidi. Makhan jumps up and lets out a loud hurrah when he lands a win, becomes droopy when he loses. Abani smiles mildly when he wins, smiles also when he loses.

Both are surprised to find Nalini all dressed up. The sari is draped in a fashionable way, with a bright-coloured blouse. Besides scrubbing her face, she has applied a touch of colour to her cheeks and kohl to her eyes.

'Where're you going?' Makhan asks her.

All smiles, she says, 'Where could I go?'

'How come you're dressed up?'

'Dressed up? You're joking. If I'm not going anywhere, should I stay at home looking like a ghoul?' Then, going up to Abani, she says, 'Do you keep my friend locked up? Why doesn't she ever come?'

Abani smiles mildly and says nothing.

'I want to go with you this time and look my friend up.' With that, Nalini actually pulls her husband's friend by the hand, one with whom until now she has had only brief exchanges standing three cubits away, and goes out without even a glance at Makhan.

Despite the frantic effort, Nalini can't hide the agitation in her. Abani's wife asks anxiously, 'What happened, my friend?'

'Nothing.'

Abani's wife has been cooking, the end of her sari perkily tucked in at her waist. She's older than Nalini, but looks very young. Always jolly, while doing her housework, she still hums to herself. Nalini feels jealous, almost tormented, whenever she sees her. Her husband also gambles, she has to run her household with greater difficulty than Nalini, and one of her two sons died. Yet she always looks as if she married just a few days ago, walking the air on her husband's love.

'What brings you, friend, suddenly all dressed up?'

'Just to see you.'

'Lucky me!' Setting the rice pot on the stove, Abani's wife comes to her smiling and sits down by her.

Their conversation does not take hold today. Nalini's fear grows with the evening, she becomes increasingly absentminded, yet mentions nothing about going home. The later it is in the night, the angrier Makhan will get, the harder his mind will be shaken up. Wouldn't there be even some slight change as a result, when his anger has subsided?

The cooking is done, Abani has eaten, still Nalini is sitting there, and Abani's wife starts feeling uncomfortable. Her jolly, smiling expression fades, her face shows a touch of apprehension.

'Do you want to tell me something, my friend?

'Tell you? No, no there's nothing to tell you,' Nalini responds shaking her head.

'Why isn't he coming to take you home?'

'Who knows! Let's not talk about him.'

After some time Abani's wife says, 'Then let the one here reach you home, no need to let it get any later. I've cooked some spicy puin greens, want to taste it before you go?'

Let it get a bit later, let Makhan get even more angry. Once she has started, she will not let go without seeing it to the end. Feeling desperate, she sits down with her friend at the same plate for a taste of the puin greens to oblige her. Both manage to eat a full meal. Since no rice was saved for breakfast there was enough; as for the lentil, fish and vegetables, no matter how little the leftovers, it's never too little when two women eat from one plate.

After the meal, with paan in her mouth, Abani's wife calls her husband, 'Could you come out of that room for a little, dear? Reach my friend home. Oh, it's eleven already!'

Nalini's heart flutters. The way she left, and now, seeing her return alone with Abani so late in the night, who knows how furious Makhan will get! Let him. It's to get him furious that she started out like this all dressed up. Would it do to be afraid now. Nalini tries hard to pump some courage into herself, but her heart's wild thumping just would not ease.

The homes of the two friends are not far apart. It takes about ten minutes in a rickshaw. Rickshaws are available at the head of the lane, not far from Abani's home. Abani is about to hire two, Nalini stops him. 'Why do you want to unnecessarily spend more money? One will do fine.'

'No, no, let's take two . . . .'

Nalini feels her voice choking. All this odd activity and unaccustomed tension are so hard to take! Still, in sheer desperation she cuts in, 'Come on, we can talk on the way.'

Little conversation takes place, the entire way both lean out as much as possible and sit silently. As soon as the rickshaw stops at the door, she quickly gets off, and says, 'Let me get him to open the door and you can go right back in this rickshaw.'

Coming to open the door, Makhan will see his wife back this late in the same rickshaw with Abani. This hope or fear that Nalini has been clutching comes to nought, though. The door is opened by the servant boy.

Going in she finds Makhan holding the baby girl in his lap and trying to put her to sleep by patting her in his unpractised way. Hearing her come, he says in a distressed voice, 'Your consideration is amazing! Left the two of them behind and stayed out this late? You could at least have taken the baby girl with you.'

Putting the baby down on the bed, Makhan goes to his side of the bed and lies down with his eyes closed in exhaustion. He shows no sign at all of being angry.

'Why didn't you send someone? I lost track of time talking with Abani-babu.'

'Whom could I send? Shambhu was taking care of the baby girl so long.'

So Shambhu had handed him the baby just two minutes ago in order to open the door; Makhan had not been held up all evening taking care of his daughter! Nalini does not ask why Makhan himself did not go to fetch her. What good is it any more? Perhaps he would not feel angry even if he sees his wife and his friend in an embrace. A quick-tempered man, who even this morning was about to hit Shambhu for taking so long to bring him a glass of water, why is he so kind to his wife? Could he not even once, in the heat of anger, slap his wife so that sometime later, prompted by repentance even if not love, he might attempt to erase the slap mark with kisses?

After checking things around the house, Nalini lies down next to her sleeping baby daughter. Makhan asks her, 'Aren't you going to eat?'

'I've eaten at their place,' she says.

Some time passes in silence. Then very quietly, almost diffidently, he says, 'I won a lot of money today.'

Nalini does not respond.

'Almost seven hundred rupees.'

Nalini still does not respond.

'I'll get you some jewellery made—it can be anything you want.'

Nalini remains silent. She weeps quietly as she thinks, 'Who wants to hear if you won or lost money, who wants any jewellery from you? Can't you ask me even once to come close to you?'

After waiting a long while for her response, Makhan finally says, 'Are you angry with me? No, no, never mind, you go to sleep now. I won't bother you any more.'

The Wife of the Leprosy-stricken Man*

God knows if there is any natural reason for this, but sometimes people's words come amazingly true. God does not spend sleepless nights trying to respect collective willpower, and the aggrieved cursing of injured people is nothing more than a declaration of stinging incapacity. Yet, once in a while, retribution comes, poisonous and terrible!

Who does not know that bringing home others' money is called moneymaking and being able to do it on a grand scale is called being rich? Like women, there is no money on earth that is not owned, except for what sneaks out of the pocket and hides in the streetside refuse. The ways of making money are thus absolutely predetermined: sweat of the brow for making less, trickery of the brain for making more. If you want to live meekly and simply, harming none, then earn a coin for five hundred drops of the sweat of your brow: everybody will pat your back and bless you. But if you want to be rich, then cheat people, ruin one and all. Even before you were born, people had divided up all the money in the world among themselves and taken possession. Empty their safes somehow—by lies, by force, by tricks—and fill your own bank account. People will prostrate themselves at your feet crying, and curse you. There is no other way to become rich.

Therefore, one has to say that Jatin's father really had no choice when he made some amount of money by ruining many. He would never have done such a thing if there had been a way of making money by doing good to people. Hence, he can't be blamed entirely for the heaps of curse and envy that collected in the nooks and crannies of his life. Still, as if to prove that virtue always wins in this world and vice comes to nought, soon after inheriting the money piled up by his father, before having the opportunity to enjoy it, at the age of twenty-eight Jatin develops symptoms of leprosy on his hand.

Exactly as people had cursed. Nothing short of leprosy itself.

'What happened to your finger?' Mahasweta asks her husband one day.

'Don't know. There was something like a little blister.'

---

* The Bengali title is *Kushtharogir Bou.*

Mahasweta checks the finger, turning it, and says, 'Not a blister. It's red all around.'

'That finger feels sort of numb, Sweta.'

'Shall I put iodine tincture on it? Or if you want, I'll put a kiss. One kiss should do.'

Kissing the finger, she smiles. 'Doesn't look like a man's finger but that of Urvashi or Menaka. Goodness! How does a man get fingers this pink! As if it's bursting with blood!'

Mahasweta then puts his arm, the arm the finger is attached to, around herself and says once again what she has said many times before, 'It's so unfair of you, you know! Because you're so gorgeous, I'm always puzzled. Can't be sure if it is you I'm in love with or your good looks. And you think that's all the trouble I have? Won't mind it if it were all. Worry eats me day and night, you've no idea what it's like. I keep burning with jealousy, you know!'

Nothing strikes as being out of the ordinary for some time after that. Not even when two or three other spots the copper colour of paisas appear on Jatin's hand, not just that finger. Mahasweta only thinks that perhaps Jatin is not too well, his blood has a slight infection and it is affecting his fair complexion—maybe he should have a tonic.

'Listen, why don't you take a tonic.'

'Why should I take a tonic?'

'Oh, why not? See if your health improves.'

Jatin takes the vitamin tonic. But tonics can do nothing for this disease. Gradually, several other fingers develop blisters. His skin begins to grow coarse, looks lifeless. The lips and the area under the eyes begin to swell, and look like unhygienic, decayed flesh. The sense of touch grows weaker; even pinching doesn't quite seem to hurt. A dull, unhealthy feeling stays with him day and night, making him melancholic and irritable. The finger which Mahasweta had kissed and applied iodine tincture to becomes the first one to catch the rot.

The doctor charging sixteen rupees a visit says: 'I hesitate to tell you, but you've got leprosy.'

The doctor charging thirty-two rupees a visit says: 'Yes, a bad type. It'll take a while to get fully well.'

'I'll get well then, Dacktar-babu?'

'Why not? No reason to be scared. If a disease can catch hold of you, it can certainly let go of you.'

But in the way the doctor says these words it is so evident that the doctor is making an effort to reassure Jatin that nobody is left with a doubt that this king of diseases will never leave.

The doctor charging a hundred rupees a visit says: 'Keeping it as localized as possible is the only thing to do. Nothing can be done beyond that. You know how contagious the disease is, you've got to be careful. I don't need to tell you not to have children . . . do you understand?'

Don't they? Jatin understands, Mahasweta understands. But if only they could have understood this six months ago.

Mahasweta feels as if she has died. She has just died from an unjust, senseless, unnatural cause, suffering an unspeakable agony. In the stupor of terror she says: 'You've got leprosy? Oh my god, leprosy!'

Jatin is still not dead, only dying. Forgetting all about the rhythm and tone of ordinary talk, he says, 'What sin have I committed that this has happened to me, Sweta?'

'What makes you think it's your sin that brought it on? It's my fate.'

Jatin lives like an untouchable in his own house among family members and relatives. No one could have stopped him, of course, if he wanted to move about. But he seeks seclusion. He keeps himself exiled and imprisoned in a separate part of the house. No one except Mahasweta has permission to go there. Friends who drop by to see him are turned back; relatives trying to express sympathy in person remain frustrated. Jatin refuses to allow anyone to see his body touched by the rot. He gets the radio in his room, books are brought in piles, and a muffled, indistinct sound link is set up with other parts of the house and the outside world through the telephone line. There's a lot of change and dislocation in the way of living daily life.

Even as he rejects all the people in the world, he can't let go of Mahasweta. One wonders how he gained the willpower to avoid even the closest relatives, but about Mahasweta he remains as feeble-minded as a baby. He follows to the letter his steely resolution to keep his infectious disease confined to his body as it drags on to death, until it turns to ashes on the pyre. Only, he seems not to have included Mahasweta in this resolution. While being careful about relatives, strangers, all, he seems to have forgotten about the danger to her. It is as if he has nothing to say if she gets a share of this horrible disease of the body now because they had shared a life for so long.

He constantly calls his wife to him, tries always to keep her close. He has her sit by him, talk to him, read books to him. If there's a nice song on the radio, he can't enjoy it unless she joins him. When he wants to talk to someone on the phone she must find the number, make the connection and then give him the receiver. If nothing else, she must sit near him so that he can just look at her.

Mahasweta obliges him. Like a human body turned into a machine, she surrenders to all of Jatin's newly aroused whims. Without any qualm, she does whatever he wishes, never tries to correct or change anything.

From the way she unceasingly does as he wishes, it would seem she has no need to bathe and eat, to be in the company of healthy people, to be alone for a while. If Jatin remembers to send her off to eat, she eats; if he reminds her, she has a walk in the garden in the afternoon. Otherwise, completely ignoring herself, she goes about satisfying his erratic wishes with untiring promptness.

Yet she doesn't do any of it on her own initiative. She watches over all Jatin's needs, comforts, and conveniences, but in the twenty-four hours of day and night, she doesn't come up with a single thought of her own to increase his comfort, give him anything beyond what he generates through his own whims.

Their cooperation has undergone a transformation. Their earlier life had a combined pace—there were certain rules of moving side by side in the course of the day. That pace is disrupted, those rules have changed. The old patterns of love, affection, and amusement have to be recast in a new mould. Four years after marriage, they face the need to set up still another relationship with each other. The established understandings they had, have altered radically.

Before the initial feeling of being overwhelmed dissipates, certain changes have taken place, changes of a nature they've had little chance to even notice. In keeping up with the arrangement for treatment, the bed is separated between the sick and the healthy. They no longer talk for just amusement—that has been dropped. What is known as conjugal conversation, which is rich in almost all the nine rasas, has died a silent death in the gap between their separate beds. Not one kiss remains in their world today in all day and night. They have forgotten the language in which their eyes talked to each other. Not entirely, though. In the look of their eyes they now reveal to each other only one disturbed, frightened question: 'What's this that has happened?' All they see in each other's eyes is a pain of incomprehension, not expressed by but transmuted into this question.

Perhaps this is the only question that Mahasweta turns in her mind day and night. Her lips stay stiff, pursed constantly. Her breathing is shallow, she takes a deep breath once in a while perhaps out of the need for oxygen. It sounds like a sigh, as if she is cursing her fate.

'Why do you behave like this all day and night?' Jatin asks reproachfully.

Mahasweta's lips mechanically move to say: 'How do I behave? I don't do anything!'

Suddenly tearful, he says, 'As it is I'm living like the dead; if on top of it you too hurt me . . . . '

Jatin forgets. Oblivious, he clasps her hands. Earlier, his sores were wrapped in a bandage, now they are left exposed to air and light. The doctor recommended washing them five or six times a day and leaving them open to the sun for as long as possible. The bandage is for nights only.

Mahasweta keeps staring at his three chapped fingers with the skin peeling off. She doesn't shudder even once at the fingers touching her hand. Her attitude seems to say that if he just asked, she would kiss the sore the size of a rupee coin which is fertile with tiny reddish boils just below his elbow.

Jatin pulls away his hand. Offended, he says, 'You're feeling disgust for me, Sweta?'

She says, 'When did I feel disgust?' Her exasperation sounds to him like an affirmative answer.

'Then why're you looking like that?'

'Looking like what?'

Is it humanly possible in this condition to deal with this sort of counter-questioning? Jatin gets up, goes to the veranda in the strong noontime sun, and lies down on his side on the deck chair left out there. The hot rays of the Baisakh sun may be unbearable to a healthy person for more than five minutes, but Jatin's ability to feel is blunted. Hour after hour he lies there in the sun. When the sun moves, he moves the deck chair with it. From his doctors he heard of the healing properties of the hidden rays of sunlight. Desperately he uses it, he can't let any of it go waste.

After some time he calls her, 'Come here, Sweta.'

When she comes, he says, 'Sit down.'

She sits close to him in the shade. Her sweaty body dries up and starts to scorch in the heat of the sun, but she doesn't get up and move. Like a radiant figure of wifely chastity, she sits still near her husband and dozes.

'I'm thirsty,' Jatin says.

Mahasweta brings him water.

'I need another pillow.'

She brings him another pillow.

'Is it enough to just bring it? Put it under my head.'

She places the pillow under his head.

Looking at her with menacing eyes, he says, 'Can you tell me what you're thinking?'

'What can I think?'

The Baisakh afternoon grows very sulky.

Waking up at night, she notices that Jatin has moved into her bed. She closes her eyes at once and doesn't open them again the whole night.

As nothing in this world quite endures, there's no reason to be surprised by the fragility of humanity itself! A person changes, and with that a person's nature also crumbles and gets remade. When someone who is a king today becomes a beggar tomorrow, the most that can be grasped is that the fellow was not always a beggar, beyond that nothing much is self-evident.

Confined to his narrow prison day and night with his own poisoned thoughts for company, Jatin grows increasingly inhuman. His horrible disease advances, and his handsome, pleasant appearance becomes ugly. The disfigurement of the outside puts its stamp on the inside too. Staying with him for even a few hours becomes impossible for the benumbed Mahasweta. His temper is completely out of control. Who knows what trouble there is with the flow of his blood to the brain, but his eyes stay bloodshot day and night, matching his bloody temper. The sound of his voice becomes hoarse, the hair on his head thins fast, the colour of his nose turns copper, the flesh on his face and body looks dead and rotten. With the frighteningly harsh behaviour of a cornered beast, he has started terrorizing Mahasweta constantly.

Jatin knows that he no longer has a place at the level of human beings. All hopes of getting people's respect, recognition and love are lost for him in this life. That no one enquires after him because he doesn't let them come near him—this self-denial he is unwilling to live with any longer. In Mahasweta's silent, unflinching surrender, he reads the expression of an uncommon hatred. Jatin has nothing more to give to people, that is why he is angry with people, that is why he has learned to be selfish. Because he is in pain, he is not hesitant to inflict pain on anyone at all. He has only Mahasweta within his reach. She is the one who has to bear the weight of both his disease and his sick mind.

She is exhausted. But her droopy, slack attitude has now changed too, significantly. The sleeping instincts of self-defence no longer seem to be asleep. She wants to try to live a little. She will not keep her husband company forever in the funeral fire, not forever.

'Do you want to go on a trip?' she asks Jatin.

'No.'

'Ocean water might help.'

Sizing her up with a crooked, suspicious look, he says, 'Help? That's rubbish off the top of your head! The doctor said no such thing.'

She gets angry. 'As if everything the doctor says is being followed to the letter!'

After some time, she says again: 'You could try taking a vow to do penance before some deity in some holy place. Perhaps you could get a divine prescription, a sort of pratyadesh.'

With bloodshot eyes Jatin stares at Mahasweta's healthy, strong body. 'Why such respect for deities from someone who got rid of her own son? Divine prescription! Deities don't speak to help the husband of a sinner like you.'

The matter is a month old. Jatin heard a summary account if it, but didn't believe it was an accident or god's design. He suspected Mahasweta, and from turning the suspicion again and again in his mind, he grew convinced of it. In extreme agitation he stayed insane for a whole day.

Mahasweta told him nothing of it. In answer to all his cross-examination, she said things he just could not believe, and saw them as her attempt to cover up. Besides, her attitude said it was entirely a personal matter of her own. Even if she had had a hand in what happened, even if she was more to blame than fate, Jatin had no right to say anything about it. He was pointlessly getting agitated by stirring up an irrelevant discussion which had nothing to do with his own life. Mahasweta was fated to suffer, it was written that she was to be deprived from all sides, so she was suffering, so she was being deprived. What was it to Jatin? Why did he get upset about it?

She can't take this accusation that he will not even receive a divine pratyadesh because he's her husband. She flares up: 'You keep raving on and on about a son. Did you read the stars to see it was a son?'

'Not a son? But they said it was a son.' Jatin's eyes take on the look of an oracle.

'As if they know better than I do!'

Jatin says nothing more at the time. He mulls over it in silence. Next afternoon, when the clouds gathering in the sky have stolen Jatin's sunshine, he calls Mahasweta to him, asks her to come close, very close. As the rain starts outside with great passion, he says to her in a long-forgotten tone of abhiman: 'Is a daughter valueless?'

'You're still thinking of that,' she says in surprise.

'How did you do it? You couldn't have strangled her, Sweta. Or, could you do even that?'

'How much senseless questioning do I have to answer? You'll keep jabbering about what you don't understand. I've calmed my mind thinking of how much it would've suffered if it had lived. Why can't you? How it is raining! Let me watch a little.'

Mahasweta gets up and goes to the window. Rain pours non-stop outside, Jatin hurls abuses non-stop inside. With her eyes she sees the monsoon, with her ears she hears her husband's shouts. When Jatin asserts that even if god himself denied it, he believed that a woman who could do such a thing could commit other kinds of crime as well, Mahasweta smiles faintly.

Once they had had the following exchange: 'What sin have I committed that this happened to me, Sweta?' to which she had said, 'What makes you think it's your sin that brought it on? It's my fate.'

The mode of their exchange is reversed today. Today he screams at her desperately: 'It's for your sin that I'm reduced to this condition, you son-eating ogress. Couldn't you die yourself? Or are your desires not yet satisfied? Is someone still offering lots of love!'

It's this suspicion that has now become his chief weapon of attack. Seeing Mahasweta's face no one could conclude she is happy. But Jatin sees it in a different manner. The haggardness of her face strikes him as beauty, the blank look in her eyes dim from exhaustion seem to him indicative of satiety, her clean and tidy look he sees as dressing up. Her lengthening backstage life away from his watch has raised in him a profound suspicion. Where does she spend all afternoon leaving him alone? Rests in another room? Jatin doesn't believe it. If all she needed was rest in another room, what was wrong with the room next to his? Why in the quiet afternoon can't she rest except in a corner room downstairs, a room someone can enter from outside and leave without others' knowledge?

'I'm not that stupid, you understand?'

Her habit of answering with a question still hasn't quite left her. 'Who called you stupid?'

Ignoring it, he stubbornly goes on: 'You can't do that sort of thing. Staying in my house, you can't go on doing that sort of thing, I'm warning you! I'm not dead yet!'

'What're you talking about?'

'About your head and my tail. Oh gosh, I'm totally ruined on all sides.'

Jatin bursts into loud sobs. Standing still like a portrait, Mahasweta watches his deformed crying. The more desperate he gets, the calmer she grows. Her eyes blink slowly, almost carefully, the pictures on the wall blur and go around her in slow motion. The sounds from outside ring in her ears, she takes them in bit by bit. Someone's crying somewhere, it seems to her.

No doubt insanity has come over Mahasweta too! It's inescapable. Doing what people don't do under ordinary circumstances is known as going insane. Her life has moved beyond all ordinary limits, she has to do these odd things. New habits form in the brain. Friends seem like enemies to some, loved ones like hated ones to others, life seems like an endless joke to still others. Confronted with sorrow, some cry their hearts out, some look on with detached eyes and wonder if missing the afternoon tea causes that reeling in the head or what sort of an amazing bird just flew across the sky!

Mahasweta doesn't stay in this room at night. She makes her bed in the next room. Jatin asks why. She says nothing, she only goes in there and bars the door to keep her answer clear through the night.

In their room Jatin stays awake, lonely and abandoned; in the other room in her empty bed Mahasweta searches, in motionless exploration, for a support to live by. She tries to think of so many things, but she can't; so many things she wants to understand, but can't; everything turns disorderly, confused. The memory of her life before marriage drifts about just outside the brain like an unimaginable sensation; thoughts of the four years after her marriage when Jatin was healthy numb her very ability to think. From that sinless, primordial celebration of life she comes right into this rotting, fermenting life centred around Jatin's decomposing body and deformed mind, a life in which a newborn baby, a well-nourished wonder, dies upon birth. Again and again it is born, again and again it dies immediately afterwards.

The lights that were on in Jatin's mind are all extinguished. In its deep darkness, superstitions he formerly laughed at have grown and multiplied. In just a few days he has become a firm believer in oracles; pratyadesh. The one who once regarded deities as products of idle imagination, religion as compensation for old age, and knowledge as uncompromising reason, starts hoping that maybe some deity will take pity and tell him of a way to health again.

But which deity? Tarakeswar, Baidyanath, or Kamakhya, where will the divination occur? He can't make up his mind. He calls Mahasweta for advice, 'Sweta, which place do you think is best for the taking of such a vow?'

Trying to recall the name of a holy place that's the farthest away, she says: 'Go to Kamakhya.'

'Me? How can I go in this condition?' Jatin is stunned with her reply.

'Who'll go then?'

'Why, you'll go, of course. When the husband is ill, it's the wife who goes to observe a vow and bring back god's cure.'

'Me? No pratyadesh will come if I go for it. I've no faith in gods and deities.'

'You've no faith?' Her words sound incredible to him.

'Not one bit. The thought of observing a vow makes me want to laugh.'

'Why, of course, you want to laugh! What else? You're busy laughing.' Jatin is furious. 'Her husband dying here, she rolls with laughter with another. You think I don't know?'

'With whom am I rolling with laughter?'

'If I knew that, would you still be living in this house?' Jatin inhales sharply, audibly, through his rotten nose, and holding out his decomposed fingers before her eyes, he says in a howl of agony, 'Don't think you'll get away, you too will get it! Even more terrible than mine. No one can hold down so much of sin!' In the ferocity of his anger, he rubs hard the sores of his finger on her hands. Overwhelmed with the violent joy of transferring the disease to Mahasweta's body like lighting fire with fire, he says, 'It's about to catch you too! You're about to get the punishment for hating me! It's coming.'

After this cursing of his, she practically abandons him. She had almost stopped nursing him, now she reduces the time for which she visits him. If she comes to see him for some time in the morning, she doesn't show up any more the whole day, except for a cursory check at night before going to sleep. Just for a second, almost in the manner of ridiculing him.

In his fury Jatin would perhaps have ended up turning Mahasweta out of the house, but in a few days he himself leaves for Kamakhya to obtain the deity's blessing for a cure. His insistent entreaties, angry demands and piteous pleas force her to agree to go with him, but when it is time to leave she can not be found in the house. One of his aunts tells him that Mahasweta has gone to Kalighat. Only a short while ago she had left for Kali's abode in Jatin's car, taking his servant along.

Her project's foundation is laid while she is still in Kalighat. It is not true that she does not believe in deities! If it had been so, she would not have been making expensive offerings to the goddess, she would not have been distributing a load of coins to the beggars.

This she does herself. Beggars sit lining the two sides of the path leading to the temple. Asking the servant and the driver to follow her carrying the large basket of coins, she walks on ahead dropping fistfuls of coins on both sides. It becomes quite a spectacle. Not just beggars but crowds of people line the path to watch her spectacular almsgiving.

Among the beggars there are lepers, of course! Some have burlap wrapped around their hands and feet, the noses of some have rotted away into horrible cavities, the bloated flesh on the faces of some is covered with monstrous boils, some have lost their forearms down from the elbows and the sore on the stub has closed smooth. One fist seems too small for Mahasweta to hold the coins to give away! A large basketful of coins is not enough for all of them.

Back home, she starts a shelter for lepers that afternoon.

The servant had managed to pick up five beggars from the temple path for her. Two of them refused to stay, despite the promise of plenty of comfort and convenience. The other three settle down comfortably. They eat, relax, sleep, and every now and then bless Mahasweta with wealth in sons and riches. Within a week the number of inmates is twenty-one.

hired servants, maids, sweepers, and a houseful of lepers, she stays alone in this house. She arranges with the doctor to come mornings and afternoons for check-ups. An advertisement is placed for two experienced nurses.

'They'll not let you open a leper shelter here,' the doctor tells her.

'Why?'

'Do you think they will allow such a shelter in the middle of the city?'

Mahasweta remarks with surprise, 'But they were roaming the city's streets. By putting them inside a house, I've reduced the risk to people.'

'Still they won't allow you,' the doctor replies with a faint smile. 'However, as you know, this sort of thing is considered virtuous. No one wants to stop it just like that. The people in the neighbourhood will lodge a complaint, it'll be investigated, then you'll be served notice. You can sit tight for two months even after that. When another notice comes, you can start making arrangements for moving it elsewhere at your convenience.'

In response to the doctor's considered counsel, she merely says: 'Leprosy is so terrible a disease, doctor.'

The doctor again smiles faintly. With the wisdom of his immense experience he says, 'There're so many such diseases in the world! It's not just one disease, you know Mrs Datta, that completely destroys man, mixes in his blood and stays on for generations through heredity.'

Heredity! For generations! Who knows how much the doctor got the wind of. Jatin was furious just suspecting, thinking that she had deceived him. The doctor is unperturbed even after knowing. Perhaps the doctor even approves of it in his mind. There must be a slight difference between someone who knows and someone who doesn't.

Jatin is back before the nurses are hired. He did not get a divine answer, but a sort of a dream that he might be cured if he got himself a white flower from the spring and wore it in a talisman. He has already put it on the talisman before returning home. He's startled to see the radical rearrangements made at home. 'What's all this you've done, Sweta?' he asks.

Mahasweta's head is now much clearer with her mind getting a lot calmer. She says: 'I've done it for your wellbeing. I came upon a sanyasi in Kalighat, he was glowing with power in a way I never saw in my life, his eyes gave off a glowing light as of fire. He said to me. Start a leper shelter, then your husband will be cured.'

The influence of taking the talisman was still strong in his mind. Awed, he says: 'Really?'

'Would I be lying to you? You haven't seen that sanyasi. If you had, you'd have had goosebumps all over! After saying those words to me he was gone, I couldn't see where.'

Regretfully he says, 'I wish you had asked him for a medicine or something, Sweta.'

Jatin takes shelter again in the part of the house where he lived. The hope arising from the talisman and the sanyasi keeps his temper noticeably softened.

But Mahasweta does not come near him. She stays at a distance the way she did before he went to Kamakhya. She has now become excitedly preoccupied with her leper shelter. When the number of inmates reaches twenty-five from twenty-one, her happiness seems to know no bounds. Day and night she attends these deformed, decomposing human beings picked up from the street. Her affection is like a mother's, her caring like a mother's. Her very ribcage seems to be made of these twenty-five sick, rotting ribs. They receive all the closeness and warmth of her heart.

Jatin protests one day, on the verge of tears. 'You take care of them all the time, and don't even look at me.'

Mahasweta stands with her head lowered, unable to say anything.

Once she loved her healthy husband, and hated the lepers on the street. That's precisely why today she hates her husband, and loves the lepers from the street. No complex psychology is involved in this. It's easily comprehensible with reasoning.

For Mahasweta is not some goddess. She's only the wife of a leprosy-stricken man.

The Wife of a Man Gone Blind*

A year after his marriage Dhiraj goes blind. There is an extremely dangerous eye disease in which the pressure inside the eye increases, and under certain conditions, a person loses vision in just one day.

The day before was their wedding anniversary. Together they spent the whole night awake! They were, of course, getting quite used to staying up late, though not exactly without closing their eyes for at least a few minutes before seeing the sun every morning. It isn't normal for even an ordinary couple in the first year of marriage to conclude their whisperings of love before two in the morning.

Dhiraj was feeling a little pain in the eyes and his vision was a bit blurry. His eyes looked quite red. But in their enthusiasm to do proper honour to their wedding night, they paid that sort of minor matter no attention at all. Sunayana said, 'You're not to use this as an excuse to sleep tonight. Sleep the whole day tomorrow and it'll be all right. My eyes are hurting too.'

'Then show me that dance of yours.'

'Close your eyes first.'

The doctor is called the next afternoon. A lot of things are then done in a great rush. But by that time it's too late. Even if something had been done in the morning when, standing on the terrace holding Sunayana's hand, he could see only faintly the newly risen sun, it might not have been useless. But who could have thought then that deep red eyes, pain, flashes of light and blurred vision were symptoms of blindness! They attributed all these symptoms to staying up all night.

The specialist does a lot of examining, but refuses to attempt surgery. 'Nothing can be done now,' he says.

Next morning, the source of light for the world appears in the sky at the expected time, but Dhiraj is not even aware of it. The light has gone out of his eyes forever.

The eye doctor said clearly that staying up all night was not the real cause of his blindness. Not being up all night would, of course, have been

---

* The Bengali title is *Andher Bou.*

better, but who can categorically say that his eyes would have been saved then? It's a terrible disease, it has ruined so many people's vision. But does human despondence want to listen to such reasoning! Sunayana keeps telling herself that had she not forced him to stay up all night, her husband's eye ailment would not have got bad so rapidly. At least, they would not have attributed the symptoms to sleeplessness; they would've been alerted in the morning and treatment would've been started sooner. She thinks of this and tears so blur the morning light that she too feels half blind.

Watching her husband's distorted face through her own tear-blurred vision, she sobs uncontrollably. 'Darling, we're ruined like this because of me.'

'What is your fault?' Dhiraj talks like a corpse.

Furiously slapping her forehead, she says, 'Whose fault is it then? Who didn't allow you to sleep even after seeing those deep red eyes? Who told you in the morning that it'd be all right after some sleep? I've destroyed your eyes—death avoids me, a luck-busted woman who eats her husband's eyes. I'll go blind too, I'll gouge out my own eyes. I swear to Goddess Kali, if I don't . . . .'

'Hush, don't say such things.'

As a troubled Dhiraj starts groping for one of her hands, she suddenly shudders and gives a muffled cry. Dhiraj's uncle is blind; when she first came to this house and touched his feet, he groped for her like this, and with a bony hand guided by guesswork he touched her head and body in an affectionate greeting and welcome.

'What're you looking for? What do you want?'

'Where's your hand?'

'Here—'

Taking her hand in his, Dhiraj says in an earnest consoling voice, 'Don't even think of those things. How'll I live if you lose your eyes? From now on I'll see with your eyes. You'll take care of me, help me with my work, read books and stuff to me . . . .'

Then letting go of her hand, he strokes her head. Sunayana suddenly throws her head at his chest with such force that it seems as if she wants to kill herself by pounding her head against it. It doesn't strike either of them as absurd that the one who is blind is caressing and comforting the other instead of receiving consolation and encouragement. Is there in the whole world any better treatment for misfortune than this blind anguish of love?

Dhiraj is not in a lot of anguish yet. He's lying in bed like a man struck by thunder, without many words on his lips, without blaming fate, or demanding explanation from god as to what sin got him this punishment, with none of the greedy child's impatient eagerness to gobble sympathy from all. As if he is still not able to believe that he has become blind forever. At the bottom of his mind, an irrational, blind hope still flickers that everything will be all right again. Already he has told Sunayana: 'There's still one thing, you know. Maybe after some time I'll be able to see a little. Of course, I'll not see very well, with glasses and stuff perhaps I'll see only nearby things smokily, hazily, but at least I'll be able to see. I must see a high-ranking specialist.'

The despair that should have possessed Dhiraj, finding no encouragement from him, takes possession of Sunayana and makes her lose control of herself. It is as if his regrets and laments are finding release through her.

She hasn't slept for two consecutive nights. One night she spent enjoying her husband's caresses, the next she is imagining the horrible inconveniences of spending life as a blind man's wife. Two nights she hasn't turned off the light, the first night to be able to see her husband, the second night from fear of darkness. It was nearly eleven in the night when Dhiraj came home from the hospital last night—a tired, worn out Dhiraj, drugged with sleep, blind. He went to bed after having just a bowl of milk. He was helped into bed by almost everyone in the family, his parents, his brothers and sisters, his father's sister, his uncle's wife, and the whole bunch of his nephews and nieces. Even the cook and the servant came up and stood at the door. The only one who did not come was Dhiraj's blind uncle. Listening to the sound of his mother's muffled crying, Sunayana's ears were suddenly struck with a noise like that made by cracked percussions played off rhythm, and the room brightly lit by electric bulb spun and went dark.

No, she didn't faint, she'd have fallen if she did, and lost consciousness. Even though she swayed a little, she kept standing there, seeing with open eyes that deep, damp darkness for nearly a minute. Then the noise inside her ears stopped; there was no sound from outside either. That stillness also seemed to her to be part of the temporary but total darkness.

Then, that deep, black darkness turned into a dense fog and gradually the fog too dissipated. The hum of words suddenly grew clear and intelligible. But then her heart started to thump with an unknown terror. The terror was not concerning Dhiraj's eyes—she had already been informed of his loss of vision. The terror she felt for a long time even after regaining her ability to think was like the unaccountable terror that overcomes one when a loud noise catches one unawares robbing one of the very ability to be aware of the reason for the terror.

With a start she was pulled into reality by Dhiraj's faint question once everyone left the room, 'Aren't you going to turn off the light?'

She had heard this question many times before. She quite often forgot to turn the light off before coming to bed, and he reminded her. Hearing this familiar ordinary reminder last night, her breathing almost choked in the sudden rush of excitement. Was he then able to see the light in the room!

No other response came from him. Then she realized—Dhiraj said that out of habit in his half-sleep. Whether the light in the room was on or off, it was all the same to him.

The abnormal thumping of the heart then subsided and tears of sorrow pushed up in her, but she couldn't let it out and cry for fear of waking him up.

Then she spent the night sometimes getting into bed cautiously and out of it again after lying down a little, sometimes staring unblinkingly at her sleeping husband's face, sometimes standing at the window holding its bars and trying to recognize the familiar objects in the neighbour's yard, and throughout all this, thinking haphazardly. Not once did she remember to turn the room's light off.

Later in the morning several gentlemen from the neighbourhood came to see him and express their sympathy. Earlier she would've gone out of the room as usual: today she just stands there insolently, a little distance from the bed. The irritation she feels at this minor imposition defies description. Seeing their faces all distorted with solemn sympathy and hearing their syrupy words of shallow politeness seems to set her on fire. When a prematurely aged, know-all gentleman says with a strange cluck of regret that homeopathic treatment instead of allopathic might have helped, then the urge to leap at him like a tigress and scratch and bite him out of the room seems harder to suppress than the urge to cry the night before.

Suddenly she hears someone say the words in her mind through her voice: 'You may go now; he'll have to rest a little.'

In wounded surprise they all look up at her, notice her dishevelled hair, anguished face and dilated eyes. Dhiraj had been politely sitting on the bed and trying to smile modestly. His smile fades away.

The prematurely aged gentleman speaks first. 'Come, let's go, time now to go to work.'

Dhiraj's younger brother Biraj ushers them out of the room. After they have all left, he comes and tells her in disbelief, 'You threw them out, Bou-di!'

Dhiraj says in a reproachful voice, 'Have you lost your mind?'

Sunayana says nothing, she only rubs her forehead with her left thumb. Biraj has been studying medicine for three years; noticing Sunayana's appearance, it occurs to him after all this time that she's perhaps ill.

'Are you feeling unwell, Bou-di!'

Sunayana shakes her head and goes out of the room. After a short while Biraj comes to her and says, 'Dada's calling you, Bou-di.'

Back in the room, she is stunned to see the transformation in Dhiraj. In just a few minutes his face has become contorted in agony, and with his right fist he's ferociously pulling at his own hair.

'What's the matter?' she asks in panic.

In an abnormally hushed voice he says, 'You've become ill right? I didn't know! If Biraj didn't tell me, I'd have known nothing. From now on when you become ill, I'll be working you to death and scolding you without knowing it—'

He suddenly screams as if from pain, 'Cheat me, go on, even you cheat me. Since I can't see with my own eyes, deceive me saying anything you like as to a little boy.' He starts crying.

Had Dhiraj said these words in a quiet manner as before, Sunayana would perhaps have flung herself on the bed next to him and started crying. Seeing his anguish and tears, she checks herself. Slowly sitting down beside him and holding his head to her chest, she strokes his head, in the same way he had stroked hers a few hours ago, and says, 'Don't act like this. Are you crazy, you think I'll deceive you? Does my brother-in-law have his senses in order? My face looks a bit wilted from worrying and staying up, and he at once assumes I'm sick. Why shouldn't I tell you if I fall sick?'

'But Biraj said you're about to have a nervous breakdown?'

'As if he's a great doctor.'

At this point, his father's sister enters their room. Biraj has perhaps chided the family members about not paying attention to Sunayana. Coming into the room, the aunt at once starts, 'What do you think you're doing, daughter-in-law, not bathing, not eating? From yesterday you've been without food. A married woman fasting . . . .'

His uncle's wife has followed her. She cuts in, 'That's enough. Come, daughter-in-law, eat something.'

His uncle's wife is a solemn, quiet woman, she doesn't mix very much with anyone. Sunayana has felt a deep compassion for her whenever she saw her. Poor woman, she has thought, living for some ten or twelve years as a blind man's wife. Today the same quiet, soft face fills her with a deep revulsion. The sincere, affectionate words arouse in her a suspicion that she's using this opportunity to taunt her. By interrupting the other aunt's mild reproach she seems to be indirectly saying: 'Don't scold her; she's now in my camp.'

A little while ago, Sunayana might have been unable to control herself and would have ended up insulting these two respected family elders just as she did the neighbourhood gentlemen. But Dhiraj's distress has plugged all the outlets for her own outburst, whether due or undue. Pulling a bit at her pallu, she silently goes out of the room with the aunt.

With just one outburst, Dhiraj's patience and self-control seem to collapse. It is as if he has finally become aware that the darkness that has descended around him is not night's temporary darkness, but fate's permanent arrangement. Sometimes he is overwhelmed with grief, sometimes restless with impatience. His mother comes in to be with her son, but seeing him in this state, she's unable to stay on and runs away with her sari pressed over her eyes. The family members come and try to calm him in their various ways, but that only makes him even more restless. In response to anything said to him, he only says in resentful grief, 'What good is living as a blind man? It's better to die.'

Patience and self-control appear in Sunayana. As if she has rounded up all her disobedient and undisciplined thoughts and put them in a prison inside her mind, letting out no hint of their existence to the outside world. From the rapid changes in the two of them, it would seem as if they had conspired to take turns interchanging their mental states. So long as Dhiraj was calm, Sunayana was crazy. Now Sunayana has checked herself, and given Dhiraj the freedom to be crazy.

The Know-it-all's Wife[*]

On their wedding night itself, Nibaran makes her shift from his right side in bed to his left.

'Could you move and lie down on this side, if that's all right with you?'

These are his first words to his new bride. Sukumari is a timid and sentimental girl, her hopes and apprehensions are both of a different kind. She could not understand what the matter is but she doesn't try to find out either. Maybe the man has an ache somewhere on his right side, and thinks it would be painful to turn on that side to engage in love talk with his new bride. Assuming some such reason, she silently changes her place in the bed.

Seeing that Sukumari does not ask any question, he volunteers the explanation. 'The wife is to sleep on her husband's left—that's the rule. Later on, of course, it won't matter whether you follow this rule or not, but at least on the wedding night . . . .'

It is then three in the morning. Does a man start a conversation with his new bride with this kind of a joke this late in the night? What would all those women with their ears to the door think if they heard him! Sukumari might be timid, but her sentimentality gets the better of her timidity and she feels a little annoyed with him. If he could think of nothing else, couldn't he start the conversation by at least asking her her name?

Nibaran perhaps thinks that just any talking is enough to bring him close to his new wife. He yawns in the manner of a familiar husband and goes on, 'So many errors were made in the wedding ceremony. From the chanting of the mantras to the women's rites afterwards. As a new groom I kept quiet, I but felt so uncomfortable that from time to time . . . .'

Hearing him talk like this, Sukumari feels her body go numb with panic. What a disaster, has she ended up with a lunatic? A little later, of course, it becomes clear that Nibaran is not quite a lunatic, probably he is only being funny.

---

*   The Bengali title is *Sarva-Vidya Bisharader Bou*.

'Why aren't you saying anything? Oh, I see, because I haven't begged you to, right?' With this he tries all over again, after all this, to get acquainted with his bride, in a manner that is a lot similar to the accounts Sukumari has heard from her newly married friends. Nibaran then seems rather sweet to Sukumari, and in the short time still left until dawn her whole body alternately shivers and feels numb—for a reason altogether different from the first time.

Within a few days of being with him, Sukumari realizes that it was no joke when he made her shift to the bed's left side and talked about errors in mantras and women's rites. Not that Nibaran is incapable of being funny; he has enough of a sense of humour, but he's not one to be funny when it comes to following rules and pointing out and correcting errors and lapses.

She was married in winter so she uses a little cream on her face. Otherwise, with her rosy fair complexion she hardly needs enhancers like cream and powder! Noticing the container of her face cream, Nibaran says reproachfully, 'Why do you use this cream? It's no good! Don't use it ever again.'

Surprised, Sukumari asks why. His answer is: 'It's not a good one, it makes the skin chap. I'll get you another kind.'

Sukumari's two brothers' wives treat their dry skin with this cream. She herself has been using it for years. Smiling just a little, she asks, 'How do you know it makes the skin chap?'

Her smile disappears the next moment realizing that Nibaran is really annoyed. Sternly he tells her, 'I *know*. Just don't use it again.'

How can a new bride obey such an order? It would have been different if he got her another cream to use instead. In the afternoon she uses a touch of the cream, and wipes all its residue off her face by repeatedly rubbing her face with her sari. Yet, home from work at eight, Nibaran somehow catches it. 'Why have you used that cream again?'

Seeing the look on his face she shrinks. Swallowing, she says, 'The skin was so chapped . . . .'

'I asked you not to use it precisely because it'll chap your skin.'

He pulls out of his pocket a new container and gives it to her. Taking a close look at the container in her hand, Sukumari is not sure whether to laugh or cry. 'I should use this cream? You think it's for women's use? It's an after-shave cream for men.'

Nonplussed, Nibaran seats himself down comfortably and says, 'That's why I bought it. Why do men use a cream after shaving? So the skin won't feel dry. If it keeps the skin from chapping after a shave, then it'll work even better with unshaved skin.'

From that day Sukumari decided to go without face cream altogether.
Not just the topic of what cosmetics young women should use.
There's no topic on which Nibaran does not consider himself an authority.
Slowly Sukumari understands why he felt uncomfortable from
discovering the errors and gaps in their wedding rituals. To keep quiet
despite seeing people make mistakes is a source of major discomfort for
him. That sort of discomfort he sometimes feels even in his own home.
Fortunately or unfortunately, as he doesn't need to keep quiet inside his
own home, he does not suffer as much. Sukumari wonders what he does
when he's outside, on the street, in his office, in his friends' and relatives'
homes.

Nibaran sets rules and prescriptions in all matters and he criticizes
the ways in which others do things. He's constantly explaining and
enlightening everyone about everything from why ants move in a line to
why his third aunt's son is a worthless chap with no future. Many of his
rules are now in practice in this household, almost all his strictures are
obeyed in his presence by those who live here. Sukumari can easily guess
that the tolerance of his opinions and respect for his rules have increased
since he became the head of the household. However, it's not that on
becoming the head of the household he has turned it into a prison with too
many rules and regulations, arbitrary do's and don'ts. He doesn't insist
on change in others' minds or force them to accept his views; he's not
angry if they are not accepted, he's not overjoyed if they are, he's happy
to just express his views. He's strict only about what he disapproves of.
Disobeying what he has forbidden makes him fly into a rage, no matter
how small the matter is. For example, he often talks about how good raw
tomatoes are for health and why, but no one else in the house eats raw
tomatoes. He doesn't even try to find out if anyone eats them or not. But
if even once he spots someone walking barefoot on the ground floor, he's
in for a showdown. It was not merely his view that everyone should wear
sandals to walk on the damp bare floor; if it had been, then he would not
be upset if all of them were walking barefoot on the damp porch all day.
But as he had ruled against walking barefoot, seeing even his widowed
aunt barefoot there makes him grumble. He bought her cloth sandals in
various designs with wooden soles with no leather and now argues with
her morning and evening to make her wear those.

His aunt protests, 'Stop it now. Put those shoes on me when you put
me on the pyre.'

He replies, 'No wonder your son is up to no good. It's all because of
your own nature.'

His aunt starts crying then. She asks whether it is right of him to
mistreat and insult her this way merely because she is at his mercy for a
bit of rice to eat twice a day, isn't she his father's sister after all! With this

her tears of grief for her dead brother well up, as they do every time Nibaran scolds her for not wearing the sandals. In this household it's only his aunt he can't quite tackle.

Nikhil is his aunt's son, as thin as he's tall, and a number one rogue indeed. While his mother is crying out loud for her dead brother, and Nibaran has given up the fight grumbling, the boy puts on a look of pure innocence and blinking his eyes stupidly, asks, 'Why does water run out of people's eyes when they cry, Dada?'

Sukumari, on her way up the staircase, stops, red in the face, wondering what fury Nibaran will now be provoked to by this mischievous taunting by the stubborn, insolent teenager. Maybe he'll throw the boy out of the house. But next moment, Nibaran's explanation reaches her ears, the same explanation she had to hear one day when she was feeling homesick and crying. She glances back and sees him pacing back and forth, body earnestly thrust forward and hands clasped behind, as he gives the boy his theory on tears.

Coming up after some time, Nibaran remarks, 'That Nikhil is getting worse every day. Did you see how he insulted me?'

Sukumari is really angry. 'Can you feel insult?' she says with eyes downcast.

'What did you say?' Nibaran approaches her angrily but is distracted as soon as she looks up at him.

'Do you have a fever?' he asks anxiously.

'No, why should I have a fever?'

'Yes, you must be running a fever. Skip the rice lunch today.'

It is with love that Nibaran asks her to skip the meal. He says it with a concerned face and in a sympathetic soft tone. At another time it would have melted her heart. But now she asks with a smirk, 'How do you know I've a fever? From looking at my face?'

Nibaran looks severe, 'I know what I'm saying.'

'You know nothing. My face gets red when I'm angry, just like anybody else's. You can check with the thermometer—I don't have the slightest temperature . . . .'

'All fevers don't show in a thermometer. Anyway, don't eat the rice and stuff today.'

It's a holiday morning. They just finished having tea and breakfast, and lunch is a long way off. Still Sukumari feels as if she hasn't eaten in a long time, and it would be really nice if she could have a plate of steaming rice with a peppery hot curry right away. The taste of her husband's caresses from the previous night still lingers in her body and mind, is it right then that she should feel so angry with him that she violates his ruling? She's not sure if it is anger. Rather, it is a pungent sort of sadness! Hasn't she felt it from the start of the day, and not just today but also on other days?

After ruling her rice lunch out for today, Nibaran leaves for the market to buy fresh food items for the day's cooking. He will return with a lot of stuff, but will a single item be bought without careful calculation? Will there be anything there which does not supply vitamins for the body, help the bones and the blood and produce energy? Something that's not good for the health but makes the mouth water?

She knows there's much work to do in the house at this time of morning and she should not be sitting in her room doing nothing. But, angry with his ruling out her lunch, Sukumari keeps sitting in her room. Five minutes after Nibaran's return with his fresh food shopping, his youngest sister Poltu comes to report to Sukumari. Poltu is pregnant in the first year of her marriage; she thinks no other girl in the world has to bear so embarrassing a fate.

'Big brother has no sense, I'm so embarrassed! He has brought all sorts of things from the market, saying those are for me and I would like them in my present condition.' With this, Poltu, almost swooning from embarrassment, leans against Sukumari, shuddering with her eyes shut!

Sukumari is surprised he has brought that sort of stuff. No small feat for him! Going downstairs on the pretext of some work to see what he has brought from the market, she hears his voice coming from the drawing room. There he's lecturing some gentlemen from the neighbourhood on topics in the day's newspaper. From the way he's talking to them, it would seem that they are just ignorant children. She parts the curtain of the drawing room window a bit, peeps in and scans the faces, searching for a smirk. They're all busy drinking tea and talking amongst themselves. While explaining the condition Europe will be in within a year, Nibaran is somehow sidetracked into India's ancient history, when suddenly something in someone else's conversation catches his ear and, without even finishing the sentence he is on, he cuts in, 'You're making a mistake, Satish-babu, if you're thinking of buying those shares! Its price is going to be half in a month. Instead, if you . . . .'

Nobody argues with Nibaran about anything now, for it will cause unpleasantness and fights during the games. On a holiday morning like this, there will be games of cards and chess. Nibaran will probably play cards with some and simultaneously instruct others' chess moves. That inevitably starts arguments which grow loud, almost as if about to turn into a physical fight! Why on earth do they come here to play!

Turning away from the drawing room window, she sees the cook hovering at its closed door.

'What is it?'

'I'm ready to start the meat curry.'

'You don't have to call him. You start it on your own today—come I'll help you.'

The cook does not have the courage; he has the order to call Nibaran before starting the Sunday mutton curry. He mumbles that he will not be left in one piece if he doesn't do that!

In that case, it occurs to her, if she disobeys him by having some rice with the mutton curry, she too will not be left in one piece by Nibaran! After all that has happened this morning, it is this thought that brings tears to her eyes.

Nothing new or unusual has happened in the household today, yet everything somehow seems to her absurd and meaningless. Nibaran's niece is practising to sing at the organ; Nibaran gives her lessons. Sukumari herself can sing quite well; the niece's false notes give her a hideous discomfort mixed with disappointment. In the porch facing the kitchen, Nibaran's mother is sitting with one of her grandchildren, feeding him his morning milk. In the little anteroom beside the storeroom, the other young women of the house are chatting over the spicy hot chanachur of fried peas and nuts that Nibaran has brought home as a concession to his pregnant sister's loss of appetite. The children are running all over the house playing. What's absurd in any of this, what's meaningless? Do they seem so to her merely because the person who carries on his shoulders the responsibilities of this large household is himself a little absurd? Not in a mood for company and not finding any work she can do here by herself, she goes back to her room and sits stitching a blouse. Nibaran has cut these two blouses. Looking at the cut of the neck, she imagines how people will smirk at her if she wears this blouse in public.

At about three in the afternoon, Sukumari's elder brother Paramesh comes to visit. She's truly proud of this brother. He's a well-known college professor, and already at his age he has written two books for students. Her tongue gets all twisted up with pleasure when uttering the degrees he holds.

She has been morosely lying in bed after gulping down some barley water and milk. By now she suspects that maybe she really has the kind of fever that doesn't show up in a thermometer. Next to her room is a large stretch of concrete roof over the ground floor. Another room is being constructed on one side of it at an angle with the rooms on this side. Nibaran is there, instructing the masons, and Sukumari from the bed is watching through the window. When Paramesh makes a self-announcing sound and comes into the room, she gets up happily: 'Come in, Dada!'

'You've a fever, I'm told?'

'Hm.'

'Where's Nibaran?'

She points outside. One of the masons, the head mason probably, has stopped work and stands facing Nibaran. The brother and sister inside the room look at each other perplexed. The mason is telling Nibaran off loudly: 'If you know everything about it, Babu, then why have you called us to do the work?'

Sukumari tells her brother in a hushed voice, 'Quick, call him, Dada, he'll now perhaps end up hitting the mason.'

One can't say what Nibaran would have done otherwise, but he turns his head at Paramesh's voice. Then he says to the mason, 'You don't have to work any more. Go downstairs, I'll pay what I owe you so far.' With that he marches back to the room.

Before they have a chance to exchange greetings and enquire after mutual wellbeing, an argument starts between Sukumari's brother and her husband. Paramesh remarks to him, 'You can't let yourself argue or fight with them, they're the lower-class folk!'

In an amazed voice Nibaran replies, 'Lower-class folk? Why do you refer to them as lower-class!'

Annoyed and hurt by the unnecessary taunt, Paramesh says, 'Oh, I didn't know you held that sort of ideology! But how come you couldn't take a bit of their criticism and fired them?'

Smiling a bit contemptuously, Nibaran says, 'I fired them not because I think they're low-class and should not criticize me. The trouble I have with you people is that reading too many books has drowned even your common sense and judgement. I'm getting a room built with my money; if they can't do it the way I want it, why should I go with it? That's the reason I fired them—not because they're low-class folk.'

This is not the first time. Several times before they have got into raging arguments that turned into angry exchanges. Nibaran, of course, starts the argument most of the time, usually by expressing some opinion on some scientific topic in the form of a question or a doubt, which then opens Paramesh's mouth. At first Paramesh patiently tries to explain why he is wrong, then losing his patience he tries to defend his side, and finally in irritation he turns to attack. Seeing him react sharply at the very first snide remark from Nibaran, Sukumari quickly steps outside the room and calls her brother, 'Dada, can you come here for a second, come fast I've to tell you something.'

When he comes out to her, she whispers, 'Are you out of your mind that you get into an argument with him? Can't you just smile and agree with him no matter what he says?'

Hearing her, Paramesh today is struck by the correctness of that advice. Why indeed, why does he enter into arguments with Nibaran? Why does he respond childishly to Nibaran's childishness? The two of them then come back into the room, and some time passes in chit-chat. The sunshine outside is suddenly wiped off by a patch of cloud from nowhere, but it is a stray cloud and will pass soon.

Nibaran then says, 'You scientists always say that nothing is faster than light. Is there any proof of that?'

Paramesh looks at Sukumari's face, a slight smile appears at the corner of his lips, and he says in an indifferent tone, 'Who knows really!'

Flustered to hear this answer, Nibaran keeps quiet for some time. Then he says: 'I was going to say that the speed of human thought may be even faster. But forget it. Let me ask you something else—during the eclipse, they've observed that the path of the light from a nearby star is bent by the gravity of the sun . . . . '

'I don't know much about that either!'

'Oh!' Nibaran this time becomes sullen. His silence prevails so long that Sukumari's face turns pale and Paramesh, starting to feel terribly uncomfortable, thinks of what to say to soothe Nibaran's offended sensibility. But his sullenness lifts by itself. The stray cloud outside having drifted away, sunshine fills the room on all sides. But the shadow of sadness on Sukumari's face does not go away. Did Nibaran shed his offended silence because he knows this is even more insulting? Is know-how the most important thing to him even in feelings of anger, love, and disappointment as it is in all other matters? The love that Nibaran lavishes on her, who knows how much of it is produced mainly by his desire to do things by just the right method!

In the evening when Paramesh takes leave, Nibaran also goes with him. Paramesh goes home, Nibaran goes out for a walk. When out for a walk, Nibaran always comes back in an hour, but tonight he's not back even after nine. The distress in Sukumari's mind brings a bitter smile on her face. Perhaps because her stomach burns with hunger, her distress also seems to intensify. The family members have come up many times to ask her how she has been feeling. They bring her milk and beg her to take some, but she doesn't. Poltu sits by her and chats till nine. Then, as soon as she is left alone, distress and disappointment grab hold of her again.

Can Sukumari deny knowing how Nibaran has brought so much variety into his lovemaking? Just as he does everything out of his knowledge of rules, so he knows the rules of lovemaking and he follows them! He brought some special food items today because he knows that a first-time pregnant girl like Poltu loses her appetite—there was no question of love, affection, compassion in that. Similarly he has seemed to her so passionate in his caressing and caring only because he knows how to satisfy a wife. Otherwise, who can expect a man like Nibaran to be capable of this kind of thrillingly sweet romantic behaviour and talk, the kind she gets when she comes into this room every night?

She, of course, doesn't realize that she too is letting her own mental processes of knowing how things work get absurdly carried away and confuse her feelings, perhaps even more absurdly than Nibaran. In her agitation she goes on persuading herself quite forcefully about a lot of things. Without a doubt she's convinced of why Nibaran has seemed to her like a completely new man each night. Each night, except the one she spent alone on a visit to her parents' place, has seemed to her, as of even this afternoon, filled with romance and thrills. All of that now feels blunted. It was all Nibaran's deceit, merely his following what he knows to be appropriate technique.

Today he's a little angry, and that's why his desire to love as the rules prescribe has evaporated. He managed to forgive Paramesh in a few minutes, but he can't forgive his starving, unwell wife. How can he? With no genuine love or affection, how can the spontaneous inspiration to forgive come?

Before her marriage, Sukumari didn't have the capacity to analyze like this. She couldn't have even imagined that a process could go on inside anyone's head which enabled one to pick through the trash pile of knowledge and experience of daily life to find just the pieces necessary to support a conclusion one chooses to believe in. She partly senses now that she should not indulge this sort of thinking, it is childish on her part, and nothing really has happened to justify her suffering such bitter pain. Yet, tossing in bed in the dark room, she can't help agonizing about how she will spend her life with a husband who prescribes one rule or another at every step in daily life, who does not even let her use her own face cream, who makes her skip lunch for no real reason, and delays coming home because he is angry with her for no real fault of hers?

Nibaran comes in after ten and turns on the light. Sukumari pretends to be asleep, keeping her eyes closed, and trying to sneak a look at what he's doing from between her lids, all she sees are the colours of the rainbow. A tear has collected in her eye. She could have seen clearly if she opened her eyes wide, but it's impossible to see anything with partly closed eyes, at least not without wiping the eyes.

Nibaran changes and goes out of the room to wash his face and hands. Sukumari quickly wipes her eyes, but now they fill with more tears. Yes, she knows, even if she doesn't know about everything as Nibaran does, she knows that he's never again going to speak nicely to her.

Nibaran comes back in. For a while she hears no sound from him. Then she hears him say in a soft voice very near her ears, 'Why are you crying?'

A shiver runs through Sukumari's body, and in one instant all the knowledge and insight she has gained is annulled. His anger left him at the sight of a drop of tear in her eyes! The anger he felt for her unforgivable act of humiliating him by conspiring with her brother. So deep is her husband's love for her, and all this time she was dying of the suspicion that nothing about anything he did was sincere!

Sitting up instantly, she clasps his feet, 'Forgive me. I've done you a terrible wrong.'

Nibaran, of course, takes her to his chest, and says, 'I see your temperature's gone up.'

'You think my temperature is up? I really have a fever?'

'You are very hot. Wait, let me get the thermometer.'

The thermometer does show some temperature, close to one hundred degrees. After putting the thermometer back, Nibaran strokes her with his loving hands. Sukumari closes her eyes in relief and comfort.

Nibaran says, 'I was really angry. But do you know why I couldn't stay angry?'

Wordlessly Sukumari nods a little, and says to herself, 'I know, because you love me.'

Again, almost touching her ear with his lips he says in a very soft voice, 'Because today I came to know that you're going to have a baby. My anger melted to water as soon as I knew that.'

Slowly opening her eyes wide, Sukumari stares at her husband's face. His anger cooled as soon as he knew! A mother-to-be should be forgiven even a serious lapse! The skin of her body smarts at those very spots which felt luxuriously comforted by Nibaran's caresses a short while ago. Her empty stomach suddenly churns with acidity, her mouth feels bitter, and her head spins.

Suddenly, she pushes Nibaran away with both her hands and goes to the open terrace. The bricklaying the masons started today for the new room is visible in the pale moonlight, not very clearly, but still visible. Yet, she stumbles full-force over that cubit-high masonry and comes crashing to the ground.

The Wife of a Seeker of Fame for Generosity[*]

It's hard to find a man as gregarious and sociable as Jatin—a short, rotund man, with an expression of joviality maintained most of the time on a flattish face covered with a smooth skin. Depending on circumstances, however, other expressions too, such as those of solemn sympathy, of apprehensive or doubtful enquiry, of unquestioning total forgiveness, of sorrow and disappointment, affection and fascination appear on his face with a clarity not found even in painted portraits. His voice sounds a little thick, but hearing him talk makes one think that it comes from a particularly generous pouring of sweetener. Not that he talks much, but what he says soothes all hearts. Good or bad, rich or poor, ignorant or learned, stupid or intelligent—everybody thinks something like this: the man definitely is not above me, maybe he's even a bit below; but considering all sides, rather seems to be of my level, like one of my own kind.

Not all approve of a few things that may be called Jatin's faults, the chief among which is a lack of discrimination in his fraternizing and being nice. Of course, he isn't a staunch believer in equality. Though he sometimes pays respectful obeisance to his old Brahmin neighbour Ramdas for no particular reason, he doesn't touch the feet of the cobbler who sits on the pavement near his house after he gets his shoes repaired, but he does sit on his haunches before the cobbler for the duration of the shoe repair and engages him in an intimate conversation. To the rich man who wants respect in proportion to the size of his bank account, Jatin perhaps gives more than his due, and to the poor man who feels very uncomfortable without an appropriate measure of slight, Jatin does not hesitate to give adequate neglect. Still, it seems equally to the rich man and the poor man that he makes himself close to each of them in the same way a relative maintains equally close relations with both father and son despite behaving differently with them. Not everyone likes this, the sting of a mild jealousy does nag some minds.

People constantly come to his house, a medium-sized house he

---

* The Bengali title is *Udaracharitanamer Bou.*

inherited from his father. On a holiday so many visit him that there isn't enough room to seat everyone in the small living-room.

'Come, gentlemen, let's all go upstairs,' Jatin invites them.

Some protest, 'No no, let's not do that. We may inconvenience the women.'

'Inconvenience?' the injured surprise with which Jatin looks at the speaker is as if a slap has injured and surprised him. His own friends' entry into the house, how can that inconvenience the women of his family!

Without giving any notice, Jatin enters the inner house with the whole group. The women quickly take shelter in the kitchen, storeroom, bedroom, and in crevices here and there. Jatin's wife Shatadalbasini, removes the pot of rice from the stove and sets a pot of water on—very soon she'll have to supply tea for all of them.

Jatin finds a break to come down for a quick check in the kitchen. 'Is the tea ready?'

Shatadalbasini says, 'I started the water. How many cups roughly?'

'Say, about forty cups. Remember to send paan with it.'

The task of dressing the betel leaves on a holiday is the responsibility of his third sister Krishna, until she goes away to another house after marriage. Waiting for the water to boil, Shatadalbasini goes to check the progress of the betel dressing and finds barely half a dozen done and, with the betel dressing material before her, Krishna absorbed in reading a letter. The handwriting is familiar, Shatadalbasini knows who it is from.

'Sister-in-law!'

Startled, Krishna transfers the letter in to her blouse and swallows, 'I'm nearly done, sister-in-law, I'll have them ready in no time.'

'The hell with your betel dressing, you've started it again? In a few days you're to be married off, and you . . . .'

'What can I do if he writes? I don't write to him.'

'You don't write, and he goes on writing letter after letter without getting a reply! This time I'm going to report to you brothers, I do have a responsibility. If something happens, they'll all blame me for keeping silent in spite of knowing about it.'

Shatadalbasini's complexion is so rosy fair that it covers up all other blemishes in her beauty, even that one eye is a bit too large and the other a bit too small. With a glum face and a reproachful look, she stares at her third sister-in-law, and Krishna prepares the paan with downcast face.

'Let me see what he has written.'

'What's the need to see, sister-in-law, since you're going to tell anyway . . .' replies Krishna in a pained voice.

'All right, I won't tell just this once. But if you exchange letters again—why don't you understand, dear, that you're going to be married in a short while . . . .'

Shatadalbasini reads the letter with profound eagerness, the hint of a smile appears at the corner of Krishna's lips, and in the kitchen over there the water for tea boils, vigorously releasing steam. The tea is delayed, the betels are delayed.

A furious Jatin is downstairs again and, almost grinding his teeth, hisses at his wife, 'You're all a bunch of langurs—number-one bears like Jambaban, the lot of you. It takes all day to make a little tea and a few betel rolls? Now see that look on your face, you going to hit me or what?'

Smiling a shy smile, Shatadalbasini says, 'Oh, how can I hit you! You say such things! My hand just got scalded from the hot water.'

'The beautiful way you work, how will it not scald? Come on, come on, get the tea ready, quick.'

Returning to the majlis, the assembly upstairs Jatin imitates his wife's shy smile and says, 'The tea got a bit held up because we're out of milk. Anyway, it's getting ready now. How can a conversation take hold without tea.'

Conversation has in fact taken hold extremely well, like the monsoon rain, when heavy clouds melt in the ceaselessly pouring streams, and its jham-jham ringing makes it seem all-pervasive. It's a large room. It was Jatin's father's bedroom, and used to be packed with furniture. Now Jatin sleeps in this room, but there's practically no furniture. The entire floor is covered with cotton durrees, in one corner of which close to the wall is his bed, the bedding rolled up. As the living room can't accommodate all those who gather some days, Jatin has got this room emptied. As the walls are not needed to seat people, a large assortment of pictures and calenders continue to hang there. In the middle of the south wall is a huge oil painting—someone who doesn't know would think it is his departed father's picture. Asked if it is so, Jatin shakes his head and says, 'It's of a friend's father.' Three years ago, the neighbouring house had a new tenant who expressed a keen desire for his father's portrait in oil. Jatin arranged for the portrait to be done and went for a month to his ancestral village. He came back to find that no one knew where his next-door new friend had moved meanwhile. Little did Jatin know that he had rented the place for just two months for the treatment of a son.

Whatever the reason, leaving his own father's likeness among several ordinary photographs of various people on the east wall, while giving so much importance to the oil painting of a mere acquaintance's father surprises everyone and makes them think: Jatin is really generous of mind, no question about it.

At this end of the house, Jatin's mother, sitting on the porch facing the kitchen turning her beads, asks, 'What was it my son came down to tell you, daughter-in-law?'

Jatin's mother is a little short of hearing. Shatadalbasini raises her voice so much to answer her question that Jatin and almost all of those gathered in the upstairs room can hear every word: 'What can he say, just asked me to put a little less milk and sugar in the tea, otherwise he's going to become a pauper just from supplying his visitors with tea.'

For this sort of misdeed, she gets punished. He doesn't find the time during the day, since many come to his place and he has to go to the places of many. Sometimes he doesn't find time till late at night, since danger, illness, and grief seem to be fond of riding people's shoulders all the time all over the world, and it takes a lot of one's time to offer help, advice, and solace to even a few of them. So, coming home after all that, Jatin wakes up his wife. With her little boy of five and girl of two, she sleeps in the small room adjoining his. He can't stand crying children and filth. There's a door between the two rooms; if he needs anything, he sometimes goes to that room, sometimes he calls her in here.

Hearing the summons on her punishment night, she at first does not realize it's for penalty, and even in the midst of the irritation and vague discomfort of broken sleep, the acuteness of expectation suddenly gives her body an electric shiver. Then coming to this room, she removes his bed, takes the of durrees outside, and shakes out the dust. She sweeps the floor, spreads the rugs, and makes the bed again. All the while Jatin silently smokes a cheroot.

When the bed is made, he lies down on his back and asks her to bring a glass of water. When she brings the water, he says, 'My feet are hurting from all the walking. Can you massage them a bit? Or, would it be insulting?'

'Oh, how can it be insulting! You say such things!'

Jatin lies down with his eyes closed and Shatadalbasini, forcing her sleepy uneven eyes to stay open, massages his feet with hands, the complexion of which blends with the golden bangles.

The odd, strangely moving lines from Krishna's letter come to her mind perhaps—how can those lines not come to a wife's mind when massaging her husband's feet, lines filled with entreaty and lament written by a crazy youth to a still unmarried girl? While recalling those lines, her sleepiness suddenly leaves as with waking from a nightmare. When the massage is over, then . . . as a reward for messaging his feet . . . .

Carefully shaking him, she makes Jatin, half asleep, open his eyes, and bringing a shy little smile to her lips, says, 'Can I stop now? I'll massage them again later, eh?'

'Is that all, for just two minutes? Told you I've a terrible leg cramp.'

There's a light in the room, and a streetlight can be seen through the window—as long as her uneven eyes remain full of tears, she holds her face up watching the room light, then as the eyes dry and grow sleepy again she looks at the street light. Along with the clock's ticking and

Jatin's wheezing exhalation, she hears many other sounds in the dead of night, not all perhaps actual sounds.

Then at one point the baby girl starts crying; woken up by her crying, the boy joins in. Pausing at her massage, she says, 'Do you hear, dear, they're up. I'm going.'

'No, you don't need to go now.'

'But they're crying.'

'Let them cry.'

He doesn't make her massage his feet any more, now Jatin lovingly locks his dear wife in an embrace. The louder the racket the kids make, the tighter his arms grasp her. Punishment indeed. For one who couldn't be made to feel penalized all this time, with the inflicting of so many penalties, the real punishment has finally started—this both of them understand, the one handing the punishment as well as the one taking it.

She knows, she understands everything, right from the beginning. Still, she doesn't want to know, or understand anything at all. She still tries for victory, she attempts to escape. 'Has your anger cooled at last?'

'When did I get angry?'

'You haven't been talking to me so long, so I thought you're angry. Tell me, when did you shave today? You didn't get even a single minute to yourself the whole day. Amazing, how hard you can work! Don't work so hard, darling, you will ruin your health.'

She smiles sweetly. With her fingers she strokes Jatin's cheeks as if to check if he has shaved. Suddenly she says in an irritated tone, 'Oh, the yelling of those two, they're killing me! Feel like flinging them to the floor. I'll go and make them quiet, be right back, in two minutes.'

'Let them cry. It's good for children to cry. I'll close the door, you stay right here.'

Jatin gets up and goes towards the door between the two rooms. Following him, she attempts to quickly get past him and slip into the other room before he reaches the door. But how can a wife outmanoeuvre a husband's embracing arms?

The door is closed, but it doesn't block out the sound of the children screaming. Soon there is the sound of thumping on the door of the other room on the porch side, and Krishna's voice with it, 'Sister-in-law, oh, sister-in-law! How you sleep! Sister-in-law?'

Krishna's wedding is about two months away. The groom is not satisfactory. His family situation is not good, his own earning is not much, he is not young in age. Of course, there's no question of Krishna's liking or disliking it, but no one else in the family likes it. The mother grumbles day and night about it, the two married sisters write letters full of regret at this arrangement, the relatives ask, 'Why settle for this groom for this girl, are there no other matches available in the market?'

Jatin says, 'So many people can't even get their sisters married, or have to settle in the end for blind or lame grooms. Does a prince have to be found for her simply because she's my sister? And how's the groom bad? Has good health, earns money—what else do they want?'

Besides, the groom has come cheap. That this is the main reason he admits only to Shatadalbasini. Financial hardship is perpetually with him. His father was quite affluent, there is some property in the ancestral village, there used to be some money in the bank, he himself gets a salary of nearly three hundred a month. Yet, with all his charity and lending, he can't balance his account. As long as there was money in the bank, he could draw on cheques, but now there's no end to their inconvenience. The income from the property comes to a couple of thousand a year. This income has saved them so far, what would have happened otherwise!

Jatin discusses this subject with his wife from time to time. Noticing the shade of anxiety on her husband's face, she says, 'If only you didn't waste money like this . . . .'

'What do you mean, how do I waste money?'

'As if you don't know. Those you lend to, has one of them ever paid back a penny, will any one? And those you give money away to—more than half of them trick you with false, tearful songs.'

'Trick me with false, tearful songs? Can you name one who has tricked me?'

How many of Jatin's friends does she know by name, what does she know of who he lends or gives to, when or on what pretext. Jatin does not come to her to discuss those things. After much head-scratching, she can think of only one example. It happened three or four years ago, about the time when Jatin's disease of charity took a lethal turn.

'Why, that time when you gave twenty-seven hundred rupees for Shanti's wedding? Her father may have had a small earning, but her big brother makes seven or eight hundred a month.'

Impatiently Jatin says, 'Do all brothers give for a sister's wedding simply because they draw fat salaries? They ran short of money, Shanti's brother refused to give anything, so I gave. Since I made them change the groom in the last minute, which called for more money, who would give it if I didn't? Didn't I have a responsibility?'

Shatadalbasini doesn't ask what the need was to bother his head about which groom someone else's daughter should be married to, and run the risk of incurring a responsibility to have to compensate with twenty-seven hundred rupees. It's useless asking Jatin such questions. She only says mildly, 'Maybe you shouldn't have changed the groom. A fat lot of good your better prospect has done, the girl's tears aren't drying. If she was married with the earlier groom instead, maybe . . . .'

'How do you know Shanti is not happy?' Jatin asks anxiously.

'Oh, how can I not know? My third sister lives in Bhagalpur. Not your sister, but mine—remember the one who at the time of our wedding snipped your tuft of hair? That one.'

Their discussion of finances doesn't hold for long; in a short time it becomes personal criticism. One-sided criticism. Jatin goes on saying how unspeakably oppressive he finds her meanness about money and Shatadalbasini listens silently. If money can't serve good deeds, what value does money have? Is money more important than people? If she loved money so much, she should have persuaded her father to get her married to a sack of money instead!

'You'll get twenty thousand rupees after I die. Why not poison me one day?'

'Oh, how can I poison you? You say such things!'

This particular exchange they had one evening in the rainy season. Three days later, in the midst of pouring rain, Jatin leaves for Bhagalpur.

'You're going for Shanti?'

'Yes.'

'That's amazing, just from what my third sister wrote or did not write, you are guessing . . . .'

'I better go and check how she is.'

After five days he returns and immediately sends one thousand rupees in the name of Shanti's father-in-law. Shatadalbasini gets to know about it only seven days later.

'Why did you send money?'

Yawning, he says, 'They were giving Shanti trouble for the unpaid part of the dowry, so I sent it.'

Simple explanation, but her uneven eyes and her eyebrows squeeze hard into a severe frown. 'Where did you get the money?'

'Why do you need to know that?'

Affecting an indifferent tone she says, 'No, what need can I have? I was merely asking if you had borrowed.'

'Why should you ask even that?'

Sensing that Jatin's temper has turned sour, she doesn't say another word for fear of 'punishment'. More than her own meanness about money, her husband's generosity sickens her, and she isn't even generous enough to feel a moment's shame or regret for that. He doesn't have money for his own sister's wedding, but can spend thousands for someone else's daughter, even borrow if he doesn't have enough. This sort of philanthropy suddenly strikes her today as excessively odd. And with the passage of a day or two, it strikes her as not only very odd, but definitely very unjust too.

All along until now she felt no great regret about a bad match being cheaply bought for Krishna. A girl who secretly exchanges letters with an unrelated young man is better married off as soon as possible with any sort of person. A girl to whom a young man of twenty-five or so, thin, tall, and stubborn, writes that sort of letter full of raving should be married off to an older portly man—she'll be disciplined. Why, Jatin also married her at an advanced age, he was no less round at the time of marriage, and has that mattered? Did she dislike her husband and secretly exchange letters with anyone? If she could be satisfied with it, why can't Krishna? Does Krishna come out any better in comparison with her either in beauty or in merit? Does Krishna have this complexion, figure, or sweet disposition? The more she thought of these things the more she believed the bad match was right for Krishna. But this time it strikes her that no matter how inadequate Krishna is in beauty and merit, or how bad she has been, she is not less valuable than Shanti, she is not worse than Shanti. If so much money can be spent for Shanti over and over again, then why can't it be for Krishna? At least as much as is being done for a stranger's daughter should be done for a daughter of one's own family. But who'll do it? Jatin is in severe financial difficulty.

From running this over and over in her mind, the golden complexion of Shatadalbasini's face grows somewhat pale; even the coal stove's heat doesn't turn it red as usual. When facing Krishna, she studies the grime collected near her collarbone, and from behind her, her swaying gait. With the pained concern of affection, she can't stop thinking: Oh no, merely for lack of money this girl is going to be sacrificed to a monkey; an old barrel-fat Jambaban, the Lord of Bears, is to be the groom for this tender young girl.

'Why's your face looking so tired, sister-in-law?'

'I don't know, really, I don't know.'

'No, sister-in-law, don't worry so much. I'll fix things for you. Has he written again?'

Whether Krishna pretends not to know even when she does, that she alone knows as she replies, 'Who will write?'

'Come on, that one of yours—the only one. You're exchanging five to ten letters a day, and you don't know who?'

'Oh, that one!' Krishna suddenly gets angry. 'What sort of you-know-what are you, sister-in-law. I keep telling you I haven't answered one letter to this day, why can't you believe me?'

Shatadalbasini too gets angry. 'Why haven't you? Are you such a saint that you couldn't get yourself to answer even one letter? Do you enjoy hurting a person's feelings for no fault of his? Women can be just like this, really.'

As if just to save the honour of womankind, Krishna says, 'I just wrote one in answer. Wrote that if he writes to me again, I'll report him to the police.'

'Oh, how can you report him to the police? You say such things!'

She feels upset, uneasy. Whenever the heat of the month of Bhadra feels unbearable, she remembers that the mild Ashwin is not far away. Krishna's wedding date is at the beginning of Ashwin. She feels as if the date for a major misfortune for herself is getting closer. Krishna finally wrote him that she'd report him to the police if he wrote to her again? She didn't answer even one letter before that? What sort of matter is this! Why did she then read the letters so eagerly, lose herself reading them? Why did she go about with the letter hidden in her blouse the whole day? Things are too complicated in this world, the ways of some people too complex.

Shatadalbasini can't understand why she feels so anxious. It is as though Krishna is engaged in an offstage battle with Shanti, and Shatadalbasini can't even bear the thought of Krishna getting defeated. If that can happen, then what good are the children and the husband in her own life, what good is this household for her, what use are all her efforts at cooking and feeding the family!

Sitting at his meal, Jatin screams, 'No salt in the lentil, the fish curry oversalted, what's happening here? I'll throw the lot of you out of the house—useless, vile creatures from some dump, come here to make my life hell.'

Although his mother is short of hearing, she hears his words of abuse very well. She speaks out, 'Daughter-in-law, why did you try to cook when you're not feeling well? This heat doesn't agree with even healthy people, and in your condition . . . .'

Jatin shouts at her, 'You keep quiet. Feeling unwell! Fiddlesticks!'

From the first-floor terrace of the neighbouring house, the porch of this house can be seen by leaning against a section of the parapet. The mistress of the house, hanging out her grandson's washed bedlinen to dry, leans over and asks, 'What's the matter, son?'

Looking up, Jatin says with a smile, 'Nothing, Aunt. Have you received Nanda's letter?'

After Jatin's 'aunt' moves away, Shatadalbasini brings him a bowl of milk, saying, 'Eat your rice today with the milk. After having Shanti's cooking for several days, my cooking must taste awful, I know.'

Lifting the bowl of lentil to throw at her face, Jatin notices that his next-door aunt has only moved behind the parapet, but not left. Hiding there, she's peering at them through a small gap. He puts the bowl of lentil down.

Shatadalbasini can see that the penalty is saved for the night. Let it be, who's afraid of penalty? All punishments come to an end, but some matters do not seem to find an end in any way at all.

Sitting down to the midday meal with her sister-in-law, she says, 'Why don't you write a letter?'

'Write a letter to whom?'

'Why, to that one of yours?'

'Oh, to him? Why don't you write yourself?'

With a grim face, Shatadalbasini eats rice coated with the oversalted fish curry sauce. After a long pause she says, 'You're stupid, sister-in-law, very stupid. You know what I'd have done in your case? I'd have run away.'

'What'd you live on after running away?'

That no doubt is a problem too. No way you can be a woman and not understand this problem. So, Krishna has written that letter threatening to report him to the police after much thought.

Krishna has stopped eating, the expression on her face is tearful. She says, 'Remember you said you'd fix everything, why don't you? Why don't you make the wedding take place within a few days?'

'Wedding within a few days! With whom?'

'The one with whom it has been fixed, who else!'

'In this month of Bhadra?'

'Let it be in the month of Bhadra.'

Her words seem to suggest she is joking, but from her face it's hard to believe she is. So Shatadalbasini keeps quiet, fingering the rice in her plate but not eating it. Impatiently Krishna says, 'Don't you have eyes? Can't you tell from looking at me?'

'I was sort of beginning to sense a little, sister-in-law, but I didn't feel sure. You said you didn't answer the letters, yet . . . you used to meet, right?'

'Yes, we used to.'

They both fall silent. It's not possible to eat any more, the fish and vegetable dishes are also quite inedible today.

After a long time she answers Krishna: 'But weddings can't take place in the month of Bhadra, sister-in-law, it just has to be delayed a month.'

At night, the children take longer than usual to fall asleep; as soon as one falls asleep, the other wakes up. Jatin has gone to bed before ten, and after putting the children to sleep Shatadalbasini waits with her ears pricked up for the summons. She'll not take the penalty today—whatever he says or does, she'll definitely revolt. Now all she needs is to be called up. Today her courage has grown large, larger than even the courage Krishna needed to go against society, customs, rules, religion, everything. The moment he calls her and says, 'Massage my feet', she'll hold her head high and say: 'No, I won't. Am I your foot-massaging maid?'

Then? Then what's to happen will happen. Krishna has accepted with open eyes so much darkness in her future, and she can't take merely a slap on her cheek with closed eyes?

The fire of lofty intention keeps burning in her mind, the self-respect she feels glows into a halo of heroism. She now seems to herself to be rather great—something close to extraordinary. But alas, the children fall asleep, the lights go off in the two houses across from theirs, the neighbourhood grows still, but no one calls her to give her the opportunity to rebel.

Then, hearing the sound of Jatin's snore, she gets increasingly upset. He has fallen asleep without calling her? She starts feeling very helpless, quite at a loss.

After a while Shatadalbasini goes in on her own and starts massaging her sleeping husband's feet.

The Priest's Wife *

The world outside, lost in the thick darkness of the night of new moon, is recognizable at this late hour only from a few mysterious sounds. Kadambini is sleepless. Sitting up in bed, she listens, ears pricked, to each bit of the night's language, hard to decipher as it is.

The sound of the crickets is so unbroken and ceaseless that from time to time you can't help becoming aware of hearing it automatically, as if it's no longer possible to distinguish it as cricket call. The wind suddenly sighs through the leaves of the margosa at the back of the room, and the dry mango leaves blowing from one side of the yard to the other seem to echo it. Foxes in the distance break into a howl. The barking of the village dogs don't stop for a long time after their agonized cry has fallen silent. The weird screech of an owl somewhere close makes the night ghastly for a few seconds; after a while the groan of the wooden wheels of a cart rises on the road not far from there, followed by the tinkle of bells tied around the necks of the bullocks pulling it.

And suddenly, rising over all these, the night's own sounds, the baby of the neighbour Ramesh Hajra starts crying, sending a shudder through Kadambini's body.

She starts to tremble, it hammers in her chest, sweat soaks her body. Ramesh Hajra's wife is very young, it takes her time to wake up. The baby cries for some time. Listening to it, consciousness loses its support inside Kadambini's head. A strange sensation of the level ground becoming wavy jolts her off her feet. Fearfully she grasps the side of the bedstead with both hands as hard as she can.

Actually it was out of the fear of hearing the cry of Ramesh Hajra's baby that this newmoon night of spring became for Kadambini sleepless and alive with sounds. Ramesh's wife was not here when she gave birth; she was at her parents' place. She came back a month ago with a four-month-old. A few days later, Kadambini for the first time heard the baby cry late in the night.

On that night, with the unbearable pain in her heart, she was lying

---

* The Bengali title is *Pujarir Bou.*

still on a mat on the porch. Gurupada was unable to talk her into coming inside. Finally, giving up, he smoked for a while, then he started to doze sitting beside her.

Sometime then, in the stillness of the night, the feeble cry was heard from the other side of the mud wall. Scrambling up, bewildered with terror and agitation, Kadambini held on to her husband with all her strength. 'My baby's crying. Can you hear it? Dear, can you hear too?'

Gurupada said, 'Ramesh's baby is crying, Kadu. Don't do that. There's nothing to fear!'

For a long while she couldn't believe his words. With eyes opened wide she stared at the pineapple bush beside the wall between the two houses, and shivered again and again, saying, 'No dear, no, it's my baby crying. I clearly heard my baby's voice—crying in that bush. There, listen, can you hear? Isn't that my baby's voice?'

Then suddenly like a madwoman she started for the pineapple bush. Gurupada held her back; it was not easy to stop her. Come back from the land of the lost, her baby was crying in the bush beside her own yard—the thought made the thin, grieving woman find an amazing physical strength as she struggled: 'Let me go and bring him. I beg you, dear, let me go. From the river's side my baby has come this far, he can't come this last bit.'

She didn't have to struggle for long to free herself of her husband's grip. Suddenly she fainted and collapsed on his chest. That was her first fainting spell. She did not come out of it before the night's end. Ramesh Hajra's wife was called up and had to come over, the baby in her arms, to attend to her. It's hard to tell what crossed Gurupada's mind as he watched her sitting on the bed by his unconscious wife's head, with her legs folded in and the sleeping baby in her lap, waving the handfan to the tinkle of her bangles. However, it was only to his eyes that night that the room's light seemed not bright enough.

Mahipati Basak is the village landlord. Gurupada is the priest at the temple in which the deities were installed in his father's time. The image in the temple is of Radha and Shyam together. It's exquisite. There's no way of knowing today who sculpted out of deep black stone this image of eternal union. But his talent lives to this day in the image worshipped daily. Day by day the stone deities were stealing Gurupada's heart. No longer satisfied with just the regular worship and offerings, even when it was time to go home after locking the temple gate, he would quietly sit before the image for a long time, time off from paid worship. He'd worship the image with his eyes—without scented flowers, incense, and sandalwood paste—for just his heart's joy.

The morning after, he was late in going to the temple. Mahipati's widowed sister Bhabini is a little crazy about the daily worship. Being of the weaver caste, she didn't have the right to go near the image. But she always kept a key to the temple with her, in a ring tied to the end of her sari. Perhaps she too was in love with the image. She couldn't resist the urge to open the temple door to look at the image from a distance even if she couldn't go near it. Waiting that morning for Gurupada to come and open the temple, she gets so annoyed and angry that, even after hearing a full account of the reason for his being late, she doesn't feel the slightest bit of sympathy.

When the worship was over, however, she said to him, 'The matter doesn't sound good, Thakur-mashai; she has suffered two losses, now she faints in this inauspicious month. I'll ask you to do this, put a prayer for Kadu-didi in two flowers, touch them to the gods' feet and take them home. Touch them to her forehead and save them.'

Many times Gurupada had sought the deities' help to keep Kadu's lap from emptying, for her peace of mind. The deities hadn't fulfilled his wish. Still, once again at Bhabini's suggestion, he eagerly placed at the deities' feet his prayer in two flowers, and took those home.

In her heart, Kadambini no longer loved any deity. How could she love those who emptied her home, her lap, her heart? Still, the flowers did her some good. Towards the afternoon she got up, served food to Gurupada and for a long time sat chatting with Kanu's Ma, visiting from another neighbourhood. In the evening she had her wash and sat down to her daily prayer. After an early supper she went to bed and didn't wake up even once the whole night.

Her feeble quietude stayed for a few days after that. An aunt of Gurupada lived in the next village, Gurupada went and fetched her. The aunt did the cooking both times of the day, but Kadambini continued to tend the cows, attend to her husband, and clean the house. Sometimes she also went to the pond to scour the pots, sometimes she brought back a filled water pot. When coming up and going down through the garden, she would rapidly glance on both sides with eager eyes. As if in the hope that her eyes might suddenly spot her two lost baby boys in some nook, in a corner around the house, or behind some tree in the garden.

'Why do you have to do the heavy chores, daughter-in-law?' the aunt protested. 'What am I doing here with my darned body! If you want, do the light stuff, or just sit down and sew baby's bedpads. The bedpads needed won't be a few! Later the shortage of bedpads will give you trouble. Before my Khemi's daughter was born, I told her so many times, "Don't spend all your time lolling, sew bedpads, as many as you can when you still have the time," but my daughter didn't listen . . . what's it dear, why are you crying so? Don't cry, crying brings no welfare, only bad luck.'

In tears Kadambini said, 'What shall I do with bedpads, Aunt?

Who'll use them? Not once did the bedpads I sew get a chance to be worn.'

The aunt, of course, offered her the customary assurance and consolation, but Kadambini wasn't in a state to feel reassured. The sun rises and sets before the eyes as expected, so people believe in the sun's rising and setting as the greatest thing in the world. Twice, not once but twice, all of Kadambini's life became focused within herself, unexpectedly, long after its time was passed, after she had lived thirstily for many, many days and nights. Both times, the joy of her life departed in a blink right before her eyes. Kadambini now believed that this combination of rising and setting was no fluke. She had understood that her babies would not live. After her long penance for a son, she had received this untimely blessing of motherhood. Kadambini now knew perfectly well that motherhood would come to her, but her child would not stay.

At some point the continuous crying of Ramesh's son becomes intermittent. After some more time, the crying stops altogether. The baby's mother is finally awake.

Kadambini's world is left without the slightest hint of sound. The stillness of sinking into one's own thoughts descends around her. Only the sound of Gurupada's exhaling makes her conscious of her actual surroundings for an instant from time to time.

Gusts of spring breeze blow in through one window and out the other. Suddenly aware that she has been feeling cold for some time, she wraps the sari carefully around her. Who knows when Ramesh Hajra's son will cry again tonight. A few nights ago, in spite of staying up the whole time, she couldn't hear the baby cry more than once. Still, she spends every moment waiting to hear the sound.

Gurupada turns on his side in his sleep. The owl on a branch of the margosa tree outside hoots harshly again. And the disappointment she feels towards her husband suddenly seems bottomless. She can't imagine how anyone can sleep so calmly every night after sacrificing two offspring. Maybe her babies never peeped in, not even once, in the world of his sleep. Perhaps that hint of a smile on his countenance is brought on by happy dreams filled with golden light.

Kadambini's heart scorches and burns. She has worshipped her husband like god so long, spent every conscious moment thinking of his comfort and needs, even her unbearable heartbreak felt instantly lightened whenever she looked at his face. She always considered herself fortunate in having the love of her virtuous, restrained, priest husband. In the twelve years of her married life, not once has she felt critical of him. Yet, all of a sudden tonight she feels an intense hostility towards him. Her mind fills to the brim with disrespect for a man who sleeps soundly in her bed of thorns.

She makes no attempt whatsoever to stop this revolt in her mind, a revolt so unprecedented, so thoroughly against all her notions of what's right. In the darkness of night her agitated mind nurses with a fierce care the thought even a shadow of which would have horrified her in the light of day. Gurupada seems cruel, selfish. It seems that the pain she viewed all this time as bestowed by god was not really god's doing. Gurupada is the one who repeatedly brought this disaster in her life. Not satisfied with dealing her the deadly blow twice, he's ready once again in the same role.

She leaves her bed and goes down on the floor. With her elbows planted on the floor and her face in her palms, she tries to brace herself against the acute, almost physical, heartache. Right here, making a bed on this hard ground, she used to lay down her two babies, while Gurupada did his scripture reading seated on the bedstead. She couldn't put her mind to work, couldn't resist seeing the sleeping baby every ten minutes, she was all ears the whole time in case he would wake up and cry. After scripture reading, Gurupada went to the temple. After his coming back from the temple, he sat with Ramesh Hajra playing chess. He would come home very late either from the temple or from chatting in someone's house. After eating the food she had prepared using the time that was her son's due, he spent the whole night in a deep sleep like this, without a care.

When her son died, he consoled her. Wiping away his two drops of tears for show he gave her consolation and advice, even tried to wipe away her tears. Could he have done it so calmly if he had felt even a little pained by his son's death?

It's this thought that chafes her the most. The burning would have cooled if he, like herself, were crazed with grief for his child, if she could at this point even imagine the grief-stricken appearance of her husband. But she can't recall having once seen him lose his composure, even after committing his son to the river. Gurupada now appears in her mind like a tormentor devoid of all pity, mercy.

Slowly, resolutely, Kadambini sits up. She can't resist the urge to take a look at his sleeping face. There is a matchbox in the wall shelf. She lights the oil lamp.

At first the light seems unbearable, she can't see a thing, her eyes hurt, she has to close them. The lamp is about to go out in the wind—the flame's red warning becomes an irritation to her eyes through the shut lids, and further intensifies her mind's agitation. She's also slightly afraid of what she'll possibly witness in this light on her husband's face, a face she has known for twelve years.

This fear doesn't go away even after she opens her eyes. She runs them all around the room, but she can't immediately look at the face to see which she lit the lamp. On top of the wooden chest she kept the shell-shaped brass spoon with which she fed the baby his milk. It looks tarnished from disuse. She keeps staring at the spoon for a long time, as if she has discovered this sorrowful inanimate object for the first time today. The grievous complaint in her heart is boiling over anew. He was such an unfeeling rock that he didn't let her keep in the house any of the babies' things except that spoon. Because she behaves crazed, hugging the baby's bed and clothes, begs god for death at the top of her voice, he got rid of those in the river's water.

With an ominous gleam in her red eyes, she holds up the lamp and stands motionless, staring at Gurupada's face with the critical eyes of an enemy. What she sees is not her husband's face, but the deformity of her own perspective. It seems to her that in every line of the sleeping man's face is revealed his oppressive nature, his countenance clearly expresses his desire for amusement from playing with her.

The lamp in her hand totters and is about to fall. Hot oil spills and rolls down to her elbow. Discovering her mind's confusion on her husband's face gives her a pain worse than death, but still she stands there, unflinching, and goes on demolishing with blind passion the only support she has left to go on living.

She's now left with no more doubt that the rest of her life will be spent like this. In a month her lap will fill again, but in six months her lap will empty and Gurupada will come home from the riverside leaving her son behind. She won't even get a chance to have a good long cry rolling in the dust on the ground. He'll wipe her tears, pat the dust off her, and bring her back to this bed. She'll not be able to stop the return of her babies to the river's side.

Gradually this horrifying picture of her entire future life grows so vivid in her mind that Gurupada's face disappears from before her eyes. She sees herself instead, herself as a son-slaughtering demoness in her husband's embrace in the death-cold air of this room. Through the nights resonating with babies' cries, she's calling up one baby at a time and strangling it to death.

She has no need to live any more, no purpose. She turns away and puts the lamp down on its stand. Using the crying of Ramesh Hajra's son as an excuse, she has spent several nights in a row in the company of her own dead babies; a faint desire to live was with her even last night. She couldn't completely give up the hope that this time the baby might survive. Tonight she no longer has the courage even to hope. Her son may live, perhaps; miracles happen in god's world. But Kadambini no longer finds the strength within herself to test her luck again. What if it doesn't live? If it dies after she has nurtured it for six months or a year, every moment holding within her the fear of losing it? How can she live, how can she go on taking it?

With a last look at the brass spoon on the chest, she blows the lamp out. She has no more desire to see his face. Her husband's closeness has become false to her. She has in her mind travelled beyond the home she has tended for twelve years, the husband she has worshipped and the nest filled with memories happy and sad. She's as if in the farthest reach of a land of half consciousness where a person knows nothing except a sense of helpless loneliness. There, a person is driven by the repeated defeat of desire, its repeated frustration in the all too concrete world of self-consciousness.

Gurupada always keeps the temple key on the shelf. The key in hand, she opens the door and steps out. She pauses for a second in the yard, then goes on, opens the gate, steps out on the path.

People have made nests crowded together in the neighbourhood. Passing by the absolutely still homes on both sides of the road, Kadambini now feels like crying. She knows each of the families living in these homes. In none of them can a woman be found cursed like her. Loss of a child is not unknown in this neighbourhood. Perhaps even at this moment a bereaved mother is shedding tears in a dark room of some home. But has anyone's son died like hers of an unknown cause, from god's incomprehensible curse? Which unfortunate one of these women knew, like her, from the time a baby came in her womb that the healthy baby will one day all of sudden start to wither away and, bow-like, bent backward, die within three days?

There's a huge pond in front of the temple. The stars, shining brighter against the sky of a newmoon night, are glittering on the water's surface. Standing on the temple steps, she looks at the wide open tranquility of the pond. She's overwhelmed for a while. Then it occurs to her that this pond should be used for no purpose other than dying. Making any other use of it would be a sin.

Unlocking the temple door, she steps in. She knows exactly where each of the things are kept. Groping a little in the dark, she finds the largest of the brass water pots. It is full. She tilts it and pours out the water. With the empty pot perched in the crook of her waist, she turns her face roughly in the direction of the image of Radha-Shyam and says in her mind, 'You've stolen two sons of mine. I'm stealing only a water pot from you. And I don't even want your forgiveness.'

Other Short Stories

The Thief[*]

Unexpected rain soaks the night. The sky was clear in the afternoon. Clouds gathered with the fall of dusk. At the dead of night the clouds melt all at once, they start to pour in continuous streams upon the still, sleeping village.

A canal flows beside the village to join up with the big river near Rasulpur. None of the gentlefolk live in the lesser part of the village that is on the east side of the canal. The village on this side consists of the neighbourhoods of milkmen, potters, and the Bagdi untouchables. A few poor peasant homes have found their bare shelters amongst them. Farther away from the canal is a large marsh. It is a bit overgrown over there, sort of like a jungle, and extremely unhealthy.

Close to that jungly area by the marsh, near the end of the milkmen's neighbourhood, the old hut topped with straw-thatch is Madhu Ghose's. Madhu has been asleep on a shabby, smelly bed atop a cot of wood boards. He came out of a bout of fever only yesterday, and hasn't recovered much strength in his body yet. Waking at the sound of rain, he sits up on the bed, wrapping himself in a torn rag quilt. Peering out eagerly into the darkness through the tiny window of bamboo strips set in a hole in the fence-wall, he says, 'Look Kadu, just look at my luck.'

Kadu has already got up and lighted the oil lamp. 'What's the matter with luck now?' she says.

Madhu sadly says, 'I still haven't had a meal, and the bugger rain comes tonight. If it'd come a couple of days later, I could have gone out for a try. The end of Bhadra now, god knows if there'll be any more good rain this year!'

The advantages in going to steal on a rainy night are many. The darkness gets thicker than on a newmoon night, people go into a deep sleep from the coolness, and no one likes to come out even if there are a hundred needs. The village dogs find shelter, stick their heads in and stay in, they don't holler at the slightest footstep. Hut bases soak in the rain and grow soft. Tunnelling in becomes easier and makes less noise.

---

[*]   The Bengali title is *Chor*.

Madhu badly needs to do some tunnelling. Four months ago in Baisakh he made some money from setting up a bangle-throw gambling stall at the Rasulpur fair with a license from the police. Since then he has not had any earning. He has of course made no attempt. Madhu can't put his mind to earning until he's broke. That is the way he has lived all these years. That is his nature. Several months every year he spends very happily. The remaining months he and Kadu suffer interminably from lack of things they need. Just before life becomes absolutely impossible, Madhu suddenly gets hold of some money again.

It's doubtful whether to this day he has earned a single paisa through legitimate means. All the covert and overt ways in which he derives his irregular income are against the law and the rules of moral conduct. But Madhu doesn't care for any kind of moral propriety. There's no act in the world he will not do for money. He has snatched gold and silver chains from babies' necks, he has taken a share of poor peasant's hard-earned cash by acting the part of a gambling dealer, he has picked pockets, he has gone to distant villages to beg from door to door in the name of his father's funeral expenses. From time to time, putting on a brief loincloth and smearing oil on his entire body, he has also tunnelled his way into some home's inner room. If he had more strength in his body and courage in his mind, he wouldn't have stopped short of open robbery.

Putting the lamp down by the entrance and unlatching the prop-up wicker door, Kadu gives him this bitter reply: 'As if you'd come back a king if you went out. They make more money working as labourers.'

Injured and annoyed, Madhu says, 'Why, in what way is my earning not enough. Didn't I buy you silver bangles the other day?'

Sharply turning her face away, Kadu says, 'Oh, the silver bangles he's given me! Four years I've been his wife, and there's no end to his talking of the few strands of silver he's given. I'll stick those bangles in a burning stove.'

She lifts the door and goes out. She brings in the basket of cowdung pats from the porch outside and puts it down, saying, 'All my likes and fancies are dumped in the stove. I kill myself making dung pats and being a slavey. What're you bragging about, giving me just a pair of bangles? Anyone else would've given a lot more.'

Madhu is surprised. He's not used to hearing this sort of complaint from Kadu. She's not the complaining type. Four years ago, he made a fat bundle from tunnelling into the home of Jatin Saha of Brindabanpur. At that time Saudamini from the potters' neighbourhood would have agreed to live with him for ten rupees a month and food and clothing, but it was Kadu he brought home as his married wife after paying two hundred rupees in bride price. Not for a day has he regretted having paid all that money earned on the risk of rotting in jail for three or four years. The money was nothing compared to Kadu's beauty and qualities. After bringing Kadu home, and with the money in hand, he spent nearly a year blissfully happy. That one year he didn't have to bother at all about making any money. He lived a life of leisure intoxicated with Kadu in a world filled with Kadu. After that they often had trouble for lack of money. At one point Madhu almost landed in the slammer. Kadu then had to go without food for half a day or even a day, but she never complained. Who knows what has happened to her over the last few days.

Looking intensely, Madhu takes in her brightly lit face as she blows the lamp out. It strikes him that an unfamiliar shadow has fallen on her face. The way she quickly glances at him from the corner of her eye, her face close to the flame, just before blowing it out, also seems unfamiliar to him.

When she climbs back into bed, Madhu tries to caress her, asking fondly, 'Shall I go out for a try, what do you say, Kadu?'

Kadu rudely rejects his touch, saying, 'Do as you wish. I'm sleepy. Don't bother me now, dear, let me sleep.'

Injured, he pulls the rag quilt over his body and lies down silently. Outside it's raining with a ringing sound. The last big performance of the rainy season. The full moon is only four or five days away. Perhaps tomorrow the moon will be out in a cloudless sky. The advantage of prowling under cover of night will be gone. Madhu starts feeling uneasy. An opportunity like tonight's may not come by in a long time. Who knows when he would be able to bring a smile on Kadu's face again. The difficulties will grow now as days pass. Once Kadu's patience gives way, her temper and irritability will get worse in proportion to their hardship.

Madhu can't sleep. Lying in bed, he keeps thinking of all sorts of things. Some time ago he heard that Rakhal Mitra of the main village has come home with a lot of cash. Rakhal Mitra's home is not made of brick and mortar, and doesn't have an iron safe to keep the money. Madhu was tempted. When Rakhal came home, Rakhal's wife wanted to hire a housemaid to be better able to attend to her husband's needs. Madhu did a lot of talking to Kadu to persuade her to go to work in Rakhal's house, to find out the location of the room. 'Go for just one day, Kadu. Get me the information. After a day, you quit work saying it's too much and come home, you don't have to go again.'

Kadu groaned. 'Oh god! Now I have to be a slavey, was this my fate?'

Where Rakhal sleeps, which room his son Pannalal sleeps in, where in Rakhal's room are the boxes and chests—all this information Kadu duly brought him. But since that day she herself has somehow changed in a strange way.

At first Madhu didn't quite notice it. He thought perhaps she was upset about being sent to work as a housemaid. It's just abhiman, pride, how long can it last? But after Kadu's harsh words tonight, the history of the odd change in her keeps coming back to his mind. He no longer feels he can dismiss it as temporary anger and irritation.

Madhu recalls that during the days he was down with fever Kadu didn't treat him well, didn't give him food in time, didn't come near him unless he called her. She was sort of absentminded all the time. The maid's work she didn't have to do for more than a day, and yet, in spite of his specifically asking her not to go, she left him in his illness and went to work at Rakhal's house. The excuse she gave was, 'They'll be suspicious if I leave the job suddenly.'

'It's my concern if they are suspicious. Don't go, Kadu.'

'Let me go for these few days left of the month. How can anyone leave a job without giving notice?'

The sort of things she said did not make any sense at all.

Meanwhile Rakhal's eldest son Panna-babu came one day—with a strange proposal.

'Raju is leaving for her in-laws' place tomorrow. You've to let your wife go with her. Not for very long, just about fifteen days.'

Madhu did not agree. But he was surprised to see Kadu's enthusiasm for going with Rakhal's daughter as a maid to her in-laws' place. For refusing permission, she didn't speak nicely to him for two days. He couldn't understand, even after a lot of thought, why for several days she was full of regret saying, 'They'd have paid ten rupees, ten rupees are lost because of you.'

After a long time Madhu becomes aware that Kadu beside him is also without sleep.

'You didn't fall asleep, Kadu?'

'No.'

Trying once again to embrace her, he says, 'Why didn't you, you sleepyhead?'

'I'm feeling hot. Let go of me.'

After the stifling heat of the day, a lovely coolness has infused the earth's air. Madhu just can't believe Kadu's words.

'Will you tell me what's wrong?' he says.

'What can be wrong? Nothing's wrong. You've come out of a fever, why don't you sleep instead of staying up all night?'

The words suggest affection. But there is such pungency in her tone that he's again hurt and surprised. Ever since he thought he guessed the reason for this permanent, inflexible irritation in Kadu, he has been feeling terribly uneasy in his mind. It's hard to say by what amazing rule of god Madhu came to love Kadu, in spite of having the nature of a wild fox. The habituated torment of carrying in his heart the burden of his own deformed secrecy, greed, and the constant fear of punishment has raised a wall of meanness around his mind. He understands nothing in the world except self-interest. Yet for Kadu he has boundless affection, under the influence of which he has made many sacrifices. His enfeebled, coward's mind is always anxious to oppress those weaker than himself. It's not true that he never had a mad urge to slap those lovely rounded cheeks of hers. But even if he does not have a trace of self-restraint in any other matter in the world, he has always subdued this urge. When angry, he has glared at her, grinded his teeth, and hurled filthy epithets. But he has never raised his hand against her.

At the sight of a tear in her eyes, he has dissolved. The same way a gentleman caresses his tearful beloved—with a deep passion, with the affinity and intimacy that springs from romantic love—he has taken her to his chest and showered her with kisses and words of love in an overwhelmed voice. 'You're my rib, Kadu, the pupil of my eyes. You're the light of my dark home, my jewel—I swear.' He has said to her, 'If I don't see you for a blink, Kadu, my heart's ready to bust.'

Kadu hasn't defaulted in paying his love back to the last paisa. She has loved him with her mind, served him with her body. Of all conceivable crafts, tricks, ruses and artfulness needed to steal the heart of a thief, she has neglected not one. Madhu has felt as though there's no one in the world like Kadu, she's incomparable in beauty, love and affection, she's his reward for some great penance he must have done unknown to himself.

Has that Kadu now become a stranger to him? Has the golden girl become rock hard simply because he gave her bangles of silver instead of gold? Learned to love money more than him?

After quietly lying down for some more time, Madhu suddenly sits up and says, 'Get up for a bit, Kadu.'

'Why should I get up?'

'Light the lamp. I'll go out.'

For a while there's no sign of Kadu getting up. She seems to be thinking of something.

Then she silently gets up and lights the lamp.

'Better not go out tonight, you're just out of the fever,' she says.

Madhu suddenly gets angry. 'Don't show your love any more, you hear me? Enough. Anyone else would've given a lot more! Why don't you go to him who'd give you more!'

Seeing her new bangles shine in the lamplight, his fury instantly turns into disappointment.

'With a fever I go out to earn in the middle of the night with rain on my head, still the girl's face stays glum like a pot's bottom. Serves her right if I get caught.'

'Who's asked you to go?' Kadu replies.

'You asked, you! Keep quiet, Kadu. When I'm angry, don't talk back.'

Slightly afraid, Kadu says, 'What can anyone do about your getting angry for no reason?'

Out of exasperation and hurt feeling, Madhu does not answer her. Why can't she beg him by clutching his feet? Can't she cry with her arms around his neck? Can't she say, Don't go out tonight you're not well, I beg you, listen to me, I'll hang myself if you go?

Madhu puts on the brief loincloth. Lying in bed he hadn't realized that there was so much pain about his waist! He gets the drilling rod from the vat in a corner of the hut used for storing bran for the cow. Looking at it he says, 'It's rusty. Couldn't you remember even to oil it one day? Bring the grinding stone, let me sharpen it before I go.'

Kadu says, 'The mud floor is soft from the rain. It'll do.'

Madhu says, 'Can't wait to get rid of me anyhow, right? Since when did you grow so greedy for money?'

She doesn't answer. Fetching him the grindstone, she sits on the bed, and after furtively glancing this way and that, she keeps her head lowered.

Madhu does not at all like this unfamiliar conduct of hers. Sharply looking at her, he says, 'I've to oil it. Give me some oil, Kadu.'

'There's no oil.'

'No oil? Why not?'

'Who knows? What can I do if there's no oil? Can I make it?'

Madhu looks steadily at Kadu. After all this time he is able to detect in her a suppressed excitement, a hidden restlessness. A seasoned thief himself, he's no stranger to the manners and ways of a thief. In Kadu's eyes and face he clearly sees an intention to steal. Suspiciously he asks, 'Out with it, what're you up to? Why're you acting like this?'

Flustered, she says, 'I'm worried. Worried for you. If you find the people in the house not asleep, don't try to drill, dear, just come back.'

Still she would not ask him not to go. The first time he was going out like this with his loincloth on and body oiled, she did all but clutch his feet to stop him. With a disappointment heightened by the memory of that night, he pushes up the wicker door and goes out. His whole body shivers at the first touch of rain, after coming from the bed warmed by him and Kadu. For a moment he thinks of going back. But reminding himself that she'll not be glad if he does, he grits his teeth and walks along the narrow path through the milkmen's neighbourhood, towards the village.

Although the rain is coming to a stop, the sky remains heavily overcast. Walking by the rain-soaked, silent, straw-roofed huts, his disappointment grows heavier. Looking at the most dilapidated hut, the thought occurs to him that the wife of this home would not let her husband go out on such a dark, rainy night even if she has been starving for seven days. The difference between that husband's luck and his is not without a reason. However poor, that one is not a thief. And he is a thief. That is why his wife does not hesitate to let him go even in the face of danger for the sake of her own comfort. After expelling her thief-husband from home, she latches the wicker door and goes to sleep herself.

In a short while, Madhu reaches the bank of the canal. Tonight, after a very long time, he feels mortified. It seems as if the notions of virtue and sin, of good and bad that had died in him and taken on another life are back in the earlier form, spreading unease . . . . Walking along this side of the canal towards the little bridge some distance away, Madhu suddenly feels like the bandit Ratnakar. He feels that he has so far lived a most contemptible life. An unspeakably detestable life. There is no end to his sins. After death he'll not find a place even in hell.

This thought makes Madhu feel utterly helpless. He is suddenly afraid, in the midst of a lost feeling he has never known before. Again he thinks of dropping it—there is no need to steal, it's better that he goes back. But this time too, remembering Kadu, he holds back the urge to return. He feels angry and disappointed with her. Still, even in this state of mind, he can't forget that she has given him beauty and youth not easily available, given him affection all this time even if not today. On that claim, she wants happiness from him. However selfish her demand is, it's not unreasonable, not unfair. He simply has to give Kadu the things she wants.

A little ahead of him is the boat landing of the potters' neighbourhood. Four or five large boats are tied there. Madhu is a little surprised to see light inside the shed of one of them. This late in the night on the canal, who could be sitting in a boat with a lighted lamp? Having roamed on and off paths for a long time, he has lost the fear of snakes. Squatting in the thick growth of tall grass and making his way with his hands, he moves towards the landing close to where the boat is. Thinking the boat may be that of a travelling jute broker and maybe he'll get lucky soon. Once on a rainy night just like this, in the boat landing of the river in Rasulpur, Madhu removed the cash box from the boat of a jute broker he knew. It had nearly seven hundred rupees in cash. He cheers up thinking that tonight too he may have an unexpected opportunity to make big. Maybe he won't have to drill into Rakhal's hut base tonight, and suffer those shudders in his spine from the fear of being beaten to death by that bullish, stubborn son of his.

Madhu is really scared of Panna-babu.

Nudged by the water's current, the boat has come close and rests parallel to the bank. Getting into waist-deep water and peeping through a tiny hole in the shed, Madhu's dream vanishes into nothingness! Inside, a bed has been made. Lying on his back and reading a book, with a lamp near his head, is Panna-babu, Rakhal's eldest son.

Madhu cannot quite comprehend how he finds none other than Rakhal's son alone in the canal's boat landing-place this late at night, reading a book, when he himself is out to steal at Rakhal's place. For some time he keeps standing in the water next to the boat, confounded.

Then it seems to him that it may not be that amazing. Maybe Panna-babu was to go to town tomorrow morning, and seeing the sky heavily overcast, he has had an early meal and come to the boat to sleep. The boatmen will come in the last hour of dawn and take it out.

But why is it that the boat is brought upstream and tied here instead of at the boat landing-place close to Rakhal's home? The reason for this Madhu is unable to guess even after a lot of thinking. But he's relieved about one thing. In Rakhal's house tonight, except for old Rakhal and his two young sons, there's no other male. Even if he makes some noise and is found, no one would be able to catch him easily.

Madhu does not get back to this bank. He swims rat-like across the canal. His heart has become lighter. Taking into consideration a number of fateful links he's convinced that success is inevitable for him tonight. His fever let up yesterday because he was to go out to steal tonight. It's for his convenience that the clouds gathered in the sky and Panna-babu decided to sleep in that boat. And Kadu's temper turned rotten this very night to force him out. Otherwise, he might have used the excuse of physical weakness to continue lazing in his hut, ignoring the call of destiny.

Tonight perhaps he is fated to be lucky.

Madhu's eyes glisten with greed. With soundless steps, moving like a dark-patch of the darkness itself, he enters the village. He is feeling cold from the frequent gusts of wind, but there's no longer any suffering in his mind. A short while ago, he took a fall to hell on being hurt by Kadu; now effortlessly he has climbed to heaven. He can no longer see anything wrong with stealing. What's sinful about it? Who in the world is not a thief? Everybody steals. Some do it within the law, some break the law. Only those who don't have the guts to set out in this line of work with nothing but courage as capital call it a sin. They're worse than thieves, they're cowardly, not men enough.

Madhu savours his self-satisfaction. In his excited greed, the justification for stealing has almost become glorious to him. There's no life like it. Rakhal has returned home after a long time, having earned money with a lot of effort in a faraway place; money with which he'll pay the king's taxes, repay loans, buy land and get his daughter married. In a few minutes in one night that money will have changed hands! When earning the money with the sweat of his brow, could the honest Rakhal have ever thought it would come to Madhu's benefit? Rakhal was killing himself with work so that Madhu could enjoy the smile on Kadu's face; it seems like a joke, it also seems like a feat on his part. A smile breaks upon his lips.

Regret and self-satisfaction. Madhu's mood swings tonight from moment to moment between heaven and hell hold nothing surprising. A thief's experience is beyond comparison; the evolution of a thief's heart follows an extraordinary pattern.

Yet a thief's life is very lonely—he really has no one of his own. Like the poet, like the thinker, the thief lives in hiding within his mind. No matter what the level of his feelings, no matter how crude and rough the boundaries of his imagination, a thief's feelings and thoughts are kaleidoscopic, variable from moment to moment. He thinks a lot, more than most gentlemen do. He's in touch with many truths in life even a hint of which don't cross the horizon of many educated, polished minds. A poet's preoccupation is woman, a thief's is stealing. Actually both these preoccupations are equally conducive to mental fertility. There are scores of honest people in the world about whom I can't write a story. There are no stories in their lives. A thief's life is full of stories, like a lover's—a lover who is erudite in forbidden, improper, stolen affections.

When entering Rakhal's room through the tunnel he has drilled, Madhu's heart is suffused with an intense, vigorous excitement; his senses all come awake with a crackling alertness. Inside the room the lantern is on, just dimmed. On the bedstead Rakhal sleeps with his small son of five or six. The bed for Rakhal's wife and marriageable daughter has been made on the floor. Standing in this dark corner, holding his breath, Madhu looks about the room. The peaceful atmosphere of people asleep in a silent room. Madhu's excitement became even more intense, even more intoxicating the moment he stepped in. Coming from the darkness outside, he can see everything clearly even in the dim light. When his scanning eyes land on Rakhal's daughter, his heart jumps. The girl is sleeping exactly as Kadu does. Do all young women sleep in this manner?

But the bangles on Kadu's wrists are of silver. This girl is wearing gold bangles. She's not full-bodied like Kadu either, her body hasn't yet had the time to flourish. Her figure is turned like a bow at the slim waist. The face is immature, flower soft. Not ripened like Kadu's. Her complexion is soothing like the light at dusk, bright like the light of morning.

It is for the marriage of this girl that Rakhal has come home with the money. Madhu had to buy Kadu with money. Rakhal will give his daughter away with money.

Madhu shakes his head wondering. For a second he has a sad, mournful expression on his face. Everyone has the right to desire. And no one in any condition deprives oneself of this right. Madhu's heart encounters no obstacle at all in feeling a profound, transient love for the sleeping daughter of Rakhal. This sudden blooming of passion in the heart is not new to him. Standing before a jewellery shop he has felt a sudden passion swelling just like this. Just as he felt sad then with the knowledge that the store's well-guarded jewellery was beyond his reach, so he feels a pain in the momentary, deep, unrequited love for this slackly clothed girl, as unobtainable as the moon, in the midst of the harsh, fear-stricken sensations of his tainted nocturnal outing tonight. He longs to touch the girl just once. To hold her once to his chest, tightly, the way he holds Kadu, with intense ardour, in his trembling eager arms—and then run away from here. He doesn't want the money.

The way a cursed god exiled from heaven becomes restless and upset when he suddenly sees a scene from heaven very close by, Madhu's deformed heart cries out for a touch of the innocent, lovely girl. It's like the appearance of a lake before a desert traveller. The knowledge that it will disappear like a mirage seems to intensify, not diminish, the desire to plunge into it.

Madhu sighs hard. Then he inhales like a troubled spirit standing outside the temple, trying to breathe the incense-bearing air, and his eyes fill with tears on looking at his own wet, almost naked body.

Suddenly the thought hits him again that he lives in hell, that he hasn't found peace for even a moment to this day. His home is dirty, smelly; his wife a fat, mean woman bought for money; his life, filled with greed and fear, is perpetually abnormal. How the gentlefolk live is not unknown to Madhu. He's familiar with the lifestyle of honest, god-fearing family men. With this sleeping family before his eyes, and love for an adolescent girl soft like tender, young leaves (Madhu's feeling is nothing short of love, though it'll disappear in a few seconds), he compares in his mind his own life with that of those who are not thieves. He is riddled with envy, distress and disappointment. He's no longer interested in stealing, he thinks of going back.

Going back and starting life anew. A restrained, beautiful, pure life. Is it too late to develop a devotion to god? Teach Kadu it's not right to be greedy, not right to stay unclean, not right to be difficult and quarrelsome? Is it impossible to convince her that there can be more happiness in silver bangles than in gold bangles? Can't the two of them stop coveting others' belongings at least out of concern for themselves in the other world? He could work as a labourer. He could buy a few cows and sell the milk. He could buy some land and farm. Or he could start a variety store in the village. Husband and wife, they could get initiated together into mantra. Rising in the morning, and bowing before the god of daylight, they could toil till dusk to earn a living, and then they could pray, singlemindedly, turning their beads. They could practice talking in lower voices. Not let themselves be frightened by sadness. With peace in their hearts they could stay calm under all circumstances. Kadu miscarried a baby because of her own carelessness. The children born from now on will live. With them they could run a happy home life.

All these years he has been stealing. What has he gained in life through stealing?

Every thief occasionally asks himself this question. Yet he doesn't refrain from stealing again. What can a thief do but steal? Everything else in a thief's life is fantasy.

So much regret, so much love for Rakhal's daughter, so eager a desire to become honest, all of it fade away from Madhu's heart in a short while. Rakhal's trunk is soon moved outside through the drilled hole. Rakhal has just this one trunk suitable for keeping a lot of money.

In a mango grove some distance away, Madhu breaks the trunk open. Rakhal probably had no proper pouch for the money; he put the notes and rupee coins in a pillowcase and kept it in the trunk. The bundle is heavy, from the great many rupee coins. Feeling its weight in his hands, Madhu's heart dances with joy.

While crossing the canal, it occurs to him once that Rakhal now would perhaps be unable to get his daughter married for lack of money. But the thought develops no further. His heart no longer has any love left for Rakhal's daughter. He has quite forgotten her.

Madhu knew that Panna-babu's boat was tied at the landing by the potters' neighbourhood. But coming close to the landing he is surprised to see that the boat has disappeared. Where could Panna-babu have taken off this late in the night, he wonders.

Reaching home, Madhu is glad to find the door unlatched. He thinks Kadu is awake, waiting for him with the door unlatched.

'I'm back, Kadu. Light the lamp.'

He has returned with enough to buy Kadu gold bangles, and the means to live in comfort for a year to a year and a half. Kadu will be so happy.

Getting no response from Kadu, his joy is a bit dampened at the thought that she's asleep. Groping on top of the wooden chest, he finds the matchbox and lights the oil lamp. The next moment the room's emptiness glares at him in the lamp's light.

With immeasurable surprise and dread in his eyes, Madhu witnesses the emptiness of his home. He is unable to grasp how someone's home can become so empty all of a sudden in the middle of the night. Kadu is not in bed. Her two daily-wear saris are not on the string. The small wicker basket atop the large tin trunk is also not there. Suddenly, with extreme anxiousness, Madhu opens the tin trunk. In it were kept a few good saris of hers, and in a brass betel-holder, her golden earrings and a ring. Those too have disappeared.

Madhu's exuberance suddenly dies out. The pillowcase filled with notes and rupee coins slumps to the floor at his feet. Staring at it, he senses that his fever is coming back. Abruptly, he breaks into a horrible laugh. The words with which he earlier had defended his occupation as thief when he was going towards Rakhal's house, come back to his mind. Who in the world is not a thief? Everybody steals.

The Ascetic[*]

Shrimat Krishnapadananda will come this afternoon, as the representative of Nagen-babu's family guru. Nagen-babu's younger son Bhupal was married about a year ago, but the bride hasn't yet been initiated in the mantra as per the family tradition. Tomorrow, after all regular ceremony, Shrimat Krishnapadananda will chant in the new wife's ear her personal mantra.

Everyone is disappointed that the gurudev himself is not coming. But in his old age he is not keeping all that well, doesn't have the strength to travel so far to give a mantra to his favourite disciple's younger daughter-in-law. Only one person hasn't felt disappointment. That is Nagen-babu's older daughter-in-law, Sumati. Within a month of her marriage, the old gurudev himself gave her the mantra, and uttered his blessing—may your minds stay in the path of dharma. Does the blessing of so great an ascetic go in vain! Within a month of that her husband had become a renouncer. He left home telling her only that his mind was not in family life, that he had made a big mistake by getting married.

He had also said to her, 'Will you come with me, Sumati?'

'Are you out of your mind?' Sumati had replied.

Ten years have passed since then, and there has been no news of Gopal in all this time. Sumati had not felt particularly heartbroken at the time for someone she had not even come to know very well in two months. But gradually, she began to feel the absence of her husband in the countless frustrations of her life; in the incongruity, the humiliation, and the misery of a married woman's life without the husband. Then she bitterly regretted not having left home with him. The desire for her husband kept getting less and less controllable, dashing itself, crashing against her heart and her mind. Even to this day she occasionally imagines that Gopal will perhaps return. Return briefly and give her once again that invitation, the meaning of which as a very young bride she had not understood at that time.

Knowing the manner in which the old gurudev's blessing took effect

---

[*] The Bengali title is *Sadhu*.

in her life, Sumati is not disappointed that his disciple is coming instead of him to initiate the younger daughter-in-law. The young daughter-in-law can do without the old man's disastrous blessing.

The men and women of the entire neighbourhood stare in amazement at the appearance of Krishnapadananda. Dressed in saffron sarong, saffron kurta and wooden thongs, he looks like a king, or a god—the return of Gopal in disguise. Gopal too had a striking figure, tall and strong, like this.

But no, this is *not* Gopal. He reminds one of Gopal, but there is no resemblance between him and Gopal. It is quite useless to entertain such a notion.

Sumati is the last one to come and pay her respects. Standing rigidly she has been watching Krishnapadanada all this time and shivers have been running through her body at Krishnapadanada's frequent glances at her. No, this is not Gopal. Like everyone else, Sumati has been searching for similarity instead of dissimilarity. No, there's no similarity between Gopal and the sadhu. When offering pranam, she discovers irrefutable proof of this. The ascetic's right toe is not crooked.

Still, in spite of not being Gopal, this saffron-clad man seems to have come to claim her, to bring to life again her first few months of conjugal love, obliterating the ten or eleven year gap in between. Sumati's heart pounds violently; she wants to pull the sari on her head over her face like a new bride. She regrets not having groomed herself properly even though that would be a laughable thing to do for a woman who has been deserted by her husband for ten or eleven years.

Gopal's mother at this point is lamenting to Krishnapadananda in a stricken voice: 'She's so very unfortunate, Father. Brought her in as the daughter-in-law, and shortly after that my son became a sanyasi. He left only two things in writing: we should take care of his wife, and she's not to blame. We've done as he asked, take a look at her yourself, Father, it almost makes one afraid to look at her. But I can't think, Father, that my daughter-in-law had no blame! I say, I brought you as his bride for your beauty, and if you couldn't keep my son at home . . . .'

'Enough! All that is as Sri Sri Thakur wishes,' Nagen-babu stops her in a tone of deep abhiman.

Smiling gently, Krishnapadananda says, 'Sri Sri Thakur has told me about her. Nothing is unknown to him. He said, "Krishnapadananda! In Nagen's home is a girl in austere devotion like Radhika; there's no other votary in the world as great as her. The girl isn't quite able to understand if her penance is for Krishna or for her husband. Talk to her, make her see." Tomorrow I'll give the mantra to the younger daughter-in-law. Then I will show her her path in devotion.'

Deep into the night Sumati comes in and sits down by Krishnapadananda's bed. A huge photograph of the guru Sri Sri Thakur, half covered with flowers, has been placed on the altar. In this room prayers and occasional large-scale religious ceremonies like kirtan singing are held. On the floor is a bed made of carpet and blankets for the guru's chief disciple, no one else has the right to sleep in this room. As Sumati attempts to examine his toe once again, Krishnapadananda sits up. 'Have you been able to recognize me, Sumati?' he asks her.

'What happened to the twisted toe?'

'It straightened with constant wearing of wooden thongs.'

'Why have the face and eyes changed?'

'Ten years I've lived as a sanyasi. You don't know how hard the asceticism is, it can completely change one's appearance.'

Sumati presses her face to his feet. 'You're lying to me.'

'I've not lied, Sumati.'

Of the large oil lamps on the guru's altar, one has gone out and the other is flickering. In its restless light neither is able to see the other's face for long. Krishnapada says again: 'I spoke one lie in the beginning. At the time of my initiation into ascetic life, I said I was a brahmachari, never touched a woman in my life. To this day that lie is ruining all my ascetic efforts, Sumati. That's why I've come to take you.'

'If I'm your wife, then why aren't you taking me openly? Why do you want to create a scandal linking you and me?'

Krishnapadananda puts out the wick burning in the oilless lamp. In a very gentle voice he says, 'I've no life prior to my ascetic life. I can't be sullied by anything. You too have to forget all about what'll happen to you in society, what people will say, and leave with me, Sumati.'

Moving closer now, Sumati lays her head on his chest. With her arms around his neck, as if seeking shelter from her husband, she says, 'I'll go with you. But you're not my husband.'

'I am your husband, Sumati. Only ten years have passed, and you can't recognize your own husband, Sumati?'

'Why couldn't your parents? I've known you for only a short time, but mother has brought you up from the time you were born. After all this time, I've finally understood everything.'

'What have you understood?'

Grasping Krishnapadananda's headful of hair, Sumati speaks so softly that he has difficulty hearing her even from this close. 'When we visited the ashram during the puja, you were constantly looking at me. Among all those disciples, you made nice arrangements for our stay. Today you've come to take me. Were you then afraid that I won't go with you just like that? Is that why you've come in the guise of my husband? Well, why don't you take me where you want to? You're an ascetic of such a high order, yet you haven't been able to forget me in all this time after you saw me—after resisting for so long you've come to take me. I'll go out with you the moment you ask me to—I'll look upon you as higher than my husband, I'll love you more than I love my husband.'

In a disappointed voice, Krishnapadananda says, 'But I'm really your husband, Sumati.'

Beyond herself with agitation, Sumati says, 'Why are you so afraid? Why do you think I'll love you any less because you aren't my husband? I've forgotten my husband. It's you I love.'

Even in the darkness it can be sensed that Krishnapadananda's voice has grown lighter now.

'That's the truth, Sumati. You haven't even seen your husband for ten or eleven years, it's not surprising that you forgot him. Yet why with me, of all people, did you fall in love?'

'I don't know. As soon as I saw you, I sort of . . . ' Sumati stops short. She feels as if Krishnapadananda is grinning to himself in the dark. Lighting one of the many lamps on the altar, she sees that indeed there's an inscrutable smirk on his face. For a moment it seems to Sumati that she has seen this smile before on the face of someone wanting to leave, the scornful smile seeing which she had burst into tears one night long ago.

'Well, go back now and sleep, Sumati.'

'Aren't we leaving?'

'Of course I'm leaving. I'll leave tomorrow morning.'

'In the morning? How can I leave in the morning in front of everyone?'

'You will not leave. I will.'

Sumati sits in stunned silence. After a long time, she says in a broken voice, 'All right, I accept you as none other than my husband. I'm the one who has made a mistake.'

With a calm ferocity, Krishnapadananda replies, 'Accepting is not enough, Sumati, it has to be believed. Making a mistake will not do, mistakes have to be shattered first.'

Krishnapadanada was expected to stay here for three days. Everyone becomes concerned when, in the morning, he expresses his desire to take leave right away.

Nagen asks him for what fault of theirs his lordship is abandoning them.

'No fault of anyone; the call has come for me to leave home,' Krishnapadananda replies.

In tears, Gopal's mother begs of him, 'Aren't you going to do something, Father, to help that unfortunate woman?'

'I have solved her problem, mother,' says Krishnapadananda in a calm voice, 'I've made her forget her husband.'

Serpent-like[*]

By the time the end of the plain is visible, it is four o'clock in the afternoon.

Ananta stops the palanquin before it enters the village. He gets off for a look and stands facing the vast plain. The path that they have covered can be seen upto quite a distance. The lonely banyan they left behind a long time ago looks even more sad and mystery-shrouded from this distance. Beyond it the end of the earth has merged with the horizon! As if that horizon has simply followed them, leaving behind it the little railway station where he got off at ten in the morning. To the right and to the left are rows of trees in a half circle, the width of the plain on the two sides not more than three or four miles. Not very far from where he stands, the water of a large pond can be seen glistening. Right beside it is some farmer's makeshift dry leaf shed, where he stays day and night guarding his barely one acre of cultivated land.

Sheltering his eyes with his palm, Ananta looks around. Who would have thought that Ketaki would write to him to drag him to a village as inaccessible as this!

But the litter bearers don't stop even at this remote village. Eliciting looks of surprise from the villagers and barked greetings from a few animals of the canine family, the litter leaves the village behind and picks up a jungle-covered dirt track. It stops after another half a mile.

The litter bearers were sent by Ketaki; so there can't be a mistake. Before him stands a house that is presumably Ketaki's most recent home.

But it's hard to describe it as a house. It has all the appearance of an archaeological site. It's an old-style three-wing house, almost all of which has nearly crumbled except for about four rooms in a row. Part of a broken wall stands here, a bit of a roof and its skeleton of beams hangs there, and the wall that once guarded the privacy of this house has disappeared without a trace. Only piles of brick rubble and jungles of weed lie all around. The portico at the entrance is in a dangerous condition, just about managing to stay up. Near the portico, a huge peepul tree, casting an

---

[*] The Bengali title is *Sarpil*.

expansive shadow, has made the abnormal quietness of the place twice as intense. A temple stands nearby.

At first sight, the temple does not seem that old, but a closer look reveals the truth. It becomes clear that the abode for the deity is not younger in age than the mansion for people that has almost become rubble today. But somehow the wear of age has not appeared on it, not one brick has fallen off. It is as if time only touched the temple for fear of the deity, did not strike it. The temple steps are broken. But that's not the work of time. How many footfalls those steps have taken over how long a period of time must be beyond calculation. Yet people can to this day use them to go near the deity; and this is what is surprising.

Ananta is not aware of Ketaki's coming and standing near him while he is absorbed watching the temple. He gives a slight start when Ketaki says, 'You've come after three years . . . .'

Seeing him startled, she pauses, smiling, before finishing her sentence, '. . . and you're standing outside looking at the temple!'

He smiles too. 'I was angry at not finding you waiting at the portico to welcome me.'

She says, 'I'd have stood and waited, but I didn't know you'd arrive so early. Usually it takes close to evening to get here.'

'Bribed with fine food, the litter bearers grew wings. Why did you send so much food?'

'It's all right that you gave much of it away, but did you have enough to eat yourself?'

'Yes I did. And while eating I was amazed how you could have remembered all that I like to eat. You didn't forget even the lime cordial.'

The sun was on Ketaki's face from a side; turning slightly and smiling at him softly she remarks, 'As if lifetimes have passed and one should naturally forget! Do you think people lose their memory in three years? Why aren't you surprised wondering how I recognized you?'

This was exactly the way Ketaki used to smile, and the manner in which she used to talk. Everything she said sounded witty, each one of her expressions was like a brief, self-contained poem.

Yet there is change in her. So much change that he barely avoided making his first remark on that very subject. That would have sounded awfully childish, like asking a mere polite question about well-being in a slightly novel way. And would Ketaki have liked having to explain her transformation in the midst of the many little questions and answers due at the start of a meeting after three years?

To really ask her about well-being is, however, something one also fears to do. With her complexion dulled, her health and body structure ruined, what has her appearance been reduced to? No more loveliness in the face, no more light in the eyes. Even though she has just had a bath at this unusual hour, instead of just a wash-up.

'Why, you've taken a bath, Ketaki. Are you going to worship in the temple?'

'Me, worship in that temple?' Ketaki seems astounded.

'No worship is done in the temple?'

'Yes. He does it.'

Now it's Ananta's turn to be astounded. Shankar worships in a temple! That fashionable atheist, Shankar! Which deity has he developed an allegiance to all of a sudden?

'Which deity's temple is it, Ketaki?'

Ketaki shakes her head, 'It isn't a god's temple. There's no god here.'

'If there's no image in there, what does Shankar worship?' Ananta asks in surprise.

'He worships an evil planet,' Ketaki says turning pale, 'the planet that rules harm. Forget about him.'

That's difficult to do. It's not possible to forget such a major statement about her husband. Ananta says, 'Can you explain to me this thing about an evil planet of harm?'

Her eyes glisten with tears. 'What can I explain? A generations-old insanity has now taken hold of him. From the moment of our coming here, he has turned an incredibly fanatic devotee of Kali. There's an image of Kali inside, but it isn't the Mother Kali he worships, only his own madness.'

After thinking a little, Ananta says to her, 'Come, I'll pay my homage to Mother Kali.'

Ketaki fearfully says, 'No.'

'Why not?'

Ketaki's face has gone pale. Swallowing hard, she says, 'It'll give you a fright. Can't even be recognized as Mother Kali. Seems like congealed darkness holding up the falchion. The eyes flash like diamonds. Even in daytime little light gets into the temple—a lamp has to be lit to see anything. And then two other lamps ignite at once, the image's two eyes. The first time I went in alone, I fainted at the sight.'

Ketaki shudders. And from just this her present physical and mental condition becomes completely clear to Ananta. But he says nothing at all. Silently he watches her controlling herself. 'Let's go into the house,' she says.

'Let's go . . . . In the letter you didn't mention any of this, Ketaki. I'm caught unprepared at each step.'

'Are these things of the kind one can mention in a letter?'

'No, they're not.' Ananta falls silent. 'These things'are matters of which he has figured out very little so far. Writing even this much is indeed impossible for Ketaki. Can a picture of this house come across in a letter! Words to convey the image of this pallid, thin and drawn face do not exist even in Ketaki's oral articulateness, let alone in the language of letters.

Coming under the portico, she says with a smile, 'Why are you looking up like that? Nothing to be afraid of when I'm with you.'

'Can't bricks come off and fall on the head of someone you're with?'

'It would seem they can't. I've been walking under it for three years and not even a bit of mortar has come off and fallen on my head. The dangers of this house avoid me, you know?'

Ananta suddenly stops there. 'Then let me ask you something standing right here. Why did the two of you need to come to this ruined shrine to make your nest?'

'How can one find peace except in the ruined shrine of generations of ancestors?'

Anxiously Ananta says, 'Whose need was it, this terrible peace? Yours or Shankar's?'

'His. A wife's peace is with her husband's peace.'

God knows the truth or falsity of this statement from her; Ananta silently resumes his walk. A narrow path twists around the piles of bricks to the rooms—a path that has perhaps come into existence just from the tread of Ketaki's and Shankar's feet.

Ananta keeps wondering—he had no idea there had been a dearth of peace in Shankar's life. It's true that many surprising changes appeared in him some time before his sudden decision to give up living in the city and go to his estate, but there was no consistent reason to infer that the cause was a lack of peace. The gravity that came over him seemed calm enough, the growing aversion he showed towards any of life's lighter enjoyments and festivities seemed calm. It seemed as if he had learned to think, to contemplate, as if he was gradually getting in touch with the inner being everyone has. It happens in the lives of many. There are certain eternal mysteries of existence and selfhood which not everyone is ordinarily aware of. All of a sudden one day, on some trivial occasion, they begin to worry deeply and move one. It would seem as if something like that had happened in Shankar's life! In fact, Ananta could also guess to some extent the occasion that might have been instrumental in his case!

But no one could have imagined it was an external manifestation of Shankar's inner disquiet. Yet today it seems beyond doubt that he had been spending his days in a terrible disquiet. Can a human being survive here? How could he, without a terrible reason, have wished to come here and make it his home! Not that long ago he spent a lot of money to buy a picture-perfect house surrounded by gardens. He left nothing lacking in the arrangements for comfort and luxury. He had all the pleasure and convenience of living in a city, he had the company of educated, sophisticated men and women, he spent evenings sweet with laughter and music. And he had Ketaki's love. The love of not this haggard, frightened Ketaki, but a smiling, graceful Ketaki as a young wife.

It could not be for no reason that, leaving that life behind, Shankar has sought the peace of the grave here. Even the desire to have the weeds cleared, the piles of bricks removed, and the few still standing rooms repaired is not in him! Running away from the most modern environment, he has buried his face in the glory of a crumbled century.

The scene Shankar created the last time Ananta saw him was something that did seem insane; but how minor that insanity was compared to this! 'Do you remember that night, Ketaki?'

'Which night?'

'Shankar wasn't well, and we stayed up sitting on the two sides of his bed?'

'How can I not remember it? That illness never left him. After tossing about for two months he came running out here like a lunatic . . . . You were going to leave for Japan the next day.'

Anxiously Ananta says, 'Yes. When Shankar fell asleep, you came out to the gate to see me off. You asked me not to write you any letter, giving all sorts of strange reasons, I still remember that clearly, Ketaki . . . . Did Shankar sleep the rest of that night?'

Ketaki shakes her head. 'No. When I went back, I found him sitting up in bed and rubbing ice on his forehead.'

Though walking very slowly, they have come near the room. In a lowered voice, Ananta says, 'To this day I don't quite understand, Ketaki, what suddenly happened to him that day.'

'An earthquake inside his brain,' answers Ketaki.

Standing by the doorway, Ananta looks in as if trying to get his eyes accustomed to the scene inside. Poverty has been carefully installed in the room. Every item seems to have a role it is playing—that of giving an impression of poverty. The bed on the wooden cot is made in the fashion of an ascetic's blanket bed. It looks like a thick shawl, and is perhaps quite soft. At the centre of the room is a small cane couch. Spread on the floor is a faded, torn rug, which perhaps Shankar himself once bought expensively for three or four hundred rupees. Against the northern wall stands a broken-door almirah packed with books.

With coarse homespun wrapped around his upper body, Shankar himself sits straight-backed on a small rug at one end of the room, reading a book. His hair is cropped short, but for a thick tuft left at the back of his head, and on his forehead is a dab of red sandalwood paste.

'Who, Ananta?' He seems terribly surprised. Noisily closing the book, he says, 'I was not expecting you. Tara! Tara! So many strange things happen in your creation!'

What a welcome! Ananta is at a loss for words.

Ketaki says, 'I wrote to him asking him to come.'

'That's nice, but you didn't seem to consider it necessary to let me know in time.'

Looking at the incredibly sullen face of her husband, Ketaki breaks into a smile, and says, 'No. If I let you know in time, you'd have asked him not to come.'

A curious smile reveals itself on Shankar's face. 'Tara! Tara! How they all misunderstand your child, Mother! Ketaki, I'd not have asked him not to come. I'd have extended my invitation too, and made appropriate arrangements to welcome him. He may be your childhood friend, but can't people become friends when older? Come Ananta, leave the shoes outside, come in and sit.'

Taking his shoes off, Ananta goes in and sits in the cane couch. Without responding to her husband's remark, Ketaki asks him, 'Will you have a bath?'

Ananta says, 'No.'

'There's some water out in the veranda, wash your hands and face. I'll bring some tea.'

Ketaki goes out. Yawning, Shankar says, 'Don't be concerned, Ananta, to hear her say that she'll bring just some tea. You'll get everything with it. All the food items that are forbidden for Hindus.'

Ananta smiles and says, 'What a thing to say, Shankar!'

'What did I say that's wrong! Is she a Hindu woman? She can do all the forbidden things. After serving you refreshments, she'll definitely sing for you, you'll see. Is there anything she can't do?'

Ananta is amazed. Quietly he asks, 'Don't you like her singing any more, Shankar?'

In a sharp voice Shankar says, 'Like it? I'm humiliated by it! Twenty-five years ago if a daughter-in-law of this house sang that sort of a song, do you know what'd be done? She'd be throttled to make her stop singing and sent back to her parents' place for good. A young wife of this house to sing love songs!'

Absolutely surprised, Ananta says, 'She sings love songs? Here?'

Absently opening the book, Shankar turns some pages with a trembling hand, and continues, 'When she starts her singing, Ananta, angry faces appear on the walls of this room. All those faces I know. My father's face appears over there,' he points a finger to an indefinite part of the north wall and goes on, 'They've such reproach in their eyes, Ananta, that after seeing it my head hangs in shame. Moving their white lips they say to me in whispers: You're a stain on this family! A stain on the family!'

Ananta runs his eyes over each wall. Is there anything at all to see on the walls? In the vague, strange marks that have appeared as a result of putting a coat of whitewash on the mildew-stained surfaces, it's not possible to discover any resemblance to human faces.

Still, one is inclined to believe Shankar's crazy description. Who can tell! He heard from Shankar himself his ancestors' history. They didn't have the remotest knowledge of what is called contentment of the soul! If awakened feeling insulted by Ketaki's singing, their frowning faces might stare out of the wall of any room, it's most likely to be out of the wall of this room.

Shankar has been studying Ananta with a fixed gaze; suddenly changing his tone he says, 'Don't tell her I told you this, my friend, she'll be scared. She scares easily.'

'I know that.'

'You know what she does? At night she gets up to look at me from the window. As if just knowing that I'm alive makes her feel less scared.'

Ananta asks in alarm, 'Does she stay alone at night?'

'Of course she does. She has a separate mahal.'

Not getting it, Ananta asks, 'What's a mahal?'

Shankar is amazed. ' . . . You don't know what a mahal is! Well . . . let me explain. No man in this Chaudhuri family, my friend, ever slept snuggling in his wife's sari. That kind of beggarliness doesn't run in this family's blood. A wife of this family would always spend her nights in her own mahal with the lamp lighted . . . if the husband felt like it, he favoured her with a visit, if he didn't feel like it, he didn't go.'

Ananta severely remarks, 'It's not a custom in this family to love one's wife, is it?'

'No, it's not,' Shankar smiles. 'We conquer women, we don't get into the business of exchanging hearts with them. Do you know that one of the ancestors was a king? Why does one get born in a royal family if one can't reign in one's own heart?'

Ketaki, back with towel and soap, has been standing near the door. Neither has noticed her. Shankar seems a bit disheartened when he does.

She asks mildly, 'May I know what revenue you collect from the kingdom of your heart at the end of the year?'

In a subdued voice Shankar says, 'Have you been listening to all that I said?'

'No, I haven't heard all of it. The little I have heard is enough. I just want you to know something: women do not fight for claim to a kingdom that has nothing but arid sand.'

She smirks to herself while saying this. It no longer remains a secret to Ananta that she derives satisfaction from speaking harshly to Shankar. This is as painful as if it were her own degradation. It was always beyond Ketaki's capability to hit even an enemy; today she can smirk after hitting her own husband.

Ananta silently suppresses a sigh!

She addresses Ananta, 'The towel and soap are by the bucket. Come, wash your hands and face. Give me your suitcase key, I'll get you a change of clothes.'

When she leaves with the key, the ten fingers of Shankar's two hands clasp each other very hard. 'Did you see that, Ananta!' he says in disappointment. 'She rolled her eyes at me and walked away, I couldn't shut her up. Did you see that!'

Ananta keeps silent.

'Took in silence the wife's rude talk. Tara! Tara! What disgrace you wrote for me, Mother!'

The dusk falls amidst a strange silence. For a long time Ketaki stands at the eastern window holding its bars, not moving, not talking. There's probably another village closer to the one through which he came here, the barking of dogs can be heard faintly. He didn't notice when the cool breeze blowing earlier in the afternoon suddenly dropped entirely. Only his disorganized, improbable thoughts keep whirling within him! The condition to which his two friends have been reduced over a period of three years seems almost too difficult to comprehend in a few hours.

Ananta has noticed the plague in Ketaki's hair. What fiery burning could be going on inside her head! How heated the top must be to make so much of her hair fall off! At one point he has an anguished desire to feel it with his hand on her head. In her adolescence, Ketaki once paid him respects by touching her forehead to his feet. That was long ago. Why she did it he can't recall today, perhaps for no particular reason. What he recalls clearly is that he forgot to bless her at the time. When taking leave this time, if Ketaki does offer pranam, even if it is for no particular reason, he'll bless her with a hand placed on her head.

But what will he say to her in blessing? What way is left open today for this woman's well-being? Will not any blessing, uttered even in his mind, seem today as utterly sarcastic?

He hears Ketaki talking as if to herself. 'The sun is barely down and the eastern sky has already turned so cloudy, look at that! Perhaps a storm will come tonight, a hard one, with those smoky dark huge clouds.'

'Why do you say a storm will come? Can't it be that it'll only rain!'

Turning her face to him, she smiles and says, 'It certainly can be, but I've a feeling it'll be a storm. Besides, have you noticed how still the air has become? I'm sweating.'

She pricks up her ears, listens, and says, 'Who is talking outside?'

'Let me look . . . .'

Going outside, Ananta sees Shankar standing in the veranda. Two men of the peasant class stand below with folded hands. One of them has a rope around the neck of a chubby male goat.

Seeing him come out, Shankar says, 'Ananta, tonight the Mother will receive a sacrifice. The rule is to sacrifice a pair, but I'd completely forgotten about it the whole day; after sending a man at a late hour, I could get hold of no more than one. I'll worship through the night.'

'Worship Kali?'

Shankar smiles calmly. 'You people know the dear goddess as Kali, we call her Shakti, in the restraint of whose power of annihilation continues the existence of creation. Who holds all the poison in one breast, and nurtures the universe with the nectar from the other breast.'

'Except that he-goat.'

With the look of a man of profound knowledge, Shankar replies, 'You don't know what destruction is, Ananta, you don't understand anything about the real nature of death. Is anything ever lost from the Mother's store? Not even the insect you unknowingly squash underfoot. The goat will be sacrificed tonight, but won't the Mother of mine nurture him tomorrow?'

With this Shankar gets down from the veranda and scratches the neck of the goat affectionately. Wordlessly watching him for some time, Ananta asks, 'But can Kali-puja be held on the eleventh of a lunar fortnight?'

'You, Anglos, how can there be a right and a wrong lunar date when it comes to worshipping the Mother?' Shankar says this without even turning to look at his face.

Responding briefly with 'You've a point there,' Ananta returns to Ketaki's room and asks her, 'Ketaki, has Shankar gone out of his mind?'

She hasn't left the window. At this direct question, she turns around in visible agitation. 'That I don't know,' she says. 'I think the disorder was there in his blood, it suddenly surfaced one day. I gave a party before coming here. Calling me aside, saying "I want to talk to you," he took me inside the cell on the first floor and latched its door from the outside. That was my first punishment. Since then I've not cried . . . but on that day I cried, and thought how far Japan was.'

Ananta gently says, 'Sit down, Ketaki, sit down and tell me.'

Ketaki sits down and says, 'You were gone then, but listen to this. The history of the last two months. After every two or three nights he'd wake up terrified from his nightmare. Trembling, he'd say, "Ketaki, get up quick, turn the light on, I'm bathed in blood." I'd find his whole body soaked in sweat. Talking about the nightmare, he'd shiver again and again. A huge sky-touching image of Kali, enormous tongue lolling over the chest, blood dripping, streaming from the two corners of the mouth—in his dream he was sacrificing a human being at the feet of this!'

Ketaki moves to the window as tears come to her eyes. Looking outside with those eyes, she says, 'And then he brought me here to be stranded and live all alone. He doesn't allow even a maid to stay with me; some nights I'm really so scared! . . . the way the clouds are growing, who knows how hard it's going to rain and storm tonight.'

'There's nothing to worry about a rainstorm!'

'Do you know that a storm of Ashwin can be worse than the kalbaisakhi of summer?' Quite clearly, the thought of the coming storm is disturbing her a great deal.

He casually says, 'It can surely be. But is no evening lamp lit in your home? It's dark!'

'Who'll light the evening lamp? Me? There's no need to embarrass evening with that!' Ketaki smiles as she makes this remark. 'The servant is going to bring a lighted lantern.'

The servant was perhaps busy with just that; presently he brings a lantern into the room. The transformation that occurs at once defies all description. The moment the room is lighted, the darkness outside deepens and totally conceals the ruins within itself. It seems to Ananta as if at the end of a terrible nightmare he has woken up in the very same room Ketaki was in three years ago; as if around this room there are no piles of rubble, no jungles of weeds, only a flower garden and beyond the garden the city's peopled, lighted roads.

From the next room come the sounds of pots, pans and plates being moved. After some time the cook and the servant together appear at the door.

'We're going now, Ma'am.'

'Have you kept all the food well covered?' Ketaki asks them. 'Oh yes, wait a little,' she adds.

Looking at Ananta, she says, 'You have the meal now and go with them. They'll arrange for you to sleep in the office that's in the village.'

'Why, is there no room here to sleep in?' Ananta asks in surprise.

'There is. But you'd better go. What misfortune could occasion your spending a night in this crumbling house?'

Even as he notices her ashen face, Ananta smiles and says, 'These poor fellow are waiting, looking really anxious. They're afraid. Let them go, Ketaki, if you don't need them anymore.'

'You're not going?'

'I will if you will. Will you?'

Ketaki sighs and says to them, 'All right, you may go.'

Seeing the way they exit the moment they're given permission, Ananta can't stop himself from laughing. Ketaki sadly says, 'You're laughing. God only knows what's going on in me. So overcast and dreadfully still it is all around.'

Ananta stops laughing. He shouldn't have laughed.

Without the sound of drum and gong, without the bustle of devotees, it's a silent worship of the priest all by himself. The sulky, stuffy weather has intensified with the night. The clouds have turned a world of stars into a full-fledged new moon night. It seems as if there's no sound, no throb of life, as if the whole universe, like the devotee meditating before the still image of stone, is in a trance waiting for the release of a fearsome, restrained force.

Some nocturnal bird or other gives an occasional call, two chameleons in the banyan tree take turns to screech horribly, the pigeons that have taken shelter in the small rectangular niches inside the temple walls flap their wings, something wades sloshing through the nearly dry, weedy pond at the back of the temple. A large beetle droning in circles around the goddess knocks its head a few times against the wall on one side and hits the floor. But the stillness is intensified, not lightened, by these varied occasional sounds and the tireless sound of crickets.

Ananta is stunned to see Shankar's face. He is sitting beside the goddess to his right, the hint of a smile on his lips, the gaze in his half-closed eyes fixed. The severity on his wide forehead is that of an arid plain. The sacrifice is over—before the image is placed an offering of a severed goat head and a drink of blood in a container. The eyes of the image glow like fire, but She hasn't drunk even one drop of the blood. It's only on Shankar's forehead that there is a thick mark of blood.

Feeling the tug at his sleeve, Ananta regains his awareness. He looks and sees Ketaki trembling. 'Come away, I'm sacred,' she says in a hushed voice.

Her words reach Shankar. 'You scared, Ketaki?' he says. 'Pray to Mother for courage.'

Again, pulling at Ananta, Ketaki says, 'Come away.'

Shankar says, 'Ketaki, go after you've paid your respects to Mother. Come let me put some of the vermilion from Mother's head on your head. With Mother's mercy, you'll forget all that's bad. This Mother of mine forgives everyone—everyone.'

It's like tormenting someone even more helpless than a baby goat by means more cruel than slaughtering. Ketaki was about to kneel and bow, with the anchal of her sari ritually wound ropelike around the back of her neck. Ananta grasps her hand and says, 'Pay your respects in your mind, Ketaki. The Mother is pleased with mental pranam alone. Let's go now.'

Picking up the lantern and holding Ketaki's hand, Ananta cautiously climbs down the dilapidated steps. A thick, black snake about three to four cubits long lies stretched out under the portico; with the light in its eyes, it raises its hooded head half a cubit and holds it fanned out, ready to strike. The two of them stop and stand still. Ketaki whispers, 'Don't move. Don't move the lamp either. It'll come speeding at you and strike.'

Ananta doesn't move himself or the lamp, but says in a low voice, 'Was it in fear of this gentleman that you were glancing about nervously? I thought your fright wasn't gone even after coming out of the temple. How long does one need to remain a statue before he'll allow passage?'

'A minute or two.'

'I see you've experience . . . . Have dangers of this kind also roamed in the house and avoided striking you for all three years?'

'As danger, snakes are nothing!' Ketaki smiles faintly.

Proof appears at once that snakes pose no danger. Within two cubits of Ketaki, another snake as thick as the other moves at leisure towards its mate under the portico. 'His wife. She's very peaceful.'

'I can see that. Even the king of death Yama is very peaceful here.' Slithering over her husband's body, the peaceful snake-wife enters a pile of bricks. Lowering his hood, the husband follows her. But the poor creature is not fated to be reunited with his wife. Before it has reached the pile of rubble, Ananta picks up a whole brick, steps forward, aims at its head, and throws hard.

With a shudder, Ketaki breaks into a muffled cry, 'What have you done?' Ananta has no time to talk now. The brick having broken its spine just under the hood, the snake keeps writhing and turning, so Ananta keeps picking up brick after brick and throwing them at it. Its hood is smashed, its bloodied body is twisted like a rope and does not move any more, only the tip of its tail waves this way and that.

Brushing the dust off his hand, Ananta says, 'That's done. Now the peaceful wife is left.'

In a choking voice Ketaki says to him, 'Why did you kill it?'

'Snakes have to be killed, Ketaki. If one is to live, this too is an unavoidable duty like repairing a dilapidated house.'

'That doesn't mean one should attempt to kill such a large snake with a brick! Had it not been hit? In a wink then . . . 'she shudders.

Ananta smiles and says, 'As the snake is dead, the question of had it not been hit doesn't arise. But your first response—What have you done?—it wasn't prompted by thought of the danger to me, was it?'

'He has forbidden it. A servant once killed a baby snake this little; he flayed the skin off his back with lashings. To this day perhaps there are marks on the poor fellow's back. In his opinion the Dakini-Jogini spirits that constantly attend Mother Kali are staying as snakes in this house—killing them is a grave sin, it causes harm and brings destruction.'

Calmly Ananta says, 'I guessed it was something like that. That's precisely why I killed it.'

Ketaki's face is drained of colour. Faintly she says, 'That's why you killed it? But you said it's only because snakes should be killed . . . .'

'Snakes should be killed, but I don't kill snakes by throwing bricks at them, Ketaki. I look for a stick. If meanwhile the snake escapes, I don't feel at all sorry about that.'

'Then? Why did you act this way now? What's it that you've understood?'

The circumference of the lantern's light is tiny indeed, a tiny, helpless glow of love surrounded from all sides by the hatred of dense darkness. Ananta keeps silent for a while, then he says slowly, 'I haven't understood anything, Ketaki. Is it possible to understand why Shankar fell so crazily in love with this ruin! He's not one to have a drop of affection for rubble and snakes!'

She suddenly smiles. 'No, he's not one to have that. He wants to live long.'

Ananta says, 'I know that. That's why I smelt carbolic acid in his room. That's why he stays in the temple worshipping through the night when he senses the approach of a storm.'

She changes the topic. 'Come and eat. Give me the light, I'll go ahead.'

Ananta hands her the light, but proceeds to walk ahead of her. 'If the snake's peaceful wife wants to avenge her husband's killing, she should have it on me, Ketaki. I pray to god . . . .'

'Why must you say such awful things? Go back tomorrow without any trouble, my dear.'

The storm rises in the last part of the night.

The truth of what Ketaki said, that a storm of Ashwin can be more fierce than summer's kalbaisakhi, is proved within five minutes of its start. Ananta had set out on the journey before dawn, his whole day had been spent in the train and in the litter. It was close to midnight when he came to bed. Sleep isn't at all willing to leave his eyes, even as sleeping seems impossible amidst this dance of destruction. In his enfeebled awareness mixed with sleep, nothing quite registers, only a sort of terror sits heavily on his chest. As if a terrible danger is closing in from all sides, and yet one is in such a numb, helpless condition that one can't even lift a finger to stop it.

Something will happen . . . it's about to happen! It is as if an unknown enemy's delayed revenge is closing in to strike from some uncertain direction. The breath of his hate can be smelled in the smell of wetted dry earth, the sound of his thousand angry knocks can be heard against the walls.

Suddenly, from a mighty blow, Ananta becomes fully conscious. For some time it seems to him as if someone has indeed punched his chest hard with a hard-clenched fist, and not one rib is left in one piece. For some time he loses the ability to inhale—with his mouth gaping, he pants feebly. Taking in air makes the ribs ache. He begins to moan in a muffled voice.

But he knows he can't keep lying like this for long. Groping in bed for the matchbox, he finds that the bed is filled with dust and gravel and next to him lies a large rectangular tile with a chunk of mortar attached.

Forgetting the pain in his chest, he sits up with a start. Now he realizes that the wail of agony that's going on in all the walls is not just the wind moaning—mixed with it is the sound of each of the bricks straining eagerly to break free.

After finding the matchbox, he lights a matchstick with trembling hands. Discerning the position of the door, he throws the matchstick away and gets off the wooden cot. Outside the door, the mad wind's play with the drops of rainwater is impossible to describe. The entire mass of darkness is being churned up by that game. Never in his life has Ananta seen a rainstorm like this. His chest has been hurting unbearably after he stood up on his feet; holding on to the wall, he advances with great difficulty. Ketaki's room is one room away—this small distance seems impossible to cross. Ananta grits his teeth and pushes ahead with all his strength.

Finally his hand finds Ketaki's door. Every now and then lightning flashes, and he notices that the door is latched from outside. Seeing the house is about to collapse, Ketaki must have left and taken shelter in the temple. Ananta at first feels relieved. If she were asleep inside, it wouldn't have been easy to wake her up amidst this awful noise all around. Knocking on the door would've been pointless, for the wind has been doing that mightily for a long time. His lungs don't perhaps have enough sound left to reach his own ears. But he would somehow have had to awaken her, it is impossible to stay on here in this storm. Good thing she left on her own to find a shelter.

But Ketaki left without calling him even once? One who was so eager this evening to send him to the village with the cook and the servant?

Ananta unlatches the door. It's flung open on its two hinges by the wind and then slammed shut. The dimmed lantern, in a corner of the room, hasn't been put out by the wind as the door was shut. Ananta sees that covered from head to toe, Ketaki lies in bed, as if asleep without a care, and across her chest lies a massive wooden beam from the ceiling.

It's not hard for him to see that she couldn't have gone to sleep in this manner with the door open from the inside. After a lot of trying and pulling, when she could not open the door latched from the outside, only then had she resigned herself to sleep like this, worrying no more. Going near her, Ananta with both his hands starts to move the beam off her.

The storm has weakened, but not quite stopped even in the morning.

With bloodshot eyes Shankar stares long at the two half-buried bodies. Then he finds a worn, half-torn basket and brings bricks in basketfuls to add to the pile that has already fallen on them. He wants to completely cover the two bodies. Let them sleep forever there in the bed in which they loved each other all night; Shankar has nothing against it. But no one must know.

How long does it take for earthly bodies to return to earth? Late in the afternoon, unable to pick up the last basketful of bricks, Shankar sits on the ground pondering this. Soaked in rain, he shivers, his bones and teeth knock inside him, and the wind growls about him from time to time.

The Accidental Death of Shipra[*]

This time, in the thirty-sixth year of the century, during the autumn vacation in honour of the annual grand worship of Durga, all three of them—Parashar, Shipra and Anindita—have converged at a village called Kokanad beside the river Padma. There is nothing special in Anindita's reason for coming to the village. For several years now her family and near relatives have been staying at their village home. Shipra too likes to be with relatives for her school break. Parashar has come in order to manage some extra money from his father. His debts this time have run a bit larger than usual. It's not easy to finance the basic minimum luxuries of two society girls one right after another over a six-month period from Baisakh to Ashwin. In spite of acting with utmost stinginess, he could not get by without borrowing. He broke up with the two girls one after another, two surgeries in the span of six months. The marks of the wounds have, of course, disappeared, but the debt has stayed and within a month grown with the interest. In earlier days Parashar did not worry. Just dropping a letter asking for more money was enough to make Madhu Bose send it, along with a heap of reproach. But now he doesn't want to open his fist easily. Getting old has made him stingy; demand for extra money makes him angry. He openly says he won't give; let his son make the extra money he needs. To change this sort of definite negative into an affirmative, Parashar has to spend a lot of energy and seek his mother's help. He's such a lazy and comfort-loving person that, to him, there's hardly any difference between burning up his energy in such persuasion and burning himself.

The letter from his mother brought him this reply, 'For over a year you've been vegetating in Calcutta without work. You never write home regularly. Your father is very upset with you. If you come for a stay, I can try talking to him about your cash needs. Yours, Ma.'

Realizing therefore that not just his father, but his mother too was very upset with him, Parashar decided to make a trip to the village. His

[*] The Bengali title is *Shiprar Apamrityu.*

fast life thus brakes to a halt and stays still for about a fortnight. And his world becomes occupied with only a motion-deprived, sullen sadness.

The reason for Shipra's coming to Kokanad is an age-old one. She's a city girl who has grown up breathing through the crevices in piles of bricks. Living within a restricted dwelling, with a limited fractional sky visible, among roads lying ahead and roads left behind, in recurrent cycles of duties and recesses! Fifty-two weeks of combining this makes her year, with hardly any difference between one year and another. If she ever takes a trip away, she does it with money saved up from her salary, and she goes, alone or with a few friends, to the hilly area west of the city or to Puri. Hiking up and down the hillside paths she pants, rolling in the seaside sand she bathes, and all the while she abstractedly ponders with a disappointed, dispirited heart about the vacation once again going waste just like her whole life. Then, desperately, one day she takes off to her aunt in Hazaribagh. After gaining a litter colour, aided by the home-cooked rice and curry and picnics in the wilderness, she returns to Calcutta. There, after dozing through the few remaining days of her vacation, when school reopens she continues teaching Bengali four hours a day from the sixth grade down to the first grade.

The inclination to spend some time in the riverine countryside she picked up from Anindita. She is seven or eight years younger than Shipra. But the gap of so many years doesn't seem to exist between them. Women usually don't let this age difference mean what it does in the case of men. After twenty, it takes them ten years to make any progress in age. From twenty they move to thirty-one, no other age is allowed to step in between. In terms of respecting the coordinates of relationship also, they don't usually follow the example of men. Those under the spell of a sense of gravity and glory, those with a high-keyed temper and a strict temperament, even though quite capable of depriving small girls of the pleasure of friendly company, find it mortally painful to maintain beyond a week a screen of reserve with a girl just past seventeen with whom they have to spend an hour each day at school. Who doesn't know that the flowering of youths is all that really counts. The one who just came to flower today is worth no less, more if anything, than the one whose flowering has worn a bit old. Women thrilled with the metaphor of flower are not capable of resisting this cruel truth for more than a week. Hence, you have to describe them as friends, even though Shipra once lived for some time at the house of Anindita's uncle as her teacher, and for an hour four days a week, sat in a chair on a raised platform facing her among thirty other girls seated on benches, teaching her Bengali. Perhaps there's an admixture of some amount of affectionate patronizing on one side and forced respectfulness on the other, but that's something to be found even in the friendship of many who are peers in age.

Anindita excels in verbal command over the language; she talks with an ease quite unobstructed. Her ability to draw pictures with the colours of expressive phrases is far from deficient. Listening to her attentively for sometime, you can follow her mental processes, her feelings and emotions so clearly and accurately that you couldn't understand her better even if the bones on her forehead and ribs were transparent enough to let you observe her brain and heartbeat with bare eyes. Hearing Anindita speak about her village, her lush green and exceedingly lovely village half a mile from a makeshift steamer stop on the erosion-prone bank of an immensely wide river, often led Shipra to wonder, 'My god, people go out ot their way to visit even such places!' That is why this time, not having the money she needed to go to Puri or to the hilly west, and the aunt in Hazaribagh being away in Karachi, Shipra has promptly accepted Anindita's invitation and accompanied her to Kokanad.

Anindita becomes rustic when she comes to the village. Even before getting off the steamboat, she sheds the city shell off her mind, and after getting home she sheds the city dress too. Not that she is relieved doing that; she isn't so rustic as to dislike the city and she doesn't consider her hostel life unpleasant. She likes the city, she loves the village. The foundation of her mind and her heart is all rural. She spent her very active childhood here, swimming in the village canal and ponds, collecting fledglings from treetop nests, pelting from a distance those she had fights with; in the indulging quietness of the mango grove she swept the leaves from under a chosen tree and set up her playthings for her housekeeping game. Even at an age when it was not considered safe for her to be outside the careful protection of relatives, she befriended the boatmen of the Padma and went alone with them in their boats out on the river. All this is history, perhaps never to return again in her life. But on her trips back from the city, being in the midst of her village aunts and girl friends, in the homes of her village uncles and brotherly dadas and her own family, she can still effortlessly reoccupy her old place. She never wages any war against rustic manners and superstitions; and although she occasionally gets herself into a tomboyish thing or two unbecoming of grown girls, she follows almost all the customs. She makes no attempt to reform things—whether inside home or outside. Things are good enough for her the way they are; she doesn't criticize any of them.

Because she transforms so well into the girl next door after coming to her village home, she seems like a stranger to Parashar who comes to his family home to live like an exile. He hasn't cultivated much friendship with her in Calcutta, and he has had no relation with her other than the one from childhood now almost forgotten. The moisture-laden wind blowing from the Padma soothes his body day and night, but he lives in a lonely capsule all his own. He could easily have enjoyed spending a few hours in the company of the Anindita of the city, but here Parashar can't find any companionship in being with the Anindita who, merging in with the colourless men and women of the village, sinks thus into the permanent stillness of this place lagging far behind the times.

If he comes to see her in the morning, she says: 'Wait a little. I'm cooking.'

'What'll you do after the cooking? Sit down to read an article on homemaking?' Parashar walks away with some such remark.

If he comes in the afternoon, Anindita says: 'Wait a little. I'm teaching them how to do their hair—how many different kinds of buns can be made without plaiting the hair first.'

Parashar snaps irritably: 'I see you had no time therefore to do your own hair!'

'That takes no time. Watch this—' Instantly she gathers up her flowing hair into a loose bun. 'Now would you like to sit down?' she asks him.

'I would. At the riverside. Not in your house.'

When finished with the hairdo lesson, Anindita goes to the riverside. Not finding him there, she thinks how spoiled the lad has become from living in Calcutta that lying comes so easily to him.

Next time she sees Parashar, she gives him a little advice. She asks him not to go back to Calcutta. She pleads with him to stay on in the village for some time.

'How many pennies did you earn this year?' she asks.

'Not even one,' Parashar admits proudly.

'Then stay in the village for a year. Your mind will get detoxified. The three or four thousand rupees you spend in Calcutta, just saving that will give you some self-respect, from seeing it as a sort of income. You just keep sinking, Montu, because you hate yourself.'

With irritation in his own tone, Parashar says: 'I told you not to learn Sanskrit precisely because you'd then learn to dispense advice of this sort. The influence of those fellows who live on a diet of raw rice and banana, it just can't go away after all?'

'You don't understand a thing, do you? If you stay, I'll stay too. You can come by every day and quarrel with me for as long as you like. That will make my taking the exams impossible this time. But for the sake of correcting you, I'm willing to make even that sacrifice.'

Anindita's request and advice aren't instances of casual, half-hearted childishness. From the very manner of her talking, it is clear that she has thought a lot on the subject. Her words are punctuated with little smiles. She casually licks at the dash of spicy pickle or seasoned tamarind she has with her, absently rubs with her left index finger the deep scar on the left side of her forehead, or moves the straying gold chain back into the neckline of her blouse. These familiar mannerisms of hers can't lighten the import of what she has just said. The temptation she offers Parashar also remains quite strong in its intent. But he has become so furious that her seduction doesn't take effect. 'Let the marriage take place first,' he replies, 'then I'm willing to spend a year here for the honeymoon. But no way I can be made to court you for a whole year sitting about in the village.'

'You don't understand a thing.'

'If my wits are getting dim, it's only from spending time with you.'

With a mock sigh, Anindita remarks, 'Women of the olden days were the happy ones. They didn't have to risk their whole lives on someone's mere words. The seven seas, the thirteen rivers, and the seven hundred ogres exacted such proof on their behalf as even modern psychology can't manage to do. The young men these days cross the seas only for winning degrees. It's no mere coincidence that we've got holes in our foreheads!'

Anindita's command over the spoken language makes her words touch a soft core in Parashar.

'You got a hole in your forehead from falling off the tree. And I didn't even push you.'

'No,' says Anindita. 'You promptly climbed off the tree and picked me up in your arms. And at that green age of eighteen, you sucked like a veteran ogre the blood from my forehead cut.'

'I thought you were dead and was kissing you.'

'Being with you is bound to make me immortal.'

Forgetting all about his sense of polished superiority, Parashar scolds her in a gnashing low voice, 'If on becoming immortal you perform penance all your life to win me over, and if being mortal I pass through five hundred births in that time, even then you won't get the chance, Ani, to be with me.'

On setting foot in Kokanad Shipra perks up quickly to what's going on between the two of them. All of a sudden, her wits seem to grow extraordinarily sharp. One night she does so much intense thinking that she goes without any sleep.

From the very next day she sets out to create a one-woman version, hers, of city life, right in this meek village called Kokanad. So abruptly does she start her astounding revolt against village life and village customs that the men and women in Anindita's family are startled as are all the other souls, young and old, in the village. There are few villages these days which don't have a shop or two within a circumference of two miles stocking such modernities as Goldflake cigarettes. Villagers these days are not likely to be disconcerted by the sudden appearance of city ways in the heart of village life. They are now used to drawing their water from tubewells and drinking the tea they prepare using that water, and if an aeroplane flies past right overhead, they look up but once and go on with their work of cutting paddy. But no one can understand the kind of citification that springs around Shipra. She seems to have no connection at all with any of the cities that people of flesh and blood construct on earth. She seems like some air-roaming fairy that accidently dropped from the sky in the previous afternoon's heavy rainstorm.

The stock of saris Shipra brought along was plentiful. From the time in the morning when she emerges for her walk, parasol in hand and dressed like a fairy, although she changes her outfit several times, never in the course of the whole day does it quite shed the impression of a fairy's costume. The swing in her walk, the manner of her talking and smiling, of her bathing and eating and resting, all these turn so extraordinary and ethereal that many are assailed by a doubt as to whether her body is made of the regular kind of female flesh and blood. She seems to be bursting with an over-abundance of lively energy, unsure of what to do with it. Within a week of coming to the village she rallies together the few college youths who have come home for their autumn vacation to get their fill of milk and rice. She chats with them, sings for them, dances before them, and flirts with one today and another the next in a way that even those unaccustomed to seeing such things would understand. With the boundless vitality of a delighted seven-year-old girl, she takes to racing them along the village path when Parashar is looking; at home in Parashar's presence she becomes for them skittish like a doe, powerful like a queen, enigmatic like an actress, reserved like a woman deceived, light as a butterfly.

Beside her, Anindita seems dull, like an oil lamp next to an electric bulb. Parashar grows worried looking at Shipra. Her notoriety spreads far and wide. An insignificant school mistress of Calcutta becomes the subject of discussion for some ten neighbouring villages. One evening when returning from her outing, a clod strikes her in the back and crumbles; one or two people even come from a village eight or ten miles away to ogle at her. After remaining timid and meek and respectful of people's opinion all thirty years of her life, Shipra elicits a lot of amazement, curiosity and hilarity as soon as she starts making the effort suddenly one day to create a desirable future for herself. Casting out all fears and worries as if to the ever flowing water, she attempts to get a hold on life with a death bite.

Anindita's father was elsewhere at the time. Anindita's mother, fearful of the goings-on, rebukes her daughter: 'What sort of trouble is this you've brought home, Ani?'

Worried, Anindita says, 'She may be having a nervous breakdown, mother.'

'I don't care if she's having a nervous breakdown or whatever, child, tell her to leave now. It's been ten or twelve days since she came, how can she still be staying so unashamedly in the home of people who are no relations of hers?'

'Let me give her a couple more days.'

But whatever Shipra may have started, she has maintained an amazing kind of control throughout. Her clothes have nothing obscene about them, her congregations are not rowdy or noisy, her flirting is confined to words and smiles. From when she gets up in the morning till the time she goes to bed, she keeps everyone excited, but she herself doesn't get excited. Her speech remains mild in tone and a touch melodious, her smile an unearthly expression of the lips, her walk in the rhythm of a slow dance. She keeps on display a sort of poetic aristocracy, a classy modernity, like an ultimate weapon of self-protection. Among the poorly educated, dimly lit men and women of the village, she has arisen like a source of light, and if they can't appreciate her, it's due to their own narrowness and prejudice and a sign of their own backwardness. Shipra has another ploy besides this. With a lot of thought and craft she has also maintained the impression that she doesn't stir them up, that they stir themselves about her. If there's anything aberrant or improper in all this, the responsibility is theirs, not hers.

Parashar at first watched Shipra from a distance. It was Anindita who introduced him to Shipra, and he held back from growing intimate with her by holding Anindita between them. But Shipra pushes Anindita out, so to speak. It becomes quite impossible for Anindita to stand the way in which Shipra carries on when Parashar's around. No sooner do those confected lines and artificial smiles of Shipra's start to sting her ears and her eyes than she flees, leaving the arena to the two of them. After that it didn't take Parashar longer than three sunsets to turn into a close friend of Shipra's, dying as he was for city life.

As soon as Shipra manages to get Parashar to herself for the morning walk, for relaxed chats in the afternoon's quiet, or for singing songs to in the evening, she gives leave to the youthful bunch. It wasn't possible for those green hearts to take leave of her for ever, nor did she think it wise to give them terminal leave. Shipra knew quite well that she wouldn't be able to keep an ultra-urbanite like Parashar happy if he was left absolutely alone with her all the time. So even though she ends the party for them, the moderate amount of visiting they continue to do meet with her acceptance and approval.

Parashar isn't stupid; he sees through it all. Shipra isn't either; she knows that Parashar sees through all of if. But even though he hides *his* pretence, she doesn't seek recourse to any deception on this point. This puts the mark of a pleasant ingeniousness in her campaign of the heart engineered by complicated processes of the brain. Parashar likes that. In this respect, he's a weak little bohemian. He prefers even a cleverly designed love game to be alloyed with a little naivette and simplicity. His coloured paper flower has to be like a real flower at least in appearance.

Before the two days are over after which Anindita was to ask Shipra to leave as she promised her mother, Shipra pulls in, her self-created city life of her own need, of her own free will. What she continues to let the common outsiders see is, though not exactly laudable, not so scandalous that she could be turned out of their house on that basis. Coming precipitously close to disaster, Shipra thus narrowly escapes it. Anindita can bring herself to attempt little more than cautioning her a bit one day.

'Why are you trying to earn notoriety, Shipra-di?'

'Getting so very old as I am, if I don't earn a little now, I won't get another chance.'

'Couldn't that sort of thing be done in Calcutta!'

It's not nice to overdo anything when staying as a guest in anothers' home—that is what she tried to tell Shipra in this toned-down way. But Shipra isn't willing to understand any such thing now.

'Calcutta is a big city,' she says. 'The competition even for earning notoriety is so stiff there, Ani, that I can't make much headway. Besides, notoriety gained in Calcutta will cost me the job if it reaches the ears of the authorities.'

Anindita, taking offence at her manner of speaking, says, 'Really, Shipra-di, your conduct has greatly deteriorated. Can't you mind your ways for a few days at least after coming to a village?'

Shipra starts humming a song. Then she says, 'After all this time, a touch of spring has come to me; don't be so jealous, Ani. Your golden dream will remain all yours.'

Anindita can't help smiling a little at this remark. 'The day Ani becomes jealous, the rest of the world will be pure loonies compared to Ani. Common sense is more to my liking than trashy sentimentality. This is the age of realism. In this day and age, can a girl get along in life without being practical?'

Shipra continues humming a tune. When in anxiety, Anindita has the peculiar habit of rubbing the scar on her forehead with her finger, and Shipra of humming a tune.

'Your understanding is still unripe, Ani. How can it do for women if there was no romance in the world? In the romantic age, women could afford to be the no-nonsense type, even being hard-boiled and practical could bring them no harm. Now men are forgetting romance, growing cynical and practical. It is the woman who needs to be romantic, sentimental, the whole works. How'll they survive otherwise? With your Sanskrit learning, you've turned into a strange sort, Ani.'

After some thought, Anindita says, 'So you're serious, Shipra-di? Not just killing time?'

Solemnly Shipra replies, 'Where's the time at this point to kill time? At my age could I charm even a young boy without being serious?'

Anindita also remarks solemnly: 'Parashar is three or four years your junior.'

Catching herself at the mistake, Shipra at once sheds her solemnity. Smiling, she says, 'Here you are, the jealousy spilling all over!'

This time Anindita doesn't object to the remark, not even for the sake of argument.

Anindita never lies, not even about herself. At least that's what she believes. In other words, like any ordinary healthy human being, she maintains a lot of misconceptions about herself. One day she engages Parashar, rather mercilessly, in a discussion about Shipra. The mercilessness was called for because the element of humiliation involved in this matter was considerable.

'To this day you've done me a lot of a wrong,' Anindita says, hiding her tears. 'But because you never tried to cover up anything, I still respected you, Montu.'

'From this you ought to know that what I'm doing now is not wrong. If it was wrong, I wouldn't be trying to cover it up before you.'

'Doing wrong? You're committing a sin!'

'You're crazy, this is love. Love is a very pure thing, a divine thing.' Parashar flashes the chosen formal smile of his. 'If you ever fall in love with someone, Ani, then you'll know how high is the level love belongs to!'

'When are you going to Calcutta?' says Anindita in response to this.

'When Shipra's school reopens, we'll go together.'

In desperation, Anindita says, 'Your father's all raging fire. Your mother cries every day.'

'So what? In old age, all husbands and wives have those kind of fits of temper.'

Anindita then realizes that though at first it was from a deeper scheme in his mind that Parashar obliged Shipra, now his mind has taken a different turn. If she made a deliberate attempt earlier to let his design work out, it would have been possible to defeat Shipra's mad campaign, but now she doesn't have even that option. Disobedient as she has been to Parashar all this time, he has turned a blind eye to everything now at the prospect of a melodramatic revenge! Like a scorned suitor of earlier times, he's about to commit nothing short of suicide, in not just words, but also in action.

But too much protest is not good. Anindita holds her tongue.

The white plumes of autumn bloom in the clumps of pampas grass by the river are less abundant this year. Chunks of silvery clouds float about the sky at a slack and slow pace, like the desires of the human heart. The muddiness still left from the rainy season impedes the clarity of reflections in the river and pond waters. Anindita cooks, does her hair, reads books, goes out to visit neighbours. The secret tete-a-tetes remain endless for Parashar and Shipra. Their secret intentions never find expression through their vocal chords, but their secret conversations carry on. Anindita hears that the staging of the play *Raktakarabi* is to be held on the night following the festivity. Until then rehearsing will go on, of the festivity and the staging, of the courtship and the drama.

Anindita still says nothing. Everyone's laments reach her ears. No one seems to find satisfaction without repeatedly telling Anindita that they had not even dreamed of the possibility that Parashar could become so crazy as to marry a shameless schoolteacher older than himself. Anindita responds with a smile, 'So what can I do about that?'

No one has asked her to do anything. But all their minds grumble at the thought of Shipra as the daughter-in-law of the Sen family of Kokanad. They convey their hearts' discontent particularly to Anindita. Her responsibility for bringing Shipra to the village becomes the focus of their collective criticism and complaints and sits on Anindita's shoulder. No one has a bad word for Anindita after the childhood she has had in this village, no one quite blames her. But all their offended and angered protests, unable to reach Shipra and Parashar, keep milling around Anindita. As if their complaints would somehow, with Anindita as the medium, set the guilty pair asunder.

When she happens to find herself before Anindita, Shipra smiles mildly. She looks so lovely that she and her smile seem almost unrecognizable. As if she has removed a layer of dead skin cells from her face, and scrubbed her body with an unknown beautifying cleanser. The improvement in her health in these few days after coming to Kokanad has been extraordinary, the harsh pallor of her complexion has softened, as if from being soaked in warm colour. Even the hair on her head has grown more lustrous as if from a change of coat. The expression of anxious restlessness and tired irritability that Anindita always saw on her face and in her eyes has now disappeared without a trace. Her look has gained depth and a reflective serenity. Only a shade of terror peeps out of her eyes once in a while when she's looking absently in Anindita's direction.

Anindita notices that Shipra has been managing, with the passage of each day, to restrain herself and reintegrate herself towards a total self-surrender to Parashar. The city life she conjured up is slowly vanishing, like a managed illusion, and she is attaining the stability of normalcy by dropping one by one all those excesses she had suddenly introduced into almost every aspect of her daily life. With relentless perseverance, Shipra has gradually made Parashar her possession, by using precisely those age-old and unalterable devices which continue to this day to remain indispensable for even the most modern girl as the means to tie a man down to a permanent relationship. The tighter she pulls and binds him to her, the more she makes herself likable. When words gush from her lips declaring that the people of the world can be happy only when no one will assert authority over another's life, and each person will be able to utilize or waste his or her life according to his or her own wish, then the look in her eyes says that Parashar is excluded from this rule. Keeping out of reach of people's eyes, she lives as a dedicated slave to Parashar out of her obsession with love, just like so many ordinary wives in this very village.

Anindita has heard her say, 'If we don't get along, we will separate of course, not stay with each other by the right of might.' And Anindita hasn't failed to realize that before saying this to Parashar, Shipra worked three days to convince him there'd be no lack of getting along for them in this life. Because, the only reason Shipra has lived a lonely life all these years is that she hadn't come across someone like Parashar, with whom she could, right from the beginning, believe in the prospect of never falling out.

'We'll rent a little flat, Ani, near the Ballygunge area,' she says. 'Every Saturday you'll come from your hostel and stay there with me until Monday.'

'How will your expenses be met?' Anindita asks innocently. 'Montu's father will not give him a paisa unless he lives here in his house.'

Shipra too replies innocently, and with a smile, 'Do you think, Ani my dear, that I'll let Montu drift after the marriage! You haven't understood him at all. He'll take on responsibilities as soon as he's given some. He can easily make three to four hundred rupees a month.'

'Did he use all these temptations on you?'

'Yes he did. But it isn't what you think, Ani. Shipra won't lose out even if all this is merely for the sake of seduction. If I stay here for a month each year, the old man will be happy enough to pay the cost of living in Calcutta for the remaining eleven months. After his son's wife has touched his feet a couple of times, do you think he'll get sleep at night without entrusting her with the key to his safe? You haven't been able to see through Montu's father either, Ani.'

'I haven't been able to see through anyone at all, Shipra-di, not even you,' says Anindita.

Lovingly Shipra places a hand on her shoulder and, looking at her with moist eyes, says in a sweet velvety voice, 'This time you learn from losing, Ani. You'll never make a mistake again. I used to be your teacher, what can be wrong with learning from me?'

Anindita removes the hand from her shoulder and closes its fingers in her fist. A smile on her face, she says: 'I'll pay you a fee, Shipra-di, that is worthy of your effort to educate me.'

'Do it after consulting me,' says Shipra. 'It feels awful to receive similar presents from two parties. Let go, let go of my hand, the ring is cutting in.'

The pressure of Anindita's closed fist makes the ring presented by Parashar produce two round tiny cuts in Shipra's two fingers. A drop or two of blood also appear.

With a slight smile on her lips, Shipra says, 'You're very simple, Ani. And therefore very stupid.'

In a day or two, more evidence comes to show that Shipra is intelligent, even if Anindita isn't exactly stupid. Shipra terminates the rehearsals for *Raktakarabi*. Parashar tries to make her change her mind. She refuses to obey him. He gets angry. She remains unperturbed. She says: 'This sort of childishness is no good.'

Making Shipra a little fearful with the sort of look people have when calculating the extent of risk involved in an undertaking, Parashar says, 'Shipra, I hope you'll not end up becoming like Anindita?'

It's easier to remain Shipra, she assures him.

Anindita comes out on her own in support of this assurance from Shipra. Not to worry, she tells Parashar. What little seems normal in Shipra is artificial, and no genuine reason for him to worry. Shipra simply went out of her mind after coming to Kokanad. Once a lunatic, even if a person sometimes stops behaving like a lunatic out of exhaustion, the lunacy never really goes away. Thus remaining a mad woman all her life, Shipra will keep Parashar's life filled to the brim with variety.

'You sure there's no sarcasm in this remark of yours!' says Parashar a bit fearfully.

'No. Take it as the remark of a true well-wisher.'

Hiding himself, Parashar says, 'Life will settle well then.'

'Yes, like ice. Cold and hard.'

'Even that isn't so bad. With ice you can make icecream, but a rock is always just a rock.'

They both feel depressed for talking like this, in bitter riddles. Forgetting to take Shipra along with him, Parashar leaves for the pond. There he floats on his back with his eyes closed. Informing Shipra of Parashar's departure and destination, Anindita sets up her easel in the vacant lot next to her home and starts painting at this odd hour.

Days go by. The moon in the sky of Kokanad keeps waxing steadily by one-sixteenths. Anindita feels mildly amused at the nightly increment of the moon, because Parashar and Shipra have announced that they will get married on the night before the coming full moon.

Shipra writes a letter to her aunt in Hazaribagh. In it she proposes that her aunt come to Calcutta and, as her guardian, take charge of the wedding ceremony—which would be helpful. The aunt answers that broke as she is now, she doesn't have the finances to rent a house in Calcutta and arrange the wedding ceremony. She can try to do it if Shipra sends her the needed money . . . . Shipra has unhesitatingly shown this letter to Parashar. 'A problem indeed,' Parashar says.

Then Shipra sets about exercising her mind to devise a solution. The essence of the solution she thinks up is that they could have the wedding in Kokanad. And if the wedding is held right in this village, then not holding it at Anindita's house would be particularly insulting to her. Isn't Anindita herself the reason for this wedding? Besides, she's a very special friend to both of them . . . . Both feel uncomfortable realizing that the imagined offer they wish to take her up on should have come from Anindita in the first place, but don't open their mouths to say anything. Although Parashar's parents have in the end given consent, they disapprove of this marriage and remain sullenly indifferent. Even the groom's arrangements are moving at a reluctant, slow peace. Parashar's family and relatives are passively going by a vague idea that the bride has an aunt somewhere on earth who will take care of the ceremonies on the bride's side. In this situation, Parashar doesn't have the courage to ask them to arrange the needful on her side too.

Shipra could take care of this difficulty if she wished to. Two solutions are possible—she could write to the aunt in Hazaribagh about the financial fluency of Madhu Bose and ask her not to worry about the money, which would immediately have sent her off to Calcutta making the arrangements! Besides Shipra has several friends in Calcutta. Writing them letters with a similar account would make them come forward to spend two to four hundred rupees for her wedding, even if it involved raising the money through contributions. But after much thought, Shipra hasn't tried anything at all along these lines. She wants to seem helplessly without recourse to anyone else in Parashar's eyes. Parashar is not just taking her out of love, but he is showing her pity. It's an act of infinite kindness on his part towards a woman without family and wealth. Shipra knows that love adulterated with compassion, like gold mixed with an alloy, is stronger than the pure stuff. Even if in the end, being opposed and wounded from all sides, Parashar wants to deny love, he'd have to concede to this inferior element. For no reason whatsoever can he abandon someone who has no one in the world.

On the ninth of the waxing lunar fortnight, she herself brings up the matter with Anindita. 'Ani, I can't carry the weight of all these responsibilities on myself any more.'

With a change of sari and a towel on her shoulder, Anindita is searching for the case for her glasses. Perhaps distracted by this chore, her words sound rude: 'Carriages and horses have been made available, haven't they?'

Sounding even softer, Shipra says, 'I have a problem, Ani.'

A problem isn't a barrier, not even the start of a disaster. Still Anindita forgets about the spectacle case she was looking for. 'What's the problem, Shipra-di? Had a fight with Parashar?'

Instead of describing the problem, Shipra gives an account, partly diluted and partly made-up, of what she and Parashar have had a talk on. She gives the impression that she herself has nothing at all to say on this matter. She's only the messenger, reaching to Anindita a request from none other than Parashar himself. The inconsistency in the phrasing with the weepy beginning about being unable to carry her own weight indicates so much impudence that Anindita turns grim.

'Let's go to the pond, Shipra-di. We can talk while bathing.'

'Which pond are you going to?'

'The Parashar family pond. We'll take Parashar along too.'

Hearing this makes Shipra's experience-filled heart suddenly forget itself. It seems to her that the unqualified knowledge she has had about every life on earth being self-centred is not completely true. Girls like Anindita can sometimes act contrary to even the harshest of the world's rules.

The pond in Madhu Bose's garden is surrounded by so many fruit trees that the warmth of the sun does not reach the cold water before ten in the morning. When the three of them are on the steps to the water, the sun is still very low in the sky, and in the thick shadow the pond's dark water has the mysteriousness of liquid night. Parashar and Shipra are making some attempts at conversation, but the one with an extraordinary command of speech is wordless today. Not just wordless, the uncomplicated, simple expression on her face is today clouded by an impenetrably pallid darkness. It isn't possible for anyone at all to infer which facial line has become complex and crooked in what way, but looking at her face makes one feel slightly afraid. Because her characteristic articulateness has all this time revealed even the rhythm of her heartbeat, and even her silence has seemed vocally expressive, it now seems quite difficult to understand her.

At the ghat, Anindita says, 'You sit here Parashar. We'll get into the water.'

'But I haven't brought my costume along, Ani,' says Shipra.

'Nor have I,' says Anindita.

'I can't swim in the sari.'

'Who asked you to swim?'

Anindita takes the absolutely reluctant Shipra by hand and practically drags her into the water. The steps just under water are slippery. Shipra tries to stop after reaching chest-high water, but she can't, Anindita's pull takes her to the middle of the pond. Panting, she says, 'Let go of my hand, Ani! Or I'll end up under the water.'

'How long can you stay under water, Shipra-di?' asks Anindita.

Crying, Shipra says, 'Not even a second, Ani, please let go. Just going back to the ghat will kill me.'

Smiling softly, Anindita says, 'What did you then learn from Parashar every morning? When the two of you spent entire mornings in the pond's water!'

Craning her neck over the water, she then yells towards Parashar, 'We're in a competition of swimming underwater, Parashar. You're the umpire. Don't be partial.'

One hand closing around Shipra's neck and the other cutting through the water, Anindita goes under. Even after taking off his shirt and going down to the water's edge, Parashar doesn't jump in. He goes back up, sits down on the cement seat, puts on the shirt, and does the buttons slowly.

Anindita and Shipra have floated up then. When Shipra's desperate, piercing scream calling his name abruptly goes silent under the pond's quiet water, he still isn't done with the last button.

When they float up again, Shipra is speechless. Anindita drags her to the ghat. 'I saved her life with a lot of difficulty, Parashar,' she says. 'She shouldn't have gone that far so soon after learning to swim. Take her up the steps, I can't come out until I manage to find the sari.'

The next day, seeing Shipra off in the steamer, Anindita tells her, 'Honestly, Shipra-di, Parashar didn't realize that you were drowning. Besides, he felt confident, quite unworried because of my being there with you. I'm so good a swimmer that I can make even Parashar drown and die. If he didn't think it necessary to jump in the water, it was simply because I was there.'

Shipra says nothing in response. She has been feeling cold from the damp air of the river. Being new to this riverine place her eyes have become red with water from the pond and from her tears. This is the stage that usually follows a sudden death from accidentally drowning in water.

Aunt Atasi*

Everyone who heard it was full of praise. Yes, definitely something worth listening to, they said. Particularly my Mejo-mama, my second maternal uncle. Rarely had I heard him praise anything with so much enthusiasm.

After hearing this again and again, I grew very curious. How well did he play the flute that everyone admired it so? One day I went to find out. I took a letter of introduction from my uncle.

I lived in Ballygunge and this flutist whose virtuosity I have been talking about lived in the Bhabanipur area. I had heard my uncle refer to him as Jatin. Today I saw the full name, Jatindranath Ray, on the letter of introduction.

When I found the house, I stared in shock. From the sort of ecstatic praise I had heard from my uncle of Jatin-babu and his flute playing, I thought the man must be quite somebody, a Krishna or a Bishnu of sorts. And it is, of course, axiomatic that a Krishna or a Bishnu must dwell, if not in a palace in Mathura or Baikuntha, at least in a good-sized and decent-looking house. But apart from the condition of the lane in which it was located, the house itself, with its exposed decaying bricks, was like an old man with one foot in the grave, a rickety ribcage of ancient bricks! If the outside looked like this, the inside must be quite unimaginable!

I rattled the termite-eaten door's knocker. The man who soon opened the door and stood before me reminded me of the bright red embers suddenly revealed when stirring a dull pile of ash.

He was very thin. And his complexion very pale. Still, it was not hard to imagine what his appearance must have been like at one time. What was still left was truly marvellous.

He looked thirtyish, maybe he was a bit younger. The lacklustre complexion was very fine, the figure great, the expression on the face pleasant. His overall appearance was very attractive. Most wonderful were the eyes; gazing into them seemed to induce an addictive euphoria.

I thought: So men too can have beauty! Seeing this man standing in

* The Bengali title is *Atasi-mami*.

the midst of the saline-stained walls of exposed brick and the termite-eaten door, was like seeing a very beautiful picture carelessly set in an awfully ugly frame.

He said, 'There's no one here but me, so it must be me you want to see. But what is it you wish to see me about?'

It was like a rude blow to my fascinated mind. What an unpleasant, rough voice! The words were nice, but the voice made it sound like an abuse. I thought, not one flawless creation was written in God's horoscope. Such good looks, but what a voice! However great a craftsman we think our progenitor is, he has no sense at all of what fits in where.

I said, 'Your name must be Jatindranath Ray? I am Haren-babu's nephew.'

I gave him the letter of introduction. Reading it in one breath he said, 'Ah! Why a letter of introduction? If Haren is your uncle, I'm your uncle too. He calls me brother. Come in, come in.'

He closed the door after me. From the door, we walked five cubits between narrow walls and came to a three-cubit wide veranda where we turned right. There was no way to turn left, as that side was blocked off by a wall.

Then a small porch, really tiny but very clean. Every porch has four sides, this one had too. On two sides were two rooms. The third side had a wall, the fourth the back of a room of another house that, with no trace of any door or window was also like a wall.

My new-found uncle called, 'Atasi, I've a nephew here to see me. Set out a mat for us in this room, that room is too dark.'

This room meant the one we were standing before. That room meant the one across, from which came out a young woman, her face completely veiled with her sari.

'What's this!' Jatin-mama said, 'Why the veil? I told you, he's my nephew.'

Seeing no sign of her removing the veil, he said, 'It's a shame if, being an aunt, you stand veiled in the presence of a nephew, looking like a kala-bou (banana-plant lady) at a ceremony site.'

This time the veil went up. I saw that my new-found aunt was a wife befitting the uncle!

Aunt Atasi unrolled a mat on the floor. The room held none of the usual furniture like wooden cot, table, chairs and so on. Only a trunk on one side, its paint peeling, and a wooden box. A string had been tied between one end of the wall and the other to hang clothes, but only a dhoti hung there; from an unoccupied nail hung a slightly soiled kurta, both Jatin-mama's property. Also on the wall were a couple of pictures from calendars of two earlier years, one with the page for the last month of Chaitra still attached which nobody had perhaps remembered to take off.

'If you've got some semolina, make a pudding for our nephew, else he'll have just tea,' he said.

'I said, 'I won't eat anything, Jatin-mama. I've come to listen to you playing the flute, the music will satisfy my hunger. Besides, I'm not hungry, because I ate before starting from home.'

'Flute? I don't play the flute now,' said Jatin-mama.

'I won't take that. You have to let me hear you play.'

'Then you've to wait, let it be evening. I don't touch the flute before dusk,' he said.

'Why?' I asked.

Jatin-mama shook his head and said, 'I don't know why, nephew, I can't play the flute during the day. I never have to this day. Well, Atasi, have I?'

Smiling softly, Atasi-mami said no.

In a tone as though relieved of a big problem, Jatin-mama said to me, 'You see?'

I said, 'It's only five now, evening will set in at seven. Let me not bother you by waiting here for that long, I'll wander around a bit and come back.'

'Tut! Tut!' Jatin-mama said in English, then added in Bengali, 'What're you saying, nephew! What's the inconvenience, eh? The neighbours have slandered and boycotted me; if you stay here, I'll feel revived from having someone to talk to.'

'How have the neighbours slandered you?' I asked.

Looking at Atasi-mami, Jatin-mama smiled. 'Shall I tell nephew about it, Atasi? You know, nephew, what the neighbours say? They say Atasi is not my wedded wife!' The smile instantly wiped out, Jatin-mama growled in anger. 'Worthless bastards these neighbours are, nephew. I've a marriage document, but who'd want to see it? All these . . . .'

Alarmed, Aunt Atasi interrupted, 'Will you mind what you're saying?'

'Right, right, nephew here is new to us, it's not correct to let him into these things. It is just that it makes me so angry.' With that he smiled. Then suddenly he said, 'How come, darling, that the two of you aren't talking to each other?'

'What shall I say?' Atasi-mami smiled gently.

'Come on! Do I have to tell you even what to say? Start with anything, and the words will roll out on their own.'

She asked, 'What's your name, nephew?'

Jatin-mama laughed heartily, then he stopped laughing to say to me, 'Now you ask her, "What're you going to cook today?" and the conversation will go fine. You have made a great start, Atasi.'

Her face flushed red. I told her, 'Don't worry, Mami, I'll never ask such an awful question. My name is Suresh.'

'Suresh means the king of melodies,' Jatin-mama joined in, 'that's why he's so keen to hear some melody, isn't that so?'

Suddenly getting up, he said, 'Oh, Bhuban-babu said he'd return those two rupees today! Let me go and get it, I haven't done grocery shopping for two days now. You sit here, nephew, and chat with your aunt, I'll be back in ten minutes.'

Going out of the room he said, 'Close the front door, Atasi. Nephew is too young, he won't be able to stop someone coveting you from barging in here.'

Aunt quickly got up and went out of the room, perhaps to hide her reddening face. I heard her low voice outside, 'I'm embarrassed, stop teasing!' I didn't hear what uncle said in reply.

Aunt came back, 'His nature is like that. In the cash box there were only two rupees the other day, he took that to buy food. I said leave one. He said, why, and went out. On the way, Bhuban-babu asked him for a loan—he gave him the two rupees and came home empty-handed.'

'He's an amazing man!' I said.

'He's like that. And listen, my brother . . . .'

'Nephew, not brother.'

'That's right! You've fixed the relationship beforehand. It'd have been nice if you were my brother instead of his nephew. Why don't you reset the relationship. It has not even been an hour, it hasn't settled yet.'

'Why?' I said, 'The aunt-nephew relationship is a nice one.'

'All right. But nephew, I've a request that you must keep. Don't ask to hear his flute.'

'What do you mean? It's to hear him play the flute that I came.'

Aunt's face turned gloomy and she said, 'Why did you have to? Did I ask you to come? Am I going to be driven by you, the lot of you, to hang myself?'

I looked at Aunt's face in surprise, at a loss for words. She said, 'Can't you see that he's killing himself to fulfil what's a mere fancy for you all? Every day one or another of you comes and asks to hear him play the flute. How long can a man live if he bleeds from the throat every day?'

'Bleeds!'

'No? Want to see evidence?' Aunt went out and came back holding a basin in her hands. There was some congealed blood in the basin.

'It came out last night, and I kept it, couldn't throw it away. I know it's useless, still . . . .'

'I didn't know this, Mami,' I said regretfully. 'If I did, I'd never have expressed a wish to hear him play. Oh, this must be the reason why he appears to be in such poor health.'

'Don't feel offended, nephew. I don't talk to anyone else so I took it all out on you. You're not to blame, it's my fate really.'

'It causes so much bleeding, and still Uncle goes on playing the flute?'

'Yes,' Aunt sighed, 'nothing in the world can stop him from playing it. I begged him so much, I shed so many tears, but he wouldn't listen.'

I remained silent. She went on, 'So many times I've thought of destroying it, but I haven't dared. Maybe he'd then finish himself by drinking instead of playing the flute, or sell all that's left there to buy another flute and then starve to death.'

Those last words that Aunt said seemed to go round the room in muffled sobs. I wanted to say something, but no words came out of my mouth.

With a sigh she went on. 'Yet except for this one thing, he never ignores what I tell him. He used to drink heavily; after our marriage, the day I pleaded with him to give up drinking, from that very day he stopped touching it. But when it comes to the flute, he listens to nothing . . . . Once I hid it,' she added. 'He became so restless. As if he had lost everything he had.'

The knocker rattled outside. Aunt went to open the door.

Coming in, Jatin-mama said, 'He didn't pay, Atasi. Asked me to come back tomorrow.'

'I knew that beforehand,' Aunt said following him in.

'Even the shopkeeper was so mean, didn't give the half pound of semolina I asked for on credit. Looks like the nephew will have to go back from his uncle's place with an empty stomach.'

'Good thing he didn't give it,' Aunt said sadly. 'The pudding couldn't be prepared with plain water.'

'Are you out of ghee?'

'When did you bring home any of that?'

'That's right!' Jatin-mama said, looking at me with a smile, a fine smile free of any embarrassment.

'Why're you troubling yourself, Jatin-mama? No food is needed, and so much formality is not right with a nephew.'

'You two make yourselves comfortable, I'll be back,' Aunt said and went out of the room.

'Where're you going?' Uncle yelled after her.

'I'll be back soon,' her reply came from the veranda.

She returned after fifteen minutes. With two little plates in her hands, each holding four rossogollas and some sandesh.

'Where did you get them from?' Jatin-mama asked pulling a plate and taking a rossogolla.

'What do you need to know that for?'

'Nothing,' said Jatin-mama calmly. 'Hungry as I am, even if you got it by robbery, I'll see no harm in that. A chaste wife goes to great lengths to save her husband's life!'

With much embarrassment I started to say, 'Why unnecessarily . . . .'

She interrupted, 'If you start that again, nephew, I'll be in tears.'

Silently I started eating. From the other room she brought us water in two enamel tumblers.

Right after swallowing the first rossogolla, Uncle said, 'Oh, the rossogolla tastes terrible. Here, you can have them or dump them. Let me try the sandesh.' Putting one in his mouth, he said, 'Yes, this is good stuff, I'll eat this.' With that, he pushed away the plate, adding, 'Go, throw these dumplings of semolina in the drain.'

Aunt Atasi's eyes glistened. His little deception was transparent to us. Sensing why such fine rossogolla became dumpling to him, I too felt on the verge of tears.

I finished my plate with downcast eyes. Looking up once while eating, I saw her saving his unfinished plate on the shelf over the door.

When the darkness of dusk thickened in the room, Aunt lighted the oil-lamp and the incense burner and with those she greeted the evening. Putting the lamp down in our room, she stood by silently, hesitating about something.

Uncle smiled at her and said, 'Don't be shy. If you skip a daily habit, you will not be able to sleep at night. There's no need to feel embarrassed before your nephew.'

I said, 'Or maybe I can . . . .'

Aunt interrupted, 'You stay here. I'm not that shy,' and with the anchal of her sari around her neck she did her pranam at his feet.

When Aunt Atasi stood up with the warm colour on her face, feeling shy, happy and satisfied, I said to her, 'Wait, Mami, let me touch your feet now.'

'No, no, that'd be awful . . .' she protested.

I said, 'It won't be awful. It may not be *my* daily habit, but I know that if I go home tonight without touching your feet, I'll not be able to sleep.' With that I did my pranam at her feet.

As Jatin-mama laughed heartily, Aunt said, 'Look at the doings of our nephew.'

'He feels respect. Learning that you pay me your respects morning and evening, my nephew feels respect for you.'

'The things you say!' Aunt ran away, adding from the porch, 'I'm off to cook.'

'Now listen to the flute,' Jatin-mama said.

I said, 'Drop it, Uncle. You'll end up bleeding.'

He said, 'You too have started nagging and whining, nephew? So what if I bleed? I'll play it anyway, whether you listen to it or not. If you wish, you may sit in the kitchen, your ears stuffed with your fingers.'

He opened the wooden chest and took the flute case out. 'Let's sit outside in the porch, the sound is too loud inside the room,' he said.

He picked up the mat and spread it on the porch. Sitting with his back against the wall, he put the flute to his mouth.

Suddenly it seemed as if a spiritual entity, insanely crazed with aesthetic purity, that was in a deep sleep within me, now stirred awake to the melody. The sound of the flute came to my ears, but its reverberations reached all the way down to the bottom of my heart. The sweetest self-expression of an acutely intense pain not only touched the core of my heart, but seemed to touch and give life to the dull walls and doors, and rise upward suffusing the air and the sky, merging into the dreamlike realm very far away where I could see a few stars just come out. The flute's melody seemed to embrace all the feelings of ecstasy that the human heart could know through the innermost pain of loss and sorrow.

I had heard a lot of fluteplaying. I had not believed that once upon a time someone playing the flute had made a tender young girl forget all about her family, honour, modesty, fear, her everything, and had made a tide surge on the river Jamuna. On that evening it occurred to me: if Jatin-mama's flute could make my entire soul awaken with a start and wring with such anguish for no reason at all, then those two deeds could not be so hard to accomplish for that cosmic fluteplayer!

I noticed that Atasi-mami had meanwhile come out silently and was sitting at the other end of the porch. Perhaps that room was the kitchen or the passage to the kitchen was through it.

Jatin-mama seemed unconscious of his surroundings, as if totally absorbed in an ascetic meditation of melody, his being all collected at the centre of an inner equilibrium.

How long the flute playing went on I don't quite remember—perhaps an hour and a half. Suddenly Jatin-mama stopped playing, and started coughing violently. Even in the dim light in the porch I saw that his eyes and his face were flushed abnormally red.

Aunt Atasi was perhaps ready, she rushed to him with water and a handfan. He threw up some blood but with Aunt's tending, he seemed to feel a little better. She laid him on the mat with a pillow under his head, and sat by him, silently fanning him.

Then at one point I got up and said, 'Let me take leave tonight, Jatin-mama.'

Before he could say anything Aunt said to him, 'Don't talk now. Nephew will come another day to eat here, not tonight; they'll worry about him at home . . . . Come, I'll close the door,' she said to me.

Before I stepped out, Aunt clasped my hand and said, 'Wait a little, nephew. Let me recover.'

In the lamplight I saw her trembling all over. After regaining composure, she said, 'This happens to me whenever I see him bleed, it could also be from listening to his flute. I'm all right now, nephew, you can go, but do come another day soon.'

I asked, 'Shall I try and see if I can make him give up playing the flute?'

'Can you? Can you do it? If you can, you'll give life not only to your Jatin-mama, but also to me.' She wept uncontrollably.

I stepped onto the street and said to her, 'Please bar the door, Aunt.'

I kept wondering why people had to pay so heavy a price for their passion. What did they get from it? The way Jatin-mama was sacrificing his life bit by bit to get intoxicated with the web of his melody. I knew there was joy in it, both for its creator and its listener. But did it have to be bought at such a high price? This creation of a dream, it's so transient, stays only for the duration of its creation. Then not a trace of the dream can be found in the harshness of reality. Why make the effort to entrance yourself in this pointless magic? The human mind is strange! I too wished I could use myself up like Jatin-mama 'casting the light of melody across the universe, spreading the fire of melody through the sky'. But there's nothing to gain. Even if there is nothing to gain.

Until then I had thought I too could play the flute. Friends who had heard it praised it. And it was not that I didn't derive enjoyment from playing it. But after hearing Jatin-mama play, it seemed playing the flute was not for me. Each person is born to do one thing, I was not born to play the flute. No one except Jatin-mama had the right to play it.

Maybe there was someone else—someone whose fluteplaying could move the heart even more, but I didn't know any such person.

One day I asked him, 'Will you teach me how to play the flute?'

He smiled and said, 'You think fluteplaying is a thing that can be taught? It has to be learnt.'

That's right. And the learning too has to be done with all one's heart, all one's being; otherwise the learning becomes fruitless, unfulfilling, the way mine had become.

I didn't forget the promise I had made to Aunt Atasi when taking leave the other night. But I couldn't think of a way to persuade him to give up the flute. Yet it was also painful to think he was killing himself with the destructive passion. What could I do? His love for his wife seemed truly deep; still if he could ignore her tears, how could I persuade him!

One day I said, 'Uncle, please stop playing the flute.'

Eyes wide with concern, he said, 'Not play the flute? Don't say that, nephew. How'd I live?'

'You've been bleeding from the throat, and Mami cries so much.'

'What can I do about it? It's all right to cry a little. Atasi! Atasi!'

Aunt came. Uncle said, 'Why do you cry? Do you want me to die from giving up fluteplaying? That'll cause more tears, not less.'

Aunt stood by quietly with a sad face.

Uncle said, 'You know, nephew, this Atasi has made life hard for me. She has come out of nowhere and settled down here, and no sign of leaving. If I was not responsible for her, I'd have travelled from place to place with my flute. My travel plans are all up in smoke.'

'Why don't you travel? Have I tied you up?'

'Haven't you?' Uncle looked at her as if he'd seen with his own eyes an attempt on Aunt Atasi's life and now she was denying it all right before him.

Tears filled her eyes. 'If you go on like that, one day I'll . . . .'

Uncle melted immediately. In front of me he held her hand and wiped her tears with part of the dhoti he was wearing. 'I was only joking, Atasi, really . . . .'

Aunt withdrew her hand and went out of the room.

'Why did you unnecessarily annoy her?' I asked.

Jatin-mama said, 'She's not annoyed. She left out of embarrassment.'

But eventually he did have to give up playing his flute. It was accomplished by Atasi-mami.

Aunt suddenly contracted the typhoid fever.

It was perhaps the seventeenth day of her fever, nine in the morning. Aunt was asleep, I was holding the ice-bag on her head. Jatin-mama was sitting on a low stool and looking on with a darkened face. He had grown thinner staying up all night, his eyes were red. His face was covered with stubble, his hair was disorderly.

Suddenly he got up and took the flute out of the chest. 'For these seventeen days it has stayed in the box unopened,' he remarked.

'What're you going to do with it now, Uncle?'

Slipping his feet into his worn-out pumps, he said, 'Sell it.'

'What do you mean?'

With a wan smile he said, 'It means I've to pay Dr Bose his fee for another house call.'

I said, 'Leave the flute. I've some money.'

He only smiled a little in reply while getting his kurta off the nail on the wall.

I had brought some money in my pocket anticipating some such need. The effort was proving futile. My own uncle had tried many times to help

Jatin-mama in times of need, but he would not accept a paisa. I told him, 'You don't have to go anywhere, I'll buy your flute.'

He turned back, 'You'll buy it, nephew? That's fine!'

'How much did it cost you?'

'I bought it for thirty-five rupees, I'll sell it for a hundred. The flute is in good condition, just second-hand that's all.'

'Didn't you tell me the other day that a flute like this was hard to find, and you found it after a lot of search? I'll buy it for thirty-five rupees.'

'How can that be! It's not new . . . .'

'Do you think I'm a cheater, Mama, that I'll want to get the flute cheap at your expense?'

I had three tenners in my pocket. I took those out and handed them to him, saying, 'Take thirty rupees in advance, the rest I will bring in the afternoon.'

Jatin-mama silently stared at the notes for some time. Then he said, 'That's all right.'

I looked away. I could not bear to see the expression on his face.

Jatin-mama called me back: 'Nephew!' I looked at him. Trying to smile, he said, 'Don't think I'm suffering too much, believe me, nephew.'

Tears came to my eyes. I quickly turned and went to sit by Aunt's head.

Aunt was still asleep and didn't know that I had just bought off the bloodthirsty flute that took Uncle's blood in splashes. I said to myself, it was false hope, a dyke of sand; he lost one flute, it wouldn't take him long to buy another; he'd only have suffered the added pain of losing his most dearly loved object.

In the afternoon, as soon as I gave him the rest of the money, he said, 'Remember to take the flute with you when you go home.'

Coming into the room I said, 'Let it be here for a few days. What's the rush?'

'No. I don't keep others' things in my home.' I understood; he could not bear the presence of the flute that no longer belonged to him.

'All right, Mama, I'll take it with me,' I replied.

He nodded, 'Yes, take it with you. Why should you leave your thing here?'

On the nineteenth day, Aunt's condition took a critical turn. Jatin-mama sat on the stool he had pulled close to her bed and, holding one of her hands in his, kept gazing silently at her face, thin from the illness, wilted like a fallen flower. Suddenly Aunt Atasi said to him, 'Darling, I don't think I'm going to live any more.'

Jatin-mama said, 'That won't do, Atasi, you've got to live. If you don't live, how'll I?'

She said, 'Don't say that, of course you'll live. Listen, if I don't live, will you honour a request of mine?'

Jatin-mama bent closer to her, 'Yes, tell me.'

'Stop playing the flute. Seeing your health get ruined bit by bit, I won't have peace even on the other side. Will you do this for me?'

'So will it be, Atasi. You get well, and I'll never touch the flute again.'

A happy smile appeared on her parched lips. Holding his hand to her chest, she closed her eyes in happy exhaustion.

I understood what a huge sacrifice he had made today for his Atasi in the sickbed. I knew, and Aunt Atasi too, even if nobody else did, how much strength there was behind those few words uttered in a soft voice. Even if his mind went insane with desire to play the flute, he'd never touch it again.

Aunt did recover in the end. The smile returned to Jatin-mama's face. The day my convalescing aunt took her first meal, he said with a smile, 'Well, darling, you said you were not going to live. That is not done as easily as it's said. Think of the ferocious uncle from whose claws I snatched you away; compared to him Yama is a nice fellow.'

I asked, 'What's this ferocious uncle business?'

Uncle said, 'You don't know? It's a long story, almost a second Mahabharata.'

Aunt said, 'Don't speak ill of your elders.'

'Of that elder, I'll speak not just ill, I'll speak worse. Why don't you show our nephew that mark across your back?'

Despite her objections, he told me the history. Her uncle was her father's cousin; Aunt Atasi had lived in his house upto the age of seventeen after losing her parents. That uncle had thought nothing of slapping and punching the grown girl, not to mention subjecting her to the other usual mistreatment. A permanent relic of her uncle's vile temper had remained on her back to this day. In the house right next to his, Jatin-mama used to play the flute and drink. Quite often his inebriation left him at the sound of her uncle's shouts and her muffled sobs late at night. Driven by sheer annoyance, he had made off with the girl one day and quickly married her.

When he finished telling his story, Aunt Atasi said smiling softly, 'Did I know then that he took alcohol? If I had known I would never have come away with him.'

He said, 'Did I know then that you'd become the jewel of my heart and stick on as if glued? If I had known, I'd never have rescued you. Besides, if I didn't booze, could I've done something as terrible as stealing a girl from a respectable home! I had thought, maybe just for a year or so . . . .'

'Stop it. Don't talk like that in the presence of your nephew.'

He smiled and stopped.

Then about two months later I went to Jatin-mama's place straight after college one day, and saw that whatever stuff they had was gathered together, all packed up and ready to go.

Surprised, I asked, 'What's going on, Uncle?'

Briefly he said, 'Leaving for my village home.'

'Village home? I didn't know you'd a village home, where is it?'

Jatin-mama said, 'Can't I even have a village home, nephew? I've some property in my village that makes five hundred rupees a year, did you know that?'

Aunt Atasi said, 'Maybe we're going away forever from you, nephew. It's my illness that has led to this.'

'What do you mean, your illness led to this?' I asked.

Uncle answered, 'It means I've sold this place. The one who bought it lives next door, he is now getting busy joining the two parts he owns by breaking down the wall between.'

In my upset voice, I said, 'You did all this, Uncle, and you didn't even tell me! When are you leaving?'

Pointing to the rolled bedding and the locked trunk, he said, 'Today. Leaving by Dhaka Mail tonight. We're rustic East Bengalis, nephew, didn't you know?' Uncle smiled. Amazing man! He could smile even in this situation.

Unsmiling, I got up saying, 'All right then, goodbye, Jatin-mama and Atasi-mami,' and proceeded towards the door.

Aunt Atasi quickly got up and clasped my hand, 'My good nephew, don't be angry. There was nothing to be gained by letting you know beforehand, you'd only have suffered. Given the kind of nephew you are, could anyone tell what sort of trouble you'd have worked up?'

I went back and sat down on the rolled bed, and said, 'If I hadn't come today, I wouldn't have known about it. Tomorrow I'd have come and seen the place empty.'

Jatin-mama said, 'No, I swear by Rama's name! How could we leave without letting you know? From Sen's pharmacy I made a telephone call to your home at noon. You would've received the message as soon as you got back home from college.'

I did not go home from there. I went to see the two of them to the train at the Sealdah Station. The time till the train left was spent in such an agitated state of mind! None of us had anything to say. Jatin-mama from time to time was saying a funny thing or two, even succeeding to make us smile. But what was going on in his heart was not unknown to me.

When the bell rang for the train to leave, I touched the feet of Jatin-mama and Atasi-mami and got off the train. Now Jatin-mama turned his face away. Perhaps it was no longer possible for him to smile.

Her head out of the window, Aunt asked me to come close. When I did, she said, 'Even though I address you as nephew or whatever, I know in my heart that you're my little brother. Come and see us if you can, pay a visit. We'll perhaps never be able to come to Calcutta, the property has suffered a lot from neglect. Come and see us there, will you nephew?'

Tears fell in fully formed drops from her eyes. I nodded my head to say yes. With the sound of the whistle, the train started. As long as their carriage could be seen, I gazed unblinkingly. When the train disappeared as a red dot beyond the red and green lights in the distance, I turned back. By then my vision was all blurred with the tears in my eyes.

It's in human nature that the pain suffered at any moment seems at the time to be the strongest, the most wrenching one. Who'd otherwise have thought that Jatin-mama and Atasi-mami, at the separation from whom my eyes filled with tears when I was twenty-one, would one day become all covered up in an obscure corner of my mind by a thousand bits of life's refuse?

A number of turns came in my life. In due course my fate took me by the scruff of the neck and put me down from the happy haven of youthful imagination on the harsh ground of reality. For various reasons our monetary condition turned bad. After having to sell even the house in posh Ballygunge to repay the debts, I got a petty job at eighty rupees a month and moved to a small rented place in the dingy Shyambazar area. Moved by my mother's tears and pressures, I even let myself into marriage.

At first, the whole world seemed to taste bitter, I lost all zest in life, and found within me not even the slightest stirrings of hope and happiness. Then gradually, things became all right. I found sources of enjoyment in my new life. In the continuous gamble that life is, how long can one hold in one's heart the memory of past losses and gains?

While these big events were occurring in my life, I became so preoccupied with myself that the thought that there was a time when I looked upon the affection of a certain Jatin-mama and Atasi-mami as my greatest treasure grew weaker and weaker. Today, seven years later, it is only on rare occasions that the thought of them comes to my mind as a faded bit of memory.

I did think of them once, about three years after Jatin-mama left for his ancestral village. The Dhaka Mail was in a collision. The name Jatindranath Ray in the list of the dead gave me a sharp jolt, I still remember that. I thought of going to look them up, but didn't manage to. Back from work that day I found my wife seriously ill. I remember I wrote a letter at Jatin-mama's village address and consoled myself thinking that it certainly couldn't be my Jatin-mama. There was no lack of Jatindranath Rays in the world. No reply came to that letter. The pressures arising from my wife's illness wiped it all off my mind.

Four more years rolled by after that. My younger sister Bina had been married off in Dhaka. They didn't send Bina for a visit home during the last Durga Puja. Two months later in Aghran, I went to Dhaka to bring Bina. I could not bring her, because her mother-in-law had just fallen seriously ill. The day before I arrived, she ran such a high temperature that the doctor suspected a case of pneumonia.

I did not have enough leave. Disappointed, I was returning alone. Getting off the steamer at Goalanda, I got into an intermediate-class carriage that looked relatively uncrowded. Just two gentlemen in it, and in a corner a woman shrouded in a shawl, perhaps the wife of one of them, for she had absolutely no luggage with her. Happily I made myself a bed on the bench, spreading a blanket and sheet over it. Sitting comfortably against a pillow, with my feet covered with the blanket, I took out an English magazine and engaged my attention on a detective story by Oppenheim. The train left on time and stopped at the next station. And started again. Though the train was the Dhaka Mail, it was to stop at every station upto Poradah, after which it skipped the smaller stations and picked up speed too.

At a stop about three stations after Goalanda, the two gentlemen got off with their luggage. But the woman remained sitting as before. What was the matter? They seemed to have gotten off without her. Never saw anyone so unmindful! People often leave behind small items, but this is an entire person, one's wife at that, how could one forgetfully leave her? Looking out the window, I saw them walking out of the station gate without looking back even once. Perhaps the husband thought his wife was following him as usual.

I shouted after them, 'Oh Mister, do you hear me, Mister?' The two gentlemen disappeared beyond the gate. The train whistled and moved.

So I returned to my seat and wondered if she was travelling alone. From the way in which she had wrapped herself, I could easily tell that she was a Bengali woman. A Bengali woman travelling alone this late in the night, and not in the ladies' carriage!

After some thought, I addressed her, 'Excuse me?'

There was no response.

I said, 'Your companions got off. Do you hear me?'

Now the wrapped bundle moved, and the face that emerged from under the shawl and the sari veil startled me.

There was nothing, almost nothing left of that face in this. This face was very different from the face of my Aunt Atasi. Still I knew this was none other than my Atasi-mami! Smiling softly, she said, 'From the voice

I could tell this was my nephew. But I couldn't hope for so much. I was afraid to uncover my face, in case my hopes were shattered.'

My surprise expressed itself in only a muffled cry, 'Atasi-mami!'

She said, 'I've changed much, haven't I?'

There was no vermilion in the parting of her hair, no sign of a border in the sari she wore. I remembered the very familiar name I saw in the list of those dead in the Dhaka Mail collision. So Jatin-mama was really no more. Quietly I said, 'I saw Uncle's name in the newspaper, but I couldn't quite believe that it was my Jatin-mama. I wrote a letter, didn't you get it?'

Aunt said, 'No. Right after that I went away from there for two or three months.'

'Where did you go?'

'To the place of a sister of mine. A distant one, of course.'

'Why didn't you send me word, Mami?'

She didn't answer.

'Didn't you remember your nephew?'

'It's not that, but what good could it do! Whatever was to happen had already happened. I stopped the flute, but I couldn't stop fate! I also heard from your middle uncle about the problems you had had. I didn't want to trouble you with my misfortune. I knew very well that you'd come running to take care of me if I sent word.'

I kept silent. What could I say? How could I complain? After reading Jatin-mama's name in the newspaper, I dispensed with my duty by merely writing a letter.

'What're you doing now, nephew?'

'I've a job. Where're you going now?'

'You'll find out in a short while. How many children do you have?'

Amazing! Of all the personal questions in the world, this one came to her mind first.

'One son,' I said.

'I wish I could see my nephew's little boy. Will you show him to me? Who does he look like? You, or his mother? How old is he?'

'He's three. Why don't you come to our place, Aunt, for answers to your other questions?'

Smiling, Aunt said, 'And if I don't move once I get there?'

'Will I be so fortunate? But, really, where are you going, Aunt? Where do you live now?'

'I live in his home village. As to where I'm going, that you'll soon find out. Oh, there's one thing I wanted to ask you, what happened to the flute, nephew?'

'It's here.'

'Here? In this carriage?'

'Yes. I had gone to see my younger sister Bina, she had asked me to bring it along. She said they wanted to listen to my playing.'

'I didn't know you could play? Can you get it out?'

I took the flute case down from the overhead rack. The moment I brought the flute out, Aunt snatched it with eager hands and stared at it with fixed eyes. With a deep sigh, she said, 'After my marriage, I thought of it as my friend, in between it became my worst enemy, today it seems like a friend again. The last three years he spent restless for the flute. Today, I think perhaps it'd have been better if I had not asked him to give up playing his flute. If he met his death through the flute, he could at least have gone in peace. He wouldn't have suffered so much mental agony in the last few years.'

Aunt put together the parts of the flute and set it to her lips. The next moment, above the rattle of the train, the flute soared in all its beauty. At the touch of an accomplished player's fingers, it magically came to life, and went on spinning out a web of exquisitely painful melody.

My surprise knew no bounds. This could not be achieved by just a little practice. It's not in everyone's hand that a flute weeps so enchantingly. Aunt's eyes slowly closed. Seeing her brought back to me the image of a melody worshipper seated with his back to the wall in a house in Bhabanipur. Seven years had passed in between. The incredible melodies of the flute I once heard Jatin-mama playing were lost somewhere in the bottom layer of my mind. Hearing Atasi-mami play tonight, those lost melodies resurfaced, resonating, softly humming in my heart.

It stopped at some point. Aunt let out a deep sigh. A sigh came out of me too.

After remaining speechless for some time, I said, 'This too you kept from me.'

Aunt said, 'He taught me to play it after our marriage. I was then so eager to learn it. Then, from the day I realized it was my enemy, I stopped touching it. Today I played it after a very long time. I thought I had forgotten how to.'

The train stopped at a station. Aunt leaned out the window, read the station's name, turned back in and said, 'I'll get off at the next station.'

'At the next station! Why?'

Aunt said, 'What's the date today, do you know?'

I said, 'The seventeenth of Aghran.'

Aunt said, 'Four years ago today—don't you see?'

Instantly everything was clear. That was right! Four years ago, it was on the seventeenth of Aghran that the Dhaka Mail was in a collision. At just this time on that night, that train like this one was dragging hundreds of unworried passengers towards death. I cried out, 'Aunt!'

Looking steadily at my face, she said, 'A little beyond the station that's coming, on the hard ground beside the tracks, he tossed in the agony of death. This day each year, I come to visit the spot. No other holy place has the slightest value for me.'

Suddenly going to the window, she pointed her finger outside and said, 'There, over there! Can't you see? I can clearly see him tossing in pain, waiting eagerly for the cool touch of love. A little water, maybe for a little water! Oh mother, where was I then!' She covered her face with both hands, moved inside and sat down.

The train slowly pulled into the station. Rolling up the bed, I said, 'Aunt, I'll come with you.' Aunt immediately said, 'No.'

'I can't let you go there alone this late in the night, Aunt.'

Her eyes flashed, 'No! You're not short of intelligence, nephew. How can I go there in the company of someone? In that deserted field, I feel his closeness throughout the night, I can't take anyone there. His last breath is in the air over there! Do try to understand . . . .'

The train stopped. Picking up the flute, Aunt said, 'I'm taking this, nephew! My claim on it is greater than yours.' Atasi-mami opened the door and got off. I gazed on, at a loss for words. Sounding the whistle, the train moved again. With a sad moan, the door slammed shut.

Poisoned Love[*]

Talk about the feeling of attachment between human minds. It can quite easily arise at any time, in any situation, with any one. Satya and Sarala did not take longer than a month to sense their mutual attraction, their affection for each other. In a case where others don't stand in the way, don't consider it necessary even to bother, an affinity of minds is usually sufficient for the kind of union which is the natural culmination of mental affinity. Love is but an affinity of minds. But owing to the very affinity of their minds, it would seem, both Satya and Sarala on their own set aside as unnecessary that kind of union. They would feel unhappy when not seeing each other, but neither realized that they had no choice but to start living together as soulmates.

Satya is the one who seems to be more indifferent than Sarala to the fact that their minds have become attached. The man is a bit reserved by nature. Moreover, his occupation is stealing—in fact, he is seeing Sarala with the plan of making away with her jewellery and money the moment he got an opportunity. With Satya, what's most desirable is that nothing about his life gets expressed. Whatever takes place stays hidden, everything from how he makes a living to the life he lives. He is not one who would consider himself lucky to find that his own heart has been stolen.

Of course, it is true that the first night he came to Sarala's room he was dressed in the standard guise of a stealer of hearts. The heart-stealer's attire he had gotten hold of some time earlier from the house of a businessman. Why businessmen stay so cautious of thieves in their own homes is a thing only they know; Satya couldn't do very well in the businessman's own room. From the room of his profligate son, he got only the attire of a nocturnal babu—dhoti, muslin kaftan, gold watch, gold buttons et cetera. But he had bought the pair of new shoes. The money for that came, of course, from the wallet of the businessman's son gone bad. Even so, as making money off others' wallets is Satya's form of earning a living, he did feel a little bad about buying expensive shoes spending

---

[*]   The Bengali title is *Bishakta Prem*.

that money. All in all, it could be said that it was out of his need for a proper pair of shoes to go with the babu outfit, that he struck upon the idea of swindling Sarala. How long can a man go on doing nothing to correct a situation in which the pleasurable squish of new shoes produces only a mild regret and unease?

Sarala has very little of what can be called beauty. This for her is a major asset—a very big attraction. A woman who does not have the looks that makes everyone say she's pretty or the looks that prompt some to say she's pretty and others to say she's ugly; a woman upon seeing whom no man feels an inescapable obligation to form an opinion about her beauty, such a woman cowardly men are absolutely crazy about. Men who by nature like to buy women are rather timid. That's why Sarala has a lot of jewellery on her body and furniture in her room.

However, the jewellery on her body is mostly gilded, the furniture in her room mostly second-hand, bought at auctions. Her real gold jewellery Sarala keeps hidden, and knowing that jewellery hidden is safer than jewellery worn, she has no regret about having to wear only the gilt stuff. The furniture consists of gifts that she exacted—knowing also that exacted gifts are usually second-hand, she has no regret about the second-hand furniture in her room. Besides, compared to her husband's room, furnished as it is with a three-generation old decrepit bedstead and a termite-eaten almirah, the attraction of a room decked out in second-hand furniture from Anglo homes bought at auctions is not small! Sarala's bedstead is not second-hand—it's the gift of love from a man who died of heart failure drinking alcohol in this room seven years ago; it was her first piece of furniture. But that's all right. In seven years, lots of memories evaporate, but an expensive bedstead doesn't become old.

This being what Satya is like and what Sarala is like, they carry on for some time solicitously trying to convince each other that neither of them has any hatred, any hostility, any dislike for the other, that they are such nice people, so simple, so exceptionally good as company when it comes to having a jolly good time, that they have an uncommon affinity.

Then the two of them do develop an affinity for each other.

But as long as the declaration was false, it was easy to convince each other. Who would believe it now? There's no point in trying to convince, there's no way to be convinced. Whether they say it directly, or convey it indirectly with gestures and hints, or make tall promises swearing in the names of gods and goddesses, the result would still be just the same. Satya's schemes and tricks to discover the location of the hidden jewellery would continue to vex Sarala. And Sarala's efforts to extract money and gifts will continue to keep Satya feeling harassed. No matter whether their hearts do or do not have an affinity, Satya doesn't have the ability to sacrifice his love of gold for anyone, and Sarala the ability to sacrifice her love of money for anyone.

Sarala keeps thinking, if only the fellow was not a thief! I'd certainly reduce my demands, I'd certainly increase the amount of love and care for him, I'd certainly try very hard to have him with me for longer periods. But the scoundrel is a thief, a rogue.

Satya keeps thinking, if only the broad was not so hardboiled! I'd certainly call off the plan to rip her off, I'd certainly hand her whatever I make, I'd certainly try to reach an understanding with her and settle down here. But the wicked creature is a seasoned Kabuli loanshark.

Thus they think, and they both keep getting annoyed. Annoyed, both keep regretting, 'I have got into the clutches of quite some person and it is making me sick with worry and anxiety.'

Regretfully, Satya decides he'll finish the job as soon as possible and get away. Regretfully, Sarala decides she'll throw him out as soon as the collection starts dropping.

One day, showing up before the afternoon is over, Satya says, 'Got some money, Sarli, let's have some fun today, okay?'

Feeling really happy, Sarala asks, 'How much money? Where did you get it?'

The face Satya makes, closing one eye, is truly incomparable. 'Got it just so,' he says.

Getting is all that matters in this world. What is gotten, by what means and from where—these are thing only the logicians sit down to argue about. Therefore, feeling ecstatic, Sarala tells him, 'You, you're going to get slammed one of these days.'

Is there never such a weak moment in a woman's life as when a man runs dangerous risks to make money and brings it to her? Sensing that Sarala's overwhelmed, Satya says in an ecstatic voice, 'If I get slammed, I'll go to the slammer, it'll be on your account, right? I don't care!'

Even more overwhelmed, she says in mock anger, 'Stop it!'

Hearing this makes him feel as if his heart is going to melt right out of his chest. All his conscious life, he has never indulged his conscience; still something seems to bite. Of course, it is like the kind of snake bite that immediately paralyzes the part of the body it strikes.

So with a sad face Satya says, 'Come, let's do something this evening, let's get a large bottle, leave it here, and go out for the bioscope show. We'll have the fun when we come back. But dress like a smasher, make them all stare at you with mouths hanging open.'

'Shall I put on the sky-blue sari?'

Satya has to think a bit to solve such a complex problem. 'Wouldn't the purple one be better? Well, go on, put on the sky-blue. Sky-blue or purple, any of the two you put on, you look so, I swear—like you're someone's wife.'

'Stop it!'

Satya suddenly lets out a yawn and says casually, absently, 'Remember to change the jewellery—people will smirk at this gilt stuff, and I'll feel embarrassed.'

This problem is indeed complex. But Sarala solves it in the blink of an eye and says, 'You think I'd not be embarrassed to go out with you in the gilt stuff? Why don't you go get the tickets, I'll send for the bottle and stuff and get dressed and ready.'

Satya lies down on his back in the almost new, seven-year-old bedstead, and says, 'Get the tickets now? As if I'll be getting those four-anna seats. We'll go out together when you're ready and buy the tickets when it's time to go in.'

But even this trick doesn't work, he doesn't have an inkling of when or how she gets the real gold jewellery from a secret spot in the room. His face turns grave.

Still, he asks innocently, 'When did you change the jewellery?'

'A moment ago.'

Satya's amazement knows no bounds. 'A moment ago! Where was it?'

Pointing her finger straight to the second-hand, auction-bought almirah she exacted as a gift, she says unhesitatingly, 'In that almirah, where else?'

The manner in which she answers is so unworried, unperturbed, and the answer so clear and direct that Satya can be sure of one thing. That Sarala's jewellery was never in the almirah, nor ever will be in the future.

Satya feels like grinding his teeth in anger, but he only bares his teeth in a grin. He feels like beating Sarala up, instead he caresses her all the more. The more his mind fills with anxiety that he has no choice but to take an extreme course, the more he jokes and makes her laugh. After taking her to the movie, he takes her to a native Anglo restaurant and treats her to stale meat patties and costly distilled liquor.

Sarala protests, 'We've some waiting in the room, why here?'

'I feel like enjoying to my heart's fill.'

'Why, what's the occasion today?'

A faint doubt, a slight apprehension appears in the tone of the question. Cautiously Satya says, 'Didn't I make a bundle today?' After saying this he stops, grinning, caressing and joking to humour her.

So, shortly after getting back to her room, Sarala asks, 'Why suddenly the glum face?' The tone of her question reveals fear and suspicion. Hence Satya becomes cautious again: 'No, I swear. I don't feel glum.'

The casual answer, without elaborate excuses, reassures her and she busies herself about having some fun. She remains unaware of when Satya mixes some powder from a paper packet in the bottle's fun poison. Good as she is at eluding him when getting out her real gold jewellery, he is no less of an expert at eluding her when getting her poisoned.

The principle that poison counteracts poison is nullified in this case perhaps because people call the bottled poison nectar, and also believe it to be so. Grimacing, she says, 'Yuck! What did you give me? Tastes terrible!'

Satya complains with concern, 'Told you not to eat those stale meat patties, you still ate them. Die of it now! Here, have a betel roll.' Lovingly he puts a dressed betel roll in her mouth.

After that Sarala drinks some more of the poison and, feeling still more unwell, says, 'Feel like throwing up. My head spins. I'm not drinking any more.'

Again in a complaining tone Satya says, 'Told you not to have the paan, still you did. Die of it now! Come, let me massage your forehead.'

After that, with her head on his lap, she tosses, moans, foams in the mouth and seems about to die. With dilated eyes she stares at his face, with arms around him she seeks relief from the poison's effect, begs for his help in overcoming unnatural death, seeks his protection. Within a short time, she grows slack in exhausted silence and puts herself completely in his hands; only her eyes remain somewhat aware and from the look in those eyes it seems as if a strange sort of stupefied consciousness has been born within her.

This is what's called laying down one's life in order to attain the fruition of one's strivings. Getting hold of some jewellery and money by taking one's soulmate close to death. His face drained of blood and looking stricken, Satya gets the jewellery off Sarala's body, one by one, and taking the keys she always keeps in a ring tied to her sari anchal, he searches out her hidden, saved-up money. But after collecting everything he wants, at the time of leaving, his legs give way from the toxic effect of a poisoned love and his head spins. He goes up to the closed door, then turns and looks back. Who can imagine from the way she lies there that she's a hard-boiled broad, a seasoned Kabuli loanshark. Satya should leave as soon as he can, but he knows no one will come to the room during the night, no one will look for Sarala until tomorrow afternoon. How long can it take to wipe the foam off her lips and splash a little water on her head?

How much nursing does it involve to just wipe her face with her sky-blue sari, sprinkle some water on her face and eyes, and wet the hair on top of her head, sparing the carefully done bun? But this little nursing produces no satisfaction even in a thief on the point of running off with the booty! Nursing is something that can be so amazingly addictive!

Starting to fan her with the handfan, a thought suddenly assails Satya's mind: what if she dies, although she's not supposed to? All poisons don't affect everyone in the same way! How unlikely is it that a poison that does nothing to one person can kill another? If she doesn't regain consciousness, if her unblinking eyes don't see again, if her heartbeat stops forever? Many here would know that he was with Sarala, and they would definitely look for him. If he leaves right now, he could, of course, have a bit more time to get away, but if she died due to his negligence, the police would be more concerned with finding the murderer than with finding the thief. If caught, the punishment too is always worse for a murderer than for a thief.

Satya knows nothing serious can happen to Sarala. Unless, after coming to some time late tomorrow, she dies of heart failure from grief over her jewellery and money. Even three times the amount of poison in her could do her no harm, but what if it did? Isn't she quite weak, quite lacking in strength? Of all the women he has seen so far, isn't Sarala the least vigorous? Is there another creature more soft and helpless than her?

Fear wrings his chest, he resents the fact that she's not strong enough to withstand the little poison supposed to kill no one, tears come to his eyes. It makes him so angry that he feels like picking her up to his chest and crushing her to death. Perhaps it is because he feels so angry that the thought of crushing her upon his chest comes to his mind, and he does not think of the easier method of strangling her.

Putting all the jewellery back on her, one by one, hiding her money back in its various hidden nooks, and tying the keys back into the sari, he now starts nursing her more energetically. It'll take Sarala time to return to a condition that will leave him in no fear about her life—no average butter doll that she is! Satya sighs. Looks like it didn't work this time. So be it, what can be done, one can't run the risk of being a murderer just for stealing. Next time he'll try something else—no more poison and stuff. After they live together for some time, can it be hard to guess one day where she hides her jewellery? Until he manages that, he'll give her the impression that he can't stay away from Sarala for a moment, that his heart is all filled with love for her.

A Widower*

It's a foggy Kartik morning in late autumn. I let out a huge yawn upon waking up. I slept well last night. On opening my eyes I discover a gecko next to the ceiling's black beam and I stare at it vacantly for some time. Today is Sunday, no hurry to get up. Although I won't be able to sleep any more, I derive ample gratification from just knowing that I can quietly lounge in bed for another hour or so.

The right side of the bed is empty. I almost never know when Sabita gets up in the morning. By the time I'm awake, she has finished washing the pots and plates and started the cooking. How does anyone manage to get up that early! Indeed, I find her quite happy even so, depriving herself as she is of the comfort of staying in bed till late in the morning. From the sort of remark she makes as she brings me tea and breakfast right after I've finished washing my face, it would seem that in her opinion there's nothing more difficult in the world than lying on one's back even for a minute once the darkness of night has cleared.

In the process of stretching, I extend my right hand to the empty side of the bed. The bed is cold there, Sabita's body warmth is all gone.

Suddenly I remember. Last night I quarrelled with Sabita.

I had completely forgotten about it so long. As soon as I remember, the pleasure of stretching the residue of a whole night's good sleep into the cool, glareless morning drains away. I pull back the limbs that recline luxuriously, unaware of doing so. How bitterly we quarrelled last night.

We quarrelled? Without taking any time to cogitate the question, I answer myself briefly. No. Call it a fight, call it a quarrel, I did it all by myself last night. Sabita took no part in it except for crying pathetically and protesting feebly from time to time. What happened between us last night can't be called a conjugal quarrel even if I add on several coats of colour.

What I did last night was discipline Sabita, straighten her out.

With my mind in a frenzy of hostility, I attacked her with rather savage cruelty. I called her by whatever name came to my lips. The more

_____

* The Bengali title is *Bipatnik.*

rude and vulgar an expletive seemed, the more I delighted in flinging it at her. Of all the words there are in the human language that strikes at the very core of a woman's heart, I did not refrain from using even one last night. Still unable to control my anger, I finally took a slipper off my feet and hurled it at her.

That was the end of it. Sabita was crying, covering her eyes with hands full of her sari. The slipper hit her in the chest that was heaving with sobs. Removing the fabric she held to her eyes, she looked once at the slipper and once at me. What Sabita saw, her eyes filled with tears as they were, I don't know. But I clearly remember the expression I saw on her face.

Yet, I had no problem sleeping well last night. If not from punishing Sabita, nor from seeing that indescribable expression on her face when she was hit with the slipper, then at least from the reason for which I got so madly furious and upbraided my wife, shouldn't I have stayed awake as if on a bed of thorns? I am amazed to recall the unalloyed peace I felt in my mind even a short while ago. How does a husband, right after hurling a slipper at his wife, while questioning her character, sleep through the night without a care and, opening his eyes in the morning, feel so comfortable? Thrilled with the feeling of winter's approach in the air?

I should, instead, have felt regretful right on waking up. I certainly was excessive last night! If one thinks calmly, nothing at all can be found to support my harsh reaction on the basis of a mere suspicion. Of course, it's good to discipline one's wife once in a while. They're such a wicked lot. They climb right to your head if you just indulge them. But why should I not admit that the chastizing should be kept within limits? I love Sabita, and not a little. The pen-pushing that I kill myself at from ten in the morning to five in the evening, for whom do I do it? Isn't it for her! It's good to discipline her once in a while, for her own good. If I had kept quiet last night, she would've been the one to pay the price eventually! People don't always know what's good for them and what's not. Especially females. Pointing their mistakes out to them, and scolding them a bit to mend their erring ways, is good for them.

But it would have done quite well if so much had not been done. It could have done no harm at all if I had at least eased things a bit before going to sleep by asking her for a glass of water or letting her do a little tending, by complaining of a leg cramp.

I turn on my side. I notice that the slipper thrown at her still lies exactly where it landed last night. After all this time, it now strikes me that I'm indeed feeling a little regret.

But it doesn't take me long to find consolation either. Whatever was to happen has happened. Like brickbats off one's hand and words off one' mouth, it cannot be retrieved. Nothing to be gained from feeling sorry or regretful. It seems that lazing in bed is, after all, not for me today. I have got to get up now and cheer Sabita up a little.

I keep lying in bed wondering what tactics I should apply in order to cheer her up. I can't ask for forgiveness. Expressing repentance to your wife, begging forgiveness—that sort of stuff doesn't go with my constitution. Even the thought of it sort of embarrasses me, makes me cringe. Rather not even bring up last night's matter. I could act as though I said nothing at all to Sabita last night. I'll go downstairs flapping and dragging my slippers the way I do every morning; at the tap, I'll wash my mouth as usual, clearing my throat loudly. At the sound, she'll take the rice pot off the stove and set the kettle on, but after the wash today, I won't walk upstairs as usual. I'll go straight into the kitchen, pull the little rug out and sit down near her. Not glumly, but with an easy smile on my face. When Sabita, shrouded in dejection and silence at being wronged, puts the breakfast before me, I'll keep talking casually of this and that while eating. Even if Sabita doesn't answer me freely, I'll pretend not to notice anything unusual and maintain the lively flow of words.

At first Sabita will be a little surprised. She'll mull over it. What's the matter? Last night he hurled abuses at me, and now he's talking to me like this! Then at some point she'll realize that her husband has forgiven her serious misdeed this time around. Last night's matter was over last night—it's not to drag on in the morning. After realizing this, she too will start talking normally. She'll grow even more devoted to her husband for taking the initiative to grant her a chance to talk and act normally—she who had no right to stay angry and could've nothing to say even if he started punishing her all over again in the morning! She'll think: My husband is like the ever-placid Shiva. For the crime I committed or was about to commit, any other husband would've finished me off. He stopped with just a little shouting. Not just that, up in the morning he now tries to save my face this way, giving due recognition to my repentant feelings.

She'll perhaps say nothing openly. The girl is not a little reticent! But her eyes will glisten with gratitude. Her face will light up with love for her husband, with pride in her husband. Her relief and joy will unmistakably show in her carrying out all the housework even more attentively.

I sit up. The regret has now disappeared from my mind and gladness has taken its place. For punishing her last night in excess of what she deserved, I'll reward her three-times today with love and caresses. The one who loves is also the one who disciplines! If it gets disproportionately large one way, then there's nothing wrong with allowing some bonus over and above what's needed as compensation. Today is going to be Sabita's lucky day, her day for windfalls.

Putting on one slipper and limping to the other that was hurled at

Sabita, I put my other foot in. To my left is Sabita's dressing-table, its mirror fogged up at the moment. I've provided her with this luxury item. Her father didn't give a dowry. I doubt if she ever saw a dressing-table before this. On the clothesrack to my left are her many colourful clothes nicely arranged. The colours are not very visible on this foggy morning, though. These, too, I've bought for Sabita, because I love her. On the bench facing me are her chest, cash box, suitcase, and her harmonium. These pieces of Sabita's property look sort of depressed due to the fog. These were all purchased with the money I earned with the sweat of my brow. Seeing all around these countless proofs of my generosity towards Sabita, I feel even more deeply satisfied, absolutely convinced that I've lavished an uncommon love on Sabita. Now I see why I lost my patience last night. It is because I love her. My love for her is so intense that the jealousy is also similarly strong. That's why even a baseless suspicion drives me out of my mind.

Sabita has closed the door after her. It opens into the covered veranda, which is like a narrow little room. The door out of the veranda is barred for the night, but the door to the room is left open; there's no need to bar it. She closes the door in the morning so as not to disturb my sleep with the clatter of removing pots and plates from the night's meal and washing and mopping.

After studying my face for some time in the mirror of Sabita's dressing-table, I open the door and step out into the veranda. First I notice the unwashed pots and plates, then the barred door to the staircase—and then Sabita, hanging.

The two large windows opening on the side of the yard are letting in plenty of light. I instantly realize that Sabita has hanged herself.

She probably couldn't reach the ceiling beam after bringing the lightweight table from the sitting room, and putting a chair on top of it. That's why she set aside the table and the chair. Probably it is by repeatedly flinging the rope that she finally got it on the hook, the hook from which was going to hang the cradle when she had a baby. But considering the amount of perseverance that was needed to accomplish this job, there's little basis to think, besides the madness of wanting to commit suicide, that she fastened the rope to the hook by tossing it up repeatedly. Perhaps she did it by some other means. Perhaps a person who attempts to die in the deep darkness of night, hiding behind people's sleep, develops so sharp an intelligence, and discovers such a technique to make an impossible task possible, so that those who hope of waking up alive each morning and sitting up on bed can't even imagine how to figure it out.

What exactly Sabita did before putting the noose around her neck, that part I'll never be able to find out or even imagine in my whole life.

It's just this problem that seems to unsettle me. It didn't take me long, nor did it trouble me, to see that she had hanged herself. But I'm distressed at not being able to understand how she fastened the rope on to the hook in that beam of the high ceiling. Helplessly I look around for a clue. My head starts to spin, not because she has hanged herself, but because she has left the step she took right before that so incomprehensible and mysterious to me. Who's ever going to explain to me how Sabita contrived to die by hanging from that hook on the ceiling beam?

Through her suicide, she has made everything quite clear to me. Why couldn't she overcome the fascination for a minor element of secrecy on this trivial thing?

I've known her well enough in all respects. What she likes to eat, what sort of jewellery and clothes she likes to wear, the sort of talking she's pleased to hear, the matters in which she derives delight from indulging her small mind, the level of life at which she can effortlessly be generous, all of these are well known to me. I've kept a full account of how much affection she held for whom in this world. I've been able even to gauge precisely the depth of her love for her husband, except perhaps in her moments of idle fantasy. Sabita was a very transparently known wife to me, an all too familiar one.

The thing about her of which I had no knowledge as of yesterday, but only a suspicion, she has given me complete knowledge of by killing herself. I'm not sorry that she has hanged herself to reveal the truth, that the suspicion I held was not baseless. But how on earth did she manage to fasten the rope on to that hook?

The Saqi Made of Mere Clay[*]

B ody without grace, mind without peace.
The poor forever lack these two—grace and peace.

But the state of lacking something does not become natural even from its perpetuity, it merely becomes tolerable some day. And even that is the cause for not a little regret!

Regret at an unspeakably unpleasant transformation of oneself.

The commuter train is to leave at seventeen-past-six and take him to Bajbaj. The train is so rudimentary that it doesn't have the added facility of a ladies' compartment. The pretty girl, getting in a few moments before the train leaves, sits down stiffly right in front of him. Even his desire to look at her face stops and hesitates. Seems almost scary! As if a moment's glance will make the delicate lips wither, the smooth cheeks become hollowed and covered with acne scars, the radiant eyes turn into the stricken, plaintive eyes of an animal dying of hunger, and on the forehead will appear a sticky sweat! At the sight of beauty, the eyes are thus overwhelmed with a picture of ugliness! The minutes become filled with such terror.

Only a ten minutes' ride, and the train is at his station. On one side of the track is the posh suburb of Ballygunge, on the other side the village of Kasba. The paved road bearing the stamp of urban aristocracy gives way right after the level-crossing gate to an unpaved one filled with cowdung and mud. The shops on its two sides, rustic in appearance, carry patches of urban pretense—sort of like a shirtless man in boots. But looking at them, Shankar almost everyday thinks that even being able to own a shop like this might not have been bad.

Shankar's home is right where the Ghoshal neighbourhood ends. It's a brick house and a two-storey one at that, but as old as it is small. Part of the uncovered stairway to the parapet-less roof atop the ground floor can be seen from the path; it looks like an attempt of the people in the house at upward mobility by stepping on some loose bricks unattached by mortar. But the location is uncramped and clean. There is a tank in front

---

[*]   The Bengali title is *Matir Saqi*.

of the house—it is small but the water is not murky with rotting things. To the south of it, after a gap of about fifty cubits of field is the house of the Right Honourable Mahadeb Bose. Since the Right Honourable had plenty of money, he bought land here cheaply and built a house. He is not alive now, his son Sukanta owns his father's money and house. Constructing large rooms, decorating them with expensive furniture, arranging a garden around it like a picture frame, and getting other kinds of renovations done, he has made the house suitable for his living. Each afternoon, he drinks tea with his wife Himani sitting in the shade of a young evergreen bakul filled with sweet-scented white bloom.

On his way back from a day's office work, Shankar watches them for the little time it takes to go around the pond to the door of his own house. The gentle laughter and talk interspersed with the little sips at the teacups, the short-legged, long-haired dog being called close and petted on the head, the random drop of a few bakul flowers here and there around them, this scene never gets stale in Shankar's eyes. Each day it seems to him as if they pick up one at a time the poems one has read during the college years, and enact them in real life.

He is familiar, but not acquainted with them, due to a lack of keenness on their side and a barrier of inhibition on his side. Shankar passes his days in his decrepit home carrying a pathetic curiosity to know how they spend their unimaginably enjoyable life.

The endless trouble with making ends meet, the children's crying, Bidhu's cooking while gasping in exhaustion and blaming fate while scouring pots, his catching the eleven-past-nine train for office and returning by the seventeen-past-six. This is all there is to his life!

It kills him with regret to think that he has become accustomed to so much variety in his life.

Today he's surprised to see that there is no one under the bakul tree. This doesn't happen usually. Even from this distance he can imagine how strong the addiction must be to come and sit in the fragrant shade of a bakul tree at the end of a hot day.

The reason for their absence becomes obvious as soon as he enters his house. The three children are standing on one side with tearful faces, Bidhu is lying on the shabby bed with eyes closed, and sitting on a stool at the head of the bed, Himani is holding two ice-bags to her head.

Taking a little time to grasp the situation, Shankar asks, 'What happened?'

Himani says, 'High temperature. She fell unconscious, she still is. Hearing the children crying and shouting, we came and found she had passed out on the floor.'

His shirt is soaked in sweat, but it's not possible to take it off before Himani—there's no undershirt. Shankar believes without a doubt that

Himani hasn't seen the bare chest of even her own husband. Loosening the buttons for air, he says, 'My office is so far away that I can't hear them even if they shout themselves to death.'

This superfluous remark is not born of rhetorical purpose, and so Himani keeps quiet.

The youngest daughter was about to cry at the sight of her father. Blocking her tearful outburst with scolding eyes, he remarks, 'Today I come home and see her unconscious, another day I'll come and see her dead perhaps.'

Making no attempt to allay the direness in Shankar's remark, Himani says, 'At this time it's important to have a female relative over to be with her.'

Shankar's tone changes at once. 'Already? It's only the seventh month! What's there to fear now?'

A dark cloud passes over Himani's face, and she speaks in an afflicted voice, 'You won't understand how dangerous a time it is for a woman. No matter how careful she is, the danger is always there. If another woman is not with her all the time, the terrible things that can happen . . . .'

She falls silent, shuddering as if from the touch of a snake in the dark. Her face has turned very pale. Such extreme concern on the part of a childless mother for a mother of three seems quite astounding to Shankar. If one began thinking like this, so many kinds of disaster would seem likely to happen to people, no matter whether men or women, in all situations; even his own demise within half an hour, falling from a dizzy spell, is nothing out of the world, but it makes no sense to worry about it! But this person's anxiety is obviously serious—even the fingers, pale from feeling cold, are trembling. It seems that the fluttering of the heart is not over either. Shankar says to her, 'You don't seem to be feeling well today.'

Concern for a newly acquainted woman's minor indisposition while skipping over his own wife's sickness does not sound quite appropriate. Himani looks up and says with a wan smile, 'I'm the same way today as I'm every day. Let's not talk about me. What good is my being healthy anyway . . . Dr Chatterjee came, he took a blood sample. Prescribed a medicine too, the first dose is to be given when she regains consciousness.'

'I can see that you haven't left anything for me to do. The doctor's fee?'

'No need for it, he's our friend.'

'I'll not insist then. But it's already late for your tea time. You can take leave now.'

Himani says earnestly, 'No, no, let me stay with her, they'll bring my tea here.'

The hurricane lantern is new—it doesn't give off sooty smoke, but the light it gives is dim because the wick is kept lowered. Himani's face is clear even in this light. Looking at her Shankar can't help wondering: could he even imagine when leaving for work that he'd come home to find anxiety and so great a surprise saved up for him! Himani's conduct today is strange. They've been neighbours for four years, but when did they care, and how much, to be involved with their poor neighbour? It's doubtful if even a word was exchanged between Himani and Bidhu in an entire year. And today she has come on her own and started attending so earnestly that she doesn't want to leave even when there's no need for her to stay. The timepiece shows ten. From one in the afternoon she has been sitting the same way at Bidhu's head; Sukanta came three or four times to fetch her, and went back almost scolded by her. What's this craving of a rich man's young darling to nurse a petty clerk's ugly wife! Nobility no doubt, indicative of generosity, but how unnatural!

Sukanta returns half an hour later. He keeps standing with a grave face and no words. Infinitely diffident, Shankar pleads with Himani, 'Don't you see there's no need for you to stay. How long will you keep sitting here like this?'

Unexpectedly, the objection this time comes from Sukanta, 'It's all right, Shankar-babu, don't try to stop her, let her do the nursing.'

Surprised, Shankar says, 'But . . . .'

Sukanta shakes his head, 'No buts. It's better for her to be here and feel at peace than go home and be restless. If you'll make it possible for me to sit down, I can watch her nursing.'

Spreading a mat on the floor and turning around, Shankar sees Himani looking up at her husband with grateful eyes. That look Sukanta greets with an inscrutable smile; then after a glance around the room, he quietly sits down.

Food comes from Sukanta's house. The children, after eating, go to sleep, cowering in a small bed in a corner of the room. Shankar sits down on the floor next to that bed. A solid block of anxiety weighs in his chest, yet suddenly the situation strikes him as hilarious. Two couples have come together in this room tonight, but what a difference between the two pairs! The one lying on the bed is a skin-covered skeleton, from whose lips even on the wedding night instead of honey he caught the odour of food particles rotting between teeth, who for over seven years now has starved his heart and supplied him only cooked rice twice a day. Near the head of the three swollen-stomached children sits a machine-pressed stick of sugarcane that happens to be alive, his life a blank page in the creator-poet's notebook of creations. And the wife who sits at the head of the ailing woman, the husband of hers who sits on that torn mat—what an abundance of beauty and youth, riches and dignity, laughter and celebration they have in their conjugal life!

Even by eleven in the night, Bidhu does not regain consciousness. Himani has been fidgeting for some time. Suddenly in agitation she says to Sukanta, 'Get the doctor once more.'

Sukanta gets up silently.

Himani adds, 'Bring two, they can consult each other.'

Sukanta's face shows not a trace of surprise, only experience and knowledge based on it. With a slight nod of the head he agrees with her suggestions as if he too has been thinking of getting two doctors.

It is in Shankar's mind that there is an urge to object, but what will he object to? From the way these two are carrying on it would be hard to even imagine that they consider any other responsibility greater than arranging Bidhu's treatment by mobilizing all the doctors of Calcutta.

Sukanta leaves, turning his flashlight on. The neighbourhood has grown still—Shankar too feels sick tonight, and the charge of nursing him seems to be with the bright moon on the thirteenth night of waxing. There is an indication of moonrise right outside the window—in the porch shines the brass pitcher Bidhu scoured by hand. Around Bidhu's toes is wrapped a piece of rag soaked in rapeseed oil; suddenly Shankar notices it. He has a major anxiety tonight: what if the moonbeams light up that foot sometime during the sleepless night once the lantern has been put out?

Himani's feet are in the shadowy darkness under the wooden cot. Only a strand or two of the gold-thread in the brocade of her slippers sparkle. Her feet seem to be golden, wrapped in darkness, their identity revealed only through a few minute holes. Are the heels of those feet chapped? Are there those whitish skin sores from constant wetness between the toes?

It seems to Shankar that his mind will forever feel uneasy if he does not pull out her feet from under the cot and check firsthand in order to eliminate this utterly improbable thought.

Shankar's eyes start smarting; this too amuses him. All he has is a bit of not-so-good vision—even those eyes give him a burning sensation.

'Won't you eat? Have something. What good is worrying!'

Shankar looks up and sees Himani gazing at his face. He does not feel the slightest bit ashamed of not thinking of his wife's illness. 'I won't eat tonight,' he says.

'It won't help her in any way if you don't eat.'

'It'll harm me if I do. I've a heartburn from acidity.'

'All suffer the same condition I see. I too get heartburn if there's the slightest acidity.'

Shankar had slumped from sitting so long; suddenly he sits up straight.

'You—you get acidity!' he says.

'And colic. The day it acts up, the pain seems to choke off my breath. Oh, the suffering!'

Shankar slumps again. When he's particularly disappointed, his spine bends like a bow.

Thinking a little, Himani adds, 'But I've no complaint about that.'

Shankar can't make out what there is to complain about colic; still he says, 'Why?'

Lowering her head she says in an unnatural voice, 'You may find it embarrassing to hear. It's my due. God has measured out a certain amount of pain for each woman; she must take her share, with her head bowed. If she avoids pain in one form, she's bound to get it in another.'

What a strange remark! Shankar lowers his head too; not from embarrassment, but from the weight of the remark. The words sound like a load of complaints—impossibly heavy like the frustrations accumulated over an inordinately long life!

But what about that reduced, bedridden woman—her complaints too remain unprojected in the lores of humanity! The prominence of the ribcage on her chest, maternal love like black cataract in her dark-ringed eyes, the endless deprivation of the inner being in possession of what is her daily life, what's the meaning then of these! The pain measured out for her by God along with the pain thrust upon her by mankind have perhaps even dulled the colour of the blood that runs in her veins.

What Himani just said he understands, though not quite as she meant. Early mornings she goes away in a car for a restful interlude in a wide open field by a quiet path away from residential neighbourhoods. She is constantly in intimate contact with scores of minds in printed pages, she awakens the sleeping ragas and raginis on the sitar with the golden touch of her fingers. She grooms her hair with perfumed oil, bathes with beauty soap, wears out brocaded Benarasi silk saris at home.

What has Bidhu got?

There is no lack of sympathy for Himani, but she does lose out in the balance-sheet of compared complaints.

Before Sukanta returns with the doctor, Bidhu regains consciousness. As soon as she opens her bloodshot eyes, she screams out, startling everyone. Both ice-bags drop from Himani's hands. The little boy wakes up and starts crying in a plaintive tone. Shankar scrambles to his feet.

The gist of Bidhu's screaming words is this:

'Oh, Ma dear, who's this witch! Khoka! Oh my little Khoka!'

After calling Khoka a few times in a throat-splitting pitch she starts wailing quite melodiously, 'Oh my Khoka . . . .'

Himani picks up the ice-bags and presses them back on her head. After some time, Bidhu perhaps falls asleep out of the exhaustion.

Himani asks, 'Which one here is Khoka?'

'He's no more.'

'No more!'

'He may be in her mind, but he's not on earth. Once on a moonlit night, Khoka fell from the roof on the cemented porch below.'

Himani gives a start and asks,'It really happened?'

'Yes. Everytime the night was moonlit, she went to the roof with the baby in her arms, I don't know why. So many times she ran up there between her cooking. If I asked, she just said she liked to look at the moonlight.'

'That couldn't be true.' There's distress in Himani's voice.

'You're right. It's impossible to enjoy just looking at moonlight. But I can't imagine why she did so much of that.'

Himani keeps silent, her face turned away. The lantern was running low in kerosene; after fluttering a few times it begins to go out. After a lot of searching about, when Shankar comes back with the bottle of kerosene, it is nearly out. He notices that there's a splash of moonlight near where Bidhu's feet were, but she has meanwhile drawn her feet in.

The flame goes completely out with the attempt to pour in the oil. In an almost choked voice, Himani asks, 'How long has it been, Shankar-babu?'

'What?'

'How long ago did Khoka, from the roof . . . ?'

Trying to light the lantern, he replies, 'About five or six months ago—in early Chaitra.'

'I didn't hear any crying!'

Shankar shakes his head, 'She didn't cry here. She went to the hospital with Khoka, from there I took her straight to her mother and left her there for a while.' Putting the lantern on the broken, crate-wood table, Shankar says in a rather serious tone, 'The thing is, you know, I can't stand the death wail, I just can't. My head spins.'

He sounds as though all others in the world except him can stand the death wail, including the person who does the wailing! As though he doesn't know that a human being is like a vessel of unbaked clay; that when it gets broken, it can be turned into soft clay with tears and remade.

Tearfully Himani says, 'The death wail is something really quite awful. But not being able to cry is even more awful. When my little brother died, I could not cry.'

'Why?' says Shankar.

'I don't know. Perhaps it was because I brought him up with my own hands. From six months I brought him up to seven years; in such a case can anyone cry when he dies?'

Shankar silently nods his head to indicate that one can't.

Himani doesn't seem happy with just that, she says in an upset voice, 'At least one shouldn't be able to. There's no difference between such a brother and a son born of one's own womb! It's all right to lose consciousness after such a death, but not to cry.'

With this she shakes her head several times to herself. Shankar keeps quiet, being unsure of which one of her many incoherent remarks this gesture of hers is meant to express doubt in.

Sukanta returns with Dr Chatterjee and another well-known doctor from Calcutta. Chatterjee has had the blood test done; he says that there are countless protozoans of malignant malaria in the blood. The other doctor, without expending words, fills his syringe with quinine.

Shankar says, 'Be careful, Doctor, the needle might break against the bone!'

The atmosphere in the room suddenly becomes horridly pathetic with this remark.

Sometime after the doctors have taken leave, Himani quite calmly goes with her husband.

From the time it takes her to come back, it's apparent that she did reach home.

'I came back to say something,' she says by way of a prelude.

'What is it, tell me,' says Shankar.

'Five to six months ago, we too often went up to our terrace-roof on moonlit nights. Haven't we incurred sin for the death of Khoka?'

With amazement Shankar says, 'Why should you incur sin?'

'Bidhu, coming up on the roof, used to keep looking at us. I don't know why she watched us. Could it be that she used to go to the roof because of us?'

Shankar says, 'It could be, perhaps. But you're not to blame for that.'

Tears were rolling from Himani's eyes. She says, 'No one but me is to blame, I'm really a witch. I've killed all my babies before they were even born; when someone's baby dies, who else is to incur the sin except me? Do you know that tonight I feel scared being out in the moonlight? What if that little Khoka of yours pulls me from behind by the anchal of my sari?'

What can Shankar do if he does? Will Khoka now care to listen to him because he's the father!

'Will you come with me just a little?' she says.

Sukanta has followed her in silence. Now he says gently, 'Don't be afraid, come.'

In the morning, Sukanta comes to ask about Bidhu. From the way he looks it's not hard to tell that he has not slept the whole night. Shankar brings him a stool and says, 'Sit down.'

'Wait, let me first go and give her the news,' Sukanta says and leaves.

He's back in five minutes, and without waiting to be invited, sits down on the stool.

In the morning light there's no hint of the night's moonlight, and that isn't an amazing thing. Yet, Shankar has at some point taken off Bidhu's foot the rag with rapeseed oil.

'You know, Shankar-babu, there's not a drop of happiness in life,' says Sukanta.

Everyone knows that; so Shankar says nothing.

'After going back from your place, the crying and shouting she started, if only you could see that. There's no lack of anything, and yet I don't know why she has lost her mind like this!'

Looking at his wife half-dead from the lack of a lot of things, Shankar this time also is unable to say anything in response.

Husband and Wife[*]

At ten in the evening, Menaka comes into the room for the night. In this household, supper and all the follow-up work is over quite early.

It's a small room, just about two cubits more in length than in width. The bedstead alone occupies half the room; it was given to Menaka's husband Gopal as part of the dowry at her wedding. Gopal's camp chair is cleverly placed at an angle with the bed so as to allow passage around the chair from all sides. With his feet up on a little stool in front, Gopal lounges on his back in this chair, smokes a combination of cigarettes and bidis, and reads books. Popular books—some written even by those who write high-brow books—the kind of books that are read to relax the mind. In a corner of the room are stored a trunk and some suitcases, made of steel, leather and tin. The trunk was received at Menaka's wedding, the paint is still bright, but one of its corners is dented from a bump against something. On the wall are several junk pictures and a large photograph of Menaka and Gopal. Except for the style of wearing the sari and the excessive jewellery, not much difference is noticeable between the Menaka in the photograph and the Menaka who just walked in. She seems to have filled out a little, but then again one isn't sure of it. The Gopal in the camp chair is, however, much thinner than the Gopal in the photograph. It's not photographic deception; Gopal has indeed grown thinner after marriage. It's hard to tell whether it is due to his marriage or due to his job, as his marriage and his job came at about the same time.

Coming into the room and barring the door, Menaka takes off her chemise. Sitting on the edge of the bed dangling her legs, she fans herself briskly and says, 'Oh, such a relief.'

Gopal lowers the book, looks at her and smiles in agreement. Then picks up the book again.

'Oh mother dear, I'm absolutely boiled.'

This time he doesn't lower the book; reading on, he says, 'It's getting awfully hot.'

'Looks like you're not going to buy that table fan.'

---

[*] The Bengali title is *Swami-Stree*.

'If you hadn't bought that sari—'

'I can't stay naked, can I?'

It is only to cool her body with the handfan that she is like this now, as though she's alone in the room and there isn't even one pair of eyes around her. After spending three months at her parents' place, she came back here seven days ago. The first night she couldn't fan herself like this. Doesn't one feel shy! Even those who become one body, one mind, one soul can't be like that after three months' separation, they can't feel oneness immediately upon seeing each other again. Three months they've fantasized each other, desired each other, sighed from sadness and frustration, endured the joy of tasting freedom and the pride in independence as though it were a punishment, stayed up nights, and sometimes the pressure of passion seemed to choke them for a few seconds. To become one body, one mind, one soul again after coming back would take one night inside a barred room, at least half a night, or a quarter. Even refitting parts of a machine takes time once they're taken apart—it takes time even if God were the mechanic.

When the sweat of her body has dried, Menaka goes to one of the two curtained windows on the east. Over the roof of the neighbouring one-storey house, there's a surfeit of moonlight. On the three-storey house beyond that, light is visible from all seven windows. Who knows when the light goes off in all those windows these days! For some time after her marriage she possessed this information. Four windows used to go dark at about eleven, two close to midnight, and in the corner window on the first floor the light went off at one-thirty or two in the morning. She speculated a lot about the person or persons in that room. Only one, and no other, possibility found favour with her; she wasn't willing to let an examinee study late into the night in that room; she somehow came to believe that in that first-floor corner room lived a couple like themselves, married a short time ago. Like themselves, they too made love unmindful of when it turned two in the morning. Of course, they turn off *their* light much earlier. Their window opens into the house and is of opaque glass; the inside of the room can't be seen but the light can be seen. Perhaps in that second-floor room of theirs, they have no problem about leaving the light on.

On the night of her return from her parents' place, they stayed up till three in the morning. But that night it did not even occur to her to look at the windows of that house. Menaka makes a faint sound of regret to herself. It was a bit excessive on that night. Things turned all hackneyed in just one night, the way they had become before she went to her parents' place after being together for six months continuously.

She was feeling sleepy. But the bit of regret now seems to repel the drowsiness. A slight flash in the sleepy eyes and a mild tingle at the centre of the back. Gopal is all attention reading. If interrupted when reading, he is annoyed. Says nothing, but is annoyed.

Returning to bed, Menaka hesitates, feels uncertain, until she remembers that Gopal's head gets overheated if he reads late. He wakes her up from her sleep and really bothers her. Then it seems as if the quiet, well-mannered man was changed, drunk or something. Makes Menaka feel so horribly annoyed! Should she run away? Should she avoid coming in the next night? Night after night? Why torment someone by waking her up—one whose health isn't that good either! Yet if any night she wakes him up to tell him something important—the night she herself can't fall asleep for some unknown reason, or when she suddenly wakes up, feeling sad and in such discomfort that she keeps tossing—all Gopal does is to say: 'Tell me all about it tomorrow, in the morning.'

If she still tries to push her face into his chest, saying in a pitiful voice, 'Listen, darling. I've a burning in my chest,' he turns over saying, 'Have some soda,' and goes back to sleep, hugging the side-pillow. Menaka then really starts getting a heartburn. It is very rarely that she can't fall asleep or wakes up at night. Even if it is only due to acidity, she has no one to talk to, and gets no caresses at a time when she needs it.

In the few minutes of hesitation, her sleep has crawled back. Yawning, she says, 'Won't you sleep? With so much reading, you'll get sore eyes tomorrow.'

'I'll sleep right after I finish this chapter, in five minutes.'

Menaka lies down and closes her eyes. Just as the awareness of the comfort of feeling the body grown numb with sleep starts to fade out, she's half-woken by the sound of Gopal getting up, dropping the book, pushing out the stool and moving the chair. Apprehensively she opens her eyes, takes a look at his face and closes her eyes again with relief. He's sleepy; his head is not heated up. She can tell from one glance. Her mind has memorized now all the signs on his face and his eyes.

Turning off the light, stepping on Menaka's feet, he lies down on his side of the bed.

In a drowsy voice Menaka asks him, 'Tomorrow is a holiday, isn't it?'

'Hm.'

The two of them have slept maybe for ten minutes, when guests come to the house in a taxi. Guests not entirely unrelated to them—it is Gopal's sister's husband's brother Rasik with his wife. Rasik got married last Agrahayan; he is taking his wife to her parents' place. They had started out by the noon train that reaches Calcutta at six-thirty and had planned to take another train at nine. Their train reached Calcutta at ten, some of the lines being closed due to an accident. Where could they go at this hour? So they came here. Otherwise, this late at night, without letting them know beforehand . . . .

'We're lucky that you remembered us and came.'

Menaka lights the kerosene stove and sets out to make some loochis. Gopal's brother takes the bicycle out to go to the sweets store. To get at least four kinds of sweets made of fresh cheese and sweet rhabri of thickened milk, and meat curry from the Sikh eatery near the crossing. They've got some eggs at home; Menaka will make omelettes. A relation by marriage has paid a visit, that too with his new bride. What a shame special preparations can't be made!

However, their train is in the afternoon tomorrow, so she could prepare a special spread for lunch. Of course, it's the end of the month, and their money has almost run out, but how can you think of money when formal relations come on a visit!

Menaka asks Gopal's aunt in whispers, 'Don't you think, Aunt, we ought to give a nice sari to the new bride?'

'Seems the right thing to do.'

Now she feels a compassion for him, rising above the flurry of entertaining unexpected guests. The poor man will have to borrow again this month. One man alone, killing himself at work, with all these brothers, sisters and aunts living off his earnings as though it were a loot. On top of that, relations by marriage turn up as guests. The helpless man can't even fulfil his desire for a table fan. And what sort of person is she that when he comes home sweaty from the day's work, she doesn't even fan him for ten minutes to cool him down! Tonight she'll sleep only after putting him to sleep by fanning. With one hand she'll fan him and with the other in his hair . . . .

Rasik is seated in the covered veranda to eat, Rasik's wife is seated in the room. The aunt keeps Rasik company, and Gopal's two young sisters sit clinging to Rasik's new bride on her right and left. While serving the food, Menaka notices that moving about here and there, Gopal is watching Rasik's bride, watching with interest. He seemed a little surprised when he saw Rasik's bride. Seemed a bit hurt when he attempted conversation and she was overcome with shyness. Seemed overjoyed when with a casual joke, he managed to make her giggle a little. Menaka has been noticing all this while frying the loochis. Now with the excuse of attending to the feasting of the guests, he is constantly hovering between the veranda and the room, running his eyes all over her body. No one else would notice anything in it. No one else would find anything excessive in his hovering around and his smiling dispensation of suitable pleasantries. They don't have Menaka's eyes. But why is he behaving this way? Because Rasik's wife is pretty? The girl has physical attraction, in a strong, vulgar sort of way. The sort that's not quite softened by clothes, but seems instead to get more stronger, more obscene. Making people in the street stop and stare. And family members spend their days worried.

And she doesn't seem to be able to step on the ground out of pride in her beauty.

Gopal likes the quiet, gentle, sweet kind of beauty—Menaka's kind. The sight of Rasik's wife is not supposed to carry him off his feet. Got to do some poking when they're back in the room, and get to the bottom of the matter, Menaka decides.

As soon as the guests have finished eating, the question of where they will sleep is discussed between the aunt, Menaka and Gopal.

The aunt suggests, 'Bhupal and Kanai will sleep in one bed and Rasik in the other, let the bride sleep in the room of Anu and Binu. It is a matter of just one night after all.'

'No, no, how can that be!' says Gopal. 'Newly married, they must have a room to themselves. They'll stay in my room.'

The aunt swallows and says, 'Do it that way then.'

Finally at one in the morning, the lights in the house are all off. Gopal lies down in Bhupal's small bed on a small cot, Menaka between Anu and Binu. Anu and Binu are beyond themselves with joy, getting to themselves under unexpected circumstances, the scarce commodity that their elder brothers' wife is. After declaring that they'll spend the whole night talking with her, they talk like gushing fountains for ten minutes, then drowsily for another ten minutes, and in half an hour both fall asleep. Menaka lies awake. So many things she had to tell him tonight, none of which could be told. This night will have to pass, this long endless night, then the whole day, a day such as doesn't seem to ever end, then at ten at night she'll get a chance to talk to Gopal. By that time, all the things to tell would have gone stale, there'll be no thrilling significance left in them. Besides, Aunt has invited them to stay over another night, as the day is not an auspicious one for travel. Rasik and his wife will perhaps stay on tomorrow, occupy her room for another night. In that case, she's not going to get Gopal to herself before the night after. What a wretched place he has rented, doesn't even have an extra room. How can it? The place is swarming with brothers, sisters, aunts. Gopal is not to blame, he's shelling out thirty rupees a month in rent for even this place. The man is killing himself slaving away for the comfort of all. He seems to have grown thinner too.

He must have grown thinner. Two nights back when he held her in his arms, he didn't hug her as hard as before! If they were close together, she could check this very night how much weaker he has become. In the morning she must take a good look at how his health is doing. From tomorrow she must feed him larger portions of fish and milk.

How about going over there now and checking him out? Bhupal and Kanai must have fallen asleep. But they may wake up if she turns on the light. And Gopal may wake up with a start if she attempts in the dark to brush her hand across his body.

Nothing is possible. Tonight she's trapped. If she's even dying of a heart failure now, she won't be getting the briefest caress from Gopal. There's no way anything can be arranged. If only there was an extra room! The silence of the night seems to produce a ringing in Menaka's ears. Leaving the fortress of excuses and rationalizations, crossing the boundaries of all reason and propriety, her thought now turns directly, openly on her desire for Gopal. Just a re-enactment of the old, accustomed union. After that, Menaka doesn't mind even dying.

'Can you hear me?'

Menaka shudders on hearing this, flushing hot and cold at the same time.

Pressing his face against the window bars, Gopal whispers a little louder, 'Are you asleep? Can you come and give me an aspirin.'

Before Menaka can answer him, the aunt says from the other end of the room, 'Is that Gopal? Are you feeling unwell?'

'No, just a headache from the heat. Want to take an aspirin. Don't get up. You just don't get up, Aunt. There's no need for you to get up.'

Menaka opens the door and comes out. 'But the aspirin is in our room,' she says.

'Forget the aspirin then. I'll go on the roof, lie there for a while. Bhupati's room is so hot.'

'Sleep under the uncovered roof! What if you get sick?'

'Nothing will happen. Spread me a palmyra mat there.'

Menaka brings the palmyra mat and pillow from the room—just one pillow. When crossing the veranda towards the staircase to the roof, Gopal stops her near the opaque window panes of their room and says in a hushed voice, 'See that? They're already asleep!'

The panes are dark. Rasik's snoring can be heard from outside. Menaka says, 'How would they not be asleep? Is it quite early in the night?'

She unrolls the mat on the roof and fixes the pillow. 'Didn't you bring your pillow?' he asks.

'Am I also to lie down here?'

As Gopal takes her hand, she sits down on the mat. 'What'll everyone say!'

As Gopal takes her in his arms, she is breathless for a while. Then she says, 'Don't feel like going up and down the stairs any more. This one pillow will do.'

The corner window of the three-story house is visible over the parapet, as the light in that room is still on in the otherwise dark building.

More Precious than Life*

Today is the day Jyotirmoy is expected to come. He's coming by plane from Delhi, the letter says that he'd stay for a couple of days where Abani lives with his family. A high-status guest, coming to pay them a visit uninvited. Shouldn't someone be going to the airport to welcome and escort him?

The problem is: who'll be able to go today? As he's Abani's friend, it would be most appropriate for Abani to go, but the problem is that events have taken such a turn that this clerk's life is all upside down. A clerk's days are no longer spent harried just with going to office, pushing pen all day, and after that, giving what's left of his life to his home and family, relatives and friends. Desperate efforts have had to be initiated with the aim of improving the rules, regulations and institutions of clerkship, basically by raising the monthly salary. There's going to be a strike at the office where Abani works, and Abani happens to be closely involved with bringing this about. He has no time at all to waste on going to receive an upper-class friend.

His cousin Subrato has an urgent students' meeting to attend.

Bani was once acquainted with Jyotirmoy, but if she goes, there'll be no one in the house to do the cooking, for Abani's aunt is ill. Bani's father-in-law, Abani's father, is old. Though not aged in years, he's worn out, prematurely aged from the mental anguish of getting no recognition after making the country independent at the cost of serving jail sentences. Saroj was always a blind believer in those grand empty dreams and ideals dating from the satya-yug; a gentleman who neither learnt to detect cheating, nor to get anything for himself by cheating. That's why in the commercial marketplace of ideals, the merit of his sacrifice hasn't sold for even a counterfeit coin. Thus, at sixty-two, the combination of heartburn and resentment has made him an invalid.

But his ideals are not the sort that are just forgotten. How far Jyotirmoy has risen in life! Not showing a high-up man like him appropriate respect will be discourteous. This feeling too springs from his

---

* The Bengali title is *Pranadhik*.

ideals. Saroj hence is the one who sees the gravity of the matter and gets all worked up.

'What're you all saying? No one will go? How can that be?'

'He's not a little boy,' Abani replies. 'He can come on his own and find the house. He'll take a taxi, what's the problem?'

'How very impolite that'd be! A distinguished man, a highly placed man, doesn't he have a prestige that ought to be recognized? If none of you can go, I will.'

Nobody has any objection if Saroj is keen on going to receive Jyotirmoy! Indeed, it's a good sign if he wants to stir out a little, shedding his undue passivity and indifference.

Only Bani says, 'You can't go alone, Father, take Montu with you.' Montu is only eleven years old, he's Bani's brother.

In pauses during the cooking, Bani goes out to the veranda for getting a bit of air on her sweat-soaked body. A short distance from there, in the little vacant plot by the roadside, the labourers who live in the slum have gathered for a mini festivity of singing and instrument playing. How high is the key to which their music is tuned, how full-bodied, lively and plain the sound they're producing. From the shadeless electric bulb in the betel shop and from the streetlight, some light is cast on their gathering; but as if to reject even borrowed light, they've lighted a carbide lantern, a cubit high, the flame of which burns sideways fighting the wind. How thoroughly has the order of things changed all around! Earlier, this unimagined prospect of Jyotirmoy inviting himself to stay in their house when he's in town would have produced excitement in their minds, they'd also have felt a bit awkward about it. Many expectations, no doubt, would've risen in their minds. Today, except for the old, eccentric father-in-law of hers, no one is particularly bothered about Jyotirmoy. They regard his visit merely as slightly puzzling, and until Jyotirmoy comes and explains, they can't make sense of this odd visit of his. His family has a huge house in the posh Ballygunge area—his brother lives there with his own family. There's no scarcity of big hotels in the city, no dearth of rich friends either. Still, Jyotirmoy is going to get off the plane and come straight to his friend's home, wanting to spend a day or two here with them, as he wrote.

Was this a fancy? A whim? Who knows what he has in mind! For Bani, it's not hard to suppose that Jyotirmoy's coming here has something to do with his remembering her, feeling an attraction to her. But as she derives no pleasure from this sort of romantic imagination, she does not like even to think about it. If this visit of his is indeed on her account, she knows what it means. At one time they were acquainted; perhaps once in a while it might even have occurred to him that the girl did not look or sound bad. It seems laughable to Bani to entertain the thought even as a fantasy that he was all of a sudden coming to see her as a result of being stirred from a distance by his remembrance of the girl she was. In any case, if Jyotirmoy is coming for her, the only meaning of it is that he harbours an ugly whim. He might be thinking that once or twice Bani had seemed desirable, yet he had made no attempt to have her then; today the wife of a poor clerk that she is, why not handle her for a couple of days.

Bani does not like to presuppose that a person is bad. But these days it's hard to think of men of Jyotirmoy's high-class status to be anything but bad. Their kind, the lot of them, are wicked.

On looking closely, Jyotirmoy recognizes Saroj and says, 'Oh, it's you? Your health has deteriorated so much. Abani hasn't come?'

'Abani had to go on some urgent work. Please don't mind, son.'

Jyotirmoy denies having any desire to mind at all. He seems rather enthusiastic, cheerful, self-confident. He pats Montu's back to compensate for not recognizing him and says, 'That was very wrong of me. You're not just his son, but also Abani's what-they-call-it, right?'

In the taxi, he says to Saroj, 'I've come on some urgent business. I made a mistake in forgetting to write to Abani that he shouldn't go around talking about my visit.'

'No-no, the news hasn't spread. After reading what you wrote—that a few days' rest at your friend's place was more the reason for your visit than the needs of work—Abani hasn't let anyone know. Don't we know, son, that people will come bothering you as soon as they know? No one can even imagine that you'd step into a home as poor as ours.'

Taking out a cigarette and looking at Saroj's thin and drawn face and nearly white hair, he puts it back in his pocket unlighted. Saroj's gladness knows no bounds, noticing that.

Jyotirmoy says, 'Let me tell you right away up front. I'll be starting an agency. I can't do it in my own name, with enemies all around, all sorts of people waiting to say all sorts of things. So I thought, who's there I can trust, to whom can I give the responsibility. Then this occurred to me. I've done so much for so many, but I haven't done anything yet for my old friend, Abani. You spent all your life working for the country, and you too haven't quite been rewarded with the happiness you deserved in later life. That's why I've decided to put none other than Abani in charge of it. He doesn't have to be at the clerk's job any more; working as my agent he'll make in commission three times what he gets in salary from his office.'

'Agency for what, son?' Saroj's voice trembles, he is on the verge of tears. After all these years, is the reward for his lifelong loyalty to ideals finally coming then? In this harshly materialistic world, his choice of nonviolence and poverty and hunger will receive some reward after all?

'I'll tell you after we get home. I'll talk about it in detail.'

Saroj sighs, inwardly muttering a few accustomed mantras and touching his joined palms to his forehead for some indeterminate deity. God is finally giving him through the roof!

'How many children do you have?' he asks.

'I've a daughter, three years old. Stays in Allahabad with her maternal grandfather. With the pressure of work you know, Uncle, I haven't even seen my daughter in a year.'

Saroj says 'bless you!' in his mind. He was a doer himself, and this one here was a doer too; having achieved so much of success at this young age, he has money, he has prestige, power and influence! But these young men don't know of moral principles, they don't understand the taking of a vow. He has just a daughter, what is this penance for then, all his striving? They don't remember that Gandhiji too had a family, he had a son, yet when the time came, he became an ascetic.

When they arrive, Bani is still alone at home. Only the aunt is in her bed, with fever. Saroj is almost furious; he shouts, 'This is incredible, no one back yet! If only they'd have some sense.'

Jyotirmoy calms him. 'Please, don't get worked up. Abani must have got tied up with the work he went for, he'll come when he's ready to come.'

But it becomes quite clear that Abani's absence has irritated him too. The next moment he asks, 'You said Abani's out on some urgent work—what is it?'

'Oh, something that concerns the office he works in.'

'Something that concerns his office?' Irritation gives way to a smile on Jyotirmoy's face. It's not unknown to him how terribly serious the office can be to a clerk.

He looks at Bani with eyes quite surprised. What he expected to see and what he is seeing, he seems to be assessing the difference with his eyes. She has been married for five or six years, a clerk's daughter and a clerk's wife! She's still so firmly made, so alive! He feels quite dismayed at not finding Bani in the eternally maternal form of a married woman prototype in the average Bengali household.

'I used to know you,' Bani says. 'I was your sister's classmate for two years. Where's Asha now?'

'Asha, Asha? She's on a little trip abroad. I mean, she was not feeling very happy in this country; an opportunity came by, and she went to America for a bit of travel.'

Bani senses Jyotirmoy's discomfort. To lighten and dismiss the matter, she says, 'She has no problem travelling. She can just take off when she wants. Why don't you change out of your travel clothes? And will you have a bath? With some special effort, I've saved two buckets of water.'

'Why the special effort?'

'There's a water scarcity. Scarcity of everything really—it's a clerk's home you know!' Bani did not have to say this. Jyotirmoy has calculated all this in coming here, he's not reluctant to put up with this sort of inconvenience and discomfort for a day or two for the sake of clinching a secret deal for a hefty profit.

He takes a long time to bathe, perhaps trying to resolve the problem of how he should adapt the conduct habitual to his own high world to suit the ordinary people's world. For a few hours he would have to do it (If he's to stay here for forty-eight hours, then ten hours can go on the excuse of urgent outside work, fourteen hours on sleep, and ten more hours being busy with letter writing, newspaper reading, thinking. That still leaves fourteen hours for home-style socializing! There's no way left but to pass ten more hours on the excuse of not feeling well. Can the total be reduced any further. On account of anything else? But that may scare them off his aim. Some pretense of friendship, love, ideals, morality, humanity et cetera is no doubt required to make Saroj's son give up his salaried job and get involved in black marketing! Something that for his own life, and for his family, is almost like a revolution!) Jyotirmoy comes out happy and smiling, a simple and casual manner, and settles himself down enthusiastically in the veranda.

Looking at the labourers' singing session in the light of a cubit-long carbide lantern, he says to Bani, 'These days only those fellows can have their pleasure! Fattening up their wages through strikes, and having their fun at a bargain. People talk only of the profits we make. No one takes account of the fact that we've to spend a thousand rupees to hear a song. Don't laugh, Bani, what I'm saying is true.'

'Is it?'

'Isn't it? Having a youth dressed as a girl, they're getting him to sing and dance, and look at how packed their gathering is! For us to have some fun listening to a girl sing, we've to give her father a cushy job. We've got to get the girl admitted in Shantiniketan and see her through; we've to have her make a name in singing on the radio and in the movies. As the singing part of it is really a hoax, we can't have fun unless we hear her sing after having her make a name first. To hear that sort of a thrilling song, we've to spend no less than a thousand, perhaps more!'

'You can do without hearing it,' Bani replies.

'No, we can't. The fellow whose daughter or wife is to sing to us also knows how things work. The machine is turned by pushing the button. Button-pushing is the main thing.'

Bani smiles at this and says, 'If that machine of yours gives such poor results, it's out of order. It'll come to no use any more.'

Saroj calls Bani aside and says to her, 'Listen, let me tell you one thing. Be cautious about what you say, how you act. He said he's going to do something for Abani. Don't ruin his prospects with careless talk.'

'I'll ruin your son's chances? What'll I gain from doing that, Father?'

With utmost generosity, Saroj controls his temper. These young women have no knowledge, no understanding, no allegiance. The poverty of their spiritual life is such that they always, in all matters, selfishly think of themselves as linked up with the husband. Let my husband prosper no matter what happens or does not happen to me—this kind of thought does not even occur to them.

Noticing the expression on his face, Bani reassures him: 'Don't worry, the man is a guest in our home, I'll do all I can to honour him and care for him.'

Two rooms and the little veranda is all they've got. Bani with her husband sleeps in the small room. Bani refreshes the bed in that room, borrowing a spread for Jyotirmoy. 'You can sit more comfortably in the bed, given the condition of the chair in the house! You'll have some difficulty.'

'That's fine, maybe I'll share the difficulty with you.'

Bani knows the expression, the tone, the patronizing display of being a generous relation. This is paternalism of the benefactor's role. Bani also senses Jyotirmoy's real discomfort. He's having to see them in a different light, his eyes are unwilling to keep within the restraints of acting. She didn't pay attention to this before, but from the look in his eyes she senses that now she has become a new attraction for Jyotirmoy. Before marriage she was supported by her father, and no matter how poor her father was, there was laziness in her life, there was some fanciful slackness. With the responsibility of her work life in her own household, the relentless self-restraint in conduct, food and leisure has within a few years brought to her body the special beauty of a labourer girl—brought it about even better because, after all, her man does not have to do the bone-crushing hard work of a labourer girl's man, and the food she gets to eat is proportionally better too.

'Haven't you had any children?' Jyotirmoy asks suddenly. Bani has no trouble guessing at the real curiosity in his mind because he has been searching her whole body with his eyes for an answer to this curiosity.

In an unperturbed voice, Bani says, 'I had a daughter, she died at two. She would not have died; there was a treatment. But it would've cost a lot of money, we couldn't afford it.'

Jyotirmoy's head is now bent a little, his eyes cast on the floor.

'Why didn't you write to me?' he says.

What can be the answer to this question? Bani keeps silent.

'If Abani's earning becomes five or six hundred rupees, will you be happy?'

'Won't I be! How can you ask!'

Jyotirmoy looks up and says, 'I'll arrange everything for it no later than tomorrow. It'll be in Saroj-babu's name, because his name has that special aura. All the managing and stuff Abani will do. He can resign from his clerk's job tomorrow.'

'Maybe he doesn't have to resign, they'll throw him out.'

'Why?'

'He's organizing a strike.'

Jyotirmoy's eyes cloud with second thoughts, 'Oh dear, does he get involved in that sort of thing?' After a pause, he says, 'Never mind, he'll need to neither do the petty job any more nor strike.'

Bani says nothing. She has vowed in her mind not to open her mouth in case it caused any harm to her husband and her father-in-law. She goes to the kitchen to finish up the vegetable dish that was cooking. Then, tidying up her sari a bit, and slipping her feet into the sandals, she tells Jyotirmoy, 'Spend half an hour talking with father. I tutor a girl in the neighbourhood, I'll have to go and check on her, show her a few things. I'll be back soon.'

Jyotirmoy is surprised, and offended. Her husband can leave his clerk's job tomorrow and start making five or six hundred rupees a month—and she can't set aside her petty tutoring job for one evening for the sake of that.

It takes Abani nearly to nine that night to come home.

'How did it go?' Bani eagerly asks him.

'They've decided for it. Unanimously.'

Abani has just finished changing his clothes while talking with Jyotirmoy. Sensing that he's back, Saroj anxiously calls him aside. When Bani went to tutor the neighbourhood girl, he has had more talk with Jyotirmoy about the agency. After learning everything, Saroj is as afraid as his agitation is heightened. He's unwilling to let his son discuss it with Jyotirmoy before he himself has talked with him and worked out an agreement. He fears that his son's conscience may stand in the way of his agreeing to Jyotirmoy's proposal for the agency; he'll perhaps snub him right away, saying, 'Don't count on me to help in your cheating business.' That'll be sheer disaster!

'Has Jyotirmoy told you anything?' Saroj's hands and feet are shaking with agitation, his words are beginning to slur.

'When could he have told me?'

'Listen then, I'll tell you . . . .'

Saroj starts telling his son about the agency in detail. Seeing Abani's tired, weary face, Bani is on the point of asking for a postponement of the discussion until after the meal, but she bites her lip and keeps silent—Abani will be able to bear the hunger a little longer, but it will not be surprising if the old man suffers a heart attack any moment unless he's able to calm down a little. Bani unrolls a mat right there and takes Saroj by both his hands to make him sit down, pleading, 'Sit down and talk, Father, please don't get so excited.'

He's so exasperated and upset that tears come to his eyes. Hunger, an attitude that life's urgent matters can be put on hold, must such weaknesses become obstacles that keep people from getting excited, from taking prompt action? Saroj concludes his account by saying, 'I've lived my whole life being mindful of morals and ideals. If I saw anything wrong in this, I'd myself have asked you to turn it down. People's morality resides in their hearts, you can't go just by external appearances. Don't be rash, don't jump and say no to Jyotirmoy.'

Abani looks at Bani! Bani knew he'd look at her in this very manner, she has been standing on the side where Saroj does not see her. Still biting her lip, Bani silently points with her eyes towards Saroj. Her signal is easy to read. It won't do to lose patience, it won't do to get upset, the old father is here, his existence too must be acknowledged. Impatience and anger did flash dangerously in Abani's eyes; had he not received Bani's signal, he might have just lost sight of whose machination it really is, he might have shouted at his helpless, desperate father.

What a terrible moment has just passed, that only Bani and Abani have understood. Those who have through the ages manipulated an emotion as terrible and as noble as indignation, and turned it very cleverly in the wrong, opposite direction to create misunderstanding, discord and despair in one home after another, their diabolic trick was once again about to succeed!

Jyotirmoy is to cheat people; to stay sheltered from the public eye, he's going to use Saroj—simple, foolish, helpless Saroj—and his poor office-clerk son Abani to fraudulently get hold of thousands of rupees. A very major blow-up was narrowly avoided between Saroj and Abani, leaving the man who is the hidden real agent quite securely behind the scene.

In a calm, gentle voice, Abani says to Saroj, 'If you insist, it'll be as you want. I'll not go against you. But what I'm worrying about is that you're saying this only for my own good. If my peace and happiness are ruined from being demeaned in the eyes of people, can you be happy?'

'That, that's the problem with you!' Saroj says in a tone annoyed and disappointed. But disappointment is a common emotion, not a dangerous one at all. The terror Saroj was stricken with thinking that his son would insensitively veto outright the reward for his lifelong self-sacrifice, just when it came home to him of its own accord, has passed. No matter if he is upset and disappointed, he has calmed down now, it's no longer likely that he'll suddenly die of heart failure.

After blowing his nose a couple of times, Saroj asks Bani for a glass of water, and taking a few sips, he says, 'What's it that bothers you? It's not a matter of stealing or defrauding, but ordinary business. Someone or other would've got the agency, Jyotirmoy has some influence in assigning the agency, and instead of giving it to someone else he has made a secret arrangement to have it himself. It's somewhat wrong, of course, that the countrymen are told one thing and in reality something else is done. But what difference will it make? Someone else would've run the agency; Jyotirmoy will run it instead through someone he knows. The main thing is running the agency. That's what benefits the country. What can you have against that?'

Abani says, 'Let it be done this way then. Jyoti wants to open the agency in your name; let him do that. You hire someone and run the agency. It's not necessary for me to be in it.'

On the radio in three or four neighbouring houses some elaborate whining is going on that passes for singing. However, the encouraging thing is that this whining is partly drowned out by the robust sound of drums and cymbals and a collection of voices.

Saroj sighs and says, 'Let me think about it. You go and eat now. I won't eat anything tonight, daughter-in-law.'

Bani quickly comes forward. 'It's better that you don't eat much tonight. I've made some thin barley gruel, just drink that and go to sleep.'

The sight of the food makes Jyotirmoy almost angry, though Saroj bought half a pound of fish specially for him and most of it is served to him. Jyotirmoy can, however, suppress anger in a situation where it can bring no gain. His concern is only with gain. Without something to be gained from it, he would not even waste anger and sorrow.

'Oh! The gourd greens taste great!'

'That's puin greens,' Bani corrects him. 'Do you know that Bengalis have been able to survive because of the puin greens—eating taro roots in place of rice, and puin greens in place of fish and meat. If the taro root and the puin greens didn't exit . . . .'

'Don't leave out the tiny shrimps,' Abani joins in.

Jyotirmoy giggles at this point. He isn't feeling at all sure of what to say, what to do.

The aunt slowly comes out wrapped in a scarf, and sits down by the door against the wall. Quietly she asks, 'Subrato hasn't come yet, has he?'

Bani answers, 'No, Aunt, he isn't back yet.'

In the same quiet voice she says, 'Before leaving, he sat down by me and massaged my forehead for a long time. I knew right then there might be trouble at the meeting, why otherwise would a son have so much compassion for a mother! He probably thought he might not return!' '

'The time for his return is not past yet.'

The aunt silently nods in agreement. But on this side, Jyotirmoy's face is suddenly drained of colour. He says, 'Who's Subrato? What meeting is it?'

After hearing the answer he turns pale. For some time he can't swallow the rice. He keeps looking up and watching the aunt's emaciated but calm face.

Before they've finished eating, Subrato comes home. 'Great!' he says, 'You've all gotten down to the business of stomach worship.'

The presence of a great man like Jyotirmoy doesn't seem to concern him in the least bit. Taking the half-dirty kurta off his sweaty body, he washes his hands, helps himself to a sitting rug, and says, 'Quickly bring my plate, sister-in-law, I'll eat first before I do anything else.'

He starts eating as soon as the plate of food is placed before him, he doesn't look at anything else. Jyotirmoy stares at him, as if astounded by this unimaginable expression of long-stored-up, fiercely alive, awesome hunger. In Abani's way of eating too, he has noticed keen hunger, but not to this extent. He probably can't quite believe that so much hunger can exist even in middle-class homes and that it has to be held back all day for the measured supply of ration-shop rice.

'How did the meeting go?' Abani asks.

'Grand! Day after tomorrow we're having a joint demonstration.'

For some time they talk just with Subrato, as if they've forgotten Jyotirmoy's presence. Saroj has gone to bed, feeling weak and exhausted; if he were present here, his heart would perhaps have stopped. A shadow of deep anxiety has now descended over Jyotirmoy's face.

After the meal is over, he lights a cigarette and fidgets. He blows his nose, clears his throat, turns this way and that in discomfort, tries sitting in various positions, and rubs his chin with his palm.

'Feeling tired?' says Abani. 'You better go to sleep.'

'Not tired. Just thinking. I'm inconveniencing you. If I knew you're short of room . . . .'

'We're not inconvenienced. Don't worry. The inconvenience is only yours.'

Bani brings water in a clay pitcher, and a glass. 'Do you think we don't have guests?' she says.

Jyotirmoy still fidgets. After drinking a glass of water, he even forgets the cigarette he put down to drink the water, and lights another.

'Oh no! There has been a mistake,' he suddenly says, 'I've got to leave, my friend.'

'Want to go out? That's quite all right. Will you be very late returning?'

'I'll have to go with all my things. Do I ever have any chance to rest? This matter was fixed up after I wrote you the letter, quite a serious matter it is. I simply have to move to a hotel, several big shots are coming to see me in the morning for an urgent conference.'

'I see!' Abani says.

Jyotirmoy tries to smile, and says, 'I had at first decided to stay in a hotel, to come from there and look you up. But when I saw your father, I forgot all about that. Seeing you after all this time, it really feels so nice. I completely forgot about the hotel reservation I had made.'

After finishing her own meal, Bani learns that Subrato has gone to get a taxi. Jyotirmoy has got his things together. When the taxi comes, a problem arises. Saroj is perhaps dozing. Should Jyotirmoy leave without taking leave of him?

'We'll explain to him,' says Bani. 'He doesn't sleep too well, as it is. Since he's sleepy, he shouldn't be woken up.'

Hearing this, Jyotirmoy sighs in relief and gets into the taxi. When the taxi leaves, Bani too sighs in relief and says, 'Good riddance. He himself solved our problem.'

'That's what they usually do,' Abani says.

Before finally going to bed for the night, Bani goes to check once on Saroj. Exhausted Abani has already gone to bed and has almost fallen asleep. He wakes up with Bani's hand shaking him, and guesses some of it from the look on her face. Silently, the two go and stand by Saroj's spare, ordinary bed made on a plain wooden cot. Abani searches for signs of life even though he knows he won't find any. Tears roll from Bani's eyes. In his sleep, old Saroj has gone to sleep forever.

Death by Hanging[*]

No question about it, the occurrence is exceedingly regrettable. Who would've imagined that after living a quiet, normal life upto his thirty-second year, Ganapati would suddenly become involved in an incident as sordid as this! Son of an educated, respectable family, a man genteel and harmless in his speech and conduct, happy in more or less all aspects of life, you could say. Such a man ends up as the accused in a shameful murder case of all things. People are shocked beyond imagination. How on earth had the murderer been deceiving them all for such a long time, wearing the mask of a gentleman of reserve and character! How horrible the man is—can you believe it? Can even a man like this exist in the world?

After Ganapati is taken by the police, the acquainted and half-acquainted and those not related seem to be far more keenly agitated than the family members and relatives, who are fearful and embarrassed, half-dead with shame and sorrow. The crowd that collects at the courthouse on the days of the hearing—one has no words to describe it! How much juicier it is to watch a sex-related murder trial in courtroom than to watch a fictional drama on stage after paying for a ticket, that only those of us know who, with curiosity unquenched from the daily reading of newspaper accounts of the previous day's trial hearings, get busy finishing the day's lunch and related activities by ten in the morning, and rush to the courthouse just like attorneys and lawyers.

Ganapati has three lawyers right at home. His father Rajendranath was at one time a famous lawyer, who made even ten thousand rupees a month sometimes—now, at the age of seventy, he no longer goes to court. The elder son Pashupati has been practising for twelve years—his reputation, although not as big as his father's, is not small either. Ganapati's younger brother is also a lawyer, though a fresh starter.

Bigtime lawyers have bigtime lawyer friends—occupational compatriots! A good number of men noted for their legal expertise put their heads together in Ganapati's defense case. That, by the way, also

---

[*]   The Bengali title is *Phansi*.

added significantly to the importance of this case. However, towards the end, even they had little assurance to feel confident about saving Ganapati. The trouble was that the case was not complicated at all. The more complicated a case, the greater the scope for men with great brain capacity in legal matters to push it towards the preferred resolution by making it even more complicated.

The incident was simple, the evidence straightforward. The door was latched from the outside and the police themselves came and undid that latch. Inside, there was the dead body, blood-covered, and Ganapati, half-crazed with fear. Except for a couple of geckoes and a few mosquitoes, there was no other living creature in the room. Mosquitoes, of course, kill people in far, far greater numbers than people do; yet for some reason Ganapati's attorneys didn't think even once of fixing the blame for the murder on the mosquitoes. They only kept trying to prove that the dead body was already in the room. Ganapati was subsequently tricked into going into the room, after which the door was latched from the outside.

'It's a serious emergency, will you kindly come for a minute?' With these words Ganapati had been tricked by a man of about forty years of age and dressed in an elegantly pleated dhoti, silk kurta and polished derby shoes. Clean-shaven, in thick glasses, and with a pale, fair complexion—the man, he claimed, looked a lot like a college professor! (When questioned as to whether a man's appearance acquired any special distinction by his being a college professor, Ganapati could give no answer—he only stared at the judge like an idiot.) Aside from this man, Ganapati had noticed three other men. They were standing in the dark under the staircase. (How could Ganapati see them if they were standing in the dark? At this question from the judge, he was stupidly silent for so long before answering that the judge gave him a suspicious look.)

The explanation Ganapati finally gave in answer to the judge's questions can't be said to be utterly impossible, for so many such funny things happen in this funny world. But the unfortunate thing was that despite all the efforts of eight or ten lawyers and barristers of countrywide reputation, his claim could not be made convincing enough. Ganapati was sentenced to death by hanging!

Hanging! The judge pronounced the sentence in English, the gist of which in Bengali was roughly that Ganapati was to be made to hang, according to the rules, with a noose around his neck until he was dead. If, however, Ganapati had any disagreement with the sentence, he could appeal the verdict.

The already short-sighted old Rajendranath became nearly blind with weeping. The crying and wailing of Ganapati's sisters and sisters-in-law turned the air over the entire neighbourhood mournful.

Ganapati's wife Rauma suffered so many fainting spells that her cheeks that looked rosy red even when she wasn't blushing, became colourless and pale like a sheet a paper. Ganapati's widowed aunt knocked her head against the floor so hard in the course of her frenzied praying that her tears were partly obscured by the blood from her injured forehead.

In due course, an appeal is filed.

After much effort and spending of money, more witnesses and evidence is brought before the court. As a result, Ganapati is given the benefit of doubt and acquitted. The police resume the search for the killer of the person for whose murder Ganapati was earlier sentenced to be hanged.

It is one afternoon that Ganapati is finally allowed to go home—the sky at the time is overcast. When there is such a heavy gathering of clouds in the afternoon, it does come to your senses as an accentuation of the coming night, the ending of the day. Ganapati has been on the verge of tears. Not from happiness, not from exhaustion or sentimental softening, but for no reason at all—in a stunned, abstracted state devoid of thought. Avoiding friends and acquaintances, he follows Pashupati into the car of barrister Mr De. Reclining in a corner of the car, Pashupati exhales noisily, reaches into Mr De's pocket, extracts a fat cigar, and puts it between his bright white rows of teeth. Mr De grins from ear to ear and says—'Well, that's taken care of.'

What gets his verdict as taken care of is not very clear. Perhaps Ganapati's trouble, or perhaps the day filled with countless people's crazy doings—or perhaps just the cigar that Pashupati has lit. Raising his ashen face but once, Ganapati glances at the smug, generous-looking face, then quickly turns away and looks out. Once he was sitting with Mr De in this very car, going somewhere he can't quite remember today. Before the car took off, Mr De had suddenly put out his hand and thrown a coin at a beggar by the pavement. He recalls how the virtue of charity shone like light on Mr De's face at the time. Today the virtue of giving life casts on his face a light no brighter than that! The expression on Mr De's face is exactly the same as it was after tossing a coin to a beggar.

Perhaps this is exactly the way it happens in the realm of human feelings—puffed rice, plain or caramelled, all the same price. Where is the expected kind of joy even in his own mind at getting back his life? Countless little dues received in life have produced in him excitement a hundred times more than this—they gave him profound peace and brought a longer-lasting sense of pleasurable enjoyment. No matter in how many ways, from how many angles he tries to imagine this reprieve, this grant of the right to live a prolonged future, to imagine talking with Rauma even for a minute on a moonlit night on the roof seems so much more expansive, replete with a far more intense pleasure.

Dropping the two brothers off at their door, Mr De goes his way. The rain has started in a heavy shower. All members of the household are awaiting him, crowding on the steps of the covered porch; if it had not started raining, many of the neighbours would've come too. After his getting off the car, the aunt patiently waits for Ganapati to touch Rajendranath's feet first. Then as soon as Ganapati touches her feet, she hugs him and cries uncontrollably. The weeping is, of course, not unexpected, they all knew that the aunt would cry in this manner! So they all stand quietly and let her cry. Ganapati feels an unnatural shyness. The strong urge to cry that he felt after getting into Mr De's car, has at some point vanished completely. Now he only wants to hide himself. Standing in the embrace of his weeping aunt in his own home, surrounded by his own family, his whole heart longs greedily for that lonely cell of his in prison. It feels as if something inside his head will snap if this goes on for some more time.

Seeing that nobody else is crying, the aunt checks herself in a while. Then Pashupati's wife Parimal remarks, 'How unwell you look, brother-in-law!'

Clearing his throat, he says modestly with a faint smile, 'Why talk of looks . . . .'

All Ganapati wanted to say was something like this—for someone who was going to lose his life, looks could not be the primary concern; but it sounded so different, as if his response to his sister-in-law's affectionate concern was an extremely rude form of being polite. Ganapati too becomes suddenly aware of this and is surprised. Why did his remark sound so strange? When a person who was about to lose his life from an illness starts recovering, and people express concern about his appearance in this manner, this is usually just the sort of thing a person says! When both sides know well why the appearance has deteriorated, this is the customary exchange on the topic of health! Yet this usual expression has seemed offensive today to the ears of so many near ones.

It seems to Ganapati that he can see why. The person who becomes thin from an illness is entitled to the degradation of his appearance, it's not the person's fault. But to become thin from going to prison after being accused of murder is something no one in the world can claim as a right—it's the result of sin. His enfeebled body and ashen face, the price of criminality, declare only one thing—that he was held by the police, charged with a terribly sordid kind of murder.

His head beginning to reel, Ganapati looks in total bewilderment at the faces before him. His eyes spot Rauma, after all this time. All the others are crowding around him. But she hasn't drawn close, she is frozen like a stone figure, standing partly hidden by the entrance door to the library room next to the porch—she's very far—separated from the rest by a great distance. As he stares at her, that distance seems to grow slowly, then gets smothered in darkness.

There's no reason for anyone to be surprised by this—that after coming home, and uttering barely a sentence to Parimal, Ganapati collapses! Oh, don't they know it is no small suffering that the poor man has gone through for nearly six months! Not just spending days alone behind the stone walls of prison but waiting for the uncertain outcome of a lottery involving his own life. And experiencing the endlessly imagined shame of having his neck twisted in humiliation before the invisible world outside. Ganapati has also—for a great many days—counted the days left before hanging to death. Hanging to death! Even thinking of it chokes the breath of anybody who has a safe, ordinary life. Of course Ganapati would faint and collapse! He should have done so much earlier on two other occasions. When he heard the passing of the sentence for his own death by hanging, and when he heard it was cancelled for the duration of this life of his. He could hold off fainting so long only because he's an amazingly tough man!

Rauma too is not short of stoic ability. For so long now she's been living as the wife of a convicted murderer in the midst of a household of pure people unsullied by sin, living in a whirlpool of sympathy mixed with amused curiosity coming from a whole horde of neighbourhood women! How many days and nights has she spent trying to reconcile herself to the prospect of widowhood on the date set for her husband's hanging! Had the appeal not worked—it would've been in no one's power to let Rauma remain a young wife. Yet, even now the manner of her standing like a stone figure shielded by the library room's entrance door can't but amaze anyone. With neither fear in her eyes, nor a tremor in her body! Her hardness seems as natural, unaffected, as that of a stone figure. Ganapati's fainting away, even that did not bother her. Let alone taking a step forward, she seems to have decided rather to take a step back into the library room to hide herself. About her husband—a husband who has returned just like Satyaban from the grasp of Death—how could Rauma lose even the inclination to see what's being done to revive his consciousness? A woman who can suppress this curiosity—her tolerance must also be truly incomparable, almost like that of Dharitree, mother earth herself—quite dead and bereft of sensation!

With the sprinkling of some water to his head, Ganapati recovers consciousness in a short while. After changing his clothes and having a bowl of hot milk, he goes with everyone to the family room upstairs and sits down. At one point Pashupati proposes that Ganapati should now go to his own room, lie down in his bed and rest. Ganapati himself does not agree to that. After recovering from the fainting spell, his desire to hide himself seems to have subsided for some reason! His head has perhaps cooled down from so much water poured over it; after all this time he feels even a bit eager to sit down and talk with everybody.

Talking about this and that, the conversation bit by bit eases considerably. In these six months, Ganapati has seen many of his family members many times; still he talks as if he did not even remotely know the history of his family in that period. He feels a freshly aroused surprise when the aunt gives him an account of events at home, even though Pashupati had briefed him about these happenings three months ago and he was surprised then. Even when Parimal describes something he himself had witnessed here shortly before going to jail, he listens as if he's learning of it for the first time today. True that memories, thoughts, feelings, imaginings and so on have in Ganapati's mind become more or less jumbled; still forgetting all about known matters is a sort of abstractedness that is supposed to come over even a prisoner sentenced to hang! But Ganapati has been enjoying acting like this. If he can go on like this, wanting to know about this and that with interest, and listening attentively to whatever people say in response, then a conviction may gradually be born both in himself and in all the others that he was just away on a long trip to a distant land. The real reason for his absence from home for so long may be almost forgotten by all.

Maybe that's what does begin to happen, and perhaps that's why when occasions inevitably arise to remind them again of that real reason, everyone seems to give a mild start. Shortly before Ganapati was taken by the police, his younger sister Renu's wedding was held with great fanfare. When at one point he asks about Renu, everyone seems to give just such a start! They look at each other—but none of the adults give an answer. Only Pashupati's seven-year-old daughter Maya says, 'Uncle, at aunt's in-laws' place, they beat her up every day.'

'They beat her up?' Ganapati asks surprised.

'It's because you killed someone,' says Maya.

As three or four scold her simultaneously, Maya falls fearfully silent. It seems as if the scolding was meant for Ganapati himself. His face shrinks even more than Maya's. Now for some time again he won't be able to look anyone in the face.

Pashupati clears his throat and says, 'They don't quite beat her, but they don't treat her well.'

Elder sister Benu says, 'Ever since they took her away after the wedding, they haven't sent the poor girl back home for a visit even once. Mahi went there twice to bring her.'

Mahipati adds, 'They didn't let her even see me briefly. They said . . . .'

In a trembling voice Rajendranath interrupts, 'Ah! Leave those things now, what's the need to tell him those things as soon as he steps into the house! He's not going to run away!'

For a while they all keep silent. The rain outside diminished somewhat meantime; now it becomes heavy again. The damp air's intimate touch is felt inside the room. This time also, Rauma hasn't come into the room, again she has kept herself hidden—at the back of the door to the next room. But she is not standing this time, she's sitting on the floor. From the ground floor kitchen the smell of flavouring boiled lentils with fried spices comes clinging to the damp air and collects inside the room; it covers up even the smell of a perfume that has been wafting so long from the body of Benu's fancy daughter Suhas. The aunt had gone to the deities' room, she returns with some of the prasad of the offerings of food and flower on a little plate. She goes to Ganapati first and says, 'Take your shoes off, son.'

When Ganapati is free of the disrespectful unholy contact with his own shoes, the aunt touches the flower offering to his forehead, then places a bit of the food offering on his upturned palm, saying her eternal litany once again in a half-indulgent half-loving tone. 'You with your not believing in gods and deities, always going around doing all sorts of irreligious things.'

No one says anything in this room; but from the back of the next room's door is heard a muffled half-cry, 'Oh Ma!'

Startled, the aunt asks, 'Who's there, daughter-in-law?'

Parimal asks from here, 'What's the matter, Rauma?'

No other sound comes from Rauma. Parimal's baby boy, who was crawling on the floor, has come within Ganapati's reach; he holds out his hands and picks him up—it is easier to hold his head down on the pretext of fondling the baby. Rajendranath says in a shaky voice, 'Go and look, Suhas, if anything's the matter with the second daughter-in-law. Has she fainted or something?'

'You stay here, I'll go and see,' Parimal says to her.

She gets up, goes and, after asking Rauma some things in a low voice, comes back and says, 'No, nothing has happened to her.'

—Nothing. Nothing at all has happened. What can ever happen to that rock-hard woman? All this time that Ganapati was locked up in jail, with no assurance even as of a few days ago, of escaping death by hanging, did Rauma even once break down with any emotion, did she once seek shelter, trembling and crying, in the arms of any of her sisters-in-law, did she give anyone the impression that she might have the slightest need for consolation? It's true that since the day Ganapati was taken by the police, she has forgotten to smile, grown almost mute from talking less and less each day, lost her golden complexion as a result of getting thinner and thinner! Well, that's no big deal! She hasn't given a share of her pain, hasn't accepted solace, hasn't broken down and cried a heart-rending cry!

Maybe she cried once. Just one time!

It was late in the night, everyone in the house had then fallen asleep, except Suhas. Suhas's husband was visiting that day, so both bride and groom suffered insomnia. Late in the night the two of them left their room and holding hands, they went past Rauma's room, to go somewhere—that is beside the point. Rauma slept alone in her room, she still does just that. A lot of persuasion, even a lot of scolding could not make her agree to sleep with anyone around her. Even the request of her father-in-law did not persuade her.

Anyway, Suhas paused at Rauma's door. Pricking up her ears, she caught the sound of a terrible moan from inside which chilled the poor girl's body warmed with her husband's caresses. Sending her groom back to their room, she then woke Parimal, 'Big Aunt, come quick, middle Aunt is moaning in her room.'

'Moaning? Go, call your Uncle, Suhas—Oh mother, what'll we do!'

With Pashupati following her, Parimal tiptoed to the door and, putting her ear against it, listened for some time to Rauma's moaning. Then she pushed at the door insistently and called, 'Middle sister-in-law, O middle sister-in-law, open the door, quick now.'

At the very first call the moaning stopped, but then even after so much calling, she did not answer, not at first. Finally she said in a muffled voice, 'Who's it?'

'It's me. Open the door, middle sister-in-law, quick.'

'What is it, sister-in-law?'

Parimal, of course, did not answer that. Instead she shouted even louder asking her again to open the door. Rauma was thus left with no recourse but to get up and open the door.

'What's the matter, Didi?'

'Why were you moaning, middle sister-in-law?'

Rauma pretended to be surprised and said, 'Moaning? Who told you that?'

The tear stains on her face were quite clearly visible in the light of the veranda. Pausing and swallowing, Parimal said, 'I heard you were crying, weren't you?'

'No, I wasn't crying! Who told you I was crying?'—With that she noticed Pashupati and pulled her sari over her head and down her face.

Then Parimal asked her nicely, 'Shall I sleep in your room tonight, Rauma?'

'Why?' Rauma retorted.

How the girl can go on demanding explanations! Endlessly!

Hesitating a little, Parimal said, 'If you feel afraid or something . . . .'

'Why should I be afraid? I don't have so much fear,' interrupted Rauma, 'I'm very sleepy, Didi, I want to sleep.' To this day this memory sets Parimal's whole body on fire.

Be that as it may; since then, many of the family members, when up and about at night, tried to listen with their ears on Rauma's closed door. But nothing could be heard on any other night!

How could anything be heard; is she a soft woman! Let her husband be hanged, she can easily snore through the night alone in a huge room. There's no need to think that something could be the matter with her today, merely because she has suddenly let out a muffled cry of 'Oh mother!'

Pashupati's throat is perhaps irritated from inhaling Mr De's strong cigar; clearing his throat again, he says to Gangapati, 'Ganu, don't worry about Renu. True, they didn't let her come, but they don't cause her suffering.'

Ganapati can't quite make out whether disallowing a newly married sixteen-year-old girl from visiting her family any more after she came to her in-laws' place does or does not amount to causing her any suffering. But he feels sad for his little sister. In a weak voice he says, 'How about sending her a telegram?'

Pashupati says, 'About you? Let it be, it's not needed, what good will it do? It may only annoy the folks in that family. They'll read all about it tomorrow in the newspaper anyway.'

The newspaper? That's right, everything about him will of course come out in tomorrow's newspaper. But is Renu in a position to read the newspaper? Those who can imprison this young a girl on account of her brother being arrested on a murder charge, are they capable of that much generosity? Ganapati sets Parimal's baby boy down on the floor and says, 'Still, if the result of the appeal could be communicated to them beforehand . . . .'

Rajendra says, 'You better do that, Pashu, send a telegram to Renu's father-in-law. And add "Please inform Renu," otherwise, that fellow may not tell the poor girl anything.'

Pashupati goes to the office room to write out the telegram.

If you search, you can always detect the real person within a person. Whether with beastliness or with goodness, who can keep oneself completely covered up? Returning to the family in which Ganapati has lived thirty-two years of his normal life, after having earned a horrific extraordinariness, he would feel particularly inquisitive and be on the constant lookout for the hidden persons in all these familiar persons. There's nothing in it to surprise. From one instant to another he keeps sensing that his folks are just not able to forget it. It's not that they're judging him or analyzing him, it's not a matter of hostility or craving, it's just memory—the remembrance that Ganapati, this person back in their midst, has acquired an unspeakable stigma, lowered their family honour in the eyes of the country and the people. Even if not proved in the court of law, his beastliness has been proved in the court of people's minds. The sentence for hanging may have been revoked, but the matter cannot end there, a lot is still left—a lot of battles of minds and honour! The person within each of these people is frightened and saddened from the thought of some unpreventable harm and danger, because this person within each of us is very cowardly and selfish. And therefore, has any of them been able to keep from thinking secretly that all problems would've ended easily if instead of this, the hanging had been gone through? Does anyone remember for long the story of the misdeed of one who doesn't exist? Does it matter even if they do? If Ganapati would cease to exist, then why would his shame cast a shadow on this family? That's not the rule. People would at the most think that a wicked man once lived in this family, one who got involved in a crime relating to some woman and ended up killing another man—but he no longer exists and this household's air is clean once again, the people living here are all right.

That's no longer possible! The evil person has come back home, his wickedness has poisoned the air of the house, and the poisoned air has made the people living here bad somehow! At least, that's just what the people will think.

These are the thoughts that roughly, if not so definitely, form in Ganapati's mind from his investigation. As he keeps thinking, his mind is suddenly overwhelmed by a profound compassion for Rauma! While he was in jail, he felt terrible pain for her, but that was only from thinking of the pain she was suffering on account of his misfortune! But now he suddenly realizes that she has not escaped with just worrying about her husband, her test of superhuman strength did not end with the torment of a dark personal future, he realizes that she has been handed a lot more. All that the outside world hands to the wife of a murderer! What those things are and how much a helpless, timid young wife has to suffer in bearing those—Ganapati did not quite have the ability to imagine and grasp. From what little he can imagine, his heart starts thrashing in violent pain.

He tries to convince himself that, well, at least an enormous anxiety has ended for Rauma. Having her husband back must have brought a flood of happiness to her heart today. Even if she suffered unspeakable pain all this time, what's to be gained from thinking of it today? He had no recourse available to remedy any of it either. If there's any injustice he committed towards her, it's only that sitting behind bars he couldn't gauge Rauma's pain exactly. But then, what difference could this injustice on his part make to her! A better appreciation of it on his part wouldn't have made any difference in terms of reducing her suffering.

About nine in the evening, when the rain stops, a few of the gentlemen from the neighbourhood and friends from elsewhere come to see him. Pashupati was against Ganapati's seeing anyone outside the family tonight—he wanted to tell them himself that Ganapati has gone to bed feeling rather unwell. But Ganapati does not heed this suggestion and goes downstairs to see the visitors and talk to them. After thinking of Rauma from a different angle, he has been feeling the surge of a new spirit of strength. He has understood that no matter what it is that happened, he can't give up control like a fearful, weak person; he'll have to rebuild his own life, familial and social, through his own strength. Simply because his home has been more or less damaged by an earthquake, he can't live the rest of his life out in an open field. He'll have to repair his home again. If he hides his face now in shame, people will start interpreting this as proof of his guilt, the reason for his shame as even more of a truth.

The visitors' motive for coming was only to satisfy their curiosity on the pretext of conveying happiness for his release. After talking with Ganapati, they go home rather surprised. No doubt the man has taken some hard knocks that crushed him, but no one gets the impression that he has fallen a long way. He himself tries in a way to remove the awkwardness in initial conversation. He doesn't talk too much, or stay too sombre; he neither dismisses obstinately the matter of getting the death sentence, nor exhibits jubilance at escaping his death by hanging! God at least is there, can He punish someone for no fault? With such amazing simplicity he says these words that he begins to gain the respect of his listeners. It strikes them that the man is perhaps not really as bad as they had believed.

This slight change in the visitors' perceptions does not escape Ganapati. His chest swells with the pride of victory and the joy of hope. Now he starts believing that he'll be able to do it—rebuild his shattered honour and image and make them intact again. The noise of the scandal raging all around him will gradually grow faint and completely fade out one day. The attitude of hatred and disrespect in people's minds towards him will die away, that of love and respect will regrow—then he'll have no more trouble living as a human being among other human beings.

The night has been getting on; after the visitors leave, Ganapati without any further delay takes a little food and goes to his own room to sleep. The intoxicated illusion of the success he has had a little while ago with a few outsiders in initiating his new life is still in his mind and this must be why he gets into an argument with Rauma in a short while.

Argument? On the night of his first meeting with Rauma after such a return—an argument? Perhaps it's not quite that; but the words that are exchanged between the two within an hour of her coming into the room sound like an argument.

Neither of them had the courage left to become emotionally effusive. So after entering the room Rauma comes to him in steps as calmly unhurried as the quiet manner in which he takes her in his arms. Her weight has become half of what it used to be, but he does not quite realize that, for the strength in his body has also been reduced to half of what it used to be.

Two teardrops slowly roll down from Rauma's eyes. After some time, she says, 'I didn't think I'd have you back with me again.'

Pressing her head to his shoulder, he says, 'I also didn't think I'd be able to come back to you in this room again.'

Not just to Rauma, his longing was to be back with Rauma in this room! While looking at Rauma, Ganapati also looks about the room. Almost nothing has changed in it! The location of the bedstead—by the twin windows overlooking the garden—is still exactly the same. Under the lamp fixed on the wall in the corner over there is her dressing table—did she use her toiletry, did she groom herself these six months? Sitting on the bed here tonight too, their reflection can be seen in the mirror: whereupon, earlier she sometimes joked, 'Who're they, tell me dear? You sure they're not watching us?' On the wall is their photograph in wedding attire, and the photographs of some members of this family and some of hers. Only where the three expensive calendars used to be, two with ordinary pictures have taken their place! During his absence, one year has ended and another started! There's yet another change. The brightness of the room has diminished. The floor is not that shiny, the photographs and the pictures have dust and cobweb on them and shabbiness has collected in many other indefinite forms.

'What are you looking at?' she asks him after some time. After almost an hour in silence.

'The room,' he says.

'What's the point in looking at the room? We aren't going to stay in this room,' she says.

Rauma gets off the bed and sits a little apart from him! Their argument has started.

A little surprised, Ganapati asks, 'Where are we going, Rauma?'

Through many sleepless nights Rauma has thought of the answer. She immediately says, 'Wherever the eyes take us—very far, to some unknown place, where no one recognizes us, no one knows our names and address—we'll go and set up our home there. This very night I'll pack our things, we'll start very early in the morning, all right? I can't stay here for even one more day.'

'Why?' Ganapati asks blankly.

Looking at him with a fixed gaze, she says, 'Can't you see why? They'll all look at us with contempt—how can we go on staying here?'

Thus starts their altercation. He argues: how can anyone talk in this crazy way, how can one leave the house and home, family and relatives and one's job? Besides, what's the need to go away? For a few days people may act a little odd, then everything will become all right. Why is Rauma worrying so much? He talks not combatively, but lovingly—in very sweet words he tries to make her understand these points. He somehow can't forget that in the drawing room, with just half an hour's effort he could almost eradicate the attitude of disrespect from the minds of several outsiders. To leave home forever for some distant land—Rauma's wanting to live by hiding their identity in the midst of unknown people—it seems to him a childish whim.

In disappointment, she finally asks him, 'You're not going then?'

Ganapati draws her back to his chest, kisses her ashen cheeks with affection, and says, 'Crazy girl, did I say I won't go? Let's go on a trip somewhere, the two of us for a few months.'

Impatiently she shakes her head: 'I'm going nowhere for a few months. Must be for ever.'

'All right, we'll talk about all this tomorrow.'

'No, tell me tonight if you'll go or not, tell me right now. We'll rise at dawn and leave.'

Ganapati this time can't help smiling. He says, 'Well, can you tell me what's the matter with you? Does anyone ever leave like that?'

Rauma sighs and says, 'All right, forget it then.'

For some more time, he soothes and comforts her, tries to make her understand. But his drained body is collapsing with exhaustion, so after about half an hour, thinking he has done enough of both comforting his immature wife and explaining the practical problems, he falls asleep.

Next morning, an awful commotion is heard coming from the house of Rajendra the lawyer. Rauma, the family's second daughter-in-law, has apparently hanged herself to death.

The Children of Immortality

1

Crowds are but natural in a populous world. Although the urge towards social formation is natural in humans, why people are so keen to pack themselves in crowds and exchange breath, body odour, infectious disease and harsh words is a question for the consideration of those who become psychologists by sitting in the confines of a room and soaking up knowledge from the printed pages of books. Ants, too, gather in crowds, not just around a bit of molasses, but also to ensure through collective efforts the survival of each one. Once they grow wings, they individually take off on those wings and proceed towards heaven.

The more the people pack together in a place, the larger the numbers in which they do so, and the more the daily occasions for which crowds become an integral part of individual life, the larger a city that place is known to be. Classes are held daily in schools and colleges, offices open at ten, meetings and assembly sessions are held every now and then; not a day passes in the playing fields without ten, twenty or twenty-five games; at movie halls people line up each day to buy one entry ticket each; people collect in eateries for tea and croquette; in Cafe de X and Cafe de Y, after ascending to the heaven of unreality induced by a bottle or two, many dance with padded-hip, flat-bosom versions of the celestial dancer Urvashi; conversations carry on and on in knots in marketplaces; inside homes ten people live in the space that is just about adequate for one-tenth of one . . . .

This is possible because not even one out of ten is a full human being. Perhaps not a human being at all!

Anupam and Shankar were both on their way to college. Anupam in a bus and Shankar in a car his family owned. At a junction, a truly big crossing, where signs of progress are found in the speed of vehicles and people, and where the world in the form of news worth a few paisas can be bought for a few paisas from under the newspaper hawker's arms, the bus and the car came to a stop together at the red light.

The huge double-decker bus could serve as an excellent home for an entire family with the seats removed. Anupam wasn't sitting in a corner, he was at a window, squeezed against it in a seat in the middle of the lower deck, looking out at the road. Shankar was sitting in the car's back seat, his elbows resting on his trousered legs and the palm of one hand on his shaved cheek. Sitting beside him was Bireswar, his grandfather, aged seventy-three-and-a-half.

Spotting Anupam's face at the bus window a few feet away, and recognizing it, grandfather Bireswar called out, 'Aren't you Anupam? Hey, Anupam!'

Their eyes had made contact a few seconds earlier. Anupam, when existing anonymously in a bus crowd, was prone to lapses in recognizing faces. Busy seeing himself, amidst so many people for so long, as apart and all alone, as inexperienced and helpless, he had so distanced himself from his own familiar mind, sort of like living incognito in a familiar world, that he made no move at all to engage the mental process of instant recall upon setting his eyes on an old man he had seen about three years ago.

'Who are you?' he asked blankly.

Bireswar frantically said, 'Get off the bus first, then I'll tell you. Get off, be quick.'

Well, this sort of thing had never happened to Anupam. Never before in his life had the occupant of such an expensive car, an elderly man with such patrician dignity of bearing, a sagely face fringed with white hair and beard, and dressed in a robelike long coat of expensive gray material, called out to Anupam and asked him to get off a bus. The light changed and the bus began to move. Anupam started to make his way to the exit. He had long practice in pushing through people to get off a bus, but now he couldn't even set a foot on its floor before the bus got to the other side of the bend. He lost his face in the eyes of a dark girl with pimples on her face and books in her arm, and heard a middle-aged gentleman, whose foot he had stepped on, spit out some vulgar insult in a boorish manner. Even as he contemplated the strange mystery of Bireswar's command to get off the bus, the bus fare gone waste kept bothering him like a lodged thorn. He'd have to buy another ticket, pay another four paisas to get to college today.

The car, rolling after the bus, stopped beside it. At once, horns blared impatiently from some twenty vehicles behind it. 'Come, Anupam, get in,' Bireswar said to him.

Anupam got in and sat in silence. A familiar person, no doubt about it, but why wasn't he quite able to place him? He hadn't thought of this before, but now, sitting next to Bireswar, he was overcome with embarrassment at his inability to recognize the bearded face! The shame of not recognizing a familiar person, an awful misdeed, like slapping the cheek of an elder who should've been greeted with a pranam instead.

'I recognized you right away, and you still can't recognize me, Anu?' Bireswar remarked. 'Such a strange lot, you young men these days! You jumble up a thousand thoughts and memories in your brain, so that not one of them is clear. I'm your grandfather.'

Bireswar smiled faintly; it showed even through the abundance of beard and moustache. Suddenly Anupam cheered up and said, 'Yes, I remember you.'

'Then tell me who I am.'

'You're Aunt Sita's father.'

'Not your father's father?'

The tone was sarcastic. Bireswar smiled at his own words, but a smile didn't come as easily to Anupam. The smile-producing factory in his mind had quite a few mechanisms out of order. Besides, his mind had become twisted like a crazy maze. Briefly, he just said, 'Yes.'

'Yes? Just yes? I'm your grandfather. It's a sin to answer me with a mere yes. This one here is Shankar, your Uncle Ramlal's son. Hope you know the relation with an uncle's son? Who knows what you know. Even God can't be sure of what you do or don't know. I better spell it out; your uncle's son is your cousin. How come you two just gape at each other?'

'I think I've seen you,' said Shankar to Anupam.

'I think I've seen you too,' said Anupam to Shankar.

'Which year of college is it for you?' asked Shankar.

'Fourth year, in sciences.'

'My fourth year too, in humanities.'

Bireswar was listening to their conversation. Suddenly he asked the driver to turn the car around and go back home. 'Aren't we going to college?' Shankar asked anxiously.

Bireswar gloomily said, 'The hell with your college! After getting home I'll lock you two in a room. And not unlock you as long as you address each other in strangers' apni. My grandchildren both, cousins, aren't you ashamed of making such formal conversation? Barely twenty-one days apart!'

Neither showed any desire to ask Bireswar who was twenty-one days younger and who older. In Anupam's mind, the grief over the wasted four paisas in bus fare had faded, but the prospect of losing a day on the class roll-call records was a still more serious waste for him. He had lost a lot in attendance percentage because of illness; if he fell short of the requisite, he'd feel very bad for having to take the finals as a non-collegiate student and, in addition, pay a precious ten rupees in fine. Still, he did not express any objection. The car headed back the way it had come. The losses? The idea of incurring a loss seemed an enjoyable thing to Anupam today. Wouldn't life become palmy, halcyon at least for a day from incurring losses by acting recklessly one day? Couldn't he incur a more serious loss today than the point in class attendance? He didn't have even a ten-rupee note in his pocket that he could throw away on the road just to suffer a big loss. He reached into his pocket for the snuff-box, but found nothing there.

He knew that it was not a momentary mood of renunciation, it was temporary madness. It happened when the mind grew too restless. It was not the act of throwing a snuff-box away, but the mind's restlessness reaching an extreme point, that made it easy for many to become renouncers.

The house was a large three-storied one, with a neat little garden in front. This part of the city was quiet and reserved, as none of the houses was a baganbari, a pleasure garden, even though almost all were homes with gardens facing the road on its two sides. No matter what the houses were like, the gardens were all like neatly arranged shops of dwarfish plants, accommodating in a tiny space as many representatives of a great forest as possible. Seeing it perhaps pleased only some eyes, considering that the number of blind with sight in this world is hardly smaller than the truly sightless.

Bireswar's plan to lock Shankar and Anupam together in a room didn't come up again, because they had started addressing each other informally by now. He took them to the interior of the house on the first floor, to a huge furniture-packed room, the kind in which the women of the house would gather after lunch to play cards, or seat the visiting neighbourhood women and join them for an informal conversation.

Aunt Sita was the first to come in there from an inner part of the house. A middle-aged widow, she was dressed in a white, very white, dhoti with a chisel-line border over a very white sleeveless chemise. The long, deep furrow on her forehead was rather prominent. It was a line not of anxiety, but of thought. This furrow had been there even seven years ago when, as a married women, she used to read little and think little. But then it had been so faint that people hadn't noticed it even if they had seen it. Then, after becoming a widow, she had taken to reading all that there was to read about human nature, everything except anatomy and psychology. All that reading involved deep thinking too. And in seven years the furrow had deepened and divided her forehead in two parts. From time to time she rubbed the line from end to end with her index finger. Maybe she pampered it, maybe she wanted to soften it and make it fade away.

She recognized Anupam as soon as he was introduced, and said, 'Oh, you're *that* Anupam! I saw you for a few days in Jalpaiguri, and yet I couldn't recognize you right away! The human mind is so strange! That was long ago though, no less than ten or eleven years ago when you were still a little boy. How old are you now? Nineteen? If I saw you ten or eleven years ago, let's say eleven, you were then . . . .'

The crease on her forehead deepened as she said to herself in amazement, 'The human mind is so strange! Nineteen minus eleven leaves eight. Yes, eight. Weren't you eight years old then?'

'I don't quite remember,' said Anupam.

'You're so much younger than me, how could you remember when I couldn't? You live in Calcutta now, do you? Where? Burra-da is here too, is he?'

'Father died last year,' said Anupam.

Bireswar, reclining on his side in a chaise longue, was listening to the conversation between aunt and nephew. At Anupam's words, he sat up straight. Then from his speechless, unmoving state, it seemed as if he had become incapable of anything beyond sitting bolt upright.

'Burra-da's no more!' It look Aunt Sita a little while to utter these words with a gasp and break into tears. How could anyone produce tears instantly at the news of the death last year of a brother whom she had seen only once in her life for a few days and from whom she hadn't received even once in those few days a sister's due? A brother who had been practically a stranger to her? Aunt Sita sat down in a chair and wept, while Bireswar only sat silently.

Today at seventy-three the news of the death of a son born to him when he was only twenty-one, and from whom as a young man of twenty-five he became separated, reached him through the lips of that son's son. Bireswar had had no experience of the grief for a son. In the seventy-three years of his life, he had seen quite a few fathers suffer a son's death, but could watching others' grief generate the experience of such a terrible event?

Shankar was not in the room at the time. After one glance at the faces of his grandfather and aunt, Anupam cast his eyes down. Bireswar's stunned silence and Sita's genteel crying suddenly set his mind on fire. These were his close relatives? Sitting in this huge house filled with such expensive furniture, what right did they have to be so distressed by the news of his father's death, when he might not have died at all if just that organ over there had been sold and the money used for his treatment?

One by one, all the other members of the family came into the room: Shankar, Shankar's mother, his three sisters and a kid brother, one of his maternal uncles and three distant relatives living here. There was also a boy of seven or eight. When Shankar's elder sister had died a year ago, this boy of hers had come to his mother's family to be brought up here.

The boy came into the room stomping loudly and then stopped short. Sita's weeping seemed to have turned everyone in the room into senseless, motionless dolls. No one knew what the matter was, but all knew that it was a serious enough reason for a middle-aged woman like Sita to cry in this self-consciously mild manner. The room's air seemed to have turned uncomfortable in some way. Besides an unfamiliar young man's presence, Sita's affected grieving, and Bireswar's stunned silence, some tragic sort of awkward sadness seemed to have created in the room an abnormal condition that could easily be sensed.

With one quick glance around, Shankar's dead sister's boy started to giggle. The boy was like this—he laughed as soon as he saw something awkward. All the major and minor incongruities in life seemed to tickle him.

'Behave yourself, Sotu!' Shankar's mother scolded him.

'Laugh again and I'll pull your ears off your head!' said Shankar.

Sotu's giggles weren't suppressed by threats. Who would touch a motherless boy in his mother's family? He knew these were empty threats. He didn't stop giggling but Sita stopped weeping when he persisted.

As Sotu was standing within his reach, Anupam reached out and pulled the boy to him, asking Bireswar, 'Who's this boy?' And Shankar's mother took a step forward, asking Sita, 'What's the matter?'

Bireswar answered Anupam: 'He's Shankar's sister Madhuri's son; she died last year.'

Sita answered Shankar's mother: 'Sister-in-law, my eldest brother died last year.'

The many people present in the room were all standing or seated at some distance from each other. Anupam drew Sotu close to him. The two of them together, they wanted to separate themselves from so many relatives all saddened by the death of one's father and the other's mother.

For some time they did just that. Sotu pulled Anupam by the hand and went out with him. Not very far, into the next room—the room in which Sita slept, hugging Sotu to her chest. Of course, she hugged Sotu only after he had fallen asleep, because when awake, he didn't like to be hugged, not even on a winter night. Not against a human chest which had some sort of strange clockwork ticking inside, and to which people desperately clasped a little boy if they could get hold of one. Sotu never indulged that sort of display of affection. It was different with Anupam, though; Anupam did not show any eagerness to crush him on his chest.

After hugging Sotu, kissing him, and asking him his name, Anupam realized that he was a strangely abnormal boy, an uncommon type of lunatic.

Asked his name, Sotu said, 'My name? You know, you're acting the way Sita does?'

'I asked you your name.'

'And I'm telling you. This is what Sita does every day. The number of kisses I've allowed her she finishes before the day's over. Then at night she sneaks up to me whispering, "You asleep, Sotu?" I lie there pretending to be asleep and don't answer. Then, putting her arm around me, she keeps kissing me, saying—can you believe this?—"Wish I had you earlier, Sotu, when you were smaller; wish your mother had died some years earlier, Sotu!"'

Clear, uninhibited, articulate talk. In the confident, precise language of an adult, without the slightest mark of his young age, Sotu seemed to be trying to communicate something to Anupam, in the way of an intimate friend, another youth; something complex and incongruous, like life losing its meaning if you were unable to go to the Greta Garbo movie today.

Anupam could say nothing in response, nor did he get a chance to. Sotu asked him his name.

'You tell me yours first, then I'll tell you mine,' said Anupam.

'I told you mine.'

'When?'

'Didn't I say Sita whispers to me at night, "You asleep, Sotu?" I said that to tell you my name. You're not smart at all!'

It did seem so to Anupam also. Sotu was such a precocious boy that, by comparison, his own intelligence was hardly worth mentioning. All he knew was the technique of hiding stupidity.

Sita came in. 'You two secretly chatting here. Strange the way the human mind works! I've been wondering where the two of you had gone. This is my bedroom, Sotu and I sleep on this bed. He can't sleep with anyone but me. Once I had a fever—the doctor said he shouldn't lie next to me, he went to sleep in my sister-in-law's bed. In the middle of the night, he sneaked out and . . . .'

Sotu was grasping Anupam's hand with both of his. Giving it an impatient jerk, Sotu said, 'Sita's constantly lying, you know.'

In a sharp tone of reproach, Sita said, 'I lie? What's the matter with you, Sotu, eh, saying all sorts of things about me? Didn't you get up in the middle of that night and come to me?'

Sotu sent savvy eye signals to Anupam while answering Sita, 'So I did.'

'Well?'

'What's wrong with it?' Sotu replies calmly.

Sita breathed in relief, and instantly softened. Resuming her mild, polished tone, she said 'That's more like it! Sometimes the way you talk scares people sick.'

A curious thought suddenly struck Anupam. Aunt Sita seemed to be affecting the speech and mannerism of a certain lady he had seen before. But he just couldn't recall who exactly it was.

Three hours somehow passed by; then Anupam started feeling a strange discomfort. There was too much groundless mental suffering among the people in this home. In the absence of any unmet material need, their minds seemed to have gone out of order; the sources of life's pleasure seemed to have frozen solid, and not easily melted by the ordinary warmth seeping into daily existence. Not quite able to make out the angle from which to look at them, to judge them or understand them, Anupam basically couldn't get past the initial wall of unfamiliarity. To think of Shankar's mother as anyone's mother at all he found quite difficult. Not because she still applied make-up on her face, or because she marred her exceptional beauty with excessive dressing and grooming, but because in maintaining an air of melancholic sadness around herself, she revealed an extreme self-centredness. Her look was sad, the expression on her face sad, her words were sad, her movement and gestures slow and heavy with the weight of sadness.

When she first walked into the atmosphere of grief, she seemed to Anupam the only one genuinely grief-stricken. Yet, despite its seeming authenticity, her excessive sadness had offended and surprised him a bit. Later on, the pall of gloom slowly lifted from all of them. The news of Anupam's father's death started getting buried under miscellaneous topics; the household's own routine started making demands upon its various members. Among those who stayed on around Anupam, the talk moved back and forth between heaven and hell, sky and underworld, but no change showed in Shankar's mother. Several times when they all laughed at something Bireswar said, she remained an image of unrelieved sorrow. Like the dark corner of a room that, blending with night's darkness, stays dark, cut off and set apart in daylight.

It's difficult to say why Anupam got this sudden urge, but at one point he said to her, 'I haven't yet offered you my pranam,' and bending forward, touched Shankar's mother's feet.

Self-deprecatingly, she shrank, and said, 'Why'd anyone bother to pay me respects!'

She was Anupam's aunt and for that reason his respectful gesture was not only her due, but to be accepted as such. But from the way she recoiled from his pranam and her words, who would say that she wasn't a beggar woman, dying of embarrassment at getting respect instead of a paisa? It seemed to Anupam as though he had not paid her the respects she was entitled to, but added insult to injury, falsely inflicting on the already dead a sacrificial falchion blow.

This odd, permanent sadness of Shankar's mother aggravated the unease in Anupam's mind. In three hours, he had thought of fleeing three hundred times. But Bireswar wanted to pay no attention to his mention of leaving, he laughed it away. And teased him. Was this some stranger's house that he was so eager to take leave?

'Not that. I've work to do.'

'What work? You won't be going to college today.'

'I'll be going home now, not to college.'

'I too will be going there. A little later in the afternoon. We can go together.'

'You'll go to our home?'

Anupam at once felt embarrassed at this unguarded expression of his genuine surprise. His question sounded unseemly, barbed with allusion to Bireswar's never having come to their place so far.

'Your father wouldn't allow me in your home, Anu,' Bireswar replied in a mild voice.

Not sure of what sense to make of this explanation, Anupam kept silent.

2

When the four of them—Bireswar, Shankar, Anupam, and Sotu—came to Anupam's home, the afternoon sun had mellowed. Shankar had a desire to come, Bireswar insisted that he come. No one had any desire to bring Sotu, but he insisted on coming along.

The paint on the front door of the house was peeling, the address was written in chalk, and by an unskilled hand at that. The discomfort Shankar had felt when starting out from their place grew rapidly from the moment they entered the narrow lane, leaving the car on the big road. Not because the lane was dingy, but because he was close to a poor relative's home. Shankar had a poor friend who once invited him to his house. Shankar would never forget the experience. That poor friend mingled very well with all when he came to Shankar's home; the minor ways in which he seemed different were neither regrettable nor embarrassing. But in a poor home Shankar was a misfit, an alien. In the exchange of polite words, he kept stumbling and causing others to stumble too. Shankar was really afraid of a poor home. He felt like a prisoner inside one, and staying in it for half an hour made him see himself as the object of contemptuous pity for all its members, young and old.

Answering the knocker, Anupam's mother Sadhana opened the door. It was so obvious that she recognized Bireswar as soon as she saw him that Anupam saw no need to say anything.

Respectfully she covered her head partially with her sari, but stood in the doorway, blocking their entry, apparently thinking of something. Then she stepped aside to ask the elderly visitor in.

Entering the house, Shankar was amazed. He had imagined a damp, unclean interior, where the air smelled foul in a dulled way, the faces had the stamp of frustrated greed, and scattered everywhere were the makeshift arrangements used to patch and mend the broken lives just to get through each day. In this home, the work-porch was not damp, just wet from washing, and the only smell in the air was that of fresh cooking. The only absence stamped on the faces of the people in this home was that of luxuries; the arrangements for daily living were only inexpensive.

Shankar had no idea that anybody could keep such inexpensive furniture and tools of daily use so neatly organized in so small a home.

Each object on the floor was in its intended place, not the slightest bit awry. The things that belonged to shelves were on the shelves, the things that belonged to the wall were on the wall, the things that belonged to the window were at the window—it was obvious that someone's meticulous eyes kept constant watch over these small and large inanimate objects, even made sure that on the window-sill used as a shelf, the tiny brass bowl of shredded betel nut on the right of the betel-leaf container never moved to its left.

Whose eyes meticulously attended to these minute details became evident when a mat was offered to seat the guests.

As soon as the tall, skinny girl rose from unrolling the mat on the floor, Sadhana corrected her: 'Half the mat's still unrolled, Nimi.' When Nimi straightened up after smoothing out the mat, Sadhana said to her, 'How did those matchsticks come into the room? Pick them up and throw them away.'

As soon as Nimi had picked up the three used matchsticks from the floor, Sadhana said, 'This is your grandfather, Nimi. Pay him your respects before you go out of the room.'

And then, after all this while, Sadhana herself touched Bireswar's feet.

No one sat down on the mat spread with so much care except Bireswar. There was a low stool in the room. Shankar sat on it and kept fidgeting, while Sotu walked about the room. Attempts were made to make him sit down, but they didn't work. In a gently reproachful voice Sadhana remarked, 'Quite a disobedient boy, isn't he?'

Shankar suddenly flared up irritably, and scolded him in a roar: 'Will you sit down, Sotu? Or I'll tear your ears off!'

Sadhana corrected him. 'No, you shouldn't scold a little boy like that. Children can't be taught obedience and manners by scolding and beating them. You've to be more patient, son. They're not born with good qualities, those who're around them build up their character—oh, no, he laughs after getting scolded!'

'Laughing is his disease, he laughs whether he's scolded or not,' said Bireswar.

'I haven't seen such a boy before!' Saying this, Sadhana tried to draw him close to her, perhaps to take a good look at his face, but with one glance at her face Sotu bounced out of the room. 'Restless, isn't he?' she remarked gently.

'Yes,' said Bireswar.

With this 'yes', the people in the room seemed to have run out of all need to talk. No one had anything to ask, no one had anything to say in answer. Shankar had seen similar situations occur in his friends' homes. In all those families, however, there was someone who would sustain the rhythm of conversation. Either the mistress of the house or a socially forward daughter of hers would come forth with a pleasant smile and bring in an old reference from somewhere and patch over the gap in conversation, which would then continue to flow on smoothly. But today, in this uneasy meeting of relatives, who was to compose prefaces to ease the conversation? In a sense Bireswar's son had just died, since he first learned of it today—only a few hours ago. Sitting before that son's wife in widow's garb, was it possible to make conversation today? There was, of course, much to say, but those words had to be kept offstage, for the heart always dwelt in the background. To bring out what was within the heart would have been an immature thing to do.

Sadhana finally said, 'You have become quite frail, Father.'

'I've reached the age, my dear, when I can only become more frail. But whatever health I've still left makes me worry about how much longer I have to be on this side of life.'

Pausing, he said, 'You knew my address, yet you didn't even send me a message?'

With downcast face, Sadhana said, 'He had asked me not to.'

In a gentle tone Bireswar said, 'You know everything from the very beginning, Bou-ma, it's not to your husband that I'm guilty of wrongdoing. If I wronged anyone, it was his mother. Still, he couldn't forgive me even in the last moments before leaving?'

'It's not that, Father,' said Sadhana. 'He told me before his death that all his life he caused you a lot of undue pain, that it'd be better to spare you this news.'

'Undue!' Bireswar sat up straight.

'That's what he said. I, too, thought that at your age, there'd be no point troubling you . . . .'

'You kept silent because you thought I'd die of old age before the news could reach me some other way, isn't it, Bou-ma?'

Now he seemed angry, as though he just couldn't forgive the wrong done to him by depriving him one whole year's grief over a son's death. Sadhana said nothing. Shankar glanced from one to the other with apprehensive eyes. Something had escaped from the cave of the past and appeared in this tiny room, something that drained the hearts of these closely related people. Although Anupam and Nimi were in the room, Shankar couldn't see them, obscured as they were by the ghost of the past. But if it angered Bireswar, why wasn't he angry when Anupam gave him the news at their place? What reason could he have to be angry with Anupam's mother?

Grasping his beard in his fist, Bireswar said, 'You went to college, right, Bou-ma?'

'Yes.'

'You've been living in the real world all this time, you've struggled alone for so long raising a family, you must then have a lot of worldly sense. You're intelligent, aren't you?'

'Why are you asking me all this?'

'Shouldn't I? Can you imagine how you altered the course of so many lives by putting your practical judgement to work? If I had been sent a message and I had come to his deathbed, then what troubled us for twenty-five years might have been resolved. Grief over my son's death? That can't be so unbearable when I know I'll soon go where my son's gone. Couldn't you have shown me more kindness by giving me a chance to make amends for the mistake I made?'

'That was not possible, Father,' said Sadhana in a voice as calm as before.

'Not possible? Why was it not possible?'

Sadhana was silent and Shankar helplessly watched Bireswar's face. What would he do now? With the seventy-three years of experience behind him, was Bireswar now going to shout at the middle-aged wife of a son with whom he had had no relationship for twenty-five years? What strange sort of quarrel were they getting themselves into today!

He repeated firmly, 'Don't be childish, Bou-ma. Tell me why it wasn't possible.'

'What's the use of explaining, Father? It'll make you suffer pointlessly.'

'Do you think my heart is so innocent of pain that I won't be able to bear the suffering that you've in store for me? Forget about my pain, just tell me in clear language whatever you have in you to say, I beg you with clasped hands.'

'It wasn't possible because I wouldn't have allowed it.'

'You wouldn't have allowed it?'

'No. I wouldn't have allowed it then, and I never will.'

Bireswar seemed to slump from exhaustion. Shankar looked out of the window and saw that the slanted rays of the afternoon sun, reflected from a mirror in the first-floor room of some house, shone on the wet patio on exactly the spot where a girl of Nimi's age in widow's clothing was about to sit down to scour a pile of plates and pots.

The help of the pool of reflected sunlight was quite superfluous. Shankar's eyes were dazzled by the very manner in which she set about her dishwashing. The dramatic dialogue going on in the room between his grandfather and his aunt had taken one quarter of a century to develop. An even more spectacular drama was created in one minute as the girl lifted a bucketful of water from the cement tank and squatted to scour the pile. She was tall and wide, her strong build like a non-Bengali girl's, her complexion an average brown, her sari stark white. It was not all this—these only made her splendid-looking—it was the incredibly, unspeakably regal manner of her going about the scrubbing of pots and plates that was so dramatic. As if a mighty sovereign, done with conquering the world, and finding nothing else to do, had turned to scouring pots out of sheer exasperation, and would return to the throne once she calmed down.

But after finishing with the pots and plates, she came in and sat down quite near Shankar, on a piece of plank with four stumps attached to it. She came in not to sit, however, but to ask for the storeroom key. She evidently wasn't interested in who else happened to be in the room. Bireswar was the one who expressed an interest in her, perhaps to put an end to the emotionally charged exchange with his daughter-in-law about his departed son.

'Who is this girl, Bou-ma?'

'She's Taranga.'

'Short for Tarangini?'

'Just Taranga,' the girl herself answered.

His attempt at light-hearted joking didn't work. Still, Bireswar asked mock-seriously, 'How's Taranga related to us?'

'Are you talking of blood relationship? I'm not related in that sense, I just live here.'

'How categorically you rule out relationship, girl! Don't you know I'm your grandfather?'

'Grandfather on my mother's side or father's side?' Taranga asked.

Sadhana then stepped in to introduce them: 'Taranga, this is my father-in-law, and this is Anupam's cousin Shankarlal,' and turning to Bireswar, 'You may not remember, Father, your son's cousin Rajani. Taranga is his third daughter.'

Taranga then greeted them both in a single vigorous joining of palms, almost in the manner of a clap, but perhaps her hands being soft, the sound made was slight. Then Sadhana asked her to sit down with them. It was an order—simple, natural, pleasant-sounding, made in the tone of a request.

'Yes, I'll stay. But lots of things are waiting to be done, Aunt.'

'Don't be impolite, Toru. So many times I've told you that when there're visitors in the house, young women have no other work; their only duty then is to make their guests feel welcome and look after their comfort. These are close relatives; if they were not, you know how uncomfortable they'd have felt at your words? They'd have thought that by visiting us they've disrupted housework and so mustn't stay for long. What sort of home is it where visitors can't feel comfortable, what sort of housework can that home have! A young woman who's able to take in her stride extra duties any time, even throughout the day, and still manage all the housework is a truly efficient young woman. From the window, I saw you sit down to wash the dishes, I didn't say anything then. But don't act like this ever again, Toru, I find it very painful if you keep forgetting what I've tried so hard to teach . . . . What time is it, Nimi? Five-thirty. Oh, there will soon be no water in the tap!'

'Shall I go, Aunt, and store the water for cooking and drinking at least?'

After a second's thought Sadhana said, 'No, you sit here. Let Nimi go to store the water. Nimi, don't take the large brass pot to the tap, you won't be able to bring it back full. Bring water from the tap in the small pot to fill the large one. Be sure to wash the lids—they haven't been washed for three days; remember to use the laundry soap to wash them, not the bath soap. There are two pieces of it on the shelf in the bathroom; use the smaller piece. And listen—why do you leave before I finish telling you all I need to? I'm getting tired of having to repeat myself to all of you, Nimi—how many times do I've to teach you the same thing? Now, what was I going to tell you? Oh, no, I've lost track!'

Sadhana smiled slightly and said ruefully, 'Don't know what's wrong with my head. Can't seem to be able to keep track of everything in the household the way I used to, the head gets dizzy worrying. Oh, yes. After storing the water, Nimi, and lighting the stove, come and let me know. Again you're leaving before I'm through! What's the matter with you today, Nimi? When starting the stove, put the pot of milk on it before lighting the spirit. And don't leave the milkpot uncovered when you come for me, the cat will put its mouth to it.'

'If the milk comes to a boil when I come to tell you, Ma?'

'How? You'll light the spirit, prime the pump and tell me. How can a quart and a half of milk come to boil in that time? Your mind's not on work today, Nimi, nothing will get done right. You stay here, I'll go myself.'

Nimi cried out in anguished protest: 'No, Ma, you don't have to go, I can do it.'

Sadhana rebuked her in a saddened tone, 'No, Nimi, don't talk like that. What I decided I didn't without thinking, without reason. Listen to me, stay here, and the two of you sing songs for the guests here. I'll finish doing these few things in a blink, how long can it take me? Nimi, you sing first—"The sunshine is strong outside . . . ." Toru, what will you sing? How about "The end of the sky, the blue of the air, and a light far away, so far away . . .?"'

Taranga said, 'All right.'

Sadhana now turned to Bireswar and said, 'All right, Father? I'll be back by the time the girls finish singing their songs.'

She asked for permission to leave. Instead, he asked her: 'You taught them to sing, right, Bou-ma?'

'Yes. I have been teaching Nimi from the time she was a kid. She can sing well, but her voice isn't that melodious. Toru started recently; her singing skill isn't perfect, but her voice is very sweet. You'll enjoy her singing more than Nimi's. That's why I asked her to sing after Nimi. Let me take leave now before the water turns off.'

The timed supply of tapwater stops and comes on again. Time passes and yet stays on. It really stays—all the time. Life stories are temporary; but being able to see the continuity in changes and cycles without the aid of repetition and sequel perhaps amounts to a crime to the pathologically naive. At least that's what the intelligent have set aside for the foolish. The rush of sensation Shankar felt from the moment Taranga came in and sat down near him was rather unfamiliar. But he didn't have the frame of mind to grasp its nature. Had it come after knowing her for a while, he would've argued that the overpowering nature of his sensation had a history to it and was therefore to an extent normal, understandable. Now he suffered within from feeling ashamed for being so turned on at the first sight of Taranga. Sotu was now back in the room. Nimi sang of the bright sun, Taranga of the blue sky. Yet Shankar's dread of impropriety left him without peace of mind.

Bireswar, too, was left without peace of mind, out of an almost similar woman-related sense of guilt. Yet his crime was socially acceptable and normal for his time—a man marrying thrice. Intemperance in Bireswar's life wasn't allowed beyond what proved to be necessary to learn from experience. To this day he didn't quite understand what could have been so terribly wrong with a man marrying three times, yet he was overcome from perceiving the unspoken censure that had accumulated in this home over a long period of time. Anupam's father and grandmother had, as it were, arranged that this sense of guilt would mingle with the permanent disquiet of his mind to punish him. They seemed to have known that some day he'd simply have to come to this almost unknown branch of his family and breathe awhile in this tiny room's air mixed with an unfamiliar, mild fragrance.

His mind's agitation almost brought tears to Bireswar's eyes. Contrary, unnatural penalties tormented human life. Anupam's grandmother did the wrong of deserting her husband, and he wasn't let off with just bearing the unhappiness all these years—now he had to lose even his self-respect.

Sadhana came back with tea and snacks—nothing much, a simple pudding of semolina browned in butter and boiled in milk and some biscuits. Bireswar didn't eat any of this. He never ate anything before the evening prayer. How about doing his prayers here and having some food? No, he had to be home at dusk to pray, and then go to bed without taking any food at all.

With dusk a feeling of being profoundly tired descended on Bireswar. He got up. Together, they all went down to the patio below. There, Bireswar asked Sadhana in a worn-out voice, 'Will you never come to my house, Bou-ma?'

'Why wouldn't I, Father?'

'Then come one day, meet the rest of the family, get acquainted with the people there. After that I'll make you a request.'

'I know what request you'll make, Father, but I don't think it'll be possible for me to keep it. For me to move to your house. . . .'

After the kind of argument they had had over a person who died a year ago, Shankar feared that Bireswar might end up shouting at Sadhana now. Bireswar had checked himself then. Now, at the leave-taking, as soon as he heard Sadhana's reply, he flared up and rebuked her so loudly it seemed as though he were paying in full, principal and interest, what was her due then.

'Bou-ma,' he said, 'I know that you've a sharp mind, that you understand everything. But show off your intelligence after you hear me to the end, keep quiet now. The cleverness of the lot of you makes it quite trying for people to go on living.'

He strode away, and Sadhana called after him, 'Wait, Father, let me touch you feet.'

'Do it when you come to my place.'

Heatedly Bireswar flung open the front door and went out. Shankar followed him. At the head of the lane, when getting into the car, he was the one to notice that Sotu had been left behind.

'Sotu is back there, Grandpa.'

Bireswar, already sitting in the car, said, 'Get him. Make it quick.'

The front door wasn't closed yet. Going in, Shankar saw that already in this short time, the coal stove had been lighted, Sadhana was cutting vegetables, Nimi kneading the wheat flour, and Taranga was at the grindstone preparing spices. Sotu, snuggling against Taranga and telling her something, fell silent upon seeing Shankar.

'Come along, Sotu,' said Shankar.

'No,' said Sotu.

How did Sotu manage to get so close to Taranga in such a short time! Seeing Shankar take two more steps towards him, he clung to her with both his arms around her neck.

'When you were all sitting upstairs, the boy came to the rooftop cell and conferred with me about not going back with you,' Taranga explained, 'he'll stay here, he says.'

Sadhana added, 'If he doesn't want to go, let him stay now. I'll bring him back tomorrow.'

'You're coming tomorrow?'

'The way father just left in a huff, it's better that we come tomorrow. My husband asked me on his deathbed not to hurt his father's feelings. You know, Shankar, I'm in such a difficult situation. The instructions my husband left me are such that if I try to follow one, it compromises another. Caught between opposite pulls drains the life out of me, son.'

Silently sympathizing with her Shankar asked, 'What time shall I send the car tomorrow?'

Sadhana was surprised. 'Why should we need a car? Tomorrow's Thursday, right? Anupam'll be going to college later, he can take us there first.'

Taranga said, 'Sotu's asking me not to go, Aunt. Says he won't go, and won't let me go.'

She said this to Sadhana with a smile, but when her eyes turned to Shankar her face at once became grim.

In this manner, the two branches of the same family came close, but did not merge. One of Bireswar's daughters-in-law went on trying hard not to waste the heat in even the bit of spirit used to light the stove, while the other, with the extravagance prompted by melancholia, went on using globs of cream on her face that cost as much a container as ten bottles of spirit. In the budget of one of Bireswar's grandsons, a paisa for a paan remained luxury spending, while the other lighted cigarettes one after another, each costing as much as ten rolls of paan.

Had Anupam's father left her with instruction only to hurt Bireswar's ego, had he asked only that none of his family ever accept a paisa from Bireswar, then perhaps Sadhana could, faced with Bireswar's arguments, commands, requests and pleas, accept at least the last and move into his house, and with a sigh of relief, recline on a soft sofa under the ceiling fan. But this separate family had been built on the vow to keep Bireswar feeling rejected for ever. For the members of this family, the spine stayed straight from strenuously pursuing the goal of conquering the temptation for a share of Bireswar's money which could be had the moment they went to him. How could all that be negated today? If was not just a question of disobeying her dead husband's wish, it was difficult for her to forget that from the time they were married he told her repeatedly like a mantra: 'If I die suddenly Sadhana, and you're in need of money, then instead of holding an upturned palm to my father, become unchaste. You've beauty and there're many rich people in the city of Calcutta.' What a terrible thing to say! But with such a passion he said those words! Sadhana knew her husband was crazy. Raised by the kind of crazed woman his mother was, it was surprising that he turned out merely crazy, not totally insane.

Besides, what'd she do with more money? The house was their own, so they didn't have to worry about a place to say. Before the money she had in savings ran out, Anupam would be ready to start making a living.

The visits were quite frequent at first, then they decreased. After every few days, Bireswar would come in his car, spend some time here, and take them all to his place. There the day's cooking and eating arrangements would become almost festive, and with Bireswar presiding, everyone would gather for conversation, laughter and stories, and turn it into a celebration of union. But how long could Sadhana carry on with these one-way visits? It was beyond Sadhana's means to incur the kind of expenses involved in having Bireswar's entire household visit her home. Besides, no matter how much laughter and merriment there was at the two families' get-together in Bireswar's house, no one once forgot that those supposed to be living there as household members were visiting as temporary guests and the day's extra talking and laughter arose only from that. The members of Bireswar's household, when visiting Sadhana's home together, didn't have space even to move, the place seemed so crammed! Shankar's mother felt the most discomfort. Stepping outside home in a sari that cost less than twenty-seven rupees would only aggravate her melancholia by adding the shame of losing face; yet the feeling that an expensive sari mocked her became too clear the moment she entered Sadhana's home, even if it stayed unclear elsewhere. Soon, she could no longer bear mocking herself with her own twenty-seven-rupee sari.

'I've a bad headache, sister-in-law. All right if I change the sari?'

Without attempting to understand the connection between having a headache and wanting to change saris, Sadhana handed her one of Nimi's saris. After changing into Nimi's plain sari, Shankar's mother still felt troubled. The perception of herself as a beggar woman, that was almost always present in her mind, now grew unbearable. 'I'm not feeling well, sister-in-law. Let me go back home instead. Is it all right if I do?'

'Want to lie down here? Why don't you lie down a little?'

But lying down cannot relieve mental agitation. In some situations, it can intensify the suffering instead. Everyone was concerned after learning that Shankar's mother was not feeling well, everyone asked her what was wrong, how she felt now, and so on. Lying down in Sadhana's bed, Shankar's mother felt she was choking. What a shame she was such a bother for everybody! Wouldn't she be better-off dead than this way?

Shankarlal's visits to this house followed a curious rule. He came alone, and after coming three or four days in a row, he didn't show up for eight to ten days. It would seem as if his craving to be here would leave him after being here three or four days in a row, and after staying away eight to ten days, he would develop such a craving to be back that he would have to come several days in a row in order to satisfy it. On that first day, the smile on Taranga's face turned to a scowl upon noticing Shankarlal's face, but now, in the manner of a kindly empress, she forgave his immature gazing and even talked to him with a smile.

'You're getting thinner every day.'

'Because the exams are getting nearer.'

'Getting thin from studying? Great! Are you sure you'll last until the exams at this rate?'

It wasn't sarcasm; Taranga didn't even know how to be sarcastic! Sarcasm didn't fit in with her speech; it was with concern that she said these words. But this time Shankar did not return for almost fifteen days. When he came after fifteen days, he had grown even thinner. But Taranga refrained from remarking any more on his health. And Shankar in his turn increased his visits this time to a full four days in a row.

Sotu came here from time to time and stayed on for a day or two. He wanted to come with everybody, and each time he came he wanted to stay for ever, but no one brought him every time or let him stay more than a day or two at a time.

The only one who didn't come was Shankarlal's father, Ramlal. He worked in the court as a lawyer and stayed out late drinking somewhere or the other. When home, he kept to himself in his room. He didn't bother anyone in the household, no one bothered him. The number of words he exchanged with Bireswar in a month could perhaps be counted on one's fingertips.

Coming home at two in the morning, if he found Shankarlal studying, he went up to his room, on steady or unsteady feet, and said to him, 'Turn off the light and go to sleep, Shankar.'

Without a word Shankarlal turned off the light and lay down in his bed.

3

It's hard to say which one of them, Shankar or Anupam, stayed up longer studying for the exams. Both had goals equally ambitious, dreams equally complex. Shankar wanted to become a scholar, Anupam a scientist. Both felt that even if he wouldn't be without parallel, he'd leave behind great achievements and rise so high that people would be spellbound with respect, awe, even fear.

Shankar's exams were over first, in the middle of a sweltering hot day. As soon as he finished writing his answer to the last question, it hit him that there was really no one in the world except Taranga, and with this his mind slipped into a grand illusion. He felt exactly as a thief felt on finding out there was nobody at home, that a great chance had come his way. Was it every day that one had the opportunity to grasp so clearly that since the whole world felt empty and false without Taranga, it must therefore be absolutely necessary to have Taranga?

It took him to four in the afternoon to reach Anupam's house. Following her routine, Taranga was at the tap scouring pots and plates. Without washing off the scrub ash all over her hands, she came to the front door and unbarred it with her elbow. Then, to save Shankar's silk shirt from getting smeared with the wet ash, she gave him a push with the same elbow. Although his shirt was saved, his hands got smeared from passionately grasping Taranga's hands at once.

'Seems you're out of your mind,' Taranga said to him.

Shankar's gaunt body, drained face and bewildered look would make one think that not just his mind, but all his body mechanisms were out of order. Even without comparing him today with the way he looked on that first day when he reluctantly stepped in through this door at about this hour, one couldn't but suspect that he had suffered a mortal illness in the meantime. The only surprising thing, it would seem, was that instead of departing for the other world he had come to this house to grasp Taranga's ash-covered hands. However, his words and gestures made it abundantly clear that a forerunner of the other world, called a ghost by folks in plain language, was sitting tight on his shoulders.

After giving the matter some thought, Taranga turned Shankar straight out of the house. 'Go home now,' she said. 'You just finished taking the exams. Let yourself recover with a regular routine of bath, meals and sleep for a few days. Then you'll realize how totally insane you're acting today.'

Shankar knew neither to communicate love, nor how to tell if someone loved him. So he didn't understand Taranga's words, or anything for that matter. Standing in the empty yard, he told her things in such a manner that though she got the substance, she failed to follow the words. He claimed that the fact that after taking his last exam he had roamed the streets in this heat instead of going home was in itself irrefutable proof that he was madly in love with her.

Agreeing with him, she said, 'That's why I'm asking you to go home now, and take rest.'

Shankar hadn't come here to listen to this sort of stuff, he paid no attention at all to Taranga's words, and went on earnestly pleading his case. Because of Taranga his studies had suffered, because of her he couldn't write his answers well, because of her he had been through so much pain. It was as if for compensation for all these damages that he was tightly holding her hands, never to let go of them. Taranga asked him once to let go of her hands; perhaps Shankar heard her, perhaps he didn't, her hands were still tightly in his grip. Her face turned sullen at this. Not just because having come here to express his love for her, he was ignoring her, not paying attention to a word she said, but because she couldn't tolerate being ignored by anyone under any circumstance.

'I'm telling you to let go of my hands, can't you hear? Why do you pretend that you are strong when there's not one bit of strength left in your body?'

'I pretend to being strong?'

'What else do you think you're doing? If you had any strength to exert, you could've impressed me, but you're shaking and still holding my hands as if you'd wrestle with me. Come, let's go to the porch in the shade, then I'll hear what you've got to say.'

Taranga's reproach slackened Shankar's grip; now she herself dragged him by the hand to the porch like an inanimate object, pointed to a stool and ordered: 'Sit down.'

His delay in obeying her order now made the residue of her concern for his silk shirt disappear; putting her ash-smeared hands on his shoulders she pushed him down on the stool. Then she went to the tap and washed her hands along with a well-scrubbed brass tumbler. She filled the tumbler with cold water, brought it to him, and said, 'Here, drink some water, the words are getting stuck in your throat. Now, tell me coherently what you've been trying to say for so long.'

'Haven't you understood?'

'Why should I? A young man of your age who can't manage to

express clearly to a young woman what's on his mind, his babble doesn't deserve any attention even if understood.'

Shankar was now angry, and said, 'A young woman of your age who can talk this way deserves to be despised.'

But one who could scour pots and plates with the majesty of a queen couldn't be upset so easily. 'That's a separate matter,' she replied with the hint of a smile.

'You're insane, Toru.'

'Who, me? What's insane about me? That I refuse to act insane in step with you?'

Seeing Shankar on the verge of fury, she quickly adopted a modest tone and said, 'Let's not talk about me. We're talking about you, let's stick to that. Will you honour a request I have for you? Go home today. Come back after a month, and tell me what you wanted to say today. In the meantime, as soon as you feel a little better with the regular bathing and meals, you'll see perfectly well how you're unduly complicating a rather simple ailment.'

Precise, unchanging advice, like a gramophone record being played. It seemed to Shankar that a record player might be as heartless, even it didn't have the capacity to be as shameless.

'Very amused, aren't you?'

Taranga immediately shook her head and said, 'No, I'm saddened. It pains me to think that the pressure of exams can so badly affect a young man like you.'

'It pains me too to think that excessive novel reading can turn a young girl like you so shameless.'

'Since both of us are so pained, shouldn't you better go home.'

'After going home, I should take to timely bath and meals and sleep, right?'

Like a mere mortal's attempt to insult a goddess residing up in the sky, Shankar's barbed question had no effect on Taranga. With the happiness of a guru who has finally been able to make a disciple understand a difficult philosophical proposition, she said, 'Absolutely. Come back when you feel better both physically and mentally. I want to talk to you! Don't stay away feeling embarrassed thinking of today.'

Getting off into the yard, Shankar said, 'I'll never again come to your place.'

'This is not my place,' replied Taranga.

The lane seemed to have now become transformed, the surroundings of the road at the end of the lane gained some novelty. Perhaps it had taken him a little longer to communicate love to Taranga than it would have to bang his head against a wall, but the effect was just the same. The world had changed. Did Shankar have any idea all this time that the world existed only in our heads? Walking along the road, he felt as though he had suddenly become a wise man, even a great man. After Taranga's rejection it felt exactly as it had felt right after his last exam—that the need to go on living was over. Now he knew that what Taranga had done was only clarify that vague, inexplicable, inscrutable feeling of life coming to an end with the exams, nothing more.

Who was Taranga? Nobody really! What was the world? Mere chemical reactions in the brain. What was life? Whatever it was thought to be.

No reason, therefore, to feel any pain. Yet, why was he needlessly feeling this pain? Was it because he was walking slowly? He walked faster. It didn't help one bit. He only sweated a little more. Was it perhaps because he was thirsty?

While putting out his thirst at a betel stand with the water of a green coconut, Shankar felt a shiver, and his head spun. It spun so sharply that he even heard the buzz of the spin. Whatever happened inside his head due to Taranga's rejection was understandable, but what sort of bizarre reaction was this? There was ash on his hand still. He washed it off with some of the green coconut water. This too was a form of Taranga's ridicule; instead of giving herself, she gave him some stove ash. How devilishly well she had mastered the art of cheating people!

Taranga's trickery had pervaded his world like floodwater. Even the betel-seller tried to palm off a bad quarter on him as if Shankar had lost the ability even to notice a bad quarter because of Taranga. Angered at the paanwalla's resentment on being shouted at, Shankar gave him a slap. It caused a commotion that lasted some time! But that was all right; when a gentleman in expensive clothes slapped a paanwalla after hurling abusive words at him, how far could things go? Some commotion, and then it's over.

After walking for some time along the side of the road baked by the sun, Shankar realized that his mind now felt quite calm. It was still restless to do something terrible, but compared to its bewildered state so long it seemed composed. No need to worry any more; now he would be able to act calmly, taking account of all aspects; nothing would cause him the slightest excitement, fatigue wouldn't take hold, effortlessly he would maintain an easy poise in his talk and conduct.

Didn't Taranga ask him to come back after reaching this state of mind? If instead of several days of a timely bath-meals-sleep regimen, he could bring about this transformation within himself in just half an hour by means of willpower, what objection could she have? If she did have anything to say in objection, what could be wrong with going back just to hear it? In matters of this sort, it was better to be without a doubt. Had he taken any notice of what she said or what she might have hinted at in the tone of her answer? Perhaps he had misunderstood her all along. Perhaps she was being playful. Scouring pots in the midday heat wasn't such a pleasant chore. Perhaps finding him there in the midst of it, she only attempted to lighten it a bit, and now she was regretting the lost opportunity. Perhaps her large eyes were filled with tears and they were dripping on the scrubbed pile of pots and plates. Perhaps she was amazed at the ignorance of a man who failed to catch the hidden meaning in the spoken words of a young woman. Perhaps she was tossing in doubt and anxiety wondering if he'd sense the real meaning of her remark, 'Don't stay away embarrassed thinking of today;' perhaps she felt like killing herself for not making the meaning clearer to him.

Shankar's heart was pounding wildly again, though he wasn't aware of it really. Walking back by the shop of the very same paanwalla he had slapped, he bought a packet of cigarettes from him. Even though he sensed that the paanwalla had by now figured out his madness, he felt not the slightest bit embarrassed. Noticing how profusely he was sweating from walking fast, he hired a rickshaw.

This time Anupam opened the door. Whichever hell he had been to, he was back in this short time. It was no longer possible to see Taranga alone. Finished with scrubbing pots, she was filling the water pots; she saw Shankar but said nothing.

Anupam said shyly, almost in embarrassment, 'I can't talk to you now. Hope you won't mind—I have physics tomorrow, two sections on the same day.' He smiled faintly, awkwardly rubbing his hands together. Hadn't he too stayed up a lot of nights studying!

'No, no. You go back to your studies,' Shankar told him.

Although Anupam went into his room and barred the door, Taranga couldn't be seen alone. Sadhana came from upstairs, Nimi out of one of the groundfloor rooms. Sadhana asked Shankar to sit down, Nimi asked him like a spoiled kid, 'Shankar-da, will you light the stove for me?'

Annoyed, Sadhana scolded her, 'Don't talk in that whining tone, Nimi, it sounds awful. Can't you light the stove yourself? Why do you ask Shankar?'

'Shankar-da does it so well.'

Annoyed even more, Sadhana said, 'Haven't I told you, Nimi, not to call him Shankar-da? That too in a tone as if you're making fun of his name? Shankar is older than Anu; you're to call him Burra-da.'

Taranga's water pot was filled, but where were the tears in her eyes, the tears supposed to be dripping on scoured pots and plates? The eyes weren't wet, the face not sad! If only she'd give a faint smile on seeing him! If she'd glance at him even once from the corner of her eyes!

Putting the water pot back in its place, she went upstairs to do something. Sadhana had just asked him a question, but without paying attention to it, Shankar stubbornly followed Taranga upstairs, and asked stupidly, 'Are you angry with me?'

'Didn't I tell you to go home?' she retorted.

With an air of self-confidence, he breezily said, 'That you did.'

'Then why are you bothering me?'

'I'm bothering you?'

'Didn't that get into your head even after so much explaining? Are you an idiot or something? Such a simple thing, even this you can't understand without having it knocked into your head with a stick? I can't imagine why the likes of you get born on earth as human beings! Do you know that it's because of all those like you that the country is going to the dogs?'

Many other things she said. Discovering in a very short time quite a few truths—that Taranga also knew how to lecture, that she wasn't a young woman despite being one, if he died today she would not sigh even once—Shankar was out again on the street. The world that was inside his head had now come outside—in the stain of betel-juice spit on the pavement that was scoured in little squares, in the dirty puddles, in the torn papers and tattered leaves, in the dogs, the people, the cows, the horses and carriages, in the houses, in the sky, in everything out here. He perceived the trick of how everything outside existed despite the whirl of nothingness inside his head. Did Shankar have any more confusion as to what reality was? Taranga was right to say that a person who wept for just one or two was unworthy of being known as a human being. One should weep, if one must, for something bigger. Only that weeping showed true love, everything else was an affectation. Some other things she said too. Shankar realized to his amazement that he had already forgotten most of the big things she had said with her large eyes dilated still larger. All these years he had been able to commit to memory so many things he read from so many books, but the things Taranga said he forgot in ten minutes? No question about his being good for nothing.

But then who wasn't a good for nothing? Suddenly his vision seemed charged with a new ray, letting it penetrate into a person—even the inside of that man who stood a hundred or a hundred and fifty yards away, smoking a cigar and waiting for the tram. By the time he reached the man, the tram came, and Shankar got in too. The men and women on the tram, the natives, the non-natives, and the hybrids, all were good for nothing. Not one face bore the mark of humanity; it was doubtful if any one of them was willing to cry for even one person, let alone something bigger and greater, so stricken they looked with the sorrow of having to part with a few coins on tram fare. Shankar didn't want to go home yet. Still, he got off at the corner of the park where he needed to catch a bus in order to get home.

A rally was going on in the park. Even without entering it, one could tell it was an assembly of this country's people held in this country's name, because collectively it had the appearance of a heap of refuse . . . a clutter of useless, rejected people swept up by the broom of cheap, trendy excitement. With the feeling now strong in him that with Taranga the whole world had rejected him, he sensed an attraction for the multitude that resembled a rubble heap of a collapsed building.

Shankar went into the park and merged with the crowd. Quite a large number of people were collected there, maybe three thousand. Looking around at the faces near him, he found that the characteristic of the gathering that struck him from the outside now appeared stamped on each face. Quite clearly, some had stopped by on the way home from office work, looking for a little variety without having to pay for it; some had postponed aimless wanderings to join the crowd; some had come hoping for a brief escape from relentless self-loathing by joining a meeting called for the country's good; some were here to satisfy an addiction to the romantic tingle of exuberance that ran in such a gathering. The old man on his right was constantly nodding his head, whether because he had a tick or was in agreement with the speaker, it was hard to tell. The middle-aged man on his left was staring dumbly at the podium, his mouth open, as if he was trying to digest the words that had already entered his ears while trying not to miss what was being said now. The young man in front of him kept moving restlessly, perhaps as a result of autoerotic habits, resenting temporary loss of the right to dwell in his body, but unable to leave the meeting to earn the right to dwell in the country.

Although Shankar felt more inclined to watch the faces around him, he forced his eyes to the dais and tried to listen to what was being said. At once it seemed to him as if he was listening to Taranga, as if Taranga herself stood on the dais shouting in an assumed thick male voice: 'Only crying for the country and the people is genuine, all other crying is silly affectation.'

It was only after seeing the second speaker that an urge to get up on the dais gripped Shankar. He knew the gentleman, but the murmur of approval that rose from the crowd as soon as he stood up indicated that he was known to many, not just Shankar. This truly amazed him. A man who only a year ago had swindled Bireswar of three thousand rupees—through legal tricks meaner than plain illegal swindling—thrilled masses of people? Was this the same Lilamoy Ghosh whose name had been appearing lately on newspaper pages? How absolutely fascinating, this lila of Lilamoy in the cylindrical shape of a side pillow!

Shankar had no permission to get up on the dais, but so what? Even the right to ascend the throne waits unquestionably only for Arjun. He was in no mood to bow down to restraint; pushing aside all obstructions and solemnly acknowledging all objections with a slight nod, he took the seat Lilamoy got up from. Lilamoy had started his speech in a detached, tearfully sweet tone. No matter what the tone was, he kept making such mean little jokes that muffled giggles and smirks rose from the gathering from time to time. This was a public speaking technique—a weepy joker was a great source of entertainment.

The bout of such appreciative titter became strong at one point, the noise didn't subside for a minute. In that pause Lilamoy asked him, 'What's the matter, Shankar?'

'I want to speak.'

'Speak? To me or to the meeting?'

'To the meeting.'

'How disastrous! Don't entertain such harmful ideas.'

Right after Lilamoy's speech, Shankar got up without any introduction and started speaking in a desperate shout. 'Friends, I'm here, uninvited, to give you some advice: please give up these affectations. You're fakers, impostors. And you know why I say that? You all cry for one, two, or three at the most, not for the many. You're unworthy of being human beings, you're beasts, you're uncivilized barbarians. Aren't you ashamed to sit here. Dedicated like animals to one or two in the crevices that are your homes, what right do you have to come crowding in this meeting? If I tell you I'm going to throw a bomb in your midst, all of you will frantically run for your own lives, at the most you'll think of taking along one, two, or three. Yet you stand here in such a solid mass, affecting such fellow-feeling and collectivity as if . . . .' All attempts to stop him, pull him into a chair, the chairman himself getting up to explain to the audience, everything failed. When four or five volunteers came up and together grabbed Shankar, he appealed to the audience at the top of his voice, 'They're making me sit down. Don't you wish to listen to me?'

The audience, fascinated with his abusive language, responded: 'We'll listen, we'll listen.' . . . 'He's all right, let him go on.' . . . 'Hey, you volunteer bastards, leave the lunatic alone.' . . . '*Bande Mataram*!' . . . 'What's the lunatic's name?' . . . 'Throw the lunatic out, beat him up, break his bones.' . . . 'Let him speak, let's hear what he's trying to say.'

After about five minutes of frantic waving of hands in the air by four or five leaders, the noise subsided a little. Then Lilamoy got up and, with hands clasped together at his chest, he slowly paced in a circle, of which he himself was the centre. After about seven such circlings on his part, the noise ceased. Then the chairman himself proposed that since there could be no meeting if everybody tried to speak at once, they should kindly pay attention and listen to his modest request. This man here, who started talking unannounced, no one knew who he was, he was not expected to give a speech here, besides, no connection existed between why this rally had been called and what this gentleman was talking about, and no purpose of a meeting was ever served if any one spoke out any time on any subject just as one wished; but still, if all those gathered here wanted to listen to him, then in deference to the collective wish he'd give him formal permission to speak; therefore if those in favour of listening to him would raise their hands instead of shouting . . . .

A large number of hands went up and by due procedure Shankar had permission to speak. But this time he found neither the words nor the air-shattering voice that came from the intoxication of disobedience. Every word seemed to get stuck in his throat. At one point he thought of calling the audience beasts once more, or at least unfit to be human beings. But where could he find the courage to say that sort of thing before so many people? What he said politely for a few minutes in a mild, diffident voice made no sense even to himself. Then he stopped abruptly and sat down. His ears were on fire and his heart gripped with the desire that Sitadevi herself once had, to respect which Dharitree, mother earth, opened up in a public gathering.

At some point the proceedings of the meeting ended. Upon hearing Lilamoy's call, Shankar followed him like a mechanical toy and got into a bearded gentleman's huge car.

'I don't understand what's the matter with you,' Lilamoy said. 'Why did you make such a spectacle of yourself?'

'I don't know,' Shankar said sheepishly.

The bearded gentleman smiled and said to Shankar, 'That's right. You wouldn't have done it if you knew why you were doing it.'

Lilamoy introduced the bearded gentleman. The name was Kedarnath Roy, owned an estate outside the city, and several houses in the city. 'Haven't you seen his name in the newspaper, Shankar, from time to time? Well, how can you if you don't really read the newspaper! If you come across a newspaper, you check the woman-abducted column, the cinema page and the sports news, that's all. Kedar-babu's name is on the rise. Give it a year, at the most two, and his name will be on everyone's lips. Not easy to become a leader, you know? So much thinking and deliberation must go before taking each step. No good barging into a meeting like you and launching those vocal chords. Kedar babu has been trying for three years, and only now he gets some recognition at meetings.'

'But he didn't give a speech today.'

'Of course he did! He spoke before all the others. There was some opposition to letting him speak first—no lack of jealous people, you know, the thought of his name appearing first in the meeting report eats up some people. But I'm not one to give in, I said that his offer of a hundred-rupee subscription would be cancelled if he couldn't speak first. That shut them up.'

Shifting uneasily, Kedarnath said, 'One hundred!'

Shankar noticed Lilamoy hint at something by poking a finger in Kedarnath's thigh, after which Kedarnath said nothing more on that topic.

Happily Lilamoy went on with Shankar, 'But, brother, I'm struck dumb by your conduct. What're you up to? Already at this tender age bitten by the bug to climb?'

Shankar was drooping, but forced himself to keep up a stance of defiance: 'At what age do you think one has no desire to climb?'

'But this isn't how one gets ahead, brother! There're standard methods for that. Consider the scene you just made, you think tomorrow your name will appear in the newspapers! Sweet success doesn't come so cheap . . . . What are you doing these days?'

'Nothing much.'

'Want to come into this line of work?'

Without waiting for Shankar's answer, he showed an effusive gladness and, taking Shankar's hand in his, said, 'Great! Don't worry about a thing, leave it all to me, I'll fix everything for you. But it isn't a matter of a few days, can't be fixed with a few words. Do one thing, come to my place tomorrow early afternoon—we'll talk. Now Kedar-da, why go home this early in the evening? Can't we go somewhere for a little—we've a young man with us, things could warm up tonight.'

Kedar asked, 'At Kanak's place?'

Shankar again noticed Lilamoy hint at something by poking his finger in Kedar's thigh, at which Kedar stopped short. A strange, indescribable feeling started growing within Shankar at the speed of a sapling in the magician's hands. His life had suddenly been taken over as if by an action-packed adventure. It didn't take him time to realize who Kanak was and why she just got cancelled. Lilamoy hadn't yet figured out what sort of young man he was, how he would take a shopping trip to the market of thrills purveyed by the person named Kanak. A shrewd, guarded man, he never took a step without calculating, and hence he left Kanak's identity unrevealed for now.

He only took Shankar to a bar in Chowranghee and handed him a glass containing a peg of alcohol. 'Man's life is dry, juiceless, he has to cross vast expanses of hard reality—doesn't he, brother?' he said. 'Poison, nothing but poison in life. That's why once in a while a man needs a little nectar—doesn't he, brother?'

'Certainly,' Shankar agreed and, draining his glass in a single gulp, clutched his throat. Lilamoy and Kedarnath both laughed at the way Shankar's face changed into a grimace. But quite clearly both were also greatly relieved that he had taken the drink and joined the club.

'Out of touch with his own pulse,' Kedarnath remarked.

'How can he be in touch with his pulse if he has never checked it?' Lilamoy equivocated.

If someone had checked Shankar's pulse at this time, he'd surely have been alarmed and sent him home at once. Not knowing the cause of the burning sensation inside, and the reeling in the head, Shankar felt only slightly worried. What a strange new life had he started this evening. Without any plan, without any purpose? Lilamoy's public-meeting mask was still on, only its top layer had peeled off. His face was still that of a juicy witty man pretending to be weepy while on the point of breaking into hilarious jokes. Shankar hadn't heard Kedar's speech, but he remembered Lilamoy's. The perfume now exuding from Lilamoy's mouth would've made his speech so much more entertaining and fascinating for his audience! Shankar smiled at the thought.

Pleased, Lilamoy asked, 'Enjoying yourself, eh? Take it easy; the evening is still early!'

Really? It was pointless to try and ascertain which phase of his life this was an early evening of. Shankar only tried to remember the phase of the earth's lunar cycle this evening was on. Close to the full moon, just before or just after. He felt a restlessness. While studying for the exams, so many times when he looked out the window and saw the moonlit nights, the desire grew intense for sitting quietly in the moonlight, on the roof, in a field, by the water, anywhere—a desire he had held back with so much difficulty for a later time, after the exams! Childish perhaps, but the value of this kind of eternal childishness never diminished in human life. Why had he come here? To drown all his softness in this atmosphere of harsh light, shrill brazenness and ruffian ugliness? The softness within himself that made the thought of Taranga so painful even now?

Did the others come here with the same purpose, all these men and women? To treat the nasty disease in which one's softness made one suffer? Soon Shankar saw, very well, that even fleshy middle-aged women came here seeking escape from the ailment. A lady came straight to their table her face artificially coloured, accompanied by an insect-like hanger-on in western dress. She was Mrs Sen, the name was Namita. That she was a specially close friend of Lilamoy became obvious when she answered his awkward greeting with a tiny slap on his neck.

With a sideways glance at Shankar, she sat down at their table. She got up after an hour, saying, 'Saw your car outside, Kedar-babu. I've had enough of this here, how about taking me out for a bit of air?'

Kedarnath promptly worked up to it, 'Certainly, certainly.'

Getting into the car herself first, Mrs Sen quickly said, 'Come here, Shankar-babu, since I am meeting you for the first time tonight, you'll sit next to me. How about going in the direction of Diamond Harbour?'

Little of the moonlight in the city, plenty of it outside. Next to the road were the railway lines, on both sides the open fields, with occasional villages solidly dark with homes, trees and shrubs. Shankar felt like crying, perhaps because today he had got his first treatment for the disease of soft-heartedness. He felt himself gone so soft that Mrs Sen's soft bulk on his right was digging into him like a witch's nails, harder than the cigarette case in Lilamoy's pocket on his left.

Mrs Sen said, 'We once came this way, had some palm juice, remember Kedar-babu? Oh, the taste of fresh palm juice—clings to my tongue to this day. Only the smell is terrible.'

It wasn't surprising that the taste of palm juice would cling to the lethargic tongue of Mrs Sen, but it was surprising that Shankar's heart should miss a beat.

Mrs Sen asked again, 'Can you recognize the village? We must be close to it. Let's go and taste some. Palm juice at night—it'll be fun!'

Shankar had a vague notion of this romantic aspect of materialism—he had heard of it from others, read of it in psychology books. For a person using expensive soap every day, rolling in dust might seem like the ultimate in being romantic. Shankar had been hating himself since this afternoon; now he started flogging himself. Still, as though spurred on by that very pain, he felt a strange impulse, a desperate urge to rebel against something as unjust as self-torment. So long he had been sitting ramrod straight; now he let his body recline, leaning towards Mrs Sen. Flattered, Mrs Sen treated him to a gentle slap the way she had slapped Lilamoy earlier. In the glowing tip of Lilamoy's cigarette, the gem on his ring flashed red, almost like a railway danger signal.

About a mile and a half up the road they came upon a village. The village lights were still on, the little shops by the path were still not closed. The toddy shop was outside the village, a little apart. They saw a small crowd not far from the toddy shop, and the police in front of the shop.

'Some sort of picketing going on,' Lilamoy said fearfully.

'Picketing?' The feel of Mrs Sen's shiver seemed to give Shankar gooseflesh all over.

Mrs Sen said, 'No need for palm juice, my goodness, let's just get back now.'

As the car was being turned around, they saw a boy of sixteen or seventeen being arrested by the police for attempting to picket.

When backing up, the rear wheels sank in the mud of the roadside drain. Kedar hurled at the driver an epithet that certainly could elicit a chorus of bravos from those who congregated each evening there to enjoy toddy mixed with foul language. Here in the car nobody said anything. Mrs Sen giggled. The way the car engine roared the next moment in an effort to get off the ditch struck Shankar as if the car were laughing too, vying with Mrs Sen.

Inside Shankar's head, everything had been turning topsy-turvy. He quite followed all that had been happening, yet everything seemed hazy and confused—where he was, how he got here, all this was in his mind, but he couldn't quite make sense of it, there was something missing that he couldn't remember. The past, from a few hours ago, seemed to have escaped his memory utterly disobediently, and careened beyond reach like the imagined future. And he kept feeling a pain he couldn't even describe, a most strange pain, as of burning and freezing at the same time.

The car got out of the drain and turned towards the city. After it had passed the village, Shankar said, 'I'm feeling sick.'

Terrified, Mrs Sen said, 'Oh no! Move over, move to that side, your mouth out that side.'

Anxiously asking that the car be stopped, Mrs Sen tried with both her hands to push Shankar away. As soon as the car stopped, she got off nimbly and ordered Shankar to come out.

When Shankar was out of the car, she said to him, 'Sit by the road and do your throwing up now. Move away a bit, I really detest vomit. Why don't one of you come out and help him. You here, can't you come out? Get off, I want to sit in front.'

Mrs Sen's companion, who all this time was quietly sitting in the front seat, got off and Mrs Sen immediately got in in his place.

Shankar said to him, 'You too get back in. I don't want help.'

Mrs Sen turned her head back and said, 'You said you wanted to throw up?'

'When did I say that?'

'Then get back in the car, I want to be back in the city as soon as possible.'

'You go on. I'm going back to the village.' He started to walk towards the village.

Lilamoy shouted after him, 'Don't act so crazy, Shankar. What will you do in the village?'

'I'll join the picketing.'

Several other calls came after him, but Shankar walked on, paying no attention, and swaying a little on his feet. After walking some distance, when he heard the car engine take off, he turned his head to make sure. Then he walked on again towards the village, a bit slowly now.

The village was not far from there. Before getting arrested by the police for picketing the toddy shop in this village, of which he didn't even know the name, he wanted to enjoy the moonlight he had postponed enjoying until after the exams. His exams were over only today.

But why should he join the picketing? Had anyone made him take a vow to do it? Shankar didn't know. The only thought that kept turning in his mind was that all day today he had enjoyed a lot of happiness in luxuries, and now he absolutely had to collect some unhappiness in hardship.

4

Taranga's father, Sadhana's aforementioned brother-in-law, Bijan, was a professor. Taranga's husband of a couple of years was also a professor, holding an even higher academic degree and a more well-known name. Taranga had learned a lot of things from these two professors. What most Bengali daughters and young wives learn, however, they are not able to practise, although while at it, the imagination of some of them travel the entire distance between the sky and the underworld and even beyond those limits. No one minds all that much if, while letting her imagination run wild, she only seems to behave absently, like an automaton. At the most, a bit of ill repute gets around for being flighty. People discuss her in asides saying, 'The girl is a bit too distracted, too flighty. Watch her, if she doesn't end up wrecking something, you're free to cut off my ear!' But if her flights of fancy so distract her that, unconcerned with what people say she proceeds to act on the basis of her imagination, then it becomes troublesome. So troublesome that it becomes impossible for her to remain sheltered for long by the half-modern relatives of a thoroughly modern man like Taranga's husband.

If on top of that she doesn't have much in terms of a parental family and knows very well that it'll be impossible to live with any other relatives of her own, then a young woman like Taranga comes to live in the home of someone like Sadhana, someone with whom her relation is neither quite based on blood nor quite imaginary, yet somehow rather close. Only, she didn't live here as a dependent relative, she paid for her room and board. Taranga's professor father and professor husband had left her some money. Sadhana was as much surprised to hear that Taranga wanted to leave the joint household of her husband and his brothers and move into Sadhana's because her parents-in-law disapproved of her ways, as she was hurt to hear that she wanted to make monthly payments covering her costs at Sadhana's place.

'Why?' Sadhana asked. 'Can't I afford to give you a bit of food to eat once a day, Toru?'

'But, Aunt, I won't eat just once a day,' Taranga replied with a smile. 'I'll eat four meals a day. I've already decided everything, the rules I'll follow in eating and moving about. It's because I wanted to follow only my rules that they all got mad at me there! But no matter what I do, Aunt, it will not cause you any inconvenience. I've come to live with you because I know you're not so stuck on silly customs.'

'How can any one live in society doing as one pleases, Toru?' Sadhana countered.

'I'm not talking of that sort of doing as one pleases. You're thinking of unrestraint, right? You'll be alarmed at the extent of my restraint, Aunt. I'd never do anything I don't need to do, eat anything I don't need to eat, think of anything I don't need to think . . . .'

Taranga went on for some time explaining to Sadhana her goal in life, her objective and her determination to pursue it. She'd complete experiencing all aspects of life in systematic stages. She was only nineteen; upto the age of twenty-four she'd persevere for total control of her body and mind, staying within the confines of her home; then upto the age of thirty she'd go from house to house teaching women confined to their homes how to live, and while doing that she'd master the technique of persuading and convincing unrelated, unknown women about various goals of life; after that she'd embark on her real mission—a powerful, open movement that would carry the whole country along, and start a creative turmoil inside every home. 'People won't listen to me until I'm a bit older, you know, Aunt.'

Listening to her, Sadhana was perplexed, and she thought, 'Poor girl! The shock of so much grief at this young age has affected her head. She surely needs a little love and care.' She didn't argue with Taranga any more on that day, didn't object to any of the things she said. She merely said, 'All right, that's for later on. You can live here the way you like, but please Toru, don't mention money. You're like my daughter, I can't stand the idea of your paying me money for food.'

'Why can't you stand it, Aunt?' Taranga said. 'If I didn't have my money, then it'd have been a different matter. Besides, I won't stay if you don't let me pay my expenses.'

Sadhana interpreted this too as a symptom of Taranga's troubled mind. She didn't argue any more.

But when she attempted giving her love and care, she found that Taranga didn't want that sort of stuff, she had absolutely no need for it. The way of life Taranga had resolutely set her mind on didn't allow any place for the heart. Happiness, convenience, leisure, pleasure and enjoyment, not one of these things was allowed any room anywhere in her daily life. Within a couple of days, she let the part-time maid go, even the sweeper who cleaned the drains and the places dirtier than the drains.

'No, Aunt, don't object,' she said. 'I need to do these things.'

All the work—scouring pots and plates, hauling water, grinding spices, cooking meals, sweeping floors, washing, sewing and mending clothes—she seemed determined to do by herself.

'How can anyone live doing so much work, Toru? You stay up nights reading too.'

'I'll do nothing excessive, Aunt. Because I don't know exactly how much work I'm capable of doing, and when, and by what methods, I need to experiment. I'm starting out this way. Gradually I'll adjust the amount of work and change the timings according to my capability. Don't worry, Aunt. I've already figured out that I can't stay up reading at night. From today, I'll do my reading in the early afternoon instead of sewing.'

Gradually Taranga did just that, she fitted her work to her ability. She let go of some chores, allowed a bit more time to the essential tasks she at first did with impatient briskness, moved some tasks from morning to evening, some from evening to morning. After about three months she even reengaged the sweeper to his job in the house.

It was for this Taranga that Shankar once did so many crazy things. Through one entire hot and humid day, he first sat in the exam hall answering the question paper, then going to exchange hearts with Taranga he ended up banging heads with her, and demonstrated his insanity before three thousand people. Then he had his first taste of alcohol in a bar, and went to jail picketing a toddy shop in an unknown village quite far from the city.

Yet, hearing this last news from Anupam, Taranga merely said, 'Only twenty-one days!'

'Would you've been happy if Shankar got a longer sentence?' Sadhana asked in irritation.

'Yes, I would've been,' Taranga at once replied. 'It's not really jail sentence, Aunt, it's medicine. Shankar-da will be saved if twenty-one days in jail dampens his sentimentality.'

'You've no sense of what you say.'

'What I say is true. Only not very nice to hear.'

'Why speak that sort of truth? What's the need to pointlessly say things that aren't nice to hear? A woman's duty is to say things nicely and get along with people. If you unnecessarily say things that annoy people, my dear, then nobody's going to be able to stand you for long.'

'But if no one says what's right, then everything is going to go on being wrong.'

'You think your saying what's right is going to make everything go the right way?'

'To some extent at least.'

Sadhana didn't like to get angry. Like a proofreader, she only corrected the errors—in people, in life around her. Perhaps, as with a proofreader not so good at spelling, her corrections were sometimes incorrect. But that didn't make her feel incompetent in her work, because she herself believed her correcting was right. But whenever she tried to correct Taranga, she felt, like a Bengali proofreader with proofs in Sanskrit, that the knowledge and skill she put to work in correcting Nimi and Anupam were irrelevant in this case. It was like trying to advice an ascetic about the rules of conducting worldly life. Hence, as soon as Taranga started arguing, Sadhana's instructions turned to entreaty and disappointment. Shaking her head, she said, 'No, Toru, the way you talk and act worries me. A young woman has to live in the shelter of someone or the other; if your words upset everyone . . . .'

Taranga didn't argue any more, she continued with her work. If Sadhana found any fault in her work, she silently agreed with her and attempted to correct it. But deep within her, Taranga felt a burning, searing dissatisfaction with herself such as she had never imagined. This was the time for her penance for self-improvement, self-preparation for a momentous future. Yet if she couldn't make someone like Sadhana understand even such simple, small points, how would she at the end of her strivings, be able to make thousands of people far inferior to Sadhana understand bigger, more profound issues?

Perhaps all this struggle she had been putting herself through day after day would end up bearing no fruit at all. She'd only remain an incongruity among people, just a poor misfit.

Tilting the washed rice in the cooking pot, she sat down to grind some mustard to season the shrimps to be steamed with the rice, and while doing that, she tried to control this overpowering feeling of discontent and frustration. Even this struggle was part of her ascetic self-disciplining. Not because she wouldn't allow pain, sorrow and disappointment any place in her mind, but because she must have the ability to control at will all superfluous sentiments, all self-pity. She was willing to analyze the problem of whether or not thousands of people would one day want to hear what she had to say. But she wasn't willing to let her mind turn sour when analyzing that. What good could feeling sour accomplish? What use was sorrow in her scheme of life, in bringing to fruition her lifelong endeavour? Could there be any rational argument at all for letting on such a feeling of sourness? Why should she indulge this unnecessary, superfluous state of mind?

The mustard grinding was done, still Tarnaga's mind did not recover its ease. A little astonished, she wondered if after nearly two years of trying she hadn't acquired the slightest command over her mind. The thought made her feel even more vexed. Then she realized that a complex whirl that had lain hidden in her mind, had been released today. In her very efforts to check the feeling of sourness, she had ended up starting a full-fledged factory producing reasons to feel sour. Today must be the day of her ultimate test.

The day was hot. It was hotter inside the kitchen. Taranga was drenched in sweat. There was a certain pain in sweating in the heat of an open coal stove on a hot day. All this time she had felt proud at being able to deliberately bear this strenuous pain; today it seemed pointless, mere stupidity, to endure needless suffering. This thought left her scorching all over with exasperation. For feeling so seared with exasperation, she also felt thoroughly disappointed with herself. And for this feeling of disappointment with herself . . . .

Anupam came with a low cane stool and sat down in the kitchen. 'When you sweat, Taranga, you look sort of amazing.'

'In what way?'

'The way it looks when it rains in the midst of sunshine.'

Taranga tested a few grains of rice to see if it was done. Washing her hand, she took out from the shelf a plate of jamun seasoned with mustard sauce and handed it to Anupam. Then attending to mixing the shrimps with salt and spices in a lidded aluminum container, she replied, 'Anyone else attempting this sort of poetry gets on my nerves, but coming from you it doesn't sound so bad. Perhaps you've a natural talent for pseudo-poetic talk, Anu-da.'

Pitching a jamun seed out in the yard, Anupam said, 'I wasn't talking poetically. Merely said what came to my mind.'

'Having such thoughts and speaking them out is what's known as poetic talk. Perhaps I can tolerate it because you do it so innocently. Besides I've given up on you, you're good for nothing. I couldn't get you off cigarettes even after asking you for two years.'

'Haven't given it up entirely because you ask,' Anupam said smilingly. 'Why should I follow your order?'

'What order?' Taranga turned her face up at him. 'When Aunt has to run the household with so much careful calculation, you shouldn't be wasting even a paisa on superfluities.'

'I don't waste my mother's money, I buy it out of what I earn from tutoring.'

'Why should you do even that? Why can't you give Aunt those few rupees you spend on cigarettes?'

Feeling a bit uncomfortable, Anupam said, 'That's exactly why I've cut down on smoking. I smoke no more than one or two a day.'

Returning to her work, Taranga said, 'Not one or two a day. Yesterday you bought a packet at ten in the morning, smoked six by the time you went to sleep.'

'Did you keep count?' Anupam asked, astonished instead of embarrassed.

'Why shouldn't I? Why do you go to sleep with the light on?'

'You count my cigarettes because I fall asleep with the light on—I don't follow.'

Taranga smiled and said, 'Last night when I went into your room to turn the light off I took the packet from your pocket and counted the cigarettes.'

'So you secretly go through my pocket.'

'But it's not to steal that I do it.'

Anupam studied Taranga's sweat-drenched face for a few minutes—with a discoverer's eyes. Then he asked quietly, 'The spare change in my pocket sometimes increases, you know that?'

'Of course I do. I make it increase, if I don't know, who would?'

'Why do you do that?'

'For Aunt's sake. You'll turn your palm up to her as soon as the pocket money runs out.'

Anupam sat red in the face—from humiliation, not from just the heat inside the kitchen.

Silently, imperviously, Taranga closed the lid of the container for steaming shrimps, took a length of thin wire from the shelf and wound it around. Seeing his face still overcast with reddish clouds, she said, 'What's there to be angry in this? Don't complicate a simple, straightforward matter, Anu-da. I've kept account of every paisa: repay me when you start earning—you may even pay me interest, three to four percent. It wasn't charity, I only lent you.'

Going out of the kitchen, Anupam said, 'Don't you dare talk to me again.'

That night Anupam went to bed with the light deliberately on. Coming in to turn it off, Taranga instead came near his bed and, with a glance at his sleeping face, said, 'You're not sleeping. Your eyelids are trembling.'

It wasn't sarcasm; she didn't know how to be sarcastic. Opening his eyes, Anupam said, 'Why are you bothering me? Can't I even go to sleep without being pestered by you?'

'I'm not sleepy either. Let's go for a walk.'

'So late?'

'Pushing through the crowds, how can one walk the city streets except late at night? Get up, put your shirt on.'

Anupam had never seen such an expression of weary severity on Taranga's face. He didn't dare argue further. He got up and put his shirt and pumps on.

She called up Sadhana who was about to doze off. 'We're going out for a walk, Aunt.'

'This late in the night!'

'Not feeling well in this heat.'

Shaking her head, Sadhana emphatically said, 'If you want fresh air, go on the roof and pace up and down there. You're not to go out this late at night.'

'Why?' Taranga asked insolently.

'Do I have to explain why? Aren't you able to understand even this much?'

'I'm not going alone, I'm going with Anu-da.'

'Anu's *not* going.'

'I'm going alone then. Close the door after me, Anu-da.'

Taranga promptly went down the stairway, opened the door and went out. After hesitating a little, Sadhana said, 'Go with her, Anu. Tomorrow I'm going to tell her straight that it'll not be possible for her to stay in my house any longer.'

Of Shankar's many deeds that day, the news of only the last one came to the relatives living in the house. Some were startled, some surprised, some amused, some sorry. They all thought it was a reaction to doing badly at the exams. Not quite shame—if it were out of shame, he wouldn't have done it right after the last exam, when no one else knew how he had done.

If it were to escape showing his face to relatives, Shankar would've gone for the slammer when the results were due—but that was far away. He must be prompted by regret, mortification—it was a 'reaction'. But how could a young man like Shankar act so insensibly? Someone so neat and well-groomed, so given to the countless small and large daily comforts. How was he going to get on in jail? Ah, the poor boy would have a tough time indeed.

Shankar's mother cried some and sought Bireswar's consolation. 'It's not for stealing or robbing after all. Do you think, Father, they'll give him tea in jail?'

'Oh! The strange ways of the human mind!' Aunt Sita remarked. 'When studying for the exams, he used to tell me that when it's all over, he'd watch three movies a day, and now as soon as the exams are over, the babu goes to jail picketing. You see, Bou-di, how amazingly the human mind works? His wish was to watch movies, he satisfied that wish by going to jail!'

As it turned out, the person most upset by Shankar's deed was Ramlal. On that evening Ramlal was in the bar, as usual. He saw his son enter the bar, saw him drink a 'peg' of alcohol. It was natural for a father to be upset in this situation.

Ramlal's feelings were rather blunted; that's why he appeared to be an unperturbed, indifferent sort of man. So indifferent that alcohol made him neither intoxicated nor sodden. His ordinary state of mind was an abnormally perpetual mixture of not liking anything and not disliking anything. The reign of alcohol only brought the aspect of his not liking anything to a normal level—that, for him, was good enough as a variation.

ing lost all taste for life, he was content just to find his life distasteful to an ordinary extent—the extent to which life was distasteful to all others. He had no choice in the matter. For one too thick-skinned to feel the light caress of the good of life, how could anything short of a beating do?

But the sight of his son drinking alcohol was no ordinary beating. After remaining stunned a while, he left the bar. His life became far more distasteful that evening in a way he had never imagined—in a strong and pungent way. He couldn't even recall when he had last felt a pain like this. He wasn't sure if Shankar had seen him there; after hearing of Shankar going to jail this doubt was removed. He even felt slightly happy at the thought that seeing his father had made Shankar's shame so unbearable that he couldn't keep from going to jail. It seemed like a consolation, a sort of proof that Shankar hadn't yet been corrupted too far—an indirect declaration from Shankar himself that he'd never do such a thing again.

But this consolation didn't last long; his feelings, blunted for so long, suddenly waged revolt and tormented him. To his question of why Shankar did such a thing, he couldn't find any good answer. Someone with a father like him would do exactly this sort of thing. That was the rule of the animal world. He couldn't blame Shankar, for as he begot him, so he also passed to him the desire to pick up a glass of alcohol.

The members of this household were as indifferent to Ramlal as he was impervious to then. But they were surprised to see the sudden change in him. He came home before evening, restlessly went from room to room, talked to them on his own initiative, made his demands for comfort and happiness, got angry with or without reason, then repentant the next moment, comforted one of the several children in the house if he had scolded a grown-up, and talked sweetly to one of the grown-ups—about all sorts of odd irrelevant things—if he had scolded a child. It was hard to tell even when Ramlal drank; but now they all knew he was not drunk, he hadn't been drinking. It wasn't for very long that Shankar was put behind bars, still it produced such an effect? They weren't aware that Ramlal's love for his son was of this magnitude.

'Why are you worrying so much, big brother? He isn't jailed for years,' Sita said.

'It's not about his jail sentence! Can you imagine what ruin I've brought on him?'

'Ruin! What ruin?'

'You won't understand. What'd you know of how powerful hereditary factors can be?'

With wounded feelings, Sita said, 'I don't know? I read so many books and think so much about the human mind, and I don't know hereditary factors! You think I'm ignorant?'

To halt her emotional outburst, Ramlal quickly said, 'All right, all right, you know that, you know everything.'

'See how strange the human mind is?' Sita remarked. 'A little while ago you said I didn't know, and now you say that I do. When I think of the workings of the human mind, Dada . . . .'

'Can't you think to yourself? Hearing you think gives people a temperature.'

Sita was stunned at this remark—exactly the way Ramlal was at the sight of Shankar downing a shot of liquor. The skin of her face wrinkled and many more lines appeared on her forehead over and above the permanent line—as if age had come to her in an instant. Like a car taking a turn without slowing, she wheeled around and went out of the room. She went straight to Bireswar. Rubbing hard the permanent line on her forehead with the tip of her left thumb, she lodged her complaint: 'It's not possible for me to stay here any more.'

'Why?' Bireswar asked calmly.

'How can I stay? You've become old, you'll close your eyes any day now. Isn't Dada then going to summarily throw me out?'

'I've not closed my eyes yet. Let me do that first, then you worry about it.'

'What good is worrying then? The future has to be thought of beforehand. You know, Father, how amazing the human mind is—because you have written away a few rupees in my name, listening to me makes Dada run a temperature. Not that many rupees you've left for me after all, have you? My big brother can't stand even that. I'll not stay here, Father.'

Bireswar smiled faintly and said, 'I'll put some more money in your name, Sita, you don't have to worry about the future. You stay right here.'

It was quite superfluous to ask Sita to stay there, as no evidence had been found so far to think that she would not stay if she weren't asked. It was in Bireswar's nature, however, to ask people to stay.

Next morning when Taranga came to him and said, 'Grandpa, will you let me stay at your place?' he asked her too to stay without any questions.

He went to see Sadhana demanding an explanation.

'I didn't do anything wrong, Father. All I said was she couldn't stay at my place if she continued to behave like that. And the girl took off immediately.'

'Why should you say even that?'

'Shouldn't I? She'll corrupt my children right here in my house and I should keep silent about it? I've tolerated it all this time, but how long is it humanly possible? At midnight the girl feels like going out into the streets for a walk!'

Bireswar kept sitting silently with a grave face. With downcast eyes Sadhana suddenly covered her face with the end of her sari and said in a voice, 'I didn't ask her to leave, Father. I didn't even think she'd ave at my just saying that. The house feels so empty now.'

With a grave, worried face Bireswar then went back home.

Shankar also came home from jail with a grave, worried face.

5

Nobody could stand Taranga. Who could stand someone who followed only her own rules and yet was at everyone else's backs? She would not do a thing in the normal way, or say a single word in the normal sense. She would constantly try to impress on others her extraordinariness, but she'd do it with such disinterested, calm restraint that it struck all as either a childish game or a drama on her part. Young women in the household and in the neighbourhood discussed Taranga among themselves. None had the slightest doubt that there could be no punishment worse than talking with Taranga for five minutes. Yet there was such an attraction in Taranga's pleasureless company that young women of the house and the neighbourhood crowded in her room in the afternoons. Taranga seemed almost like a theatre or jatra performance all by herself.

Indeed, for them Taranga's attraction was merely that. What she actually said or did had not the slightest value to anyone; it was to watch why and how she did what she did that all felt deeply curious. By attempting to infuse in young women's minds something bigger and greater—though what exactly, Taranga herself didn't understand very clearly—she infused merely curiosity. A curiosity similar to that which makes us watch in fearful fascination the snakecharmer tease the snake, and the eager enthusiasm to satisfy that curiosity that drives us to the theatre or to a jatra show.

This enthusiasm fascinated Taranga. She wondered if the aim of her life was already starting to be fulfilled? How auspicious was the moment she left Sadhana's house and came to live here? The neighbourhood women there didn't throng to her like this, show such eagerness to listen to her. Here, anyone who came to her once couldn't help coming again and again. Yet how little had she revealed of herself? How much had she really tried to recast women's lives in a new mould?

What Taranga felt was really pride. But as she had forbidden herself to entertain pride, she interpreted this feeling as one of happiness. The prouder she felt, the happier she considered herself. She didn't bother to remember that even feeling happy was forbidden by her strictures.

Not just that. Taranga didn't even realize that nobody could stand her. Perhaps she had the intelligence to understand that it was possible for ple to feel a desire to talk to someone they disliked, but she neither wanted nor tried to understand this. Innumerable indications were all around that she was nobody's darling, but she neither accepted nor paid attention to any. Taranga's willpower was of no ordinary calibre!

It seemed even Shankar did not like her any more. As if his romantic feelings had ebbed away and a tide of desire to study was now in his life. The moon rose in the sky, Taranga was in a room in the same house, yet the light stayed on in Shankar's room late into the night. He didn't do anything beyond what he had been doing all these years. He ate, he slept, and he studied late into the night.

Ramlal was relieved to see this. Reassured, he went back to his old custom of slaking thirst in this or that watering hole and coming home late at night. But he no longer asked Shankar to turn off the light and go to sleep. Perhaps he thought it was just from being unable to stay up studying as late as he wanted, due to his interference, that Shankar had gone to a bar and downed some alcohol. Let him stay up, instead of going to a bar, let him stay up at home as long as he wished . . . .

Taranga asked him, 'Why so much studying now?'

Shankar retorted, 'Is there a right and a wrong time for studying?'

'There're no exams now.'

'I don't study just for exams.'

With a slight smile Taranga said condescendingly, 'Always living in self-deception. What am I going to do with the lot of you?'

'You've to do nothing with the lot of us.' Saying this Shankar exited the scene in such a brusque manner that any other girl would have felt quite insulted. With her complex sensibility, what Taranga felt was quite beyond the standard definitions.

There was no lack of clarity, however, in what she felt when Anupam came and left. Seeing him made her happy, his departure made her sad. She could no longer turn off the light in Anupam's room; maybe that's why when turning off the light in her own room, it occurred to her that when Anupam left it was like a light being turned off. It was not as though Taranga's world was steeped in darkness once Anupam left—she decided that darkness had an advantage, it helped understand essential matters. Taranga simply had to grope in the darkness of her own mind in order to be able to grasp the connection of her distinctly feeling happy and sad with Anupam's coming and leaving.

That's why she thought of Anupam often. Almost constantly.

Not because she felt any desire to think of Anupam. That would be a shame! Taranga did not indulge that sort of weakness. Was she like the other, ordinary girls, that merely because she came close for some time to a college-attending, cigarette-smoking, half-baked poet of a young man, she would spend sleepless nights in bed dreaming of the fellow? She thought of Anupam because she wanted to know just why she missed him a little as she did. There was absolutely no other reason!

A lot of people lived in this household. When Anupam visited there was too little opportunity to talk to him alone. That made Taranga angry, and getting to the bottom of this anger was another reason she thought of Anupam. How could she afford not to? For someone whose goal was to create a greater and nobler level in her life through a temporarily destructive but ultimately beneficial revolution by means of infusing the existing layers with an indomitable strength gained from self-discipline, for someone whose constant striving was to earn the power to keep the heart and mind unruffled even through life's disruptive kal-baisakhis—how could such a person bother not to find the reason behind feeling angry at not having the opportunity to be alone with a particular person? And if she was to search out its reason, how could she bother not to think of the person who was the reason for the anger?

Taranga had become a little detached, so it seemed. Her strict and inflexible adherence to her own rules in daily life had grown a little slack. The movement of her limbs seemed a little languorous. The look in her eyes a little eager.

With this change came also a mitigation in the vehemence in her odd non-conformist behaviour. Though some softness and flexibility appeared in Taranga, the result proved to be quite terrible in another way. Taranga's wayward novelty now diminished very rapidly in the eyes of other young women. Her distracted moodiness was, of course, new, but when was there a scarcity of distracted, moody young women? Mere distracted manners couldn't exert the attraction that drew people even to the uncomfortable company of someone whose talk irritated them, produced resentment and antipathy in their minds, someone with whom it was impossible to exchange a few words about the regular, maudlin kind of pleasures and woes.

The young women of the family and the neighbourhood discussed her much less now, and attrition set in their eager visits to her. With the weakening of Taranga's magnetic combination of peculiarities—such as labouring away like a housemaid with the bearing of a queen, instructing like a schoolmistress with the modesty of a beggar woman, and following all sorts of strange rules but none of the normal ones—their feeling of distaste asserted itself more and more strongly.

The early-afternoon gatherings in Taranga's room no longer became impressive. With a look of surprise and injury, she watched the gathering get smaller and smaller. The realization that many of the young women had started just avoiding her set her mind raging like fire.

The restraint she thought she had built in herself for so long with her proud self-confidence, without taking anyone's advice, asking none for

...rections, now seemed all set to catch fire like a stack of dry straw.

Sadhana came to visit one day and said to her, 'Want to go back, Toru? Why don't you come with me?'

'No.'

'But I didn't ask you to leave. Did I?'

'No.'

'Then why did you leave in such a huff? Come back with me.'

'No!'

'No, no, no! If you were a little girl, I would've treated you with a good beating.'

Anger, regret and hurt feeling brought Sadhana to the verge of tears. What a strange girl! Leaves her long-standing shelter without a word of explanation, goes on living day after day in a stranger's home, apparently without feeling the slightest bit uneasy. Her conduct would make anyone think she had completely forgotten that she had lived in Sadhana's home as her own for so long.

Keeping sullenly silent for a while, Taranga all of a sudden said to her, 'Aunt, why doesn't Anu-da come here?'

'Stays busy with all sorts of work, doesn't find much free time.'

As soon as she heard this, Taranga flared up. As if it was in order to blow up today with an innocuous remark like this that she had all this time practised self-control so assiduously.

'Stays busy with work, does he? Doesn't find the time? Tell him, Aunt, that I too keep busy with work and if he ever comes here to bother me, I'll throw him out, sweep him off with the broom—and if I don't . . . .'

Taranga left the spot stomping, and Sadhana's heart pounded like a hammer. She had just been able to make Taranga out. But Anupam? Her own son Anupam?

'The girl is crazy,' Sita remarked. 'But the human mind is so amazing that though she does seem crazy, it's still not convinced that she's really crazy.'

Sadhana went back home with her face darkened with anxiety.

Taranga went up to her room, closed the door, and dropped on her bed. She breathed hard, she was panting even though stomping to her room in the heat of anger hadn't caused her all that much strain. As the agitation subsided, self-mortification raised its beastly head—stronger and more mortifying than what she had felt at Sadhana's house the day before she moved here!

That night when Anupam sat down to eat, Sadhana said to him, 'Don't go to Shankar's place so much, Anu.'

'Why do you say that?'

Without giving any reason, Sadhana asked, 'What's the need?'

'I understand that I've no particular need to go to Shankar's place, but there must be a reason why you're asking me not to go.'

After thinking a bit, she said, 'Visiting rich relatives too often is not the right thing to do.'

Anupam stopped eating and said, 'From what you just said it seems to me that something has happened, you're keeping it from me. Tell me what happened. Don't hide it from me, Ma.'

Feeling a bit harried, Sadhana said, 'What could happen? Nothing has happened.'

'Come out quick, Ma. I'm going to sit here by the food and not eat until you tell me what happened.'

'Nothing specifically,' Sadhana said after some thought. 'I was at their place today—the way they talked and behaved made me think, perhaps they don't like us to go to their house.'

'That must mean they've insulted you.'

'Who could insult me? It merely occurred to me from their general behaviour, that's all.'

'How can it occur to you for no reason? They must have insulted you, you're hiding it.'

Sadhana now felt annoyed. 'Heavens! I can't argue with you any more, Anu. If I open my mouth on a little thing, I've to kill myself giving explanations. What if they did insult me, what's it to you? Don't go to their place any more, that's all I ask. Stop chattering now and eat.'

The very next morning, Anupam went to Shankar's home. Grimly and without speaking to anyone else, he asked Sotu where Taranga was.

Sotu wasn't that good at providing information. Still Anupam gathered that yesterday sometime in the afternoon, Taranga had gone into her room and closed the door, and had not come out yet, not even in response to the others' repeated, insistent calling.

Anupam didn't have to do much calling. Taranga came out. Her face wilted, she looked as though instead of spending the whole night in her room, she had been out trekking in the sun.

Even so, Taranga didn't neglect to put on a slight smile. 'What's it, Anu-da?'

'I came for some information from you. I gather my mother was insulted here yesterday.'

'Insulted? Who insulted her? I don't know anything! Oh yes, I remember. I insulted her.'

'You?'

'You seem surprised—can't I insult anyone, Anu-da? You want to know what happened yesterday? I asked Aunt, "Aunt, why doesn't Anu-da come?" She said, "He has so much work that he finds little time." As soon as I heard that, I lost my temper.'

'Why? What's in it for you to lose your temper?'

'That's the funny thing; I too have thought of it through last night. What I discovered from that thinking you need not hear today, just listen to what happened then. Furious at hearing what Aunt said, I said, ''If Anu-da ever comes to this house I'll sweep him out with the broom.'' So you see I didn't insult Aunt, I insulted you. But as you're her son, the insult hurt her.'

Smiling, Anupam said, 'So that's it. Why haven't you thrown me out like you would sweep refuse with the broom?'

Taranga smiled too and said, 'Today I'm going to throw you out in a plain, regular way. Don't come to this house again for a few months.'

'I don't understand any of this, Taranga, I'm totally puzzled.'

'You'll understand everything when I'm dead. I'll leave a letter for you explaining it all.'

'What do you mean by you'll be dead?'

'What do I mean by I'll be dead? I mean I'll kill myself. Whether by hanging myself with a rope tied to that crossbeam, or taking poison, I'll go straight to heaven. Be sure you don't come here for about two months. Let me see if I can manage without killing myself.'

Roughly two months passed. It shouldn't seem astounding that Taranga, conceited as she was, thought she could cure the illness of her mind by not seeing Anupam for two months. And Anupam here, he was no fool either. During those two months he dropped by many times to see Taranga. But Taranga neither acknowledged his presence, nor relented to talk to him nicely. Then one day she summoned him up to her room and lashed out at him so sharply and with such a temper that for some two months after that he didn't take one step in the direction of this house.

When he came after a couple of months, Taranga was in her room, hanging from a rope tied to the ceiling beam, her body not even taken down yet, as they awaited the police. She hadn't forgotten to leave a letter for Anupam. The envelope with his name on it was in the custody of Sita who, weeping, handed it to him. The envelope was fat, heavy; its heft in the hand told him at once that Taranga had not only written a letter for him before departing, but it was a rather long letter.

6

A nupam,

So, I've decided to hang myself for you, haven't I? Because I love you? What a profound pleasure you must be deriving from this! But don't feel too repentant about it, don't roast in the flames of self-mortification. If you can, shed a few secret tears for me. No harm in trying, is there? But in the grip of your deep sorrow if you find an even deeper joy in thinking that I'm now dying for you, then sit down to analyze your own mind in a scientific way. I do believe if you'd only open any book by a German psychologist and embark on self-examination, you'd receive full marks. Your idiocy has a certain genius about it.

It's not right to hang oneself. Still quite a few do hang themselves. While mentally debating the question of whether or not to hang oneself, one isn't even aware when one has absently put the rope around one's neck. Not being aware only means—surely you know what it means—how can one be aware after one has hanged oneself? But, bothered as I am by you, I can't even hang myself the way others do. In the planetary configuration of my birth sign, you're the wrecker Saturn; before dying, it's with you of all people that I feel furious. The more I imagine you thinking that love for you gave me cancer of the heart and, unable to bear its pain, I took a trip to heaven hanging on to just a few yards of rope, the more I feel like murdering you first before taking whatever step I want to with myself. I know there'll be much discussion of me and plenty of research, and you'll deduce all kinds of theories, but I don't care about any of that. Let all think as they please, imagine whatever they like—but if even one person in this world believes that Taranga has hanged herself for love, then what good to Taranga can this hanging of herself be?

You've known me closely for a long time, at least you should know it's not possible for Taranga to harbour in her heart anything but total scorn for love. Yet you're the one who'll believe that Taranga has killed herself for love. You're such a prize idiot!

This is the reason why I'm having to write and leave behind such a long letter for you, of all people. Of course, I don't know exactly how long the letter is going to be, but I've no doubt it'll be very long. Read patiently to the end. It's beyond my competence to explain in a few words to an idiot like you why I'm killing myself. If we may compare intelligence to a sword, then yours has become so blunted with the constant grind against the stone of misunderstanding, that the original blunt side has ended up being sharper and you've no recourse other than using the wrong side.

Are you offended? Don't be. Whatever the level of your intelligence, take it as a major compliment that I've admitted that you've any intelligence at all. Who knows, maybe it's only because I have a bit of affection for you that I wish to think you're intelligent. Affection is the worst of the weaknesses of human beings.

Anupam, women's minds sizzle at the very mention of the word affection, and so do the minds of effeminate men, those who are male but not men. If your mind sizzles at the mention of this affection thing of mine, then light a cigarette and singe your own skin once. This affection or tenderness is not love. Taranga does not care for romantic love.

I'm not ashamed to admit to you that I don't quite understand how it came about, whatever it's that came about in me. All I can say is that the house of cards that I built with a lot of care has collapsed from my own breathing. I'm so freakish a deadly snake that by biting my own tail, I'm dying of the venom from my own head. If the poison had stayed in my head, I'd perhaps have lived, as many people do, the poison almost like ambrosia to them because it's possible to kill others with it—a poison that can give such a satisfaction is nothing less than that in this day and age of violence! But as my head doesn't work right, I tried using my poisonous fangs on myself.

You know what an incongruity my life is. Whether my life

hasn't cohered because I'm a misfit or I've become a misfit because my life is so odd—it's pointless to bother about this puzzle. Let my puzzle stay mine; and when it's time, I'll tie it well in the rope's knot. What reason could there be for me to hang myself other than love for you: that's the puzzle for you. I'll only answer your puzzle before I leave. For if I don't, Anupam, then you'll jump to some conclusion by yourself that I won't be able to stand even when I'm dead.

My father used to read thick books, talk in high-flown language. He received a fat remuneration for teaching college students. His temper too was quite sharp. When my father, wearing his high-power lenses, flared up lecturing the man who was to become my husband on subjects like society, religion, civilization, philosophy of life, science, theories of history, and my future husband also got all worked up on these subjects, I used to be fascinated with both of them. I felt a deep love.

No, not love in the sense you understand it. Neither my father nor my future husband believed in love in the sense in which you understand it. On love, my father's view derived from the new theory that had refuted the view of seven German psychologists who were specialists on love, and my future husband's view was based on an adaptation of the view of those seven German scholars to the indigenous cast of our society. His was no mere translation, but a transcreation of the essence. That's why the view my future husband held was more appealing to me.

Not just on love, but on almost any subject my future husband had this sort of amazing ability to translate the essential aspects. Indeed, that's precisely the reason I granted that mahatma the right to become my husband.

Otherwise, for a girl like Taranga, who is without parallel, who has to be compared not just to a swan but to no less than the queen of swans if all other young women of the entire world are cranes, can the husband be just anyone, anyone except that kind of a great man?

O Anupam, you cigarette-smoking, emotionally fragile boy, you're nowhere near that husband of mine! Compared to him, you're the tiniest of insects. You're like the newspaper office translator's translation of English news items; and that one of mine was like a literary writer's transcreation of English literature in poetry and stories. You get the analogy? Let me explain in a way that makes it clearer. He fell in love with me because at that time I could smile in an authentic Indian way the smile of western film stars, and you fell in love with me when I had learned to smile in the western way the smile of native film stars.

I'm not exaggerating. My future husband said to me on his birthday, 'Taranga, I want a present from you for my birthday.'

I said, 'What'd you like. It's only nine in the evening. I'll go and buy it myself.'

He said, 'Not that sort of present. You've to come with me, alone, for a movie.'

I said, 'Let's go.'

He said, 'Go tell your father.'

I said with a smirk, 'What's there to tell my father? My father is not one who'll toss and turn worrying whether I'll be able to retain my virtue going out with some bad fellow to watch the 9.30 movie show. Do you know, the Taranga that I am has been moulded by my father?'

After the movie he took me for a walk in the quiet open and proposed. He said that my smile was like so-and-so's, my face like so-and-so's, my talk like so-and-so's, my walk like so-and-so's. I haven't named those so-and-so's because not all of them are film stars.

Well, then do you remember the time you first became overwhelmed in my company? That evening you didn't want to go home after taking me to see a native movie, but took me on a trip to the suburb. That evening you too told me in an ecstatic voice that I looked like so-and-so.

I replied, 'What's the fee your so-and-so charges?'

How deeply injured you were by that! Once I saw the mother of a little boy on a ghat by the Ganga—she slapped him on the cheek when for some reason he kept insisting that he wanted to drown and die. The way the boy then, on the brink of tears with pouted lips, checked himself from crying—you had that same expression on your face when, wanting to drown and die in your own sentimentality, you suddenly got a slap from me verbally.

Today I keep thinking that you must have a similar expression on your face hearing I've hanged myself. If only I could see it!

Don't think that even if I could see it, I'd have gained anything except the satisfaction of mere curiosity. I've shed the erroneous idea that it'd do you great good to prevent you from drowning in false romanticism mistaken for Manas Sarovar, the purest lake high in the Himalayas. There's some difference between drowning like that and dying by beating one's head against the rock of reality, yet both are unnatural deaths. There's a lot of difference between my hanging by the rope and your dying some time later from tuberculosis, spewing blood—yet both are tragic, unnatural deaths. Hearing that I've hanged myself will deal you a hard blow, and that blow will make you come down from the hollow, meaningless, unreal world of make-believe to the concrete world, at least for a while—this thought would have made me happy earlier. I would have felt rewarded by the expression on your face—like that of the sentimental boy his mother slapped. It would have made me think I've been of some use to at least one person and my life wasn't entirely in vain like all those others'!

But today I can see that it's worthless to force you down to the concrete world that way, and I've no right to do it. I won't be able to show you the way to live. I myself don't know the way. Groping as I am in impenetrable darkness, how can I tell you not to travel the melodious, flowery path of poetry, but come instead to the noisy, rocky road of striving, how can I tell you that this is where life's fulfilment lies? What's the melody of poetry and what's the din of action, what're the flowers and what're the rocks, what's the right way and what's the wrong way, all this is confused in my mind. What's a human being, what makes us human, what do we want in life, why do we want what we want, what should we want instead and why, these have all turned into such weird problems for me that I can't even understand if these are really problems or if some kind of craziness lodged in my brain makes me see simple, clear things as twisted, distorted! Yet only a short time ago, I thought I had found the answers to some of life's puzzles, and with trying for some more time, I'd be able to discover the answers to the rest as well. Sometime ago, when I first had doubts about my capacity, do you know the kind of strange thoughts I had? It might interest you. I wondered, was I born with this amazing talent to find answers to puzzles without knowing that life itself is a puzzle, without considering whether the puzzles were part of life or of the sort that pose in a competition for a prize? Was this uncommon ability bred in my blood? Or was it the upbringing and education I had since then that turned me into a woman so improbably odd?

But, listen Anupam, today I can't find an answer even to a very simple puzzle I've asked myself a thousand times. For some time a question has been ploughing my mind, but I've no conviction I'll find an answer to it from any one. You know what I'm thinking? I'm thinking, the kind of upbringing I had is not that exceptional, many grow up in a similar way in similar situations. Then why did this sort of mishap occur only in my case? Why did I trouble myself with matters that are outside my reach, inaccessible to my intellect, beyond my capacity? Why is my mental state in such a turmoil today that, unable to fit in livably with the world, I'm having to kill myself?

Anupam, I feel my heart pounding wildly as I write to you of these things. Have I really grown so strange? Am I really what some time ago I described myself to be—a hopeless misfit?

Are the reasons that have made me this way perhaps the same ones that turned many others out like me? Perhaps my difference from them is only in trivial matters of detail—no more significant than the apparent distinction of each human being from another despite their essential similarity. Anupam, who can tell if the real reason for my hanging myself is not the same as what made many others hang themselves? Could it be that the force that spurred me on to commit suicide did them too—only we aren't able to figure out the true nature of that force, how, when, and in what disguise it does its lethal work?

When I was staying in your house, a youth in Bhudeb-babu's house in the neighbourhood died from taking potassium cyanide. You came and said to me, 'Taranga, the boy killed himself because he caught an ugly disease. Good thing he did. That sort of chap is definitely better off dead.' With my sarcastic smile I replied, 'Maybe it isn't *that*, Anu-da, maybe he was sick of depending on others for food year after year and decided to go to heaven for a change. Ugly disease? Nonsense. If he had a way to earn money, you'd have seen that with ugly disease and all he'd have gotten married and carried on fine with home and family life.'

I told you some other things too, Anupam, things I don't fully recall. Perhaps the reason that youth killed himself is also the reason I'm about to do it. I don't have an ugly disease, I don't have to depend on others for food, but this is what I'm thinking—hear me out. Since I'm not alone in the world, since I live among people, the influence of the surroundings works on me just as it does on others. On account of that, the destinies of all the people in the world are inter-connected. If a person somewhere is driven to suicide by hunger, we can't take that for an isolated event, as the reason for that suicide is bound to stay around in the world in various forms. If that's so, Anupam, then the collection of causes and effects from the time of the birth of that unemployed youth in Bhudeb-babu's house—perhaps from ages before his birth—which finally led up to his suicide, is also the collection of causes and effects in my life that makes me take my own life. But where exactly is the connecting thread? What is the nature of the close connection between that youth's life and mine? A connection established by the laws of nature as mediated by all men and women, birds and animals, insects and plants, climates and soils of the society, maybe even of the whole world? I don't know, Anupam! Just writing these words to you makes my head reel. Where's the power of intellect with which I can find this crucial link? Since I don't know, it troubles me that the thoughts on the basis of which I'm about to hang myself may also be wrong—I may not even have the ability to see what's *not* wrong! Do I?

But you know, Anupam, I've at least this consolation—that it's impossible for me to go on living. Even if all the reasons why I've decided I should kill myself were wrong, this much is true that no one taught me the skills to go on living among you, with all of you. I've no choice but to die.

All this time, I've looked around me with the idea of reforming and correcting; and thus I could tolerate what I saw, I accepted a lot of things as only temporary; I thought it wasn't impossible that there could be a worse lack of grace and harmony in life than what I had seen so far. I thought, people were still people and they more or less knew the rules of life, it's only due to their own stupidity that they lost some humanity and acquired some bestiality, it's only by making mistakes in following some of the basic rules of living that they brought confusion into their lives.

Oh no, in the end I realize that the mistake is mine, mine alone!

In just about everyone's life there's too much injustice today, too many unmet needs, too many faults, too much immorality, too much disorder. Had people consciously accumulated all this in their lives, even that might make some sort of sense. But, unknowing and unaware, they're squandering their own lives, ruining themselves with great gusto. The blind are leading the blind. And those who themselves are living like this are advising others: do this, do that, do the other. Anupam, do you realize where we've come today? Even the efforts of a person who wants to make life beautiful, less faulty, less incomplete, are proving to be futile—one is not even finding the path to life's fulfilment, not succeeding to resist the countless hostile forces from the outside shoving one by the neck down wrong paths.

Take me, for example! What education did my father and my husband give me! The light of knowledge flared up like the will-o'-the-wisp, but didn't come to anyone's use, didn't even come to my own good. After taking me through one wrong path after another, it has ended up pulling me towards unnatural death.

Taranga's letter was incomplete. It was quite clear that she wrote a lot more, but someone had torn off the rest of her letter. Anupam at first didn't notice if the envelope was sealed or open. Now from a closer look at the envelope he realized that someone had opened it with unskilled hands by wetting it with water, and closed it again with utter negligence.

Sita admitted. 'Yes, I opened the letter. You don't mind, do you? I came to love the girl so much in this short time, Anu, that I couldn't keep myself from opening it.'

'Where's the rest of the letter?' asked Anupam.

'I tore it off,' said Sita calmly.

'Why?'

'If a young girl impulsively writes all sorts of things just before killing herself, how can everyone be allowed to read it? You tell me, can it be allowed?'

'But didn't she write those things for me? You opened the letter and read it, didn't even think it necessary to ask me. And then you tore off and kept half the letter. Bring it out from where you kept it.'

'You think anything's left of it? I burned it,' Sita calmly answered.

The shock of Taranga's death had so long barred Anupam's mind blocking his anger; now in his fury he lost all his bearings. He looked at Sita the way one driven by rage to murder does, and said, 'You burnt it? You think it's a joke, eh?'

Forgetting that Sita was older and in a relation to be treated with respect, even a vile expletive came to the tip of his tongue which he had to hold back with enormous effort!

Aunt Sita seemed to have undergone a personality change. Today she was a calm, patient, intelligent and mature woman—no trace of demented absurdity in her words and conduct. On the contrary, it was as if she had known for a long time, even before Taranga hanged herself, that Anupam would do something as childishly crazy as getting furious about her tearing off part of Taranga's letter, and she had from that time also taken on herself the task of restraining him. In a calm, quiet, grave voice, she said, 'Don't be childish, Anupam. Taranga left the letter in my care; if I liked, I could've burnt all of it without giving you any part of it. That's what I wanted to do, but I kept half of it for you only because I couldn't quite ignore Taranga's last request. Well, Anupam, does it matter more to you that you couldn't read part of her letter than that she left us in this manner?'

In an agitated voice, Anupam said, 'It's precisely because she left us in this manner that I'm so eager to read the whole letter. What did she write in the rest of it?'

'You don't need to know that.'

Nothing could make Sita divulge the contents of the rest of the letter. Keeping a secret was impossible for Sita, but the things Taranga wrote in the rest of her letter to Anupam she seemed to have hidden inside her heart; no one got even a hint of what was there. All that could be figured out was that the rest of what Taranga wrote was not very nice. She had rather viciously insulted herself and everyone in the world. Even about herself she had written some things that . . . .

'What were those things?'

'I can't tell you, dear.'

That Taranga's nature wasn't normal was quite clear from the part of her letter that Sita kindly gave Anupam to read. Now she seemed to have left many others going out of their minds too. In all their lives she had introduced such a problem, such a mystery, exerted such a strange influence that the violence of her dramatic self-destruction kept tunnelling into everyone's mind—even when they were not thinking of her—like a thief trying to steal the calm and peace that might still be inside any of them.

Whatever calm and peace was or was not left in anyone else's mind, Anupam was left with nothing but unrest. What had Taranga said in her letter? Of the puzzle she had created, what clue had she herself provided in the part that Aunt Sita entrusted to the fire? Aunt Sita's rhetoric seemed gradually to come true—it became more important to Anupam that he couldn't read the last part of Taranga's letter than that she had left them in this manner. He kept on imploring Aunt Sita, getting furious with her, threatening her, raving and ranting at her—but he found that on just this matter Sita was very hard to crack or pry open.

Shankar was in a daze for some time. The fact that Taranga left a letter for Anupam dealt him a hard blow. Although he had begun to dislike Taranga, still why did she write to Anupam when he was near at hand? Was it then for Anupam that she humiliated him? What other meaning could there be of her leaving a letter for Anupam despite his being here?

Such thoughts kept Shankar thoroughly miserable. One day Lilamoy came rushing to him and said, 'You've any money, Shankar? Mrs Sen wants some.'

'Where's Mrs Sen?'

'That same place. She wants you to come too.'

'How much does she want?' Shankar sounded as if he had an endless stock, and anyone could get as much as one wanted.

Smiling from ear to ear, Lilamoy said, 'She wants you to come prepared on the high side. She said the need is very urgent, she'll return it in a week.'

In the same bar, the same room, the same atmosphere, Mrs Sen in the same jolly way was entertaining her friends and companions. At an eye signal from Lilamoy she left their company to sit down a little apart from them.

Shankar asked directly, 'How much money do you want?'

Smiling sweetly, Mrs Sen said, 'The need is for a lot really, but why don't you tell me how much you can give!'

'One hundred.'

'Only one hundred? Well, give me that.'

'I didn't bring it with me today. I'll give it to you tomorrow.'

'Tomorrow when?'

'There's a meeting tomorrow at Sradhananada Park right? You too are giving a speech, I read in the newspaper, aren't you?'

Mrs Sen nodded in affirmation.

'I'm also thinking of giving a speech. I'll give you the money afterwards.'

At this, Mrs Sen looked worriedly at Lilamoy.

In great discomfort, Lilamoy demurred: 'Getting up to lecture all of sudden like that without deciding beforehand what to say or not to say . . . .'

'I won't do anything crazy, don't be afraid,' Shankar said calmly. 'I'll say only what can be said. That sort of immaturity has blown over me.'

Lilamoy still pleaded desperately, 'Why not let go of tomorrow's meeting? If I don't get you to address the next meeting, then do what you want. That's better, all right? I'll release your name in advance to the newspapers, and part of your speech you'll find in the following day's newspaper report on the meeting . . . .'

'You think mere promises can make parched rice tender all the time, Lilamoy-babu!' Shankar replied. 'Why don't you go and telephone the newspaper office right now . . . ask them to add my name to your list of speakers? And include my name in the meeting report the day after. Maybe I'll give some more money.'

Mrs Sen and Lilamoy exchanged ocular messages. Clinging to Shankar's upper arm, Mrs Sen then said in a voice at once caressing and demanding, 'Why're you behaving like this, Shankar? Why not let tomorrow go? There'll be many like that. I myself will . . . .'

But Shankar had turned into a rock, he refused to be stirred at all. The matter was indeed a bit complicated. Calling the newspaper office wasn't enough, a little negotiation with others in the party was necessary. What if tomorrow they objected to a young outsider getting up on the podium and behaving childishly, what if they all got annoyed with Lilamoy?

'You're putting me in trouble,' Lilamoy said with a worried face. 'I've to make uite a few telephone calls. It's not free here.'

With a sl ght smile Shankar said, 'Go on, make those calls. I'll pay what it costs.'

Mrs Sen added, also with a slight smile, 'And what about this evening's entertainment costs?'

'That too,' replied Shankar.

Shankar seemed to have matured into a dry, hardened veteran. All the tricks to make a name, get ahead and acquire fame were as if mirrored on his fingernail. He knew there were many other things behind the so-called public life of Mrs Sen and her cronies—things uglier, things even more contemptible and complex. But he also knew that if he could properly apply what little knowledge he had gathered, he'd gradually pick up all there was to pick up and put all he had learnt to work for his own advancement.

His own advancement? Shankar's heart was given to sentiments. Mrs Sen's mildly surprised, mischievous look and smile, her companions' disgusting jokes, his own slow suicide to deceive his hungry, unsatisfied heart—all this produced a rather adverse reaction in his mind. With the mental processes he was deliberately inducing in himself, their actions and the simultaneous reactions were now on a ferocious rampage through his brain. Was this his advancement? Maybe he'd make himself famous for a day, maybe people would listen to him eagerly for a few minutes, but what would come of it? If he had to contract a horrible disease in order to put on expensive clothes, what'd he gain from wearing those expensive clothes?

Late night's acute pain kept sleep away from Shankar. The sorrow tasted particularly bitter, because now he was left with only the reaction. Even without finding the highway of life, he had so far moved happily along the lanes and bylanes, but today, in attempting to satisfy the craving to walk the slimy, slippery gutters of life, just one fall gave him a terrible bodyache.

Shankar's mother was going insane over the suicide of Taranga. A bit of a nervous wreck even in normal times, her energies were taxed to the limit by the constant struggle to suppress the urge to find self-expression in abnormal behaviour. Now came, on top of that, this big opportunity to let go. In a few days she grew haggard without any evident physical illness; then she suddenly started throwing tantrums, screaming, shouting abuses and banging her head. This was novel for Shankar's mother. For the timid, numb, prematurely aged women that she was, utterly devoid of any life force, this sort of fierce excessiveness was both incongruous and terrifying.

The doctor prescribed medication. But what would medication do? Drugged, Shankar's mother merely spent the nights lying in bed like a corpse. The medication was of course for sleep, and her lying in bed like a corpse was of course mistaken by all for sleep; but who could give genuine sleep to someone whose sleep had been snatched away by mother nature?

The doctor said, 'A change of air might do good. City noise is very bad for this kind of a patient—perhaps she'll do better in a quiet and peaceful atmosphere . . . .'

Arrangements were made for her to go to a well-known health resort for a change of air—a place where so many people with so many diseases went seeking a change of air that it was turned into a warehouse of illnesses, and crowded like a city with droves of sick people.

'I'd like to go to the village home,' she begged. 'I so miss being in the home village.' She clutched Bireswar's feet and burst into hysteric weeping.

Bireswar said, 'Don't cry, daughter, don't cry. What's there to cry about going to the home village? We'll leave tomorrow.'

The doctor gave his consent. Bireswar himself, with Shankar's mother, Sita and Shankar, left for a lengthy stay at their ancestral village house.

Shankar went with his sick mother to the village for about three days. He was scheduled to speak in a gathering, but what could he do, how could he refuse to make such a small sacrifice for his sick mother. Shankar's mother absolutely refused to go on the trip without her son; she started a terrible commotion at the very suggestion, crying and banging her head.

And as soon she had come with her son to the ancestral home, she became as quiet and inert as an inanimate object. Returning after all those years to the ancestral home, where once long ago she had lived a long time in shy modesty, surrounded by in-laws and relatives, brought back in her a new bride's pleasingly shy modesty converted, as it were, into lifelessness.

But Shankar was shocked to see the village. He had seen villages. As a boy he had come several times even to this village, he had some faint memories. Besides, so many times on trips to the city's outskirts, and going somewhere else in a train, he had seen villages on both sides go by endlessly before his eyes. And he had read about villages in so many books.

What sort of a village was this? The paths, the homes, the vegetation, the ponds and ditches, nothing matched the image he had of a village, the people who lived here weren't of the same kind as those who lived in his mental village, the gap between the village life of his romantic imagination and life in this village was like that between a book of poetry and a newspaper.

Instead, the village took after the city in a way. Here too, one killed oneself like Taranga.

A young wife she had been, about Taranga's age, though not as beautiful, nor as healthy. In front of her home was some jungle-like overgrowth, at the back some sickly paddy crop in fields as sickly-looking as most of the village people, to the right was a mango grove, and of the four crumbling rooms of the neighbour's house to the left, one was long collapsed but not repaired. In these amazingly natural surroundings, she had copied Taranga in the cowshed of her decrepit large home.

It was not hard to guess that there had been no cow in the cowshed for a long time. The people in this home didn't drink milk. Not even the weak baby boy of five or six months crying in a feeble voice in the arms of an elderly woman standing in front of the cowshed. Where did he get any milk? It was not possible that there could be any milk in the breasts that were only two folds of loose skin on the skeletal mother who was hanging from a rope in the cowshed.

7

Coming to the village seemed to have opened Shankar's eyes to the real character of the city after all these years—that the city was a vast dormitory, an escape-seekers' haunt. People went to the city to contemplate destruction, they loved to be in the city out of an affinity for all sorts of abnormal deaths, minor and major. When life became tasteless, people developed a taste for renunciation; when life became poisoned, they developed a desire for city life.

Those unable to go to the city, those who had to live the deprived life of prisoners in a village, cursed their fate and tried to bring into their village life as many city attitudes as possible. Like all those city-dwellers, the villagers didn't live knowing, intending what they were doing—neither urban nor rural people had that much discerning capacity. Not knowing nor understanding, they destroyed themselves and their own future generations bit by bit, like fools, thinking all the while, 'I'm living by the rules that befit the times,' and wallowing in the deep despair of living only out of a need to stay caught in the trap of social, political, economic, and moral binds.

After seeing the village people, after seeing its soil, its trees and plants, the crops in the fields, the cattle, the cats and dogs, it was only on account of the people that Shankar felt depressed. The thought strangely tormenting him was that although people came to the world to live, they didn't seem to want to live. Neither in the city nor in the village did people want to learn the rules, the signs, the methods to wage life's battle, all seemed to be just reluctantly going through some bizarre, incongruous play-acting that missed the real purpose of life.

What else could one make of not following the methods and the ways that did exist for living a life?

What method, what way? He himself didn't know!

A trap was laid, as it were, in this area of his thought—it was the amazing mind-snaring trap of the hunter that life was crafty too, like the presiding deity of a great poet's world. Shankar thought so highly of his own intellect, but caught in this trap, his mind twittered helplessly like a sparrow.

'Shankar-babu!' Bireswar addressed him with a grave face, and a sarcastic voice.

'Yes, sir.'

'Yes, sir! Never in my life have I heard you being so proper, grandson!'

'Learnt it after coming to the village,' Shankar said, trying to smile a little.

'What else have you learnt after coming to the village?'

'That in order to live, people have to eat only half of what they need, they've to quarrel and fight, they've to spend their food money on luxuries, addictions, and sins of the flesh . . . .'

'Stop, rascal, stop there!' Bireswar smiled. 'So that's what happened—you caught the disease of nationalism! You're worrying about the people of the land! And here I'm worrying who the girl is the thought of whom so wears you out. Little did I know that you're busting your heart with compassion for compatriots. Is that why you've started hanging out with Lilamoy?'

'Is it wrong to think of the country?'

'Yes, for you it is.'

'Why? Don't I have the right to think of my country?'

'No,' Bireswar replied at once.

'Why?' Shankar too countered at once.

'Because the more the likes of you think of the country, the more the country will be ruined, because a lot more people die of quackery than of no treatment. Do you know how to think, have you been trained to think? Is your mind healthy, is it normal? To this day have you done a single thing which can prove it's possible for you to live, even for a single day, as the young of absolutely genuine human creatures? Write poetry if you like, fall in love if you like, become a scholar if you like, weep and mope and behave crazily for the country if you like, but don't even think of the country. Your mind is like water; thought of the country is like oil and it will never mix with your mind. Sooner or later those like you are bound to exit, and one day those capable of thinking of the country are bound to rise, maybe one or two already have—leave the thinking for the country in their charge. You're like an outbreak of septic boils on the nation's body; don't try to suppress yourselves with the ointment of patriotism; please, come to a head and drain. Some infected blood and pus will get out of the nation's body.'

It had to be taken as no less than a speech from Bireswar. The words smarted with pain, agitation, yet the tone was almost sarcastic, the face was calm yet serious. Shankar had never heard him talk in this tone about this kind of subject. Overwhelmed, he kept looking at Bireswar's face for some time. He saw himself as somehow immature, inexperienced, and impure by comparison.

'I'm not alone in being a septic boil.'

Bireswar said, as if consoling him, 'If that was the case, would there be a reason to worry, dear chap? What can a couple of septic boils do to the country?'

After a while in thoughtful silence, Shankar said, 'Septic boils need treatment, don't they?'

'Treatment to absorb a boil back in the body? It is better not to take that sort of treatment. You know, Shankar, no holy task should be performed by a sinners' hands—that shelters the sin and contaminates the holy task.'

'But if everyone is a sinner, and sinners are never allowed to do anything except sin, then how'd the future of mankind see the light of day.'

Bireswar suddenly smiled at this remark, a smile of mild distress. He knew and enjoyed playing tricks with words; nothing worked more cleverly to make men dance like monkeys, nothing worked better as a means to defend men. But when faced with not just tricks of words, but words framed in a forceful statement, this spirited grandson of his at once lost his foothold and started to flounder in doubt and conflict, such a great man was he! Yet he had formed quite large an image of himself, from absorbing day after day the elixir of self-deception! His selfhood had simply been swept away in a flood on his *sense* of selfhood!

Bireswar was sitting in the veranda upstairs talking to Shankar. In the yard below in front of the room in which Shankar was born, a mangy dog was hurriedly swallowing some inedible stuff. Watching the dog at it, the trace of distress disappeared from his smile. Seeing Shankar about to open his mouth, he cut in and said: 'Sin diminishes only with penance—and, Shankar, do you know what the penance for sin is? More sin! Is there a worse punishment for the sinner than committing more sins? In the course of an age, or a hundred ages, the sinners' sins are eroded through constant sinning. The poison that infects the country is also exhausted one day once the septic boils have all burst and drained off.'

'You're a great sinner yourself, Grandpa,' Shankar suddenly broke into a laugh.

'What makes you think so?'

'You're joking and mooning about the topic of the country.'

Aunt Sita too remarked, 'You're becoming sort of strange, Shankar.' To clarify what she meant, she remarked again, 'Your face looks so wilted.'

Swallowing hard once, she quickly lowered her eyes and said shyly, 'I know I shouldn't be telling you this sort of thing, yet how can I not? Don't pine for Taranga, Shankar. The awful mess the girl got herself into, in a way it's good that she died.'

Shankar sternly said, 'Okay, I won't pine, but let me hear what mess Taranga got herself into?'

'Oh dear, I can't tell you that.'

Aunt Sita had found quite a thrilling game. Using various pretexts, she had started telling all of them one by one that she knew something quite terrible about Taranga, but what exactly it was, oh dear, she couldn't talk about that. Perhaps Aunt Sita did feel sad thinking of Taranga, her eyes even grew moist from time to time. But what could she do, how could she afford not to make proper use of such a major, dramatic incident? What an unimaginable good fortune had befallen her, being the only one in the world who knew a mysterious, dark secret about Taranga, something no one else knew! The very thought sent a shiver through Aunt Sita's body. Even seeing Taranga hanging from the ceiling didn't produce that sort of shiver in her!

Aunt Sita seemed particularly eager to discuss Taranga with Shankar, using all sorts of excuses. She forgot, so it seemed, the level of her relationship with him. 'Taranga has been saved by death, Shankar. Had the girl lived . . . .' Starting a conversation along some such line, the sight of the shadow of pain across his face filled her mind with deep gratification! She, of course, had also to taste a sharp feeling of pity for Shankar suddenly tugging at her heart. But what could she do if the plain and simple feelings of life didn't live up to her imagination, sate her appetite?

Finally it was to escape Aunt Sita that Shankar ran away to Calcutta. He was, of course, due to address a large meeting. For the sake of his mother, he had lost one opportunity to give a speech; this time he'd be back in Calcutta on time. But it was still a few days away. Just as Aunt Sita was deriving happiness from pitying him, he was deriving a similar happiness from pitying the deprived men and women of the village. Had Aunt Sita not been at his back so much, he'd have stayed on a few more days in the village.

Shankar found out that he had gained some mastery of the technique of public speaking; he could orchestrate his delivery quite well along the high notes and the low notes. He received a lot of applause too! From just a few experiences he figured out that speaking was quite easy once he shed his inhibition by imagining the audience to consist of little boys.

A couple of days after Shankar left, Sadhana suddenly came to the village house with Anupam. She said she had been craving, like Shankar's mother, for a visit to the ancestral home, and after hearing that they were here, had decided to come for a day or two. But from her conduct it seemed that she craved less to be in the ancestral home than to be with Bireswar. It wasn't possible for her to stay in his house in Calcutta. Her strong spirit and sense of self-esteem did not allow her to go against her departed husband's instruction. But it was different with the ancestral home. Her husband had not left her any instruction about it; and there was nothing incompatible between her coming for a short stay in this house, despite her argument with Bireswar not so long ago, and her rudely turning down his invitation to forget past quarrels and move into his own house.

'I'm terribly worried about Anu, Father.'

One look at Anupam could tell him why his mother was worried about him!

'Perhaps it'll gradually get better, my daughter.'

'Day and night he sits and broods, or he wanders the streets aimlessly. Pays no attention to his bath and his meals, hardly sleeps at night—you've seen how he looks!'

Bireswar agreed in silence.

'Is he going out of his mind or something?' Sadhana asked in the tone of a muffled scream.

'He's acting this way because he is out of his mind.'

Sadhana's self-confidence was all gone. She seemed totally disintegrated. In a distressed, beseeching tone, she went on, 'Do something, Father, I concede defeat. No one but you can hold him back. I can't bear so much anxiety, Father; will I too end up hanging myself like Taranga!'

Anupam was born in this very house, in the same room Shankar was born in. From this veranda on the second floor, the mud huts of the village could be seen to the far distance, with a brick house or two standing out in their midst. It was doubtful if any of the inhabitants of all these homes had peace of mind, but the atmosphere of the village was very peaceful. Peaceful wretchedness so pervaded the scene that those not used to it might feel thoroughly uncomfortable. Today, moreover, the stench of something rotting assaulted the nose—the wind direction had suddenly changed. The wind till today had merely seemed like the muggy, stale air of a closed-up room—it hadn't brought in such an acrid, oppressive smell.

With a dim face, Bireswar continued to sit in silence, thinking. Did he have the ability to talk Anupam into becoming a calm, healthy, normal person? This madness of Anupam's was never going to leave—only the extreme pitch now reached could slowly diminish, if no new reason arose to intensify it. What could he tell Anupam? Pieces of his own life history came back to Bireswar's mind—in a different way he too had done many insane things in his life. From time to time in some abnormal situation, his own madness had often anchored itself on some specific thing or other and become similarly excessive. At other times it expressed itself in various forms in most areas of his life. He was not, however, as terribly bewildered and devastated as Ramlal, Shyamlal, Shankar and Anupam were. In his time, people were not so terribly crushed in the grindstone of their environment, their lives did not become pulverized like this. What would the children of Shankar and Anupam become like?

Talking to Anupam, Bireswar found that it was impossible to persuade him about anything. He was so calm and quiet yet abstracted that he seemed almost unable to hear anything at all.

Besides, he had also become terribly shameless. 'Taranga has left me ruined in every sense, Grandpa.' While saying this, Anupam was unable to lift his head, but to Bireswar it seemed as if he had never seen anyone as shameless.

But Anupam was a good boy in his studies. His exam results turned out quite good, though not as good as Sadhana had expected and Anupam had imagined. Taking into account the condition he was in for so long for Taranga, it was an achievement no doubt.

When Shankar's mother's urge to be at the ancestral home was satisfied and they returned to the city, Sadhana invited them all for a meal one day to celebrate her son's doing well at the final exams. She found Bireswar alone at one point to tell him, 'What you said, Father, turned out to be correct, he has gradually recovered quite well on his own.'

At Sadhana's special request, Anupam paid Bireswar respects properly by touching his feet. It wasn't clear if Bireswar uttered in his mind any blessing for him; outwardly he only said, 'Where did you learn to do pranam so perfectly, dear chap?'

But Aunt Sita was terribly upset to see Anupam's health improved and his madness diminished. She kept thinking that Anupam had deceived her, cheated her. Done something very wrong, an absolutely unpardonable crime. Didn't Taranga write Anupam such a long letter before taking her own life? How dared he forget her like this within a few months? How could the distinction between right and wrong, proper and improper be allowed to be erased like this? Aunt Sita was particularly troubled that none of what she had imagined actually happened. Anupam was supposed to go on shedding secret tears, his pillow to be found sopping wet in the morning; when in company, his eyes were to well up from time to time; he was to become haggard day by day and thin as a stick; his conduct and mood were supposed to make all constantly fear that, unable to bear the pain, he'd wear saffron and leave home to become a renouncer! Instead, what sort of odd conduct was this on Anupam's part! He seemed to be slowly shaking himself free of the malaise the way people come out of a bout of fever.

Indeed, Anupam was quite enjoying the visitors' company. He talked to them with a smile, he laughed and joked with his neighbourhood friends; sitting down to eat with them, he ate well; in the afternoon, he arranged on his own a little singing session at the house, without waiting for any request. A mood of festivity filled their home.

Sadhana was smiling happily. Aunt Sita's chest was ready to explode with resentment.

Why did it turn out this way? Why did Anupam leave her no scope to sit by him, stroke his hair, and tell him in a tearful voice that Taranga had specially asked her to see to it that Anupam didn't get too depressed and do something extreme? Good heavens, Anupam seemed to be denying her the opportunity to perform the dramatic piece Taranga left her in an exclusive position to do!

By dusk, Aunt Sita was no longer able to hold it. She called Anupam up to the cell-like room—unhealthy, uninhabitable—in which Taranga had once chosen to live, and said to him, 'Anu, I can't keep it from you any more.'

'What's it, Aunt?'

From somewhere in the neighbourhood rose the sonorous triple blowing of the conchshell.

'What Taranga wrote in the letter for you—in the part I burnt. So many times you wanted to know and I didn't tell—I couldn't. Today my heart breaks looking at your face, Anu.'

Anupam grew pale. From what she could see in the hazy darkness of the change of expression on his face, Aunt Sita's heart started to hammer.

She stood there waiting for Anupam to ask. But Anupam remained silent, didn't express the slightest interest to learn the suppressed mystery of Taranga's letter.

Left with no other recourse, Aunt Sita volunteered: 'Taranga loved Shankar.'

Anupam still remained silent.

'It's for Shankar that she suddenly left your house and moved to that house.'

She had disclosed Taranga's secret, given a proof even of its validity, yet Anupam did not let out even a muffled cry. Aunt Sita was on the verge of tears. Suddenly, pushing Anupam out of her way from the cell that used to be Taranga's room, she hurried downstairs. Her feet got entangled with each other and she fell. Rolling down the staircase, she got stuck at the bend halfway down. Aunt Sita screamed, and from another home came the deeply peaceful sound of the conchshell, three times. To this day, in at least three or four homes in the neighbourhood, evening was greeted with the blowing of the conchshell.

8

'Someone who can read the sacred *Chandi* is viewed as not uncommon, someone who can stitch shoes is also viewed as not uncommon, but someone who can both read the *Chandi* and cobble shoes impresses people as uncommonly talented. People are overcome by a fascination for that person. The human mind has some perverse quirks; living in a world regulated by rules, eternal or temporal, people are overwhelmed on seeing opposites combine. There's no reason why one can't know how to mend shoes because one knows how to read the *Chandi,* yet a person who has skills ranging from scripture reading to shoemaking seems to us superhuman. It's easy for us to worship humans as gods, easier still to hate humans as beasts, but when we find a person read the scriptures with his lips while sewing shoes with his hands, it strikes us as an exception; a phenomenon.

'So much so that we've made out of it an idiom of sarcasm prevalent in our language. We're a sarcasm loving lot. As you know, the sarcasm that's most effective has a sharp contradiction to the context—when you say heaven and mean hell, the sarcasm sets like thickened milk. What can be more sarcastic than calling a beggar a king? The direct meaning of saying that someone knows how to read the scriptures as well as how to make shoes is that there's nothing the person doesn't know how to do, but is that what we mean when we use the phrase? We mean that the person knows nothing at all! Now the education we get in our schools and colleges is also like learning everything from scripture reading to shoemaking, yet it's amazing that . . . .'

The young listeners at this point, did not exchange nervous glances, they clapped as hard as they could! The huge hall of the college resounded with applause. Those with weaker nerves even got gooseflesh. That an ex-student of their college could think so well filled quite a few young chests with pride.

But the applause jolted Anupam back to his senses. He hadn't wanted to come to the annual reunion of the college, but came at the insistence of two enthusiastic students. Nor had he wanted to speak to the gathering of invitees who had just been 'entertained' by the current students with poetry recitation, caricature, muscle control demonstration and so on; he got up to say 'something' only at the prodding of those two enthusiastic youths. But he hadn't intended to talk about scripture reading and shoe making, nor to criticize college education. It was not customary to talk about these things on such an occasion. It would have sounded well and served custom well to mumble something to the effect that he would never forget the memories of happy days spent in college and the deep joy at being able to join today's reunion took his words away.

Instead, what were these things he was saying? And why were the students so happy to hear such utter nonsense? Perhaps students were entertained by anything said sarcastically in a tone of complaint—by irrelevant but juicy name-calling and criticism! That didn't seem unlikely to Anupam. Considering the kinds of singing, reciting and muscle control demonstrations that had drawn applause from the whole audience.

But then, Anupam didn't stop even after sensing that the college principal, the professors and the invited gentlemen were feeling rather uneasy; he went on blasting without reserve college education and college-educated youths. The students were thrilled to hear him! Among the thirty or so girls sitting on one side, the eyes of many gleamed with excitement, and as a result of forgetting in their happiness to smile with lips closed, the dull uneven teeth of some were exposed when they smiled.

That's how it began. The next day two associations enlisted Anupam as a member. One was called the Students' Association for the Protection of Everybody's Rights Including Students'; the other had a vernacular name that translated as the Association for Education, Society and Literary Reform. The president of the first was a young professor, a gentleman who seemed, at least from his looks, not advanced in years. He held a western degree, but always brimmed with the exaggerated modesty of one who thought he knew everything. He liked the students; they came running to consult him before any meeting, association, or celebration.

Accompanied by two admirers and association members, and equipped with printed pamphlets, cards and so on, he appeared at Anupam's house to induct him. Smiling genially he said he was Sarasilal Bhaduri, the president of The Students Association for the Protection of Everybody's Rights Including Students'. His tone seemed to suggest that if his world-famous name hadn't yet reached Anupam's ears, he could assume that Anupam was the most worthless person in the whole world.

Left without recourse to the usual polite gesture of asking the guest to take a seat, because he had already sat down, Anupam merely said, 'Yes, I see.'

'You've to become a member of our association.'

'Fine.'

The executive chief of the second association was a student. His name was Brahmananda Chakrabarty, age about twenty-four, and his looks amazingly good. He always seemed angry, but with whom or what even he himself didn't understand very well. The moment he started to explain anything, his face flushed crimson with anger. He said to Anupam, 'If even those like you don't join our association, and like all the rest, think of looking after only your own comfort and happiness . . . .'

Anupam said, 'Have I said I won't join?'

But Brahmanada's anger couldn't be assuaged so easily. Why easily, it never was assuaged anyhow. 'You may not have, but many like you do,' he said, 'as if to secure a job after getting a degree and have a family after getting married constituted life's sole responsibility.'

'Are you married?'

'Me? Me married!' Brahmanada was speechless from outrage.

In this manner the motion of Anupam's life and that of Shankar's got directed along the same path. Shankar started his journey right out on the open thoroughfare on his own will. Anupam started his in a narrow lane at others' behest. Shankar had to make his way through the crowd by sheer bluffing; Anupam was pushed on by a bunch of immature youths' senseless enthusiasm.

But Anupam, as it turned out, made quicker headway. Whereas Shankar was killing himself to gain the right to move alongside notable men, Anupam was heading there without even trying. The young liked Anupam; his fame kept spreading in the circles of female and male students. No matter what sort of event they organized, they almost dragged him there. And Anupam had to say 'something'. What he said wasn't easy to follow, because he said anything that happened to come to his head. But to the students, used to hearing explanation-focused lectures from school teachers and college professors, Anupam's slightly diffident random talk stole hearts. His posture, the impression he gave of feeling uncomfortable with his hands and limbs while he spoke, the way he scratched the tip of his nose from time to time, all this made the students feel a deep compassion for him. Anupam seemed like someone from their own homes. The girl students mostly listened with a smile, some even developed an affection for him.

At least Ashalata did, there could be no doubt about that. Not so long ago, the sight of a likable young man inspired only romantic love in her. But after having once moved along the path to motherhood for about three months, all because of a little carelessness, she no longer felt anything for boys other than maternal affection.

Ashalata took the initiative to introduce herself to Anupam. She said, 'One can tell the moment one sees you that you've something that's rare among people these days. Simplicity, spiritedness, devotion to ideals, natural poise . . . .' She seemed to all but pat Anupam's back. Then she added, 'Will you come to my home one day? I want to have a good talk with you.'

'Certainly.'

'Why don't you come today? It's not even eight yet.'

Trying to look sad Anupam said, 'Today? You've to excuse me today. My mother at home isn't too well . . . .'

Ashalata at once was overcome with anxiety. 'Your mother's not well? Go home, go home as quickly as you can. I'll be here, you'll be here. You can come to my place some other day. How could you leave your mother and come here!'

It was just a fever. A slight temperature. She had been in bed around noon, but had got up later in the afternoon. Another day Anupam would've made no solicitous remark. But tonight, maybe because Ashalata's eager concern was still ringing in his ears, he echoed it: 'Why're you up with a fever?'

'Who'll do the work?'

'Didn't the maid come?'

'Does the maid cook?'

'I asked you to hire a cook . . . .'

'Don't talk like a nawab, Anu.'

Clearly Sadhana's temper was higher than her temperature. The cooking of the meal done, she was boiling some barley water for herself.

Diffidently Anupam asked, 'How about bringing Nimi over for a few days?'

'Can you tell me what you think, Anu?' Sadhana asked back. 'Why'd I have had her married if I was to bring her over and keep her back here?'

There was no answer to this. Because, there were unspoken things behind it. When Sadhana finished boiling the barley water, Anupam got himself a rug and sat down on the floor to eat.

Serving him rice and stuff, she said, 'Have you ever considered, Anu, how many years it's been that not one paisa came home from outside? He didn't plant a money tree!'

Anupam ate silently. Sadhana proceeded: 'Do you've the time you can afford to waste this way, Anu? It's all right for Shankar, his grandfather is rich, it's not for you! If you want to study further, study; if you want to do something that'll get you ahead in the future, do it; I'll manage somehow. A teaching position is open, I'll work for a few years if I need to. But if you wander around aimlessly like this . . . .'

Sadhana swallowed hard and said, 'Don't stop eating. I've cooked in a sick state, I'll not take it well if you get up without finishing.'

Anupam stayed up late that night and resolved in his mind at least a thousand times that he would not wander aimlessly any more. Next day in the afternoon he changed into good clothes and went to Ashalata's place, having decided that this did not belong to the category of aimless wanderings. Going to Ashalata's place was indeed one of his aims.

'I didn't imagine you'd come today.' Ashalata seemed a little disappointed. From much experience she had gained at least the knowledge that those who came to her running eagerly like this didn't have anything much to offer. Those who were gentlemen enough to be tied down were also gentleman enough not to appear at the place of a young woman seen just once at a meeting only the day before. How could someone who was simple, idealistic, in possession of natural poise, find it in him to take advantage of an opportunity as soon as it presented itself, unless he was a thief, a cheat?

Still, she didn't neglect to receive him. The house was small. It was quite obvious that trying to introduce a modicum of modernity in the living-room had nearly killed the head of the household. Because, in what little of the inner house was visible through a gap in the window curtain from his seat in the old sofa, there was no attempt at all to cover up the family's real economic condition. Someone used a suitable opportunity to sneak up and close the gap in the window curtain.

Anupam was familiar with this sort of deception in educated middle-class families; it didn't trouble him. This cheap pretence of affluence in the living-room of a non-affluent home didn't strike Anupam as incongruous. Just as it didn't seem unnatural to see the women of a household showily dressed in expensive saris when out to view the images of the goddess at the sites of public worship, despite knowing well that the very same women of the very same house scoured pots through the year in shabby raglike clothes, mopped the floor, cooked, and during leisure popped between nails the lice picked from each other's unkempt hair. It was quite in order, it was the custom.

'How's your mother?'

'My mother? Oh, my mother is all right,' Anupam said, looking at Ashalata's face a little surprised. The face looked rather sombre. She had met him only the day before, not even seen his mother yet. He couldn't quite grasp the reason for this amazing concern of hers for his mother.

But the grave look on her face didn't last long. While absently letting out a sigh of sadness, she managed with fascinating ingenuity to break into a smile, 'I was thinking of something.'

From then on, one step each week, Anupam progressively became more intimate with Ashalata. He had no idea what sort of staircase he was climbing or towards what end, but precisely for that reason the climbing seemed to him more exciting.

Ashalata talked to him on various topics—society, religion, politics, literature, nothing at all was left out. In the pauses between these wide-ranging conversations, she asked him the important questions, one or two at a time. 'What're you planning to do now?' she asked.

'Look for a job, what else,' Anupam answered vaguely. Ashalata wasn't happy with that.

'Why don't you study further? Taking a job now means becoming a clerk or a schoolteacher. You've been doing well at the exams throughout, don't ruin the future.'

For another week or so Anupam kept his real situation from her, and then he revealed it all, though he himself didn't quite know why he did it!

With a grave look on her face, Ashalata thought for some time, watched Anupam take sips from the cup of tea, and proceeded to hold a biscuit to his mouth, saying, 'Your grandfather didn't abandon you, your father is the one who abandoned him, right?'

Anupam agreed silently.

'Doesn't your grandfather now try to take you back in? Doesn't he want to help you?'

'What good is his wanting? My mother isn't willing to take his help.'

Ashalata fed Anupam another biscuit. 'If you go to your grandfather and ask for money to study further, won't he give it to you?'

'He'll, but . . . .'

'If you ask for some money for no particular reason, won't he give it?'

'He'll, but . . . .'

'If you go to him and say, "Grandpa, I want to go to England, give me ten thousand rupees, not at once, but in five or seven hundreds over ten months?"—won't he give it?'

'He'll but . . . .'

'But, what?'

'When my mother comes to know of it, she'll never look at my face again.'

Smiling softly, Ashalata said, 'Can a mother keep from seeing her son's face? You're so childish.'

'I can't hurt my mother's feelings,' Anupam replied stubbornly. 'Besides, what my father told my mother on his deathbed, doesn't that have some value? I'd rather work as a clerk all my life than take my grandfather's money to . . . .'

Ashalata calmly broke in, 'Yes. That'd be a shame! Of course, you can't do such a thing. Don't I know you? Working as a clerk is better than doing well in life by sacrificing humanity.'

The dark cloud that was coming over Anupam's face cleared up. As he groped in his pocket for a handkerchief, Ashalata wiped his face with her own sari and then suddenly went inside the house, at which he also somehow felt greatly obliged.

Two more weeks later one day, coming with Ashalata to a general meeting of the students' association, he noticed Shankar sitting on the dais, among the major and the minor, the known and the unknown leaders.

Although a students' meeting, it was like an open public gathering. Anupam had neither the desire nor the courage to speak here. But caught in Brahmananda's clutches, he was forced to say 'something'. Without even asking him, Brahmananda got up at one point and announced that the famous student-leader Anupam-babu would explain the position of the Association for Education, Society and Literary Reform on the topic under discussion. After doing this, he brought his flushed face close to Anupam's and whispered, 'I forgot your last name. Why're you still sitting? Why don't you get up and say something?'

In a stricken voice Anupam said, 'You're the association's president. Why don't you?'

Getting redder with anger, Brahmananda said, 'Would I ask you if I could? Get up now!'

Anupam's speech didn't go well. Listening to his own faltering, broken words, his ears started getting hot. Once or twice his ears caught even a sniggering remark or two. After a few minutes of explaining in the most unintelligible way whatever came to his mind about the purpose and ideal of the Association for Education, Society and Literary Reform, he stopped. While returning to his seat, he noticed that Brahmananda had usurped it. He was telling Ashalata something and she was gazing at his handsome face with fascination and amazement. Sitting a little apart, ashen-faced, Anupam stared at the two. Anger, sorrow, and humiliation made him wish to go, by whatever means, straight to that vast empty space where Taranga was invisibly merged.

Seeing his face, Ashalata leaned closer to Brahmananda, talking in a more intimate fashion.

While Anupam considered getting up and leaving, Shankar got up to speak. How well he delivered his speech! What a roar of applause arose from the gathering from time to time!

So be it, Ashalata had already killed Anupam; these were only falchion blows on a corpse. Still, he didn't know that even a corpse could suffer so much from these blows! Anupam recalled what Aunt Sita, in the hazy darkness of dusk in Taranga's cell-like room in their house, told him about Shankar and Taranga. That Shankar could speak so well? And that too in a meeting in which a short while ago Anupam had people laugh at his attempt to say a few simple things! It seemed to Anupam as if Shankar's speaking so well was to show off and humiliate him intentionally.

When the meeting ended, Ashalata said to Anupam, 'Let's go now.'

Brahmananda said to her, 'You're going home? Come, I'll reach you home.'

Ashalata said drily, 'Please don't mind, Brahmananda-babu, we've to go the market.'

Brahmananda said, 'I'm also going to the market.'

Ashalata said, 'We'll go to someone's house first, can't come with you.'

Not to anyone's house, not to the market, but straight into a wide open park's anonymity. Seeing that Anupam's corpse hadn't revived even with her rejection of Brahmananda as vivifier, Ashalata said, 'Come, let's sit down a little.' In the softly gathering darkness underneath a tree, nestling against Anupam, she then remarked, 'You're so childish, darling.'

Hence, ten days later Anupam got married to Ashalata.

Anupam suggested waiting for some time: 'Let me find a job first.'

Ashalata said, 'Don't worry. Everything will work out fine.'

If Anupam knew what'll work out fine, he'd perhaps have shuddered with horror, but it's doubtful if he could have prevented the disaster from happening.

9

After trying for some time to win Sadhana's approval, Ashalata found the job too difficult. Sadhana was not easy to trick. She was simple, quiet and affectionate, but hard on pretences. Even if she let a bad person come close, she'd have nothing to do with anyone trying to get somewhat intimate with her in the guise of a good person.

All the techniques Ashalata knew to gain people's confidence she tried on Sadhana, but the result turned out worse than what would have been the case if no such attempt had been made. By attempting to win Sadhana over, she had only revealed her true nature more clearly to her.

Ashalata was upset about her own foolish attempts, she was also angry. Angry at Sadhana. If Sadhana was clever enough to catch out each one of her tactics, then was it right of her to act like a plain and simple person and produce a false impression in her mind? Was it nice of her to trick thus someone who was her daughter-in-law, her only son's wife?

Also, seeing the way Anupam acted like a guilty child before Sadhana for marrying Ashalata set her ablaze with irritation. Had she begged at his feet to marry her? Her age was a little on the high side, her conduct not exactly what Sadhana would adore, but was she the one to be held responsible for this? Hadn't Anupam picked her out, fallen in love with her, proposed to marry her, all on his own? Besides, she was the one who had virtually done Anupam a favour. Considering the condition of his family and himself, didn't the fact that she knowingly agreed to marry him reveal her uncommon magnanimity, indicate her immense self-sacrifice, prove her non-materialistic, generous love? The kind of love that put a woman on the level of a goddess?

But, no matter how angry she felt, how scorched and vexed she was, Ashalata wasn't so stupid as to express any of it openly. She did give up trying to win Sadhana over, but she avoided confrontation. Silently she took the ignoring from Sadhana, who was deeply injured by her son's doings, and stored up bitter hostility in a secret corner of her mind.

In the mirror of Sadhana's transparent nature, Ashalata saw her own meanness and narrowness reflected again and again, but she wasn't particularly troubled by that. What bothered her most were the very subtle and indirect expressions of Sadhana's fathomless mother-love for

Anupam in the commonplace, small matters of daily life which she sensed every now and then.

Ashalata had no complaint against the simple truth that a mother was bound to love her son. When Sadhana's love for Anupam was expressed directly, she didn't suffer, or see Sadhana as her enemy. But it was those expressions that weren't apparent, except to a person having the insight of mother-love, that produced in Ashalata a strange, inscrutable pain. At those moments, Sadhana seemed like an enemy, as if she had encroached upon Ashalata's personal right, expropriated her most precious possession for herself and left her deprived.

Ashalata didn't quite understand this curious facet of her own mind. She knew that Sadhana didn't have the power to take Anupam away from her; no matter how diffident he felt before Sadhana and how unwilling to hurt her feelings, he didn't have much strength of mind. And that's why Ashalata had far greater power over Anupam than Sadhana had. Just as one can understand a mother-in-law's apprehension about her daughter-in-law turning her son into a stranger, one can also understand a daughter-in-law's jealousy of her mother-in-law's greater authority over her husband. But what could be the reason for a daughter-in-law's fiery resentment of her mother-in-law's maternal affection for her son? Especially when the daughter-in-law knows that she could make her husband humiliate this mother-love any day she wanted to?

After becoming conscious of this baffling mystery of her own mind, for a few days Ashalata searched within herself for a comprehensible explanation. And during those few introspective days, an unprecedented natural sweetness infused her conduct, which surprised Sadhana and fascinated Anupam.

For a while at least Ashalata seemed to become a new person. It seemed to Anupam that after so long she had finally learnt to give herself and turn off that relentless process of receiving him, finally understood a little the need also to receive caresses from him instead of only caressing him. Perhaps she had understood just a little, very little.

But even that, it seemed, might do for Anupam. Of the illusion that Ashalata aroused in him he found no fulfilment from her; in the depth of its non-realization, his illusion only grew more and more intense. She showed him affection, tended him, caressed him, overwhelmed him from time to time with deep and genuine emotion, met all his demands with a smile—yet it seemed to him as if she gave him nothing, while depriving him in every way.

What he desired from Ashalata and didn't get, why the pain of a terrible lack of satisfaction cut him and slashed him as with a sharp instrument, Anupam could not understand. Sometimes it seemed to him as if Ashalata was not exactly his wife, but someone else who, wearing the mask of his wife, had made herself a place in his bed next to him, to set up some other relationship with him. She seemed to embody all the female relations a man could possibly have in life—mother, sister, maternal aunt, paternal aunt, and a woman friend moreover—and on top of all that, a lifeless inert lump of flesh. But nothing else.

Late nights were filled with the stillness of the city noises turning down. At the command of Ashalata's very soft, very gentle pleading, Anupam lay in bed with his head on her lap, despite knowing that sleep would not come to him. For staying up late was supposed to be bad for his health.

Ashalata talked, moved her fingers through his hair, looked at him with deep affection in her half-closed eyes, smiled gently, enchantingly. Anupam also talked, fingers of one hand locking those of the other. Holding the hands together on his chest, he gazed on her face almost unblinkingly. The electric current fastened to the wall, transformed as light, stayed fixed on Ashalata's face; the shadow of the face stayed beside the face, the shadow of the nose beside the nose, the shadow of the eyelid in the half-closed eyes. In that glare-and-shadow, her face seemed horribly frightening to him. Anupam shuddered. With one ear he heard the soft murmur of Ashalata's voice, while in the other ear someone seemed to keep cutting into the rhythm of that murmur with, 'This is not Taranga, this is not Taranga!'

Presently, Anupam would have to pretend to be asleep. No matter what Ashalata was talking about, he knew that in her mind she was reciting the lullaby calling the sleep-aunts to bring sleep to his eyes. What could he do but pretend to fall asleep! Taking a deep breath he would shut his eyes; after waiting a little she would softly ask, 'Are you asleep?' He would not answer. After waiting a little longer, she would carefully and correctly put his head on the pillow. Turning off the light, she would even more carefully lie down beside him. It would seem to him as though the stagelights were finally turned off.

The stagelights were turned on and off, but the curtain that Ashalata rang down on Anupam's trips to the rostrum never rose again. Brahmananda came for Anupam one day and went back red-faced without him. Coming for him another day, he was tackled by Ashalata: 'Neither I nor he has the time, Brahmananda-babu, to join in those frivolities of yours.'

'Frivolities! You, you . . . .' the intended expletive got stuck like a hard object in Brahmananda's throat.

'Would you like some tea?'

Brahmananda left without having tea, and after a few days an unsigned letter came for Anupam. It carried some allegations linking

Ashalata with Sarasilal Bhaduri, the president of The Students'
Association for the Protection of Everybody's Rights Including Students'.

'Let me see whose letter it is,' Ashalata said.

After calmly reading the letter from beginning to end, she laughed
and said, 'Oh, what a satanic young man! He's taking revenge, because I
insulted him the other day and threw him out. You know whose
handwriting it is? Brahmananda's.'

Even after seeing Anupam's face become sullen she didn't drop her
own lightly joking tone. 'So, what're you waiting for, aren't you going to
do some checking?' she remarked.

'Don't be silly,' replied Anupam.

By the yardstick of ideals, life's worth was going down, but Anupam
had no idea that life could become so cheap. The colourful reflections of
unrealistic dreams, which were called ideals, had been getting wiped out
of life one after another since Taranga's suicide. Anupam had more than
superficial attachment to those. Of the ideals that tinged not just his own
life, but the lives of many he knew, why the dyes were of such poor quality
that at the slightest touch of real life they faded and turned ugly—this
question was too large for Anupam's intellect to find an answer to, but it
often came to him in vague forms. Today, it suddenly occurred to him
that the answer was that humanity itself had lost its hold on human life.

Sadhana finally said to him one day, 'It won't do, Anu, to just play the
role of the guilty. Something needs to be done! Have you thought of what
to do?'

'I'm thinking, haven't decided anything yet.'

'You'll never be able to decide. You don't have the slightest strength
of mind, Anu.'

Sadhana seemed very tired, and helpless. As if drained of all strength,
in her body and in her mind. After all these years, she was forced to accept
total defeat in life's struggle—exactly when she was supposed to have the
glory of victory at the battle's end. From the time of her husband's death
to this day, she had virtually been doing penance for self-reliance, the
penance to respect her husband's wish, to overcome the temptation to seek
the luxury of Bireswar's shelter. From the way Sadhana gazed now at
Anupam's face, it would seem as if she was trying eagerly to assess
Anupam's worth and from that the worth of her own long, hard struggle
to keep her vow. As if she just wasn't able to believe in any way that it
had all been futile.

'How could you become like this, Anu!'

Her expression sounded more like despair than complaint.

She asked herself, as though in bewilderment, 'Why's it that I tried so hard and still couldn't bring up my son? How's it that all the efforts I made for so long went in vain?'

Anupam's heart felt stricken. He knew that Sadhana had not all of a sudden started considering him a failure because of Ashalata. He knew it so clearly that he couldn't even take advantage of the opportunity to feel a bit annoyed with Sadhana and ventilate it by blindly supporting Ashalata. After silently hesitating awhile he returned to his room. There he found Ashalata sitting in wait for him. She lost no time to ask.

'What was mother saying to you?'

'Just wondering how come she ended up making a monkey's image when she tried to make Shiva's.'

Ashalata at once saw that Anupam was angry, but not quite with whom.

'Did you tell mother about it?'

'No. I can't tell her that.'

She showed no disappointment to hear this, only smiled a little in the manner of dealing with an infant's disobedience and said, 'You're so childish. The slightest problem puts you off.'

Sadhana thought he was good for nothing, Ashalata thought he was childish. Anupam's own view of himself didn't match either's. He saw himself as a complete void in a human form, just a void that contained neither good-for-nothingness nor childishness.

Ashalata had seen Bireswar about four times, twice when he came to this house and twice when he invited them, took them all to his house. In just four meetings Ashalata had figured Bireswar out to the extent she needed; she knew she had nothing to worry from his side. Her worries concerned only Sadhana. However, from hearing Anupam's accounts of her amazing mental strength and stubbornness, the apprehension she had about Sadhana was now largely gone. She sensed that Sadhana had reached the stage in which a person battling oneself started breaking down. It would have been better to wait some more time and have her reduced to a more feeble state, but after Brahmananda's unsigned letter Ashalata didn't dare to delay things any further.

Taking Anupam along, she went out one afternoon. She started a bit early, because the things she wanted to get done were many. Coming out on the road she said, 'Where can we wander in the roads? Let's visit a few friends' homes instead. Haven't seen them in a while, didn't invite them at the wedding either, they must be feeling very offended.'

'Isn't it better to go see a film?'

'We'll see a film another day.'

The two houses to which she dragged him were clearly such that

Ashalata might be acquainted with the families there but was quite unlikely to be in a relation of close friendship with them. Nor did any proof appear as to her currently having any relationship with them. On the contrary, it didn't seem that anyone in these two families, even any of their servants and attendants, lacked the knowledge that a girl like Ashalata could be made ecstatic with a single invitation to tea. Ashalata herself wasn't dressed particularly well today, nor was Anupam. Sitting stiffly in soft-cushioned seats in those two almost indistinguishable capsules of dream-life and listening to the detached bits of polite conversation in polished tones, it seemed to Anupam as if even the fancy ashtray was mocking at this wife-accompanied Anupam-babu.

Coming out of the second house, they walked alongside the clean asphalt between two rows of aristocratic homes, towards the tram lines. Ashalata had been watching the expression on Anupam's face and at one point she said lightly, 'They mentioned reaching us home by car—but just once! They knew that the first time we would say no out of politeness. If they asked once more, I'd have come out saying, "Many thanks, if you so insist".'

'Why, you have trouble walking?' Anupam remarked harshly, resentfully.

'I've no trouble walking—just could've had the fun of riding an expensive car for some time.'

'People don't become happy just by riding an expensive car.'

'That's true.' Ashalata said with a sigh. 'Being happy is that hard!'

With the reins loosened for some more time, she let Anupam have a round by the lake in the city's posh area, and then pulling the reins in again, she got him before Bireswar as dusk fell.

After listening to everything, Bireswar said, 'Who gave you this advice, Anu?'

'No one gave me advice, Grandpa, I'm old enough to make a decision about by own future.'

'But from what you're saying, that doesn't seem to be the case! I can see the point of your going to England to study—but why must you take your wife along?'

Ashalata had taught Anupam the answer to this question. With a grim face he said, 'There's a reason. I can't tell you, Grandpa.'

Also with a grim face Bireswar replied, 'The two of you'll go to England with my money, and you can't tell me the reason?'

Anupam said, 'No.'

For a long time, Bireswar sat silently and thought. Then he shook his head and said, 'No. Not exactly my money. You're demanding your father's share of the money, aren't you, Anu? The money that I'd have spent for your father as I did for Shankar's father, had he not cut me off in his rage, isn't that right? Since you know that you can't get *your* share of whatever I've got until I die, you've come to exact from me the money that I owe to your father, isn't that it?'

Anupam earnestly said, 'No, Grandpa, no! It's really not that. I'm only asking for your help.'

'Have you thought of your mother, Anu?'

'Mother will, of course, be angry with me . . . .'

'Not a little angry, perhaps she'll never look at your face again.'

'But I can't ruin my future worrying about my mother . . . .'

Bireswar suddenly flared up, 'What's a person's future, you monkey, if it excludes his own mother? Your father once gave up the temptation for my money for the sake of his mother, and today you're giving up your mother for the sake of that money? My daughter-in-law couldn't bring you up right, Anu.'

Anupam knew that.

Bireswar's outrage took some time to subside. Then in a tired, helpless voice, just like Sadhana's, he said, 'I'll give you the money, Anu, since you've asked for it! And what good will it do to Bou-ma even if I don't? No matter by what means, you're bound to finish her off.'

Coming out of Bireswar's room, Anupam paused on the veranda. Ramlal's room was dark, he was still not back from emptying at the bar his daily bottle of medicine for his sickly life. Shankar's room was also dark. Of the women in the family some were moving about, some putting babies to sleep, some reading novels. The children were doing their school or college lessons. Food was being cooked in the kitchen for all of them.

Standing at the far end of the veranda, Aunt Sita was telling Ashalata something in a hushed voice. Who knew if it wasn't Taranga's life story? The staircase leading to the room in which Taranga hanged herself started from that end of the veranda. The sari cover had come off Ashalata's head as she listened attentively to what Aunt Sita was saying. Though her hair wasn't like Taranga's, puffing it up she somehow got a bun almost as large as Taranga's. Seeing her face in profile in the dim light from this distance, it suddenly seemed to Anupam as though someone had taken a patch of that pale, grotesque death-mask from Taranga's face and pasted it on Ashalata's.

When returning home with Ashalata, Anupam forced himself to look out at the streets in order to avoid looking at her face.

Back home, he wasn't able to look at Sadhana's face either. But that was for a different reason. He had planned and speculated much with Ashalata on how they'd build their future life. Today he was just back from arranging the most important element to accomplish Ashalata's plan, and it was today that he felt more than ever that he had finally made his life completely aimless. All these years he had done little aimless things.

Now with fanfare he would embark on the greatest aimless task of his life, and with that he would render Sadhana's entire past and future life pointless. Until now, a corner of Anupam's mind held a bit of hope of his need for self-consolation. Sadhana hadn't been able to raise him right, he was good for nothing; but perhaps one day he'd be a worthy man, find a purpose in life and a path to achieve it. The day he would be able to prove his worth, it would also be proved that Sadhana's lifelong work had not ended in total failure.

Today, even that nearly groundless hope within Anupam's mind has committed suicide.

Sadhana was sitting in the porch alone. The part-time maid had left after doing her work. After cooking for dinner, Sadhana was waiting in the empty house. 'You're so late, Anu!' she said.

Ashalata knew how confused and distracted Anupam now was, and to finish off the whole business tonight, without giving him the time to calm down and think, she answered on his behalf. 'We went to the other house, Mother.'

Anupam had neither the desire nor the courage to tell Sadhana anything tonight. Yet in answering Sadhana's question as to why they went to the other house, and in picking up the thread of one or two of Ashalata's comments, he ended up telling her everything.

Sadhana went to bed and lay down like a corpse. Next morning, she left alone, with a small suitcase, for their ancestral village home.

After some time, everyone from the other house started to appear, everyone except Bireswar. After getting wind of it, they all came to find out more about what had happened. After learning that Anupam had demanded his father's share of the money from Bireswar and been granted it, they left, all with dour expressions on their faces. Aunt Sita was almost in tears.

Shankar came later, around noontime.

Ashalata was greeting them all by herself; she greeted and seated Shankar too. Anupam didn't say a word.

'Could you give me a glass of water? I'm very thirsty,' Shankar said to Ashalata.

'Would you like some cordial?' she said. 'The one I make tastes just like ambrosia!'

Ashalata went to make her ambrosia-like cordial, and Shankar and Anupam sat there, staring silently at each other's face.